The Fatal Eggs

AND OTHER SOVIET SATIRE

The Fatal Eggs

AND OTHER SOVIET SATIRE

Edited and Translated by

Mirra Ginsburg

GROVE PRESS, INC., NEW YORK

Contents

variety and range. But Soviet literature still has a very long way to go before it catches up with its own past. And this is particularly true of satire.

Throughout the years of eclipse, the cry was raised repeatedly: "We need laughter!" This was invariably qualified: "We need healthy, positive, life-affirming laughter, clearing the way to a Communist future." The makers of a grimly humorless society demanded humor—but made to their own specifications and serving their own ends. Another problem that bedeviled Soviet writers generally and satirists particularly was the fear of "generalizations," particularly "negative" generalizations, which might be construed as inimical to the regime, and the problem of the "positive" and "negative" hero. Endless discussions went on about the kind of hero needed and properly portrayed in literature. In the end, even the satirists began to introduce positive characters to lecture and put in place the offenders who were their original target.

Through all this, appeals from above continued to call for "new Gogols and Shchedrins." They stubbornly failed to appear. After the elimination of the great satirists of the earlier period, all that was left was the obedient writer of the so-called *feuilleton*—half skit, half didactic fable, often based on actual incidents, with an obvious, very elementary, and very explicit point, illustrating whatever social ill, "corrupt relic of the past," or "contagion from the West" was currently under attack. The authors of these *feuilletons* were and are journalists rather than makers of literature, and the most widely published among them are, significantly enough, the least witty and the least talented. Their writings appear in newspapers and magazines and subsequently are collected into innumerable little volumes and anthologies that are appalling in their flatness and mediocrity.

Nevertheless, a few among these "satirists" have managed, under stifling conditions, to retain a measure of talent, humor, and a sense of the absurd. The stories for the later period selected here are examples of the best of the genre.

Thus, while the stories of the 1920's and early 1930's included in this volume are representative of the wealth, brilliance, and diversity of satirical writing in the Soviet Union in those years, those of the later period are, unfortunately, not representative: they are incomparably superior to the general level of writing in their field during the last three decades.

A few final words about the choice of material for this collection. In selecting the stories, I was completely unobjective. I chose stories primarily because I liked them. Beyond that, my criteria were: essential value as literature; good writing; genuine wit; independence of official policy (this, of necessity, had to be modified for the later period); and contemporary reference. I chose stories dealing only with the current scene in Russia, omitting historical satire or satire directed at the "capitalist West" or America, particularly since the latter bears the heaviest stamp of official policy.

I hope that the reader will have as much fun reading the stories as I had translating them.

The Fatal Eggs

AND OTHER SOVIET SATIRE

Panteleymon Romanov
(1884 - 1938)

Born in Tula Province, the son of a petty landowner, Romanov
began to publish in earnest only after the Revolution. The
author of the novels Comrade Kislyakov and the panoramic
Russia, Romanov was at best in his short satirical stories.
During the 1920's, when he was at the height of his popularity,
he published a number of collections that reflected with
extraordinary wit and vividness the confusion of the people
in the face of the cataclysmic social change around them.
Called "an artist of the first rank" and "a worthy heir to Gogol
and Goncharov," he was treated from the first with uneasy
ambivalence by the official critics, who alternated between
claiming him as a supporter of the Communist Revolution and
criticizing him for being alien and hostile to it. Comrade
Kislyakov (1930), which satirized the new officialdom, was
bitterly attacked and withdrawn from sale soon after publication.
Romanov was unable to publish anything again for several years.
A few of his sketches appeared in magazines between 1936
and 1938, when he died of heart disease. His books were deleted
from circulation, and his name, like Mikhail Bulgakov's and
Yevgeny Zamyatin's, was deleted from history. Unlike Bulgakov,
he has not been accorded even partial rehabilitation in the
post-Stalin era, and remains virtually unknown in Russia today.

About Cows

Epoch of 1918

by Panteleymon Romanov

Trofim the plasterer came to the meeting at the District Soviet House and asked anxiously, "What's this I hear, that all the women are being scrapped?"

"What women?"

"Well, the legal wives . . ."

"Woke up. . . . That happened last week. Those who were married before the Soviets, they're done for, finished."

"But I've been living with my old woman for thirty years," said the stovemaker. "What am I supposed to do with her now?"

"Whatever you want, but she's got to go," said the redheaded Mitka.

"Dumbhead! If you have no understanding of a thing, keep quiet," said the member of the Soviet. "Nobody's chasing them; the only thing is that you've got to get the stamp applied to it properly."

"Applied to what?"

The other thought a few moments, then said, "To whatever it's got to go on."

"No, but they were also saying something about the old wives," said the plasterer.

"Well, the only thing about the old ones is that you have a right to divorce them."

"That's it. . . . But, then, it was the same in the old days— about the divorce, I mean."

"In the old days, you had to tag after the woman with witnesses for three years, maybe, before you caught her at the good deed.

3

Today you can divorce her any time you wish. Just make an application and give the reason. And she can leave you for mis-treatment."

"What kind of treatment?"

"Well, let's say, if you thrash her."

"How's that? You mean a man can't give his own wife a beating any more?"

"No, you haven't even got the right to swear at her."

"My own wife?" cried several voices.

"God-given?" cried Prokhor Stepanych, who served in church in place of a deacon.

"Nuts to your God," the soldier, Andryushka, said irritably. He had come to get some information from the member of the Soviet. "You mean, if I want to divorce my woman, I can give the reason that I beat her?" he asked.

"No, that's the reason she has to give against you."

"She?"

"Yes, she."

"Well, I never. . . . And what about the property? Suppose I divorce her and we have a cow. Who gets the cow?"

The member of the Soviet was silent again for a while, then he said, "If you show that your wife's at fault, you get the cow."

"And what about the new one?" asked Andryushka.

"What new one?" cried the member of the Soviet impatiently, waving away the plasterer, who was also trying to get his attention. "Talk louder, I can't hear a thing! . . ." Wrinkling his face, he stretched his neck toward Andryushka, who sat in a back row.

"I say, if I marry again and the new wife has a cow, to whom will it belong?"

"To both of you . . . while you're together . . . and . . . natu-rally, the man's the head of the house."

"And if I get rid of the old one, will you people marry me to the new one?"

"We don't marry anyone. The priest does that. We only put the stamp on it."

"So you slip out of the law and there's no getting you back?" several voices asked at once.

"What law are you talking about?" cried the member of the Soviet. "You're to live in civil marriage."

"Maybe I live in the civil marriage every God's day!"

"Maybe you do, but without the stamp. . . . And if she has a cow, you've got no right to touch it. You must get the stamp first. Understand?"

"I understand. . . . It's enough to make your head spin. . . . Like walking in the woods, God help me."

"Lots of people are suffering. The other day the carpenter divorced his old woman—it was a pity to see. They'd lived like doves together. . . . He burst out crying himself."

"What made him do it?"

"He found himself a new bride. Two cows, a sheepskin coat—almost new—and fifty poods* of rye. . . ."

"Two cows?"

"Two. . . . And, then, the woman was too good to let by . . . round-faced, hefty, strong enough to knock down a wood goblin . . . picks up a five-pood sack like a man. And the old one, she was a good woman, quiet, but smaller. He brought two cows of his own, and the new wife's got two."

"You don't say!"

"But will it stick?" asked Andryushka.

"What?"

"About the property, I mean."

"Have you got a lot with her?"

"With the old one?"

"No, the new one."

"One cow, fifty yards of homespun, a cloth jacket, and about ten pounds of sugar."

"Did you have a fight with the old one?"

* A pood is approximately thirty-six pounds.

"No, but she's puny. Can't even lift the sack of flour when she's baking bread."

"That's different."

"Last week Ivan Andronov came home from the army and took one look—no wife, no cow, no sheepskin coat, nothing. His woman went off and married another man and took everything with her. Ivan's suing her now. The other day he met her new husband. 'Give me back the cow and the sheepskin,' he says, 'and the devil take you altogether!' So the man says, 'And what will I have left?' 'What d'you mean "what"? And the woman?' 'What do you think,' he says, 'I took your woman for nothing? She can't even plow. You can have the woman if you want.' Wouldn't give him either the cow or the coat. It's up to the court now. . . . The poor man's fit to do himself in. . . ."

"What are you palavering about?" asked the blacksmith, coming in.

"Oh, nothing much, about cows."

"They're not dying off again?"

"Heaven forbid. . . . No, we're talking about divorce."

Inventory

by Panteleymon Romanov

After the inventory of livestock, some of which was later requisitioned for meat, more people came down to the village from the city. They called a meeting and announced that they had come to make up lists of children of preschool age.

The peasants, standing huddled in the schoolroom, which was as dark and sooty as a bathhouse, looked at one another.

"How's that? You will be taking inventories of the young ones now?"

"Not inventories, lists," answered the visitors.

"Same difference."

"Who asks them to come . . ." muttered someone in the back. All heads turned anxiously.

"First they go at the livestock, now they're getting at the children."

"So you'll be confiscating kids now?" a mocking voice asked from the back.

The visitors, busy with their papers, did not answer.

"Maybe they won't confiscate them, but there's sure to be trouble."

"This is how you're to make up the lists . . ." said one of the visitors, taking a sheet of paper from the table and looking at it.

The peasants became quiet and crowded forward in a close knot, as if afraid to miss the explanation.

". . . up to five years, separately; up to seven, separately. The others needn't be listed at all. Do you understand?"

Everybody was silent.

"Never mind. We'll go from house to house and make a record on the spot, or you will muddle things up so we shall never make head or tail of them afterwards. The meeting is over."

"May I ask what is the purpose of this?" asked the storekeeper, a member of the village Soviet.

"To collect information for purposes of social welfare, statistics, and pedagogical uses. Further instructions will follow later," answered the man with the sheet of paper, without glancing at the storekeeper. And he began to gather up the papers from the table like a judge who had just pronounced a sentence subject to no question or appeal.

"Again they're *collecting*. . . . Will there ever be an end to it? . . ."

"You may go. Prepare the children at once."

The women dashed out of the schoolhouse and ran across the common toward their streets with such a frantic air that some peasants who were passing by in carts slowed up their horses and looked around anxiously, as people do when the fire bell rings.

"I'm going crazy, I don't know where to put him!" a woman's voice lamented from a doorway.

"You never know where the next misfortune's coming from."

Within five minutes, the peasant women, their kerchiefs awry on their heads, rushed from their yards, colliding with one another, each dragging something into the back alley in her hands or under her arms, as though her house were on fire. And from the hemp fields in the back, there rose a steady chorus of children's voices, howling and crying.

"They're coming! . . ."

The women rushed out of the hemp fields and took up positions at their thresholds, panting heavily, waiting for the visiting commission.

When the commission arrived at the first house, accompanied by the storekeeper, the visitors spread their sheets on the table and prepared to write. But the home turned out to be childless. The other households were also without a single child. Occasionally, there was a child, but rarely, and then only an older one, twelve or thirteen years old.

"How come none of you have any children?"

"When could we have them? . . . First there was the war, then . . ."

"And who's that crying out there?"

"That's next door, my good sir."

"What the hell, if nobody has any children in the village, where's all this howling from?"

"Some kids must have crawled in from the lower village."

When the visitors came to the last house, they were barred in the doorway by a frightened young peasant woman, who kept repeating, "He's no good, sir, he's no good at all. . . . He can't lift an arm or a leg."

"Who's no good? What isn't he good for? . . . It doesn't matter; if he is sick now, he'll get better."

"These fellows aren't choosy; they don't care," said a voice from the crowd that silently followed the commission.

Kuznechikha was the only woman in the village found to have young children—five of them. When the commission entered, she was sitting on the floor searching for lice in the hair of her seven-year-old. She was too stunned to rise.

"They've got her," somebody said in an undertone.

All five were registered. A young neighboring woman gave their ages; Kuznechikha herself could not utter a word.

"And where are your young ones?" the storekeeper asked one of the women in a perplexed tone.

She flashed her eyes at him and, showing him a fist under her apron, said quickly, "I've never had none. They were my sister's."

"The devil knows them," said the storekeeper, shrugging his shoulders.

"Wasn't worth bothering here in this village," said the visitor, glancing at his list.

When the commission had gone to the storekeeper's for a glass of tea, the hemp fields again became the scene of feverish activity. Some of the women dragged the cribs back home, others ran about anxiously, still others shouted, "What do you want here, trampling other people's hemp!"

"I've lost my young one! . . . Merciful God, I put him down right here, right near the furrow."

"They should've put them all in a heap instead of poking 'em away all over. They'll never find them now. All the hemp they're spoiling, the devils."

"Here's somebody's baby!" a woman cried from one side.

Another woman rushed over, threw up her hands, and turned back. "Not mine . . . mine wore a red cap."

"They've crawled off all over the hemp field. . . . Such trouble!"

"Where the devil'd you get off to! I put you down there and stuck a nipple in your mouth. Why couldn't you sit still? . . . You devil's imp!"

"What's the matter with you? Wait till I give it to you on the backside, then you'll know better," cried another, pulling a three-year-old boy by the hand. The boy's mouth was twisted, his fist was at his eyes, and he barely managed to keep up with his mother.

Only the owners of infants carried their bundles calmly, occasionally glancing with disapproval at their frantic neighbors.

"A hell of a life. One day you're driving out the cattle, the next you're hiding the children . . . no end to it," said a young woman with an infant.

"It's easy enough for you—just slip the crib under your arm and go. I'd like to see you manage in my place: two in my arms, two holding on to the skirt, and a fifth one lost."

"No, but we put it over fine! We've learned our lesson after the livestock inventory. Got the kids out of the way in five minutes!"

"Trouble is we didn't catch on at first, or we'd . . ."

Everyone was pleased except Kuznechikha, who sat on the grass near the well lamenting loudly: all the young ones she had, each one of them registered; they'd caught her with the goods. The others gathered in a circle and looked at her.

"Poor woman, they got her all right," said somebody.

"She'll know to be more careful next time. Spilled out a whole slew of kids and thinks she can get away with it. . . . No, sir, those days are gone."

"Still, it's a lot easier with children than with livestock. What if they crawl away? It's no great misfortune. But dragging off a yearling bull on a rope! Before you know it, he'll butt you in the rump, your eyes will fair jump out on your forehead."

"It's sure handier with kids."

"They got a lot of livestock that time all the same."

"They catch you unawares. Give you no time to think."

The storekeeper came down the street. "Those who registered their children are to go into town on Saturday."

All heads turned involuntarily to Kuznechikha.

"What for?"

"They'll get assistance for the seven-year-olds—shoes, clothing. . . ."

Everybody was silent for a long while. Finally someone spat angrily and said, "A hell of life! You never know what they're up to!"

And Kuznechikha was again surrounded, this time by envious neighbors: she was the only one in the village who had not miscalculated.

1919

Inefficiency

by Panteleymon Romanov

A man in a cap and carrying a wicker basket, of the kind you take to market when you go shopping for food, approached a locked store. Shading his eyes with his hands, he looked in and knocked on the grimy, dusty window, in which a bullet hole had been mended with a wooden patch.

Another man, in a leather jacket, looked out of the door and said, "Wait a minute. I'll finish cleaning the piano, then we'll go together."

The door closed, and the man with the basket remained outside, waiting. He put his basket on the step and began to roll a cigarette.

An old woman walking on the other side of the street with a knitted cord shopping bag in which several carrots were rolling around stopped at the sight of the man waiting near the store. She looked up at the sign over the door, then at the other signs nearby, and hastily ran across the street, as though afraid that someone might get there before her. Peering closely at the man who was standing at the door, she took up a position behind him with her carrots.

"Have you been here long, dear man?"

"No, I just came," the man answered glumly and reluctantly.

The old woman wanted to ask something else, but she only looked at him and did not dare to speak.

"Merciful heavens," she said a few moments later, "what they've brought us down to—you can't get anything anywhere. You run around all day from one line to another. Yesterday I passed a line without stopping, and then I heard they'd gotten soap."

"You've got to stop each time now; can't afford to let things slip," said a little old man with a pipe, who came up after the old woman.

"That's how it is. . . . You see, we haven't been here more than two minutes and there are three in line already. And here's a fourth one."

"They'll keep coming now."

"What are they selling here?"

"We don't know yet."

"They'll have something. They wouldn't be collecting folks for nothing."

A disheveled woman with a bag came running from the house across the street. She hoped to take the fifth place, but two men who had been passing by stepped in before her.

"People are gathering . . ."

"They will . . . the other day the line outside our store stretched all the way to the boulevard. Their stocks ran out; those who were last in line had to go away empty-handed."

"That's what you're afraid of most of all."

"What is the line for?" a corpulent lady in a hat asked breathlessly.

Everyone looked at her with hostility. No one answered.

"You'd better take your place instead of asking questions, or others will get in ahead of you and you'll be left with nothing."

"Asks questions like she was a boss or something," the disheveled woman grumbled to herself. "People came before her and they keep quiet. And this one—make an announcement for her right away."

"Didn't I tell you?" said the little old man when three more people lined up behind the lady.

The man with the basket, who had come first, looked back at

the line behind him and asked, "What are you standing here for? What are they going to distribute?"

"God knows," the old man answered. "They'll announce it when the time comes."

The man with the basket looked at the old man, said nothing, turned, and peered through the keyhole into the store. "A fine 'minute,'" he said to himself, glancing at his watch. "It's twenty minutes already."

"It's the same everywhere, dear man, you wait and wait."

"What are you blocking the whole sidewalk for—are people supposed to walk through you?" cried passersby, stopping at the line.

"Where are we to go?"

"Where! . . . Stand along the wall, instead of taking up the whole street."

"Heavenly Father, where do all these people come from?"

"You'd think they smell it out somehow."

"One man finds out, and all the others follow," said the little old man.

"Some bright heads thought this up. In the old days, you'd go and buy what you needed, and that was that. Nowadays you stand and stand, and nobody knows what for. Nobody knows when they'll open up, either."

"Maybe somebody should go and ask?"

"That won't make it any sooner."

"No, but maybe if everybody gets after them, they'll move a little faster."

"If they set it for a certain hour, that's the hour they'll open."

"And what's the hour?"

"How would I know, what do you want from me?"

"Hey, there, citizen, out front, ask when they'll start to let us go, you're right at the door."

"It's none of my business," the man said sullenly. "You want to know, go and ask."

"The devils—won't even lift a hand for their own sake. He'll stand there two hours, but he wouldn't go and ask if you push him. Came before anybody else, too."

"Those bastards, they don't give a damn about people; they'll make you line up first thing in the morning and won't start selling before noon."

"Stop pushing there; you're mixing up the line! Now you can't tell who was standing where."

"They do it on purpose. Now the back ones will shove up front."

"They ought to make lists or something. With all this mob, how can you keep track of who stood where? If they know there will be such a mob, they should have lists or something."

A woman ran up, all out of breath and all covered with chalk figures: on her back there was a large 5; on her chest and sleeves, other figures.

Everyone looked at her silently. The lady moved away and said, brushing her sleeve, "Don't lean against me, please."

"They didn't start yet?" the woman asked.

"No."

"How come you're standing unmarked?"

"Who knows . . ."

"Must be a new store. We were also getting mixed up all the time. People even got into fights. Now the manager comes out and marks everybody in order. You get your number on one line, and you go off to another."

"We'll get things straightened out right away," said a burly fellow, taking a piece of chalk from his pocket. "We'll do it without the manager."

"Thank God there's one sensible man. Make it bigger, dear."

"Don't worry, auntie. There you are," the fellow said, drawing a big 20 across an old woman's back.

"Makes you feel better right away."

"Sure thing; now there's order."

"What's all those figures on you?" the little old man asked the woman with the figures.

"This one is for sugar, number 15; this one is for kerosene, number 10; this, for cloth . . ." said the woman, looking down at her chest and pointing with her finger. "Oh, my Lord, I hope I don't miss this one!"

"Look here, now, where can I write when you don't have a free spot on you?" said the burly fellow, approaching the woman with his chalk.

"Maybe there's room on my back, dear?"

"The back's all right."

"Good, my dear man, write it on the back."

"If the managers had heads on their shoulders," said the woman in the hat, "they would arrange some system by alphabet. Everybody would know his time, and people wouldn't have to be marked up with chalk like convicts. And you wouldn't have to stand for hours, either."

"Again she is complaining," said the disheveled woman, offering her back to the fellow and looking up with animosity at the lady with the hat.

"They aren't used to waiting," a mocking voice said from the crowd.

"You stand here shivering in nothing but a jacket and never say a thing. And that one's got a storeful of clothes on her, but her dainty little feet are chilled, you see."

"Where are you shoving? The devil take you! . . . Spilled out all the way into the middle of the street . . . and then I have to take the blame!" cried a soldier with a gun. "Look out or you'll get it with the butt. What are you waiting for?" he asked, glancing at the sign over the store.

Everybody merely looked at him with fear. No one said anything.

"Swallowed their tongues. Line up along the wall."

"Oh, merciful heavens!"

"There's no efficiency. If people had some sense, they'd go in first thing and find out properly when they were opening and what they had to sell, instead of standing here an hour without sense."

"There's sure no order. They kick you around, the devils; they don't give a damn about people. Today they'll sell you products in one place, tomorrow in another. Come to think of it, I've never seen them use this store before. There is some kind of music standing in there."

"That won't stop them none."

"Damn it, where the hell's he disappeared to!" said the man with the basket in front of the line, and he knocked on the door.

"Right away, right away," a voice cried from the store.

"About time," said people in the crowd. "Stood there an hour before he had the brains to knock."

"We're lucky at that. Yesterday we waited six hours," said the little old man with the pipe.

"They're opening up. Watch your numbers. Hey, woman, where do you think you're going?"

"The devil knows her—she's got figures all over her."

"Stop pushing there! Cover themselves with figures half a yard long and think it's so much fun. Keep leaning on you and getting chalk all over you. A nuisance!"

The door opened, and everybody, forgetting all about the numbers, rushed to the door in a solid mass. Those in front swept aside the man with the basket and began to push their way into the store, where the man in the leather jacket had been cleaning a piano.

"What's this? Where are you going? Have you all gone nuts?"

"Get through, cut through the middle; you'll get there quicker that way."

But the man in the leather jacket rammed his knee into the stomach of the lady in the hat and managed to force them back.

"People have gone clean off their heads lately," he said to the angry crowd, coming out of the store. He padlocked the door and started down the street with the man who had waited for him.

"Where'd they go to?"

"Hey, there, where are you going? Making fools of us, or what?"

"Who told you to line up here? Lost your wits?"

"They make your life miserable, the devils. Did you ever see

the like of it?" cried the disheveled woman. "Kept us standing
here a whole hour, with everybody numbered. Then they come
out, and off they go as though it wasn't anything at all."

"Trouble with inefficiency. Somebody should have gone up in
the first place to find out properly why they're keeping people
lined up and when they'd start to sell."

"A whole hour! Everybody marked up with chalk like nuts, and
they just wag their tails at you, and good-bye!"

"Lucky at that, only an hour," said the little old man. "The
other day we stood six hours in a single line."

1920

A Mistake

by Panteleymon Romanov

To combat the obsolete prejudice of religion, the Komsomol announced that it would hold its own Easter celebration.

Feverish work went on all morning at the district education
committee. The Young Communists pasted, painted, combed flax
for the Lord's beard, sewed a *sarafan* for the Virgin Mary.

Every five minutes or so, the director came running in, and
with the naïve arrogance of a superior official to whom everything
seems easy, exclaimed, "Hurry up, hurry up, boys! You're falling
asleep on the job!"

The stage manager, in felt boots and trousers covered with paint
drippings, had not eaten since morning. He snapped back angrily
at every criticism. "We were supposed to carry torches, but when
I went to the department for kerosene, they tell me, 'Where were
you before? Why do you come on a holiday eve?'"

"Why so few saints?" the director asked.

"Why? Did they give us flax for beards? What are we to do, send them out with shaved faces?"

"Make the beards out of hemp. Where am I to get flax for you?"

"Hemp! Give them propaganda, overthrow God, and they . . . just tell me, what kind of parody is this on the Almighty?" the stage manager said, stepping back and looking from a distance at a gloomy, listless fellow with a beard tied to his face. "And nobody knows what to make the devils with. Besides, no one will come, anyway."

"There will be a mob of people," said the director, "because it's ideological propaganda. There are posters all over town, and admission is free for everybody."

"So nobody will come. They don't give a damn in the Center. All they know is to send in resolutions, and we can wear our feet out trying to get everything we need. Where's Mary disappeared? . . . Oh, there you are. Where are you running off to all the time! Am I supposed to follow you around with the glue? Where shall I paste it on now?"

"Come on, come on, get moving, or we'll be late. . . . What are you doing there, putting on the damned cloak inside out!" cried the stage manager. "You devil's doll!"

"Who knows it?" said the gloomy fellow.

" 'Who knows . . .' Can't you tell by the stars! Do you expect them to be inside?"

He stood before the gloomy fellow with a jar of paste in his hands and looked at him with irritation. "And where's your orb?"

"Here, they brought the round glass lampshade from the library."

"The asses! Are you supposed to march around with the lampshade in the dark? You'll smash it, and there won't be anything at all to read by. As it is, there's only one lamp left for the whole reading room. Are the posters ready?"

"The devil knows them," said the director's assistant and went to the next room, where a group of young men were busy painting posters on the floor and on the tables.

A tousled fellow with fair, almost white, hair wiped the brush on the tail of his shirt and glanced around at the others, like a painter in a studio, changing his brushes to give himself a moment's rest. The letters in his poster grew smaller at the end of every line, and the lines dripped downward.

"Can't you calculate beforehand, you nitwit!" the director's assistant shouted at him. "And look what you're writing here! 'We don't need hevenly papas.' What did you do with the 'a'—swallow it? It's written out here for you. Can't write a single line without mistakes, the fool!"

The fellow looked at the slip of paper with the writing, then at his poster, and grumbled, "Who can keep up with every letter?"

"Ivan Mitrich," the stage manager cried with irritation, coming up to the director's assistant, "look at the devils' tails they've given us! I asked for thick rope, and they sent us twine. What is this, are they making fun of us?"

"Twist several thicknesses together; it will do. Is the Chinese Buddha ready?"

"He's ready. He was the most difficult to do. They copied him from a teapot."

"Good. But Buddha has to squat. Where is he? Do you hear, Buddha? Don't forget to squat."

"Ready?" cried the director. "I ordered a cart for you. You'll ride to the monastery. Such weather tonight, God help us! The devils ought to put something on in the meantime, or they'll freeze."

Everyone crowded out.

"Wait, wait! You'll pull it off!" a frightened voice cried in the dark.

"Pull off what? You're blocking the way! Go on."

"You're stepping on my tail. Let go, I tell you!"

"Spreading it out all over the place! Throw it over your arm."

A cart stood waiting in the street. Somebody sat huddled sideways in it holding the reins.

"Did you take the posters?"

"We did. What the devil do we need posters for? It's pitch dark!"

"All right, then. Start now! Buddha, don't forget to squat."

"We're going, but who the hell knows what for?" said the stage manager. "You cannot see your own nose, and here we are, all rigged out in makeup and with placards."

"They shouldn't have said anything about ideology; nobody'll come," said the director's assistant, "especially for the first time."

"Maybe not . . ."

The cart, jolting on the rocky ground, went down the street. In the thick, low fog, from which large drops of rain fell now and then, some windows glimmered dimly, and the infrequent street lights were barely visible.

"Yes, too bad they spoke about ideology . . ." somebody said again.

"I won't squat any more. To hell with it!" said Buddha.

The devils were already beginning to freeze. Their teeth chattered. When the cart approached the monastry, everything there was dark and silent. They sent the horse back and, choosing a drier spot, began to jump up and down to warm their feet.

"Naturally, not a damned soul showed up," said the stage manager with exasperation. "Now the makeup will be ruined in the rain, and we shall all look like the devil."

"What the hell got into him to write about ideology?"

"Yes . . . Now listen: we'll wait until they start coming for matins, then we'll begin."

"If they would only start soon," said the Almighty, shifting the lampshade from one hand to the other and hiding his free hand in his pocket to warm it. "Stuck me with this blasted shade. Froze all my fingers with it."

Everybody huddled together in the dark, empty square before the monastery, dancing up and down with the cold. A shadowy figure emerged from the gateway of the house across the street, but vanished instantly.

"But when will matins begin? It's half-past eleven already."

"In half an hour. At Easter the service always starts at midnight."

"If we could only step in somewhere and warm up, but it's awkward somehow. Go ask the gatekeeper when it will start. It's queer, just half an hour to go and nobody is here yet."

One of the devils ran, holding up his tail, to the gatekeeper's hut, knocked at the window, spoke to someone through the glass, carefully staying out of the shaft of light, and returned.

"That's a fine mess! A bit better than ideology! The service is at twelve according to the old time, but now, with the clock moved, it starts at two."

"Hell! We'll perish here till two o'clock. And wouldn't you know it, they let the horse go back. Our feet are soaking wet. Let's get into that barn to warm up a little. At least it's drier there."

Everybody filed in through the gates of the barn facing the square, found in the dark a pile of last year's straw in the corner, and crouched down, huddling together for warmth.

"Wait till the owner comes at us with a pitchfork," said the stage manager, "then we'll have a show!"

"Damn! Cooked up a situation. At least, if a single damned bastard had come out—after all, everybody must have seen the announcement."

A cart drove past across the square. The actors heard the splashing of the mud and melting snow under its wheels. After a while, the cart returned.

"Where are you, fellows?" they heard the director's voice.

"Here."

"The service, it turns out, is at two."

"Turns out!"

"And here I am driving all over the square looking for you. What are you huddling in there for?"

"Huddling! Try not to huddle."

"The devil, such a mix-up. Nobody came?"

"Not a soul. We should have had music first, then painted the fellows every color and let them march around. And we should have told everybody that attendance was restricted."

"You're right, I guess. I'll bet you're frozen?"

"What do you think? We're wet like dogs."

"All right, get in now, hurry up, we'll give it up this time. The devils must be altogether chilled. Buddha, sit down properly. Everybody squat down!"

"I'm too numb, my knees won't bend."

Everybody silently began to pile into the cart. Suddenly there was the sound of broken glass.

Somebody spat and said, "There! The devil take it!"

"What is it?"

"The orb got smashed."

"Eh, butterfingers! The last shade . . ."

"Come on, get in, get in. Damn it, I sat down on something wet!" ·

"It's my tail," said one of the devils.

"Tear it off, damn it! Spreads it out all over, when people are soaked through as it is."

They rode back silently.

The director shook his head and said, "What the devil got into me? I just don't understand it."

"What?"

"Such a stupid mistake. Mentioning ideology."

1922

A Gift of God

(A Story of 1920)

by Panteleymon Romanov

Three elderly peasant women rode between the cars of a freight train, perched on a board they had laid across the buffers.

Two of them carried sacks of flour. The third had only a small bundle.

They had hopped the train quietly, late at night, and settled on the board they had stolen at the station.

"Oh, God, I went three hundred verst to get some flour, and then they stole my money," said the woman with the small bundle, and she began to cry.

"Such trouble," responded her neighbor, an old woman with white wrappings around her legs, neatly tied with string. "And I've had luck; the good Lord helped me. I haven't slept for nights, my eyes keep closing, but when I think I'm bringing home some flour, my heart jumps up for joy. And I got it, if I may say so, for a song. There was a man there, same as you—all his money cleaned out, to the last kopeck, so he sold it to me for a thousand."

"A gift of God, straight from heaven," said the woman with the small bundle. "And I . . ."

The old woman with the flour sighed sympathetically, fingering her sack. Then she settled herself more comfortably, propping her foot on the buffer.

"Holy Mary, what's one to do?" said the woman with the small bundle. "How will I face the old man without flour? He's eating linden leaves."

"I didn't get much. Still, I'm bringing home a bit of flour," said the third woman, looking at her sack, half the size of the other's.

"I carried my sack and kept crossing myself," said the old woman.

"Naturally. You can tell it was the hand of God, such a sack for a thousand."

The train rushed downhill at full speed. The cars were swinging violently from side to side. Then something happened. . . . There was an inhuman scream. Something rolled down under the wheels and disappeared.

The old woman's foot had slipped from the buffer, and her companions saw only the flash of her shawl and her feet in the white string-tied leggings under the wheels.

The woman with the bundle looked back from around the corner of the car and cried out, covering her eyes with her hands.

Between the rails, at the curve of the road, something bloody heaved and fluttered like a slaughtered hen.

The woman with the bundle, beyond herself, began to scream, calling for help.

"Don't, it is all the same now," said her neighbor. "Run over?"

"Run over! Lord, it was a fright to see," replied the woman with the bundle, pressing her hands to her cheeks and staring with wide-open, horror-stricken eyes. "Flopping around . . ."

"Merciful heavens, the times we're living in!"

For a while both were silent, shocked by the accident.

"If she was hit, it must be all over now."

"One moment you're alive, the next you're gone. . . . And back home they'll be counting the days, waiting for the old woman to get home with some flour."

"She was crossing herself, she said, carrying the sack, thinking it was a gift of God. Didn't know she was carrying her death on her shoulders."

"Good God, I'll have nightmares all week now. I took one look at her, flopping around, the poor soul . . . Maybe she's still alive; we should have stopped the train."

"Not likely," said the woman with the flour. "If she was run over, she wouldn't have lived long, anyway. It was God's punishment for taking advantage of another's misfortune. She bought a bargain, you see, thought she was lucky."

The two women fell silent again, sitting motionless for a while. Then both glanced at the old woman's sack; their eyes met, and they looked away.

"Oh, Lord . . . There will probably be a frost at night."

"Looks like it. Last year we had snow in October," said the woman with the flour. The train was approaching a station, and she wanted to put her sack on the old woman's.

"Uncomfortable there? Let me move the sack over this way."

"No, no, it's all right."

"I'll move it over, then you can sit closer."

"No, I'll just put my little sack on top here, then I can move."

"What are you doing there, putting it on the clean sack? Don't you see yours is all muddy?"

"What do you care? It isn't your flour, is it?"

"It's not yours, either."

"I didn't say it was."

"Well, there's no need to get it muddy, anyway."

"Mind your own business—it isn't yours."

And the woman put her small sack on the larger one, which made it seem at once that both sacks belonged to her.

"Look at her, piling them up, the old witch!" cried the woman with the bundle. "Take it off right away, it makes it awkward for me sitting here."

"Oh, hush."

"Will you take it off or not?"

"Trying to get your hands on it, I see?"

"I'm not trying anything, but I'll bet you are. Wait till we get to the station, I'll tell everybody how you told me not to scream!" The woman with the bundle was now shrieking at the top of her voice. "You've got a whole sack, but it's not enough for you. Now you're trying to rob the dead. Take it off this minute, or I'll chuck it under the wheels!"

The woman with the bundle made a move to throw off the sack.

Her neighbor clutched at her hair. "So that's what you're up to!"

And the woman with the bundle, ignoring her enemy's hands in her hair, seized her by the throat with both hands.

The other began to gasp and, releasing the hair, merely tried to pull away the choking fingers with one hand, convulsively clutching the sack to herself with the other. She could have freed herself by using both hands, but she was afraid to let the sack go.

The train rushed downhill once more. The board on which the women sat jumped up and down, and the crossties flashed below with dizzying speed.

At last the eyes of the woman with the sack began to bulge, and her clawed fingers spread out helplessly.

The woman with the bundle continued to hold her for a while, giving her a shake from time to time, which made her enemy's head, with its bulging eyes, drop backward. Then she released her throat and quickly pulled over the old woman's sack.

"Will you try it again? I'll push you down under the train altogether. Old carrion crow! One bag isn't enough for her . . . grabbing another's."

The woman with the flour began to cry, sniffling like a child, her whole body shaking with sobs. "Give me half of it, at least, you bitch!"

"Try and get it! No wonder . . . the woman might be still alive, and she says, 'Don't yell.' Trying to put her hands on somebody else's goods. Got a head on her shoulders, figured it out quick. . . . The rotten scum."

The woman with the flour said nothing, but went on crying weakly, bitterly.

In the distance, around the curve of the road, flashed the water tower of the station.

The woman with the flour dried her tears, blinked, and, still shaken by dry, continuing sobs, pleaded in a submissive, wheedling tone, "Auntie . . . say, auntie, let me have just a little, just ten pounds."

There was no reply.

"After all, it was I who stopped you. If you'd yelled, they would have taken the flour away, in any case, if she was still alive. And she was, I'm sure she was. The train had just cut off her arms or her legs. She would have spoken up, anyway, about the flour."

But her neighbor sat upright like a statue, without a word, looking stubbornly before her. Her hands firmly clutched the sack.

The train had barely stopped when she jumped off, heaved the sack onto her shoulders, and, hurriedly, without a backward glance, walked away with it in the opposite direction.

The woman who remained looked down at her sack, exactly half the size of the other, and her eyes began to blink again, rapidly and helplessly.

Through the blurring tears, she looked after the retreating figure. And for a long time, in the dim light of the gathering, dismal
evening, the woman could be seen walking away from the railway
tracks, weighed down by the heavy sack and crossing herself continuously with a wide, joyous gesture over her unexpected good
fortune.

1925(?)

Valentin Katayev

(1897 -   )

Son of a high-school teacher and grandson of a priest, Katayev
was born in Odessa. His younger brother was the celebrated
humorist Yevgeny Petrov (see Ilf and Petrov's "How the Soviet
Robinson Was Written"). Many of Katayev's earlier stories
were satirical burlesques. In 1926, he published The Embezzlers,
an amusing novel of the years of the New Economic Policy in
the 1920's. The author also of a number of plays, including
Squaring the Circle, and the novel Time, Forward, which
glorified the industrialization of Russia, Katayev quickly adapted
himself to the stylistic and thematic demands of the Party
critics and has been one of the more successful Soviet writers.
He joined the Communist Party in 1958. As editor of the
monthly Yunost ("Youth") in recent years, he was one of the
more liberal forces on the Soviet literary scene, until removed
from the post in January, 1962.

The Beautiful Trousers

by Valentin Katayev

There were two of them—a prose writer and a poet. Their names are unimportant. But they ate.

And in the next room in this huge, run-down hotel, which resembled a chest of drawers forced open and thrown into utter disarray by a burglar, a hotel full of dust, heat, the clanking of cavalry spurs, and the tramping of infantry boots, Master of Arts Zirlich sat naked on a striped mattress and read Apuleius in the original. He had graduated from the university with a degree from the Department of Romance Studies; he could read, write, and speak many languages; he worked in the diplomatic service; and he was very hungry.

His coarse cotton shirt, with laces instead of buttons, and his trousers, made of sacking and still bearing the stamp of the automobile transport depot where the sacks had done their service to begin with, were hanging on a nail. The philologist Zirlich owned nothing besides these trousers and this shirt, and he guarded and preserved them as carefully as a young lady preserves her ball gown.

His neighbors ate. He visualized perfectly how they ate and what they ate. Imagination, which is not ordinarily a quality associated with philologists, this time drew for him unforgettable Flemish still lifes. Not less than four pounds of excellent black bread and coarse salt. Very possibly, a samovar. At any rate, the sound of a falling cup was indescribable.

Zirlich leaned his crooked, gourd-shaped head on both hands and listened. They were chewing.

Zirlich swallowed his saliva. It was unbearable. Then he swept the bare room with his dusty eyes. A hopeless formality. Emptiness is emptiness. There was nothing edible about. He hurriedly licked his lips and stole on tiptoe to the keyhole.

They sat at the desk, ladling up with their spoons a salad of tomatoes, cucumbers, and onions. The salad bowl was very large. Next to the bowl lay a damp, bricklike loaf of bread. Over the samovar hung a cloud of steam and a thin buzzing sound as of a swarm of mosquitoes. The sun glared through the cotton shade, burning out on it the cross of the window frame.

"Gorging themselves," the Master of Arts thought sorrowfully.

He hesitated a moment, then he quickly slipped into his trousers. He knew what he had to do. He had to knock politely on the door and ask, "May I come in?" And then, "Tell me, my friends, do you happen to have a pen? Mine broke."

To knock politely!

He had knocked politely yesterday, the day before yesterday, last Wednesday, last Friday, and Saturday. No, it was impossible.

Zirlich sadly removed his trousers and hung them up on the nail. Even hunger should know its limits! But hunger knew no limits. They were eating. The philologist clutched his head and quickly put on his trousers.

He knocked politely.

"Come in!"

The Master of Arts cleared his throat, arranged his face into a worldly smile, and entered. They were sitting at the desk, but on the desk, piled with huge sheets of newspapers, there was nothing edible. Even the samovar was gone.

Swine! thought the philologist. They've managed to hide everything away. Bare as a field. Could they have put the samovar into the washstand?

He chewed a little with his lips and tied the laces at his throat into a pretty bow. "Good afternoon, my friends."

"Good afternoon, Professor."

"Listen, my friends . . ." Zirlich puffed out his cheeks and blew up at his own nose. "The point, my good comrades, is . . . You see, dear fellow writers . . . hm . . ."

He looked once again at the table and suddenly noticed the

edge of the bread showing from under the papers. And Zirlich could no longer take his eyes from it, just as a bird cannot take its eyes away from the emerald eyes of a boa constrictor.

"What is it, Zirlich?"

The corner of the black loaf showed with absolute distinctness against the telegrams of the Russian News Agency.

"I am very hungry," Zirlich said quietly. He caught himself. He shook his head and cried gaily, "You know, I am very fond of bread, and I am very fond of tomatoes and cucumbers. I want some tea."

The prose writer turned pale. How careless of them.

"Here, I can offer you a little piece of bread. I've just received my ration. At the artillery courses. As for tomatoes, well, you know . . ."

No, no, he could not have noticed the salad. The salad was camouflaged too well.

The poet smiled with melancholy. "Yes, Zirlich, have a piece of bread. But tomatoes, so help me, we have none. We haven't eaten anything ourselves for three days . . . I mean two."

Zirlich hastily broke off a piece of bread and stuffed it into his mouth.

"Sit down, Zirlich."

Zirlich sat down. His eyes were expressionless, his cheeks bulged as he chewed.

"How are you, Zirlich?"

Zirlich swallowed hard, and his Adam's apple jumped. He shook his head and spread his hands.

"Bad?"

Zirlich nodded and gagged.

"Don't they give you rations at work?"

Zirlich wiped the drops of sweat from his nose with his sleeve. "In extreme-ly lim-ited quan-tity," he brought out with difficulty, staring at the bread. "Yes, my friends, in very limited quantity. I receive one quarter of the diplomatic ration a month, which constitutes . . . hm . . . if I am not mistaken . . . If you permit me, I'll pinch off another little piece."

"Pinch it off, Zirlich," the prose writer said through clenched teeth. "Pinch it off. Why not?"

"Thanks, fellows . . ."

"A man should write propaganda plays, Zirlich, that's what one should do," the poet said gloomily, opening the wardrobe. In the huge, empty, echoing wardrobe hung a pair of new, blue, very beautiful trousers. "You see?"

"I see, a pair of trousers."

"There you are, trousers! Blue. Beautiful. New. A masterpiece, you might say."

"You bought them?"

"I bought them. Today. Yes. And so I say—a man should write plays, Zirlich."

Zirlich raised his eyebrows. "They buy them?"

"Oho, and how they buy them! Just write them!"

Zirlich became very agitated. "But do you know, that's an idea! Propaganda?"

"Propaganda."

"Seriously?"

"Couldn't be more serious. You saw the trousers?"

"It's an idea, friends! Only, how shall I put it, I'm not sufficiently experienced in the dramatic form. Of course, it is possible to reconstruct a thing or two from memory. I am thinking of Molière's theater, in the history of French—"

"No history, Zirlich! To the devil with Molière!"

"My dear friends, really, it's an idea!" Zirlich exclaimed with joy. "But you must help me a little, brothers."

"All right, we'll help."

"But what does one write about?"

"About hunger. But make it simple. One, two, three."

Zirlich excitedly finished the bread, looked with admiration at the beautiful trousers, blew at his nose, and went off to write the play.

All night the prose writer and the poet heard the rustling of paper, the scraping of a pen, puffing, panting, and the pattering of bare heels in the next room. Zirlich was writing. At dawn he politely knocked at the door. He was admitted.

He waved his pen excitedly and an inkspot settled on his trousers. "Forgive me for disturbing you. The play must be uncomplicated?"

"Uncomplicated. The simpler the better."

"You have no bread, my friends?"

"None."

Zirlich stood a while, shifting from one foot to the other, then he left. Zirlich wrote all morning, all day, and all evening. Hunger made his ears hum, and magnetic needles twitched before his eyes. They were eating cucumbers and round onions. At night Zirlich loudly knocked at the door.

"Come in."

He came in. In his hands fluttered a sheaf of paper covered with writing. In high excitement, he sat down on the window sill, took a peace of bread from the table, put it into his mouth, and said, chewing, "I've written a play, fellows. I want to read it to you."

"Is it long?"

"Short. One act."

"Read, Zirlich."

And Zirlich read his play. The play was as follows: a vast, hungry steppe; railroad tracks in the distance; an abandoned baby, five months old, in the midst of the steppe. A crow flies over the baby; wolves, a dogess, and a gopher circle around it; and on the ground beside it crawls a wise snake. The above-mentioned animals conduct a dialogue in the spirit of Maeterlinck on the subjects of hunger, the abandoned infant, and the lack of political consciousness in society. The wolf wants to eat up the baby. The snake reproaches him for cruelty. The gopher weeps. The crow prophesies imminent deliverance. The dogess begins to feed the baby from her own breast. Then a train arrives. The locomotive flashes its fiery eyes. A nurse emerges from the long row of hospital cars. She is not too late! The infant is saved. The wolf lopes off. The snake is triumphant. The hospital train bears the inscription: "All as one to the aid of the hungry population of the Volga region."

Zirlich finished reading his play, put the manuscript on the table, and looked with feverish eyes at his listeners. "Well, comrades, what do you say?"

The poet hid his eyes. "What can I tell you, Zirlich? It's a play, as plays go. A good play. The concept is interesting, but . . ."

Zirlich felt a chill.

"Yes, Zirlich, the idea is interesting, but it would be difficult to produce."

"Do you think so?" asked Zirlich, blowing up at his nose.

"Yes, I think so. Look, you have a whole hospital train in it!"

Zirlich imploringly untied the laces at his throat. "But it's only a set. Of cardboard, you know. It's only painted!"

"All right, let us suppose the train can be managed. But the infant, the infant! How can you bring a three-month-old baby into a play, Zirlich?"

Zirlich threw back his head. "It's five months old, and besides it doesn't speak. It is a silent role, you see. They can even use a doll, just make one up for the part."

"Hmm, perhaps, if you use a doll. And what of the wolf and the dogess? Why did you bring them in? And incidentally, why a dogess? What sort of animal is a dogess?"

" 'Dogess' is feminine for 'dog'—an ancient usage, a Slavicism."

"I see. A Slavicism! But who will agree to play a dogess, did you think of that?"

"I thought of it. He'll use stage makeup; he'll get down on all fours and walk around that way. Oh, that's a point I've given very careful thought."

"Very well, let us say it will pass. But the crow, the crow! How can the crow be played? And then you make it fly in your play, Zirlich!"

Zirlich was silent for a long while, then he said in a flat voice, "And what about Rostand, in *Chantecler*? He has hens in the play. And I have a crow. After all, the difference is not so great?"

"No, not so great. All right. That can still pass. The crow, the gopher—it is not too important, after all. But the snake? Zirlich, just think about it—a snake! Do you understand it—a snake on the stage! That's impossible. The snake kills the whole thing. The Department of Political Education will never buy a snake."

Zirlich broke into a beady sweat. He whispered hoarsely, "Yes. I never took the snake into account."

A painful silence followed.

"So what is to be done, my friends?"

"Throw out the snake; replace it with something else."

"No! Impossible. Without the snake, the whole composition falls apart. The snake is the reasoning element." Zirlich wilted gloomily. "But maybe," he said, scratching his nose and dully staring at the ceiling with his dusty eyes, "maybe . . . somehow . . . they can make a snake from a fire hose. . . . And have the prompter . . . speak for it? What do you think, fellows?"

"No, Zirlich, the snake won't do."

The poet glanced at the table. There was nothing edible on the table. The table was piled with newspapers.

"Try to write something else, Zirlich."

"I'll have to try. Good night, my friends. . . . I'll go and try."

"Try, try. Good night."

Zirlich went to his room, took off his shirt and his trousers, sat down on the striped mattress, and clutched his head. He felt dizzy. He had no strength. They were eating. Zirlich stole up to the key- hole. On the table stood a bowl with salad. There was bread. And a round onion. Zirlich returned to his table, pressed the pencil into the bridge of his nose so that it left a violet dot, and sat so for a long time. Then he began to write a new play. He wrote all night. Green wheels were flying before his eyes. His hands dropped. He wanted to eat so much that he felt nauseous. From the courtyard came a smell of roast. He wrote all night, all morning, and half the day. At noon he lay down on the striped mattress and imagined a large piece of bread with butter, a cup of milk, and an omelet. The market was not far; at the market, they sold cabbage soup and fried sausage. At the market, there were plaited breads and milk. He had nothing to sell. Zirlich held his head, sighed, then rose and stole up to the wardrobe, his white, flabby body reflected like a slanting shadow in the mirror. He heard the tapping of his toenails on the floor, and his heart clattered like a typewriter. He opened the doors. The beautiful trousers hung in the huge wardrobe like a suicide in a vast and empty hall. Zirlich did not think about the sin of stealing; he forgot that he was a Master of Arts, that he could read, write, and speak many languages. Zirlich thought only of how much he would get for the trousers; he also thought that he would get a beating if he were caught.

Zirlich felt very ashamed selling the stolen trousers. But after that, he walked about in the market for two hours—eating. He ate bread and onions; he ate cabbage soup with cream and sausage made of dogmeat; he drank milk and smoked cigarettes.

When he was full to repletion, Zirlich cautiously made his way back to his room and sewed into his striped mattress three pounds of bread, a hundred cigarettes, and a large number of cucumbers and onions. He removed his shirt with the laces and his trousers with the stamp of the automobile transport depot and hung them on the nail. After that, he sat down cross-legged on the mattress and devoted himself to Apuleius.

In the evening, they came home and ate. They were probably eating round onions and bread, but it was unimportant. After a while, without hurrying, Zirlich put on his trousers, assumed a suffering mien, and knocked.

He heard the sounds of panic behind the door, and two minutes later he was admitted.

There was nothing edible on the table. It was piled with newspapers.

"Look, my friends . . . I mean . . . I am very hungry. Can you give me a little piece of bread?"

"Alas, Zirlich," sighed the prose writer.

"Well, if you have none, you have none," Zirlich shrugged sadly.

"You must write a play, dear fellow! A play!" the poet pronounced gloomily and went to the wardrobe. "Here, if you please! take a look. Such a pair of trousers. A beauty!"

And he opened the wardrobe.

Zirlich was tying the laces at his throat with a sorrowful air, looking down and off into the corner.

1922

The Suicide

by Valentin Katayev

On the part of the Citizen, it was a swinish thing to do in every respect.

Nevertheless, he made up his mind to it, especially since suicide was not punishable under the criminal code.

In short, a certain Citizen, disillusioned with Soviet realities, decided to turn his face toward the grave.

It's sad, but it is a fact.

He hurriedly collected his severance pay and the wages due him for the vacation he had not taken. Then he penned a feverish note to the Local Committee, bought a large and beautiful nail, a piece of toilet soap, and three yards of rope at the government store, and went home. There he pushed a chair over to the wall and climbed up.

Cr-rash!

"The devil! What a seat! It can't even support the weight of a young, intellectual suicide. And they keep talking of their fight for quality! They call themselves the Wood Manufacturing Trust! Phooey!"

But the Citizen was not a man to bow before the blows of fate, which is nothing but the theory of probabilities, anyway, nothing more!

He managed somehow to climb up on the windowsill, held the nail against the wall, and hit it with a paperweight.

Cr-rash!

"Some nail! In pieces! Their fight for quality, indeed! A decent man has nothing to hang himself on, may the Lord forgive me! I'll have to tie the rope directly to the chandelier. At least that's still a product of the old regime! It will not let me down!"

The Citizen tied the rope to the chandelier, tied an elegant noose, and began to soap it. "Some soap, I'll tell you! First, it does not lather; second, it smells of goat, if you'll pardon the expression, instead of lilies of the valley. It even makes you sick to hang yourself with it."

Suppressing his disgust, the Citizen put his head into the noose and jumped off into the unknown.

Cr-r-ra-sh!

"A million curses on it! Broke, the beastly thing! It dares to call itself a rope! In the most interesting spot, too. Take a look for yourself. . . . Quality! I'll say!"

"To hell with it! Let me try something simpler. Ah! A kitchen knife. 'Will I fall,' as the song says, 'pierced by the arrow, or is it going to fly past?' "

Cr-r-r-rash!

The arrow flew past indeed: the handle in one direction, the blade in another.

The Citizen burst into wild laughter. "You may be sure! Ha-ha-ha! Quality! Well, how can you keep from killing yourself after all that?"

"To die is to die! To hell with the knife, that relic of rotten medieval romanticism! Experienced suicides say that matches can be very, very useful for suicide. You grind up fifty matchheads into a glass, drink them down—and Eureka! An excellent idea. How come I didn't think of it before?"

His spirits restored, the Citizen opened a fresh box of matches and merrily began to snap off their heads. "One, two, three, ten, twenty. . . . Hm . . . there are only twenty-eight matches in the box, and there should be sixty."

The Citizen broke into muffled sobs. "Comrades, dear friends! What is this? I can understand if they say quality. But where is it written that an honest Soviet citizen should suffer like this over quantity?

"To the devil with matches! I'll bang my head with all my might against the wall, and that's that. With our own heads, as the slogan goes, we'll push our way toward our goal!"

The Citizen closed his eyes, took a running start, and—

Cr-r-rash!

The solid wall of the brand-new cottage cracked wide open, and the Citizen flew out into the street. "Well, well! *Merci!* Hurrah for quality which is quantity! Hurrah! Ha-ha-ha!"

Nevertheless, he did not lose his mind and was not taken to a hospital.

The Citizen looked at the jar and sighed with relief. "There. At last! Exactly what I need. Acetic acid. Now, this will surely work. I beg to state that no one is to be held responsible for my death . . ."

The Citizen greedily brought the jar to his fevered lips and gulped down its contents. "Hm! A pleasant beverage! Like grape wine, only milder. Shall I try another?"

The Citizen drained a second jar, grunted with pleasure, and waved his fingers before his face. "A piece of sausage would be just the thing now. Or some caviar. . . . And I was trying to kill myself, like a fool. Life is so beautiful! There's quality for you! Marya, my dear, run down and bring me two more jars of acetic acid—and don't forget some sausage. I've worked up a devilish appetite."

"Wel-ll, and now, after our little snack, we can sit back and dream a bit about the joys of liv— But what is this? What's hap-

pening in my stomach? Oh, and my eyes! It's turning dark. . . .
The sausage, it's the sausage! My friends, I've fallen in the battle
with quality! And life is so beau . . ."

And with those final words, the Citizen lay down with his belly
up and died.

Which, however, was exactly what he had been after to begin
with.

1922–1925

A Goat in the Orchard

by Valentin Katayev

An enormous unshaven man in a sinister-looking tailcoat clambered up onto the stage of a provincial club.

After loudly clearing his throat he asked in a hoarse whisper,
"But where is the accompanist?"

"Why, comrade lecturer," said Sasha anxiously, "this is a lecture on home brew, on *samogon*. And our fight against it. What
do you want music for?"

"A lecture? Hm. . . . And maybe I'd better sing something,
eh? Something, say, from the *Demon*?"

"Ho-ho! But this is a lecture!"

"Honest, I'd rather sing. So help me. . . . Something . . . you
know . . .

>   "On . . . the earth all hu-oo-man-kind
>   Wo-*hor*-ships one divi-*hi*-ni . . ."

"But please, please! This is a lecture. Anti-*samogon* and temper-
ance and such. . . . That's what the announcement says."

"Really? Oh, well. Hm, hm!"

The man in the tailcoat let out a deep cough, put his hand on his throat, shook his head, and stood in position.

The chairman rang the bell. "Comrades, you are called to order. Our comrade from the Center will talk on the subject of home brew, and so on, and so forth. The subject is most important in social significance for workers, and if there's any that prefer dancing, they can leave the hall right now. The comrade from the Center has the floor."

The lecturer looked around him with pale, bluish eyes, bent forward, and said, "Comrades! At this dire hour, when the Soviet Republic groans before the machinations of the hirelings of world capitalism, we cannot remain indifferent. All as one! Am I right?"

"Right," disapprovingly affirmed the audience.

"Yes, comrades! We, all of us to a man, must join in the fight against home brew. Thousands of people drink it, and thousands of people are poisoned every day by this harmful poison that destroys the organism. Am I right?"

"Some get blind, too," said a brisk female voice from the hall.

"Cor-rect, citizen! A v-very apt remark. Exactly, they get blind. It happens. And deaf. Hon-est. . . . And so, comrades, we see that home brew is a terrible poison and a scourge. And why?"

The lecturer gave the hushed audience an annihilating look. "And wh-hy?"

He held out an effective pause. Then, after savoring the silence to the full, he raised his voice: "And the reason, dear comrades, why home brew is so harmful is that we haven't learned as yet to purify it properly. And what can be simpler than to purify home brew? It's a cinch. To one pail of brew, take three pounds of common, ordinary, completely unremarkable salt—"

"Coarse or fine?" quickly asked someone in the hall.

"Fine is best. But, of course, you can use coarse salt, too. Well, then, you put this salt into the brew and cover the pail with something warm. A blanket, say."

"Will a pillow do, comrade lecturer?"

"You can use a pillow, too. It's even better with a pillow. Yes, dear comrades. Then take, say, five or six pounds of plain, elementary cranberries—"

"Cranberries!" ecstatically shrieked a woman in the third row, slapping her thighs. "Well, I never! Cranberries!"

"Exactly, cranberries," triumphantly exclaimed the lecturer. "Plain, simple cranberries; then cook said cranberries on a slow fire, adding some yeast, chalk, and soda!"

"A lot of yeast?"

"And soda?"

"Comrade lecturer, and what if—"

"Easy! Easy! Let us hear. Don't push. How much yeast should you add?"

The hall was in an uproar. The people in the rear pushed those in front. Women squealed. Notes flew to the stage.

"Comrades, not all at once! Order, please. This note asks: 'Can you add some pepper and tobacco to the brew to make it stronger?' I answer: Of co-ourse not! Pepper and tobacco do create an impression of strength when added to the home brew, but in reality they do not make it stronger, and your head aches like the devil afterwards. Well, then . . . I continue. And so, dear comrades, when the cranberries are thoroughly cooked and discharge their juice, take a strainer, the simplest, most primitive kitchen strainer, which—"

The chairman was pale. "Comrade lecturer, a little nearer to the subject, please."

The public roared: "Let him speak! We demand, we demand! Don't interfere! How much soda? Ground chalk or in lumps? Let him tell again about the strainer."

The lecturer, with lowered head and half-closed eyes, continued. "Then, dear comrades, rub this whole business through the strainer into a recipient . . ."

"Sip it! Oh, Lord, sip it already?"

"Isn't that something?"

". . . into a clay recipient, where you have first put . . ."

The chairman clutched his head and bounded off backstage. Sasha stood leaning his cold, sweaty forehead against the window.

"Sasha," the chairman howled in anguish, "he is demoralizing the audience. He doesn't look like a doctor, either. Maybe you made a mistake and brought somebody else?"

"I made no mistake," said Sasha dully. "I went to the hotel myself, room number 8."

The chairman began to tremble. "It was 18, not 8! Help! Drag him from the stage! Not 8—18! Curtain! Curtain! You've got it all mixed up. The fellow in 8 is an actor. Blockhead!"

Sasha convulsively pulled at the curtain.

But it was too late. The lecturer was now standing in the middle of the hall, surrounded by the enthusiastic audience and answering the notes.

The chairman bent down and peered through a slit in the curtain. For a moment his face expressed despair. Then it brightened. Anxiously he swung forward and suddenly shouted hoarsely into the hall, "Comrade lecturer! And what, for instance, if you put too much yeast into the brew and it thickens, the scurvy thing?"

And with these words, he plunged into the thick of the knowledge-seeking crowd.

1925

The Struggle Unto Death

by Valentin Katayev

The director opened the newspaper and a cold shiver ran down his spine. "Call the secretary!" he cried hoarsely into space, pressing his clenched fists to his temples.

"You wanted me, sir?" the secretary asked, delicately sidling into the office.

"I did. Sit down. Did you read?"

"I did, sir," the secretary sighed politely.

"Well, what do you think of it?"

"I think, sir, that it must be fought, sir."

"Bureaucracy?"

"Bureaucracy, sir. Yes, sir."

"Right! Exactly! It must be fought. We must fight bureaucracy. Or what does it come to, comrades! It is outrageous, comrades! The young Soviet apparatus is permeated, comrades, by the old-style, moldy, malodorous red tape and bureacracy, and we are sitting here and paying no attention! It's a hell of a thing, comrades, if you'll pardon the expression! Even newspapers are talking about it. In short, we must take the most resolute steps to extirpate bureaucracy! Root and stock! Am I right?"

"You're right, sir. It's the holy truth, sir."

"There! You will take care of it, comrade secretary, issue instructions. There must be no more bureaucracy. Starting right now. It's a crash assignment. Urgently—immediately—personally. . . . No admission without permission. . . . I mean, what the devil! What am I saying? My head is going round. . . . That's all we need, to have them come and find bureaucracy in our organization. And whose fault will it be? It's impossible, comrades! You'll run me into the ground, comrades. Don't you understand?"

"I understand, sir."

"Go to work at once, my dear man! Draw up a plan for the immediate extirpation of bureaucracy, then submit it for signature to my deputy and to me; correlate, coordinate, process it; multiply it, mail it out, post it up, get the receipts. Handshakes are abolished, no admission without permission, the throwing of cigarette butts on the floor strictly prohibited. . . . I mean, hell! . . . What am I saying! I'm getting all mixed up. In a word, get to work on it!"

"Yes, sir."

"Coordinated?"

"Coordinated, sir."

"Correlated?"

"Correlated, sir."

"Ventilated?"

"Ventilated, sir."

"Duly processed?"

"Duly processed, sir."

"Did my deputy sign it?"

"No, sir."

"And wh-hy?"

"Because, sir, he is on vacation, sir."

"On vacation? Hm. . . . And who is deputized to take his place?"

"You, sir, you are deputized, sir."

"I?"

"Yes, sir."

"Hm. . . . In that case, give me the plan. I'll look it over and sign it as the deputy, then you will register the signature and submit it to me as the director. Is that clear?"

"It's clear, sir."

"Very well, go on."

"Comrade deputy director, here is a little plan that needs to be looked over and signed, sir."

"What plan?"

"Concerning the struggle against bureaucracy, sir."

"Good. Leave it. I'll look it over."

"Yes, sir."

"Well, did my deputy sign the plan?"

"No, sir. He told me to leave it. He promised to look it over, sir."

"Outrageous! Red tape! Bureaucracy! I shall write him a memorandum at once on the inadmissibility of such outrageous red tape in a matter of nationwide importance. Take the memorandum. Put it through the records department. Stamp it and take it to my deputy. Get his receipt."

"You mean yours?"

"Not mine, my deputy's."

"But you are the deputy of your deputy, sir."

"Silence! I know! In private life I may be I, but officially I am not only I, but also my own deputy and the deputy of my own deputy. Is that clear?"

"Very clear, sir."

"Comrade deputy, a memorandum to you from the director."

"Give it to me. Leave it. I shall look it over at home."

"Did my deputy read the memorandum?"

"No, sir, he didn't, sir. He kept it. He promised to look it over at home."

"The scoundrel! Call him here."

"But, sir . . . how . . . sir, if you and he, sir . . . are one and the same person, sir?"

"Silence! Officially there can be no such thing as one and the same person. Here all persons are official! Call him!"

"Yes, sir. Comrade deputy, the comrade director wants to see you, sir."

"Tell him I'm coming."

"They asked me to say, comrade director, sir, that they will come at once, sir!"

"Very well, you may go."

An hour later, the visitors who stood in a long queue outside the director's office heard the loud voice of the director in angry conversation with himself:

"Is it correlated?"

"It's correlated."

"Coordinated?"

"Coordinated."

"Processed?"

"Processed."

"Did you sign it?"

"I did not sign it."

"Why?"

"Because you should sign it first."

"I am your superior! I will not sign first! You must sign first!"

"I will not!"

"I will dismiss you."

"And I will complain!"

"You wretched bureaucrat!"

"Look who is talking! Miserable red-tapist!"

"What's going on?" the visitors asked the messenger, Nikita.

"Oh, that's our director, fighting bureaucracy."

And from behind the doors of the office came wild shrieks:

"First priority! Most urgent! Incoming and outgoing! Coordinate, correlate, process, verify. No admission without permission, butts on the floor strictly prohibited, no advances issued! . . . Ha-ha-ha-ha. . . ."

1922–1925

Mikhail Bulgakov
(1891 - 1940)

Born in Kiev, Bulgakov graduated from the Medical College of Kiev University, but very soon abandoned medical practice for writing. His first major novel, The White Guard, serialized in a magazine in 1924, was a study of the disintegration of a noble family under the impact of the Revolution. Because it did not castigate the Whites, it was never published in Russia in book form. Bulgakov's dramatization of the novel, presented as The Days of the Turbins (1926), was shown with great success, but before long it too was banned. The ban was eventually lifted, but was later reimposed.

Bulgakov was also a brilliant satirist of great verve and imagination. Bold and original, he was under constant attack from hostile Party critics and censors, who began to hound him long before the general campaign against all independent writers. By the early 1930's, he could no longer publish his work, and he found refuge with the Moscow Art Theatre, mostly in the capacity of a literary consultant. He wrote a number of highly successful plays (which usually brought him into conflict with the censors), dramatized the novels of other writers, and wrote opera librettos.

His death was not reported in the Literary Gazette, and his name was omitted from literary histories.

In 1963, in a belated gesture of "rehabilitation" and recognition, the magazine Moskva published several of his unpublished early stories. The introduction calls him "a writer with a great and original talent," whose works are directly linked with Russian classical literature, with Gogol and Chekhov.

"The Fatal Eggs," which prophesied such dire events for 1928, was published in 1925.

The Fatal Eggs

by Mikhail Bulgakov

CHAPTER 1   Professor Persikov

On the evening of April 16, 1928, Vladimir Ipatievich Persikov, professor of zoology at the Fourth State University and director of the Zoological Institute in Moscow, entered his office at the Zoological Institute on Herzen Street. The professor switched on the frosted overhead lamp and looked around.

The beginning of the frightful catastrophe must be traced precisely to that ill-fated evening, and the prime cause of this catastrophe can be laid to none other than Professor Persikov himself.

He was exactly fifty-eight years old. His head was remarkable, shaped like a pestle, bald, with tufts of yellowish hair standing up at the sides. His face was smooth-shaven, with a protruding lower lip, which lent Persikov's face a permanently pouting expression. His red nose was surmounted by old-fashioned tiny spectacles in a silver frame. His eyes were small and shiny. He was tall, with a slight stoop, and he spoke in a high, croaking voice. Among his other peculiarities was his habit, whenever he spoke of anything emphatically and with assurance, of screwing up his eyes and holding up the forefinger of his right hand, curled into a hook. And since he always spoke with assurance, his erudition in his field being phenomenal, the hook appeared very often before the eyes of Professor Persikov's listeners. As for any subjects outside his field, which included zoology, embryology, anatomy, botany, and geography, Professor Persikov had little interest in them and scarcely ever troubled to speak about them.

The professor read no newspapers and never went to the theater. His wife had run away from him in 1913 with a tenor from the

Zimin Opera, leaving him the following note: "Your frogs make me shudder with intolerable loathing. I shall be miserable for the rest of my life remembering them."

The professor never remarried and had no children. He was extremely short-tempered, but cooled quickly; he was fond of tea with raspberries; and he lived on Prechistenka, in a five-room apartment. One of the rooms was occupied by his housekeeper, Marya Stepanovna, a shriveled little old woman who looked after the professor like a nurse after a child.

In 1919 the government requisitioned three of his five rooms, and he declared to Marya Stepanovna, "If they don't stop these outrages, Marya Stepanovna, I shall emigrate abroad."

Had the professor realized his plan, he could easily have obtained the chair of zoology at any university in the world, since he was a truly outstanding scientist. With the exception of the professors William Weccle of Cambridge and Giacomo Bartolommeo Beccari of Rome, he had no equals in the field bearing in one way or another on the amphibians. Professor Persikov was able to lecture in four languages in addition to Russian, and he spoke French and German as fluently as Russian. But his intention to emigrate was never carried out, and 1920 proved to be even worse than 1919. Events succeeded one another. First, Great Nikitskaya was renamed Herzen Street. Then the clock on the building at the corner of Herzen and Gorokhovaya stopped at a quarter past eleven. And finally, the terraria at the Zoological Institute became the scenes of wholesale deaths: the first to die, unable to endure the perturbations of that famous year, were eight splendid examples of the tree frog; then fifteen ordinary toads gave up the ghost, followed, finally, by a most remarkable specimen of the Surinam toad.

Directly after the toads, whose deaths decimated the population of that first order of amphibians which is justly known as tailless, the Institute's watchman, old Vlas, who did not belong to the class of amphibians, moved on into the better world. The cause of his demise, however, was the same as that of the poor beasts, and Persikov diagnosed it at once: "Lack of feed."

The scientist was perfectly right: Vlas had to be fed with flour, and the toads with mealworms, but since the former had disappeared, the latter had also vanished. Persikov thought of shifting the remaining twenty examples of the tree frog to a diet of cockroaches, but the cockroaches had also disappeared somewhere, demonstrating their malicious enmity toward War Communism. And so, the last examples also had to be thrown out into the garbage pits in the Institute's backyard.

The effect of the deaths, especially that of the Surinam toad, upon Persikov defies description. He put the entire blame for the misfortune upon the current People's Commissar of Education.

Standing in his hat and galoshes in the corridor of the chilly Institute, Persikov spoke to his assistant, Ivanov, a most elegant gentleman with a pointed blond beard. "Killing him is not enough for this, Pyotr Stepanovich! What are they doing? They will ruin the Institute! Eh? A magnificent male, an extraordinary example of *Pipa americana*, thirteen centimeters long!"

As time went on, things went from bad to worse. After Vlas died, the windows of the Institute froze over altogether, and the inner surface of the glass became encrusted with patterned ice. The rabbits died, then the foxes, the wolves, the fish, and all the grass snakes. Persikov went about in silence all day. Then he caught pneumonia, but did not die. After recovering, he came to Institute to lecture twice a week in the amphitheater, where the temperature for some reason remained a constant five degrees below freezing regardless of the weather outside. Standing in his galoshes, in a hat with earflaps, and a woolen muffler, exhaling clouds of white steam, he lectured to eight students on "The Reptilia of the Torrid Zone." The rest of the time Persikov spent at home. Covered with a plaid shawl, he lay on the sofa in his room, which was crammed to the ceiling with books, coughed, stared into the open maw of the fiery stove that Marya Stepanovna was feeding with gilded chairs, and thought about the Surinam toad.

But everything in the world comes to an end; 1920 ended, giving way to 1921. And the latter year witnessed the beginning of a certain reverse trend. First, Pankrat appeared, to replace the late Vlas. He was still young, but he showed great promise as a zoo-keeper and janitor. The Institute building was now beginning to be heated. And in the summer, Persikov managed, with Pankrat's help, to catch fourteen examples of the *Bufo vulgaris*, or common toad, in the Klyazma River. The terraria once again teemed with life.

In 1923 Persikov was already lecturing eight times a week—three times at the Institute and five at the university. In 1924 he lectured thirteen times a week, as well as at workers' universities. And in 1925 he gained notoriety by flunking seventy-six students, all of them on the subject of the amphibians.

"You do not know how the amphibians differ from the reptiles?" Persikov would ask. "It is simply ridiculous, young man. The amphibians have no pelvic buds. None. Yes, you ought to be ashamed. You are probably a Marxist?"

"I am," the flunked student would answer, wilting.

"Very well, come back for reexamination in the fall, please," Persikov would say politely. Then he would turn briskly to Pankrat: "Next!"

Just as amphibians revive after the first heavy rain following a long drought, so Professor Persikov revived in 1926, when the united Russo-American Company built fifteen fifteen-story houses in the center of Moscow, starting at the corner of Gazetny Lane and Tverskaya, and three hundred eight-family cottages for workers on the outskirts of town, ending once and for all the frightful and absurd housing crisis which had caused the residents of Moscow so much hardship from 1919 to 1925.

In general, it was a splendid summer in Persikov's life, and he often rubbed his hands with a quiet and contented chuckle, recalling how crowded he had been in two rooms with Marya Stepanovna. Now the professor had all his five rooms restored to him: he spread out, arranged his 2,500 books, his stuffed animals, diagrams, and specimens in their proper places, and lit the green-shaded lamp in his study.

The Institute was also unrecognizable: it had been given a coat of ivory paint, a special pipeline had been installed to carry water to the reptiles' room, and all ordinary glass was replaced by plate glass. The Institute was also provided with five new microscopes, glass-topped dissecting tables, 2,000-watt lamps with indirect lighting, reflectors, and cases for the museum specimens.

Persikov revived, and the whole world learned about it in December, 1926, when he published his pamphlet entitled "More on the Problem of the Propagation of the Gastropods."

And the summer of 1927 saw the appearance of his major opus, 350 pages long, later translated into six languages, including Japanese, *The Embryology of the Pipidae, Spadefoot Toads, and Frogs,* State Publishing House—price, three rubles.

But in the summer of 1928 came those incredible, frightful events. . . .

CHAPTER 2   The Colored Spiral

And so, the professor turned on the light and looked around. He switched on the reflector on the long experiment table, put on a white smock, and tinkled with some instruments.

Many of the thirty thousand mechanical carriages which sped through Moscow in 1928 swished past the Institute along the smooth paving stones of Herzen Street, and every other minute a trolley, marked Route 16 or 22 or 48 or 53, rolled, grinding and clattering, from Herzen Street toward Mokhovaya. Reflections of varicolored lights flashed through the plate-glass windows of the room, and far and high above, next to the dark, heavy cap of the Cathedral of Christ, hung the misty, pale crescent of the moon.

But neither the moon nor the noise of Moscow in the springtime was of the slightest interest to the professor. He sat on a three-legged revolving stool and with tobacco-stained fingers turned the adjustment screw of the magnificent Zeiss microscope, examining an ordinary undyed preparation of fresh amoebas.

As Persikov was shifting the magnifier from five to ten thousand, the door opened slightly, affording a view of a pointed goatee and a leather bib, and the professor's assistant called, "Vladimir Ipatievich, I have set up a mesentery. Would you like to see it?"

Persikov nimbly slid off the stool, leaving the knob halfway, and, slowly turning a cigarette in his hands, he walked to his assistant's room. There, on the glass table, a frog, half-dead with fear and pain, was crucified on a cork plate, its translucent viscera pulled out of its bloody abdomen into the microscope.

"Very good," said Persikov, bending over the eyepiece.

Evidently, he could see something very interesting in the frog's mesentery, where living blood corpuscles ran briskly along the rivers of the vessels. Persikov forgot his amoebas and for the next hour and a half took turns with Ivanov at the microscope lens. As they looked, the two scientists kept up an exchange of animated comments, incomprehensible to ordinary mortals.

Finally, Persikov leaned back from the microscope, announcing, "The blood is clotting, that's that."

The frog moved its head heavily, and its dimming eyes were clearly saying, You're rotten scoundrels, that's what you are.

Stretching his numbed legs, Persikov rose, returned to his laboratory, yawned, rubbed his fingers over his permanently inflamed eyelids, and, sitting down on the stool, glanced into his microscope. He put his fingers on the knob, intending to turn it down. But he did not turn it. With his right eye, Persikov saw a blurred white disk, and in it, a number of faint, pale amoebas. But in the center of the disk there was a colored spiral resembling a woman's curl. Persikov himself and hundreds of his students had seen this spiral many times, and no one had ever taken any interest in it. Indeed, there was no reason to be interested. The multicolored swirl of light merely interfered with observation and showed that the microscope was not in focus. It was therefore ruthlessly eliminated with a single turn of the knob, bringing an even white light to the entire field of vision.

The zoologist's long fingers had already taken a firm grasp on the knob, when suddenly they quivered and withdrew. The reason for this lay in Persikov's right eye, which had in turn become intent, astonished, and then widened with something like alarm.

No, this was not some wretched mediocrity at the microscope. It was Professor Persikov! His whole mind, his whole life, was now concentrated in his right eye. For some five minutes the higher creature observed the lower one, tormenting and straining his eye over the preparation outside the field of focus. Everything around was silent. Pankrat was already asleep in his room off the vestibule. For a single moment the glass doors of the cabinets rang musically and delicately in the distance: Ivanov was locking his study before leaving. The front door groaned after him. And it was only later that the professor's voice was heard. He was asking, no one knows whom, "What is this? I do not understand."

A truck rolled down Herzen Street, shaking the old walls of the Institute. The flat glass bowl with the forceps tinkled on the table. The professor went pale and raised his hands over the microscope like a mother over an infant threatened with some danger. There was no longer any question of turning the knob. No, he was afraid that some outside force might push what he had seen out of the field of vision.

It was bright morning, with a strip of gold slanting across the ivory entrance of the Institute, when the professor left the microscope and walked on his numb feet to the window. With trembling fingers he pressed a button, and the thick black shades shut out the morning, returning the wise, learned night to the study. Sallow and inspired, Persikov stood with his feet spread wide apart, staring at the parquet with tearing eyes. "But how can this be? But it is monstrous! . . . It is monstrous, gentlemen," he repeated, addressing the toads in the terrarium. But the toads slept and did not answer.

He was silent for a moment, then he raised the shades, turned off all the lights, and glanced into the microscope. His face became tense, and his shaggy yellow eyebrows came together. "Uhmm, uhmm," he muttered. "Gone. I see. I see-e-e," he drawled, looking like an inspired madman at the extinguished bulb overhead. "It is very simple."

He swished the shades down once more and lit the bulb again. Glancing at the bulb, he grinned gleefully, almost rapaciously.

"I'll catch it," he said with solemn emphasis, "I'll catch it. The sun might do it, too."

Again the shades flew up. The sun was coming out. It poured its brightness on the Institute walls and fell in slanting planes across the paving stones of Herzen Street. The professor looked out of the window, calculating the position of the sun during the day. He stepped away and returned, again and again, hopping slightly, and finally leaned over the windowsill on his stomach.

He busied himself with important and mysterious tasks. He covered the microscope with a glass bell. Melting some sealing wax over the blue flame of the burner, he sealed the edges of the bell to the table, pressing down the lumps of wax with his thumb. Then he turned off the gas, went out of his study, and locked the door with the patent lock.

The Institute corridors were still in semidarkness. The professor found his way to Pankrat's room and knocked on the door for a long time without result. At last there was a sound behind the door resembling the growling of a chained dog, hoarse coughing and mumbling, and Pankrat appeared in a square of light, in striped underpants tied at his ankles. His eyes stared wildly at the scientist; he was still groaning with sleep.

"Pankrat," said the professor, looking at him over his spectacles. "Excuse me for waking you. Listen, my friend, don't go into my study this morning. I left some work there, and it must not be moved. Understand?"

"U-hm-m-mm, I understand," Pankrat answered, understanding nothing. He swayed on his feet and growled.

"No, listen, wake up, Pankrat," said the zoologist, poking Pankrat lightly in the ribs, which brought a frightened look into the watchman's face and a shade of intelligence into his eyes. "I locked the study," continued Persikov. "Don't go in to clean up before I return. Do you understand me?"

"Yes, sir-r," gurgled Pankrat.

"Excellent, now go back to sleep."

Pankrat turned, disappeared behind the door, and immediately tumbled back into bed, while the professor began to dress in the vestibule. He put on his gray summer coat and soft felt hat. Then, recalling the picture in the microscope, he stared at his galoshes for many seconds, as if he had never seen them before. Then he put on the left galosh and tried to put the right one over it, but it would not go on.

"What a fantastic accident, his calling me," said the scientist, "or I should never have noticed it. But what does it promise? . . . Why, the devil alone knows what it can lead to!"

The professor grinned, squinted at his feet, removed the left galosh, and put on the right one. "Good God! But one can't even imagine all the consequences." The professor contemptuously kicked away the left galosh, which irritated him by refusing to fit over the right one, and went to the door in one galosh. He dropped his handkerchief and walked out, slamming the heavy door. On the stairs, he searched for a long time in his pockets for matches, patting his sides; then he found them and started down the street with an unlit cigarette in his lips.

The scientist did not meet a single soul all the way to the cathedral. There the professor lifted up his face and gaped at the golden cupola. The sun was gaily licking it from one side.

"How is it I have never seen it before, such a strange coincidence? . . . Damn it, what a fool." The professor bent down and fell into deep thought, looking at his variously shod feet. "Hm . . . What's to be done now? Go back to Pankrat? No, he won't wake up. A pity to throw it away, the vile thing. I'll have to carry it." He removed the galosh and carried it squeamishly in his hand.

An ancient little car with three passengers turned the corner from Prechistenka. There were two tipsy men in it and a garishly painted woman sitting on their knees, in silk pajamas of the latest 1928 style.

"Hey, daddy!" she cried in a low, hoarse voice. "What dive d'you leave the other one in?"

"The old man must have loaded up at the Alcazar," howled the drunk on the left, while the one on the right stuck his head out of the car and cried, "Hi, grandpa, is the all-night tavern on Volkhonka open? We're heading there!"

The professor looked at them sternly above his glasses, dropped the cigarette from his lips, and instantly forgot their existence. Slanting rays of sunshine cut across the Prechistensky Boulevard, and the cap of the Cathedral of Christ was aflame. The sun had risen.

CHAPTER 3   Persikov Caught It

The facts of the situation were as follows. When the professor brought the inspired eye of genius to the eyepiece of the microscope, he noticed for the first time in his life the presence of a particularly thick and vivid ray in the multicolored whorl. This ray was bright red and emerged from the whorl in a little sharp point, like a needle.

It was simply a stroke of bad luck that this ray happened to arrest the expert eye of the virtuoso for several seconds.

Within this ray, the professor caught sight of something that was a thousand times more significant than the ray itself, that fragile accidental by-product of the movement of the microscope's lens and mirror. Because his assistant had called the professor away, the amoebas remained for an hour and a half subjected to the action of this ray, and the results were these: while the granular amoebas outside the ray lay about limp and helpless, strange phenomena were taking place within the area illuminated by the tiny red dagger. The red strip teemed with life. The gray amoebas, stretching out their pseudopods, strove with all their might toward the red strip, and, reaching it, revived as by a miracle. Some force seemed to infuse them with living energy. They swarmed in flocks and fought each other for a place under the ray. Within it went on a frenzied (no other word can properly describe it) process of multiplication. Defying all the laws that Persikov knew as well as he knew his own five fingers, the amoebas budded before his eyes with lightning speed. They split apart within the ray, and two seconds later each part became a new, fresh organism. In a rew instants, these organisms reached their full growth and maturity,

merely to produce new generations in their turn. The red strip
and then the entire disk quickly became overcrowded, and the
inevitable struggle began. The newborn amoebas furiously attacked one another, tearing their victims to shreds and gobbling
them. Among the newly born lay the tattered corpses of those
which had fallen in the battle for survival. Victory went to the
best and the strongest. And these best ones were terrifying. To
begin with, they were approximately twice the size of ordinary
amoebas. Secondly, they were distinguished by extraordinary
viciousness and motility. Their movements were rapid, their
pseudopods much longer than those of the normal amoebas, and
they used them, without exaggeration, as an octopus uses its arms.

On the following evening, the professor, drawn and pale,
studied the new generation of amoebas. He had not eaten all day,
and he kept himself going only by smoking thick cigarettes, which
he rolled for himself one after the other. On the third day, he
went on to the prime source—the scarlet ray.

The gas hissed quietly in the burner, the traffic swished and
clattered on the pavement outside, and the professor, poisoned by
his hundredth cigarette, threw himself back in his revolving chair.
"Yes. Everything is clear now. They were revived by the ray. It is
a new ray, never studied, never discovered by anyone. The first
thing to be done is to find out whether it is produced only by
electric light or by the sun as well," Persikov muttered to himself.

In the course of the next night he had the answer. He caught
three rays in three microscopes, but had obtained none from the
sun. And he said to himself, "We must conclude that it does not
exist in the sun's spectrum . . . hmm . . . in short, we must conclude that it can be obtained only from electric light." He looked
lovingly at the frosted lamp above him, spent some time in inspired
meditation, and then invited Ivanov into his study. He told him
the entire story and showed him the amoebas.

Assistant Professor Ivanov was astounded, totally crushed.
Damnation, how was it that such a simple thing as this slender
arrow had never been noticed before! By anyone? Why, even by
himself? But it was really monstrous! Just look! . . . "But just look,

Vladimir Ipatyich!" cried Ivanov, his horrified eye glued to the eyepiece. "Look what is going on! They're growing before my eyes. . . . Look, look!"

"I have been observing them for three days," Persikov answered ecstatically.

A conversation ensued between the two scientists, the results of which may be summed up as follows: the assistant professor undertook to construct a chamber with the aid of lenses and mirrors that would produce a larger ray—and outside the microscope. Ivanov hoped—indeed, he was entirely confident—that it would be quite simple. He would obtain the ray, Vladimir Ipatyich need not doubt it. And here there was a slight pause.

"When I publish my work, Pyotr Stepanovich, I shall indicate that the chambers were constructed by you," Persikov put in, feeling that the pause needed to be resolved.

"Oh, that's unimportant. . . . However, of course . . ."

And so the pause was instantly eliminated. From that moment on, the ray utterly absorbed Ivanov as well. While Persikov wore himself out sitting all day and half the night over the microscope, Ivanov puttered in the physics laboratory, which gleamed with lights, combining lenses and mirrors. He was assisted by a mechanic.

After a request to the Commissariat of Education, Persikov received from Germany three parcels, containing mirrors and an assortment of polished lenses, biconvex, biconcave, and even convex-concave. In the end, Ivanov constructed the chamber and had indeed captured the scarlet ray in it. And in all justice, it was an expert job: the ray was thick and rich, almost four centimeters in diameter, sharp and powerful.

On the first of June, the chamber was installed in Persikov's room, and he avidly began to experiment with frog roe, exposing it to the ray. The experiments produced staggering results. Within two days, thousands of tadpoles hatched from the roe. And it took only a day before the tadpoles developed into frogs, but they were so vicious and greedy that half of them immediately devoured the others. And the survivors began without delay and without regard for time to spawn, so that before another two days were gone, they had produced a new generation, this time without the aid of the ray, and in countless multitudes. The scientist's office became the scene of something unimaginable: the tadpoles crawled off everywhere throughout the Institute. From the terraria, from the floor, from every nook and cranny came loud choruses as from a bog. Pankrat, who had always been afraid of Persikov, was now inspired with a single feeling toward him—mortal terror. After a week, the scientist himself began to feel that his mind was reeling. The Institute reeked of ether and prussic acid, and Pankrat, who had thoughtlessly removed his mask, had barely escaped poisoning. The teeming swamp population was finally exterminated with the aid of poisons, and the rooms and offices were thoroughly aired.

And Persikov remarked to Ivanov, "You know, Pyotr Stepanovich, the ray's effect on the deutoplasm and the ovum is quite remarkable."

Ivanov, ordinarily a cool and reserved gentleman, interrupted the professor in an unwontedly heated tone. "Vladimir Ipatyich, why talk about petty details, about deutoplasm? Let's be frank—you have discovered something unprecedented!" Then, obviously at the cost of great effort, Ivanov brought himself to conclude, "Professor Persikov, you have discovered the ray of life!"

A faint color suffused Persikov's pale, unshaven cheeks. "Now, now, now," he muttered.

But Ivanov continued. "Why, you will gain such a name. . . . It makes my head spin. Do you understand," he went on passionately, "Vladimir Ipatyich, the heroes of H. G. Wells are nothing compared to you. And I had always thought his stories were no more than fairy tales. . . . Do you remember his *Food of the Gods?*"

"Oh, a novel," said Persikov.

"Why, yes, good Lord, a famous one!"

"I don't recall it," said Persikov. "I read it once, but I don't remember it."

"You don't remember? Why, take a look at this." Ivanov picked up a dead frog of incredible size with a bloated belly from the glass-topped table and held it up by the leg. Even in death its face preserved an expression of utter malevolence. "But this is monstrous!"

CHAPTER 4   The Deaconess Drozdova

God knows how it happened, whether through Ivanov's indiscretion or because sensational news transmits itself somehow through the air, but everybody in gigantic, seething Moscow suddenly began to speak about Professor Persikov and his ray. At first this talk was haphazard and extremely vague. The news of the miraculous discovery hopped through the gleaming capital like a wounded bird, now vanishing, now fluttering up again, until the middle of July, when a short item about the ray appeared on the twentieth page of the newspaper *Izvestia*, under the heading of "News of Science and Technology." The item stated merely that a well-known professor of the Fourth State University had invented a ray which greatly stimulated the vital processes of lower organisms and that this ray required further study and verification. The name was, naturally, misspelled and turned into "Pevsikov."

Ivanov brought in the newspaper and showed the item to Persikov.

"Pevsikov," grumbled Persikov, puttering with the chamber in his study. "How do these windbags learn everything?"

Alas, the mispelled name did not save the professor from the flow of events, which began on the very next day, immediately upsetting the entire course of his life.

After a preliminary knock on the door, Pankrat entered the office and handed Persikov a magnificent satin-smooth calling card. "He's out there," Pankrat added timidly.

The card bore the following legend, printed in exquisite type:

ALFRED ARKADIEVICH BRONSKY
Contributor to the Moscow journals
Red Spark, *Red Pepper*, and *Red Projector*
and the newspaper *Red Evening Moscow*.

"Send him to the devil," Persikov said in a monotone and threw the card under the table.

Pankrat turned and walked out. Five minutes later he came back with a suffering face and a second copy of the same card.

"Are you playing a joke on me?" Persikov croaked and looked terrifying.

"The gentleman's from the GPU, the gentleman says," Pankrat answered, paling.

Persikov seized the card with one hand, almost tearing it in half, and with the other hand he threw a pair of pincers on the table. On the card, in curly handwriting, there was a message: "I beg sincerely and apologize, most esteemed professor, to receive me for three minutes in connection with a public matter of the press, and contributor to the satirical journal *The Red Raven*, publ. by the GPU."

"Call him in," said Persikov and gasped for breath.

A young man with a smoothly shaven, oily face bobbed up immediately from behind Pankrat's back. The face struck the onlooker with its permanently raised eyebrows, like a toy Chinaman's, and the little agate eyes beneath them, which never for a second met the eyes of anyone their owner spoke to. The young man was dressed immaculately and in the latest fashion: a long narrow jacket down to the knees, the widest bell-shaped trousers, and unnaturally wide patent-leather shoes with toes like hooves. In his hands the young man held a cane, a hat with a sharply pointed crown, and a notebook.

"What is it you wish?" asked Persikov in a voice that made Pankrat retire behind the door at once. "You were told I am busy."

Instead of answering, the young man bowed to the professor twice, once to the left and once to the right, and then his eyes ran eagerly over the room, and he jotted a quick entry in his notebook.

"I am busy," said the professor, looking with revulsion into the guest's restless little eyes, but without effect, since the eyes were impossible to catch.

"A thousand apologies, my most esteemed professor," the young man began in a thin, high-pitched voice, "for bursting in upon you and taking up your precious time, but the news of your world-shaking discovery, which has reechoed throughout the world, compèls our journal to beg you for whatever explanations—"

"What kind of explanations throughout the world?" Persikov squeaked in a falsetto, turning yellow. "I am not obliged to give you any explanations or anything of the sort. . . . I am busy . . . terribly busy."

"But what is it exactly you are working on?" the young man asked in sugary tones, and made another notation in his book.

"Oh, I . . . why do you ask? Do you intend to publish something?"

"Yes," answered the young man, scribbling furiously in his notebook.

"To begin with, I have no intention of publishing anything until I complete my work—and particularly in those sheets of yours. Secondly, how do you know all this?" Persikov suddenly felt that he was losing ground.

"Is it true that you invented a ray of new life?"

"What new life?" the professor snapped back. "What kind of nonsense are you babbling? The ray I am working on is still far from being fully investigated, and, generally, nothing is known about it as yet! It is possible that it may stimulate the vital processes of protoplasm."

"How much? How many times?" hurriedly inquired the young man.

Persikov was completely unnerved. A type! What the devil! "What kind of stupid questions are these? Suppose I say, oh, a thousand times. . . ."

A gloating, predatory spark flashed through the beady eyes of the visitor. "It produces giant organisms?"

"Nothing of the sort! Well, it is true that the organisms I obtained were larger than normal. . . . Well, they do possess certain new characteristics. But the important thing is not the size, but the incredible speed of reproduction." Persikov allowed the words to slip out to his misfortune and was immediately appalled. The young man had covered a whole page with his writing, turned the page, and scribbled on.

"But don't write!" the desperate Persikov pleaded hoarsely, already surrendering and feeling that he was entirely in the young man's hands. "What are you writing there?"

"Is it true that you can obtain two million tadpoles from frog roe within two days?"

"What quantity of roe?" Persikov shouted, infuriated again. "Have you ever seen a grain of roe . . . well, let us say, of a tree frog?"

"From half a pound?" the young man asked, undaunted.

Persikov turned purple. "Who measures it like that? Damn it! What are you talking about? Of course, if you take half a pound of frog roe, then . . . perhaps . . . well, what the devil, perhaps about that number or even more."

Diamonds sparkled in the young man's eyes and he covered another page in a single swoop. "Is it true that this will cause a worldwide revolution in stockbreeding?"

"What kind of a blasted newspaper question is that?" howled Persikov. "And, generally, I'll give you no permission to write nonsense. I can see by your face that you are cooking up some swinish trash!"

"Your photograph, Professor, I beg most urgently," the young man said, closing his notebook smartly.

"What? My photograph? For your vile little journals? To go with that rot you've scribbled there? No, no, and no! And I am busy. I will ask you—"

"Even an old one. We shall return it instantly."

"Pankrat!" the professor shouted in a rage.

"With my compliments," the young man said and disappeared.

Instead of Pankrat, Persikov heard the strange rhythmic creaking of some machine behind the door, a metal tapping on the floor, and a man of extraordinary bulk appeared in his study. He was dressed in a blouse and trousers made of blanket material. His left mechanical leg clacked and rattled, and in his hands he held a briefcase. His shaven round face, filled with yellowish jelly, presented an amiable smile. He bowed to the professor in military fashion and straightened up, which caused his leg to snap like a spring. Persikov went numb.

"Mr. Professor," the stranger began in a pleasant, ·slightly husky voice, "forgive an ordinary mortal who ventured to invade your privacy."

"Are you a reporter?" asked Persikov. "Pankrat!"

"By no means, sir," replied the fat man. "Permit me to introduce myself: sea captain and contributor to the newspaper *News of Industry,* published by the Council of People's Commissars."

"Pankrat!" Persikov screamed hysterically. At this moment the telephone in the corner flashed a red signal and rang softly. "Pankrat!" repeated the professor. "Hello, I'm listening."

"*Verzeihen Sie, bitte, Herr Professor,*" the telephone croaked in German, "*dass ich störe. Ich bin ein Mitarbeiter des Berliner Tageblatts.*"

"Pankrat!" The professor yelled into the receiver,"*Bin momentan sehr beschäftigt und kann Sie deshalb jetzt nicht empfangen!* . . . Pankrat!"

In the meantime, the bell at the front entrance of the Institute was ringing incessantly.

"Shocking murder on Bronny Street!" howled unnatural hoarse voices diving in and out among the stream of wheels and flashing headlights on the warm pavement. "Shocking outbreak of chicken plague in the yard of the widowed deaconess Drozdova, with her portrait! . . . Shocking discovery of Professor Persikov's life ray!"

Persikov recoiled so violently that he nearly fell under the wheels of a car on Mokhovaya, and he snatched a newspaper.

"Three kopeks, citizen!" shrieked the newsboy, and squeezing himself into the thick of the crowd on the sidewalk, he howled again: "*Red Evening Moscow*, discovery of X ray!"

The stunned Persikov opened the newspaper and leaned against a lamppost. From a smudged frame in the upper left corner of the second page there stared at him a bald-headed man with wild, unseeing eyes and a drooping jaw—the fruit of the artistic endeavors of Alfred Bronsky—with the caption: "V. I. Persikov, discoverer of the mysterious red ray." The article below it, under the heading, "World Riddle," began with the following words:

" 'Sit down, please,' the venerable scientist Persikov said to us affably . . ."

The article was signed with a flourish: "Alfred Bronsky (Alonso)."

A greenish light flared up over the roof of the university. The fiery words "SPEAKING NEWSPAPER" flashed in the sky, and Mokhovaya was instantly packed with a milling crowd.

" 'Sit down, please,' " the loudspeaker on the roof brayed suddenly in a most repulsive high-pitched voice, an exact replica of the voice of Alfred Bronsky, magnified a thousandfold, "the venerable scientist Persikov said to us affably! 'I have long desired to acquaint the proletariat of Moscow with the results of my discovery! . . .' "

A quiet mechanical creaking was heard behind Persikov's back, and someone tugged at his sleeve. Turning around, he saw the round yellow face of the owner of the mechanical leg. The man's eyes were moist with tears and his lips trembled. "You refused to acquaint me with the results of your astonishing discovery, Professor," he said dolefully, with a deep sigh. "Good-bye to my two smackers."

He looked gloomily at the roof of the university, where the invisible Alfred was ranting in the black maw of the speaker. For some reason, Persikov was suddenly sorry for the fat man.

"I never said any sit down please to him!" he muttered, angrily catching the words from the sky. "He is simply a brazen scoundrel of extraordinary proportions! Forgive me, please, but—you

understand—when you are working and people break in . . . I don't
mean you, of course . . ."

"Perhaps, sir, you would give me at least a description of your
chamber?" the mechanical man begged humbly and mournfully.
"After all, it's all the same to you now."

"Inside of three days, such multitudes of tadpoles hatch out of
half a pound of roe that it's impossible to count them!" roared
the invisible man in the loudspeaker.

Too-too, the cars boomed up and down Mokhovaya.

"Go-go-go . . . Did you ever! Ga-ga-ga . . ." rumbled the
crowd, gaping up.

"The scoundrel! Well!" Persikov hissed to the mechanical man,
trembling with indignation. "What do you say to that? Why, I
shall complain about him!"

"Outrageous," agreed the fat man.

A dazzling violet ray struck the professor's eyes, and everything
around flared up—the lamppost, a strip of tiled pavement, a yellow
wall, curious faces.

"That's for you, Professor," the fat man whispered ecstatically
and hung himself on to the professor's sleeve like a lead weight.
Something clicked rapidly in the air.

"To the devil with all of them!" Persikov exclaimed hopelessly,
tearing through the crowd with his ballast. "Hey, taxi! To Prechistenka!"

The dilapidated old car, vintage 1924, gurgled to a stop at the
curb, and the professor began to climb into it, trying to shake off
the fat man. "You crowd me," he hissed, covering his face with his
fists against the violet light.

"Did you read it? What are they saying? . . . Professor Persikov
and his children were found with their throats slit on Little Bron-
naya! . . ." voices shouted in the crowd.

"I have no children, the sons of bitches," Persikov screamed and
suddenly found himself in the focus of a black camera, which was
shooting him in profile with an open mouth and furious eyes.

Krch . . . too . . . krch . . . too, screeched the taxi, plunging
into the thick of the traffic.

The fat man was already seated in the car, warming the professor's side.

CHAPTER 5   The Chicken Affair

In a small provincial town, formerly called Troitsk and currently Steklovsk, in the Steklov District of the Kostroma Province, a woman in a kerchief and a gray dress with pink cotton posies came out onto the steps of a little house on the former Cathedral, and now Personal, Street and burst into tears. This woman, the widow of the former deacon Drozdov of the former cathedral, sobbed so loudly that soon another woman's head, in a downy woolen shawl, appeared in the window of the house across the street and called out, "What is it, Stepanovna? Any more?"

"The seventeenth!" the former Drozdova answered, sobbing bitterly.

"Oh, dear, dear," whimpered the woman in the shawl, shaking her head. "What a misfortune. Truly, the wrath of God! Is she dead?"

"Take a look, take a look, Matrena," muttered the deaconess, sobbing loudly and deeply. "See what's happening to her!"

The gray, sagging little gate slammed to, a woman's bare feet pattered across the dusty ruts of the street, and the deaconess, streaming with tears, led Matrena to her poultry yard.

It must be said that the widow of Father Savvaty Drozdov, who had died in 1926 of antireligious heartaches, did not lose courage, but founded a flourishing poultry business. As soon as the widow's affairs began to prosper, the government clapped such a tax upon her that her chicken-breeding activities were on the verge of coming to an end. But there were kind people. They advised the widow to inform the local authorities that she was organizing a workers' cooperative chicken farm. The membership of the cooperative consisted of Drozdova herself, her faithful servant Matreshka, and her deaf niece. The tax was immediately revoked, and the chicken business expanded and flourished. By 1928, the population of the widow's barnyard, flanked by rows of chicken coops, had increased to 250 hens; she even had some Cochin Chinas. The widow's eggs appeared in the Steklovsk market every Sunday; the widow's eggs were sold in Tambov; occasionally they were even seen in the glass showcases of the store that was formerly known as Chichkin's Cheese and Butter, Moscow.

And now a precious Brahmaputra, the seventeenth that morning and everybody's favorite, walked about the courtyard vomiting. "Er . . . rr . . . url . . . url," the hen gurgled and rolled her melancholy eyes to the sun as if she were seeing it for the last time. The working member of the cooperative, Matreshka, was dancing before the hen in a squatting postion with a cup of water in her hand.

"Here, darling, here . . . tsyp-tsyp-tsyp . . . drink some water," Matreshka pleaded, following the hen's beak with her cup; but the hen had no desire to drink. She opened her beak wide and stretched her neck to the sky. Then she began to vomit blood.

"Holy Jesus!" cried the guest, slapping herself on the thighs. "What's going on here? Poor slaughtered blood! I've never heard of such a thing, may I drop on the spot, never seen a chicken ailing with her stomach like a human being."

And those were the last words heard by the poor creature. She suddenly keeled over on her side, helplessly pecked the dust a few times, and turned up her eyes. Then she rolled over on her back, kicked her feet up to the sky, and remained motionless. Matreshka broke into a baritone wail, spilling the water in the cup. The deaconess, the chairman of the cooperative, followed suit, and the guest leaned over and whispered into her ear, "Stepanovna, may I eat dirt, but I'll say your chickens got the evil eye. Who's ever seen the likes of it? Why, there ain't no chicken sickness of this kind! Somebody sure bewitched your chickens."

"The enemies of my life!" exclaimed the deaconess to the sky. "Are they trying to drive me out of this world?"

Her words were answered by a loud crowing, after which a lean, bedraggled rooster flew out sideways from a chicken coop, like an obstreperous drunk out of a tavern. He goggled his eyes at the people, stamped furiously up and down on one spot, spread his wings like an eagle, but did not fly off anywhere. Instead, he began to run in circles around the yard. In the middle of the third circle, he stopped and became sick. Then he began to cough and wheeze, spewed bloody stains all around him, tumbled, and pointed his claws at the sun like masts. A new outburst of feminine wailing filled the courtyard, answered by anxious clucking, flapping, and noisy fussing from the coops.

"Well, isn't it the evil eye?" the guest cried triumphantly. "Call Father Sergy; let him hold a service."

At six in the evening, when the sun sat low like a flat fiery face among the round faces of the young sunflowers, Father Sergy, the prior of the Cathedral Church, was divesting himself of his robes, having completed the service. Curious heads stuck out over the crumbling old fence and peered through the cracks. The sorrowful deaconess kissed the cross, shed copious tears on the torn canary-yellow ruble note, and handed it to Father Sergy, in response to which he sighed and mumbled something about the Lord's wrath.

After that, the crowd in the street dispersed, and since hens retire early, nobody knew that three hens and a rooster had died at the same moment in the coop of Drozdova's next-door neighbor. They vomited, just like the Drozdov hens, and the only difference was that their deaths took place in a locked coop and without noise. The rooster tumbled off the perch head down and died in that position. As for the widow's poultry yard, by evening her coops were deadly quiet—the hens lay on the floor in heaps, stiff and cold.

When the town awakened in the morning, it was stunned as by a thunderclap, for the affair assumed strange and monstrous proportions. By noontime, only three hens were still alive on Personal Street—and those belonged to the last house, where the district financial inspector lived. But even they were dead by one o'clock in the afternoon. And by evening the town of Steklovsk hummed like a beehive with the dread word "plague." Drozdova's name appeared in the local newspaper, *The Red Warrior*, in an article headed "Can It Be Chicken Plague?" And from thence it was carried to Moscow.

Professor Persikov's life took on a strange quality, restless and disturbing. It was no longer possible to work. On the day after he had gotten rid of Alfred Bronsky, he was compelled to disconnect his office telephone at the Institute by taking the receiver off the hook. And in the evening, as he rode home by trolley along Okhotny Row, the professor beheld himself on the roof of a huge building with a black sign—"WORKERS' GAZETTE." Crumbling and flickering and turning green, the professor was climbing into a taxicab, and behind him, clutching at his sleeve, lumbered a mechanical globe in a blanket. The professor on the roof, huge on the white screen, shielded himself with his fists against a violet ray. Then a golden legend leaped out upon the screen: "Professor Persikov in a taxi, explaining his discovery to our famous reporter Captain Stepanov." And, indeed, the wavering car flicked past the Cathedral of Christ on Volkhonka, and in it the professor rolled helplessly, with a physiognomy that bore an expression remarkably like that of a wolf at bay.

"Devils, not men," the zoologist hissed through his teeth as he rode past.

That same evening, when he returned to his rooms on Prechistenka, the housekeeper, Marya Stepanovna, handed the zoologist seventeen slips of paper with telephone numbers that had called during his absence, along with a verbal declaration that she was plumb worn out. The professor was about to tear up the notes, when his eye caught the words, "People's Commissar of Public Health" on one of the slips.

"What is this?" the learned eccentric asked in bewilderment. "What has come over them?"

At a quarter past ten the doorbell rang, and the professor was obliged to receive a certain citizen in dazzling attire. The visitor won admission by his calling card, which stated (without name or initials), "Plenipotentiary Chief of the Trade Departments of Foreign Embassies to the Soviet Republic."

"Why doesn't he go to hell?" growled Persikov, throwing down his magnifying glass and some diagrams on the green cloth of the table. Then he said to Marya Stepanovna, "Ask him here into my study, this plenipotentiary."

"What can I do for you?" Persikov asked in a tone that made the Chief wince. Persikov transferred his spectacles from the bridge of his nose to his forehead, then back, and peered at his visitor, who glittered with patent leather and precious stones. In his right eye sat a monocle. What a vile physiognomy, Persikov thought to himself.

The guest began in a somewhat roundabout way. He begged permission to light his cigar, in consequence of which Persikov most reluctantly invited him to sit down. The guest proceeded to offer extended apologies for coming so late. "But . . . the professor is quite impossible to catch . . . hee-hee . . . pardon . . . to find during the day." (When he laughed, the visitor sobbed like a hyena.)

"Yes, I am busy!" Persikov answered so shortly that the guest twitched again.

"Nevertheless, he permitted himself to disturb the famous scientist. Time is money, as they say. . . . Is the cigar annoying the professor?"

"Mur-mur-mur," answered Persikov. "He permitted? . . ."

"We understand that the professor has discovered the ray of life?"

"In heaven's name, what life! It's a reporter's fiction!" Persikov became more animated in his anger.

"Oh, no, hee-hee-hee. . . . He understands perfectly the modesty which is the true adornment of all genuine men of science. But why beat about the bush? There were many communiqués. All the world capitals, such as Warsaw and Riga, already know everything about the ray. Professor Persikov's name is on the lips of the whole world. The world follows Professor Persikov's work with bated breath. But everybody is aware of the difficult position of scientists in Soviet Russia. *Entre nous soit dit.* . . . There are no strangers here? . . . Alas, in this country they do not know how to appreciate scientific work. And so he would like to talk things over with the professor. . . . A certain foreign state is offering, quite disinterestedly, to help Professor Persikov with his laboratory work. Why cast pearls here, as the Holy Writ says? The said state knows of the difficulties the professor had to endure in 1919 and 1920, during this . . . hee-hee . . . revolution. Well, of course, in the strictest confidence . . . the professor would acquaint the said state with the results of his labors, and in exchange it would finance the professor. Take, for example, the chamber which he has constructed—it would be interesting to become acquainted with the blueprints for this chamber . . ."

At this point the visitor drew from the inner pocket of his coat a dazzlingly white sheaf of bills. "A trifling advance, say, five thousand rubles, can be placed at the professor's disposal at this very moment . . . And, of course, there is no need of a receipt . . . Indeed, the Plenipotentiary Chief would feel offended if the professor as much as mentioned a receipt."

"Out!" Persikov suddenly roared so loudly that the piano in the parlor made an answering sound with its high keys.

The guest vanished so quickly that Persikov, shaken as he was with rage, began to doubt whether he had been there at all. Could it have been a hallucination?

"His galoshes?" Persikov howled a few seconds later from the hallway.

"The gentleman forgot them," said the trembling Marya Stepanovna.

"Throw them out!"

"Where can I throw them? He'll come back for them."

"Take them to the house committee. Get a receipt. I don't want the sight of them here! Let the committee have the spy's galoshes!"

Crossing herself, Marya Stepanovna picked up the magnificent rubber galoshes and carried them out to the back stairs. She stood for a few moments behind the door, then hid the galoshes in the pantry.

"Did you turn them in?" Persikov raged.

"I did."

"The receipt!"

"But, Vladimir Ipatyich, you know the chairman is illiterate. . . ."

"This—very—instant—I—want—the—receipt—here! Let some literate son of a bitch sign for him!"

Marya Stepanovna merely shook her head, went out, and returned fifteen minutes later with a note: "Received from Prof. Persikov 1 (one) pair galo. Kolesov."

"And what's this?"

"A tag, sir."

Persikov trampled the tag underfoot and hid the receipt under the blotter. Then some idea darkened his lofty forehead. He rushed to the telephone, roused Pankrat at the Institute, and inquired whether "everything is in order." Pankrat growled something into the receiver, from which the professor was able to conclude that everything, in his judgment, was in order.

But Persikov felt reassured only for a minute. Frowning, he clutched the telephone and poured out breathlessly, "Give me . . . oh, whatever you call it . . . the Lubyanka. . . . *Merci*. . . . Which of you there should be told about this? . . . I have suspicious individuals hanging around here in galoshes, yes. . . . Professor Persikov of the Fourth University."

The line was abruptly disconnected. Persikov walked away from the telephone, mumbling and swearing at someone.

"Will you have some tea, Vladimir Ipatyich?" Marya Stepanovna asked timidly, poking her head into the study.

"I don't want any tea . . . mur-mur-mur . . . and to hell with them . . . a bunch of maniacs. . . . I don't care."

Exactly ten minutes later the professor was receiving new guests in his study. One of them, amiable, rotund, and very polite, wore a modest khaki-colored military jacket and riding breeches. On his nose perched a pair of pince-nez, like a crystal butterfly. Generally, he looked like an angel in patent-leather boots. The second, short and extremely gloomy, wore civilian clothing, but the fit suggested that it constrained him. The third guest behaved in a peculiar manner. He did not enter the professor's study, but remained in the half-dark hallway, which afforded him a full view of the well-lit, smoke-filled study. The face of this third visitor, who was also in mufti, was graced with dark pince-nez.

The two in the study carefully examined the calling card and wore Persikov out completely with questions about the five thousand and with repeated demands for a description of the earlier visitor.

"The devil knows him," croaked Persikov. "A revolting physiognomy. A degenerate."

"He doesn't have a glass eye?" the short man asked hoarsely.

"The devil knows him. But no, it isn't glass; his eyes keep running."

"Rubinstein?" the angel said in a low, questioning voice to the short civilian. But the latter moodily shook his head. "Rubinstein wouldn't give any money without a receipt, never," he mumbled. "This is not Rubinstein's work. It's something bigger."

The story of the galoshes provoked a burst of the liveliest interest in the guests. The angel uttered a few words into the telephone of the house office: "The State Political Administration invites the secretary of the house committee Kolesov to report at Professor Persikov's apartment with the galoshes." And Kolesov appeared instantly, pale, and with the galoshes in his hands.

"Vasenka!" the angel called quietly to the man who sat in the hallway. The latter rose limply and ambled into the study like an unwound automaton. His smoky glasses swallowed up his eyes. "Well?" he asked laconically in a sleepy voice.

"The galoshes."

The smoky eyes slid over the galoshes, and for a second it seemed to Persikov that there was nothing sleepy about them at all; in fact, the eyes that flashed sideways for a brief moment from behind

the glasses were astonishingly sharp. But they immediately faded
out.

"Well, Vasenka?"

The man they addressed as Vasenka drawled out lazily, "Well,
what's the problem? They're Pelenzhkovsky's."

The house committee instantly lost Professor Persikov's con-
tribution. The galoshes disappeared into a newspaper. The angel
in the military jacket was overjoyed. He rose, began to press the
professor's hand, and even concluded with a little speech, to the
effect that "it does the professor honor. . . . The professor may
be sure that no one will trouble him again, either at the Institute
or at home. . . . Steps will be taken; the chambers are completely
safe."

"Could you shoot the reporters while you're at it?" Persikov
asked, looking at him over his glasses.

His question provoked a burst of merriment among his guests.
Not only the glum little man, but even the smoky one smiled in
the foyer. The angel, sparkling and glowing, explained that this
was impossible.

"And who was that scoundrel who came here?"

At this everybody stopped smiling, and the angel answered
evasively that it was nobody, a petty swindler, no one worth
troubling about. Nevertheless, he strongly urged the professor to
keep the evening's incident in complete confidence. And the guests
departed.

Persikov returned to his study and his diagrams, but he was not,
after all, allowed to go on with his work. The telephone flashed
on again, and a female voice inquired whether the professor would
like to marry an attractive and ardent widow, with a seven-room
apartment. Persikov bawled into the receiver, "I advise you to
take a course of treatment with Professor Rossolimo!" The telephone rang again.

This time Persikov was somewhat abashed: a sufficiently well-
known personage was calling from the Kremlin. He questioned
Persikov sympathetically and at great length about his work and

expressed a wish to visit the laboratory. When he left the telephone, Persikov mopped his forehead. Then he took the receiver
off the hook. At that moment there was a sudden blast of trum-
pets overhead, followed by the shrieking of Valkyries: the director of the Woolen Fabrics Trust in the upstairs apartment turned
on his radio to a broadcast of a Wagner concert from the Bolshoy
Theatre. Over the howling and crashing that poured down from
the ceiling, Persikov shouted to Marya Stepanovna that he would
sue the director, that he would smash the radio, that he would
leave Moscow and go to any damned corner of the world, for it
was obvious that people were dead set on driving him out of
there. He broke his magnifying glass and went to bed on the sofa
in his study. He fell asleep to the gentle ripple of piano keys under
the fingers of a famous pianist that came wafting from the Bolshoy
Theatre.

The surprises continued on the following day. When he arrived
at the Institute, Persikov found an unknown citizen in a stylish
green derby stationed at the entrance. The citizen scanned Persikov closely, but addressed no questions to him, and therefore
Persikov ignored him.

But in the foyer, Persikov was met by the bewildered Pankrat
and a second derby, which rose to greet him courteously. "Good
morning, Citizen Professor."

"What do you wish?" Persikov asked menacingly, pulling off
his coat with Pankrat's assistance. But the derby quickly pacified
Persikov, whispering in the tenderest tones that the professor had
no cause to be concerned. He, the derby, was there for the sole
purpose of shielding the professor from any importunate visitors;
the professor could set his mind at rest in regard not only to the
doors of his study, but also to the windows. Upon which the
stranger turned for a moment the lapel of his coat and showed
the professor a certain badge.

"Hm . . . I'll say you're well organized," Persikov mumbled,
and added naïvely, "and what will you eat here?"

The derby smiled and explained that he would be relieved.

After that, three days went by in splendid peace. The professor had two visits from the Kremlin. His only other visitors were students who came to take their examinations. The students flunked to a man, and their faces showed that Persikov was now the object of literally superstitious dread among them.

"Go and get jobs as conductors! You aren't fit to study zoology," came from the office.

"Strict, eh?" the derby asked Pankrat.

"A holy terror," answered Pankrat. "Even them that pass come out reeling, poor souls. He sweats the hide off them. They stumble out and head straight for the tavern!"

Engrossed in these minor affairs, the professor never noticed how three days flew by, but on the fourth day he was again recalled to reality. The cause of this was a thin, falsetto voice from the street. "Vladimir Ipatievich!" the voice shrilled from Herzen Street into the open window of the office.

The voice was in luck. Persikov was exhausted from all the events of the recent days. At the moment, he was resting in his armchair, staring weakly out of his red-rimmed eyes and smoking. He was too worn out to work any more. Hence it was even with some curiousity that he glanced out of the window and saw Alfred Bronsky on the sidewalk below. The professor immediately recognized the titled owner of the satiny calling card by his pointed hat and his note pad. Bronsky tenderly and deferentially bowed to the window.

"Oh, it's you?" the professor said. He did not have enough energy left to become angry, and he wondered with a faint stirring of interest, What next? Protected by the window, he felt secure from Alfred. The ever-present derby in the street instantly cocked an ear to Bronsky. A most disarming smile bloomed on the latter's face.

"Just a couple of minutes, dear Professor," Bronsky said, straining his voice from the sidewalk. "Only one tiny question, a purely zoological one. Will you permit me?"

"Go on," Persikov answered briefly and ironically. He thought to himself, There is, after all, something American in this rascal.

"What will you say as for the hens, dear Professor?" cried Bronsky, folding his hands into a trumpet.

Persikov was nonplussed. He sat down on the windowsill, then got up, pressed a button, and shouted, poking his finger in the direction of the window, "Pankrat, let in that fellow from the sidewalk."

When Bronsky appeared in the office, Persikov stretched his favor to the extent of barking out, "Sit down!"

And Bronsky, with a rapt smile, sat down on the revolving stool.

"Explain something to me," began Persikov. "You write for those papers of yours, don't you?"

"Yes, sir," Alfred replied deferentially.

"Well, it seems incomprehensible to me. How can you write when you don't even speak correctly? What sort of expressions are these—'a couple of minutes,' 'as for the hens'? You probably meant, 'about the hens'?

Bronsky broke into a thin, respectful giggle. "Valentin Petrovich corrects it."

"Who's Valentin Petrovich?"

"The chief of the literary department."

"Oh, well. Besides, I am not a philologist. Let's forget your Petrovich. What was it specifically that you wanted to know about hens?"

"Everything you might tell me, Professor." Bronsky armed himself with a pencil.

Triumphant sparks flashed in Persikov's eyes. "You needn't have applied to me. I am not a specialist on the feathered kingdom. You had best speak to Emelyan Ivanovich Portugalov, of the First University. I myself know very little."

Bronsky continued his adoring smile, as if to indicate that he understood the dear professor's joke. "Joke: little," he jotted in his notebook.

"However, if you are interested, very well. Hens, or pectinates . . . Order, *Gallinae*. Pheasant family . . ." Persikov recited loudly, looking not at Bronsky, but somewhere beyond him, where a thousand people were presumably listening. "Pheasant family, *Phasianidae*. Birds with a fleshy comb and two lobes under the lower jaw; hm . . . sometimes, of course, there is only one in the center of the chin. . . . What else? Wings, short and rounded. Tail, medium, somewhat serrated, the middle feathers crescent-shaped. . . . Pankrat, bring me Model No. 705 from the model cabinet—a cock in cross section. . . . But wait, you don't need this? Never mind, Pankrat. . . . I repeat, I am not a specialist; go to Portugalov. Well, I personally am acquainted with six species of wild hens—hm . . . Portugalov knows more—in India and the Malay Archipelago. For example, the Banki rooster, found among the foothills of the Himalayas, throughout India, in Assam and Burma. Then there is the swallow-tailed rooster, or *Gallus varius*, of Lombok, Sumbawa, and Flores. On the island of Java there is a remarkable rooster, *Gallus eneus*. In southeast India, I can commend to you the very beautiful *Gallus souneratti*. And in Ceylon we encounter the Stanley rooster, not found anywhere else."

Bronsky sat with bulging eyes, scribbling furiously.

"Is there anything else I can tell you?"

"I should like to know something about chicken diseases," Alfred whispered meekly.

"Hm, I am not a specialist. Ask Portugalov. . . . Well, there are intestinal worms, flukes, scab mites, red mange, chicken mites, poultry lice, or *Mallophaga*, fleas, chicken cholera, croupous-diphtheritic inflammation of the mucous membranes . . . pneumonomycosis, tuberculosis, chicken mange—there are all sorts of diseases." Sparks flashed in Persikov's eyes. "There can be poisoning, tumors, rickets, jaundice, rheumatism, the *Achorion schoenleinii* fungus . . . a most interesting disease. It produces little spots on the comb resembling mold."

Bronsky mopped his forehead with a brightly colored handkerchief. "And what do you think, Professor, is the cause of the present catastrophe?"

"What catastrophe?"

"Why, haven't you read, Professor?" Bronsky cried with astonishment and pulled out a crumpled page of the *Izvestia* from his briefcase.

"I don't read newspapers," answered Persikov, frowning.

"But why, Professor?" Alfred asked tenderly.

"Because they write nonsense," Persikov answered without a moment's hesitation.

"But what about this, Professor?" Bronsky whispered mildly, unfolding the newspaper.

"What is this?" asked Persikov, and even rose a little from his chair.

The sparks were now flashing in Bronsky's eyes. With a pointed, lacquered nail he underlined a huge headline across the entire page: "CHICKEN PLAGUE IN THE REPUBLIC."

"What?" Persikov asked, moving his glasses up to his forehead.

CHAPTER 6 Moscow in June of 1928

She gleamed brightly, her lights danced, blinked, and flashed on again. The white headlights of buses and the green lights of trolleys circled up and down Theater Square. Over the former Muir and Murrilis, above the tenth floor built up over it, a vari-colored electric woman jumped up and down, throwing out letters of many colors, which added up to the words, "WORKERS' CREDIT." In the square opposite the Bolshoy Theatre, around the glittering fountain that sent up multicolored sprays at night, a crowd milled and rumbled.

And over the Bolshoy, a giant loudspeaker boomed: "Anti-chicken vaccinations at the Lefort Veterinary Institute bring excellent results. The number of chicken deaths for the date decline by half."

Then the loudspeaker changed its timbre, something growled in it, a green stream flowed and flickered, died out and went on again, and the speaker complained in a deep basso: "Special commission set up to combat chicken plague, consisting of the People's Commissar of Public Health; the People's Commissar of Agriculture; the Chief of Livestock Breeding, Comrade Fowlin-Hamsky; Professors Persikov and Portugalov; and Comrade Rabinovich! . . . New attempts at intervention," the speaker laughed and wept like a hyena, "in connection with the chicken plague!"

Theater Lane, Neglinny Prospect, and the Lubyanka flared with white and violet streaks, sprayed shafts of light, howled with horns and sirens, and whirled up clouds of dust. Crowds of people pressed around the walls covered with large posters lit by garish red reflectors.

"Under threat of the most severe penalties, the population is forbidden to consume chicken meat and eggs. Private dealers who attempt to sell these in the markets will be subject to criminal prosecution and confiscation of all their property. All citizens who own eggs must promptly turn them in at the police precincts."

On the roof of *The Workers' Gazette* chickens were piled sky-high upon the screen, and greenish firemen, sparkling and quivering, poured kerosene on them from long hoses. Thin red waves flowed over the screen; unreal smoke billowed, tossed about raggedly, and crept in swirling rivulets; and fiery words leaped out: "Burning of chicken corpses on the Khodynka."

Among the madly blazing show windows of stores open till three in the morning (with two breaks for lunch and supper) gaped the blind holes of windows boarded up under their signs: "Egg Store. Quality Guaranteed." Very often, screaming alarmingly as they overtook the lumbering buses, cars marked "Moscow Health Department—First Aid" sped hissing past the traffic policemen.

"Another one has gone and stuffed himself on rotten eggs," the crowd rustled.

On the Petrovsky Lines, the world-famous Empire Restaurant gleamed with green and orange lights, and on its tables, next to the portable telephones, stood cardboard signs stained with liqueurs: "No omelet—by decree. Fresh oysters."

At the Ermitage, where tiny beads of Chinese lanterns glowed feebly amidst the artificial, cozy greenery, the singers Shramms and

Karmanchikov on the eye-shattering, dazzling stage sang ditties composed by the poets Ardo and Arguyev:

> "Oh, Mamma dear, what will I do
> Without eggs?"

while their feet tapped out a frantic dance.

Over the theater of the late Vsevolod Meyerhold who died, as everybody knows, in 1927, during the staging of Pushkin's *Boris Godunov*, when a platform with naked boyars collapsed over his head,* there flashed a moving varicolored sign announcing a new play, *Chicken Croak*, written by the dramatist Erendorg and produced by Meyerhold's disciple, Honored Director of the Republic Kukhterman. Next door, at the Aquarium Restaurant, scintillating with electric advertisements and bare female flesh and resounding with wild applause, the diners watched, amidst the greenery of the stage, a review by the writer Lazier entitled *The Hen's Children*. And down Tverskaya marched a procession of circus donkeys, with lanterns suspended from their heads and gleaming signs announcing the reopening of Rostand's *Chantecler* at the Korsh Theatre.

Newsboys howled among the wheels of motorcars: "Shocking discovery in a cave! Poland preparing for shocking war! Shocking experiments of Professor Persikov!"

At the former Nikitin Circus, in the oily brown arena, which smelled pleasantly of manure, the dead-white clown Bom was saying to Bim, bloated in checkered dropsy; "I know why you are so sad!"

"Vhy-i?" squeaked Bim in a falsetto.

"You buried your eggs underground, and the police of the fifteenth precinct found them."

"Ga-ga-ga-ga," the circus roared, chilling the blood in the veins with joy and anguish and making the trapezes and the cobwebs sway dizzily under the shabby cupola.

---

* Meyerhold's actual death was considerably more tragic. Arrested in 1939, he died in a concentration camp in 1942.

"A-ap!" shrilled the clowns, and a sleek white horse leaped into the arena, carrying on its back a woman of astonishing beauty, with long slender legs in scarlet tights.

Looking at no one, noticing no one, unresponsive to the nudging and the soft and tender invitations of prostitutes, Persikov, inspired and solitary, crowned with sudden fame, was making his way along Mokhovaya toward the fiery clock at the Manège. Here, seeing no one, engrossed in his thoughts, he collided with a strange, old-fashioned man, painfully stubbing his fingers against the wooden holster of a revolver attached to the man's belt. "Oh, damn!" squeaked Persikov. "Sorry."

"Sorry," answered the stranger in an unpleasant voice, and they disentangled themselves in the dense human stream. Turning to Prechistenka, the professor instantly forgot the encounter.

CHAPTER 7   Destin

We do not know whether it was owing to the success of the Lefort Veterinary Institute's inoculations, the skill of the Samara roadblock units, the effect of the stringent measures applied to the egg merchants of Kaluga and Voronezh, or the efficient work of the Extraordinary Commission in Moscow, but two weeks after Persikov's last interview with Alfred, the chicken crisis in the Union of Soviet Republics was already a thing of the past. Here and there a few desolate feathers still lay about in the dusty backyards of provincial towns, bringing tears to the eyes of the onlooker, and a few greedy people were still in hospitals, recovering from the last spasms of bloody diarrhea and vomiting. Fortunately, human deaths did not exceed a thousand for the entire republic. Nor were there any serious disorders. True, a prophet had appeared briefly in Volokolamsk, proclaiming that the chicken plague had been caused by none other than the commissars, but he enjoyed little success. In the Volokolamsk marketplace, a crowd beat up several policemen who were confiscating chickens from the market women, and some windows were smashed in the local post-and-telegraph office. Luckily, the efficient Volokolamsk authorities promptly took the necessary steps, resulting, first, in the cessation of the prophet's activities, and, second, in the replacement of the broken windows.

Having reached Archangel and Syumkin Village in the north, the plague stopped of itself, for the good reason that it could go no further; as everybody knows, there are no hens in the White Sea. It also halted at Vladivostok, beyond which there is only ocean. In the far south, it disappeared, petering out somewhere in the parched expanses of Ordubat, Dzhulfa, and Karabulak. And in the west, it halted miraculously exactly on the Polish and Rumanian borders. Perhaps the climate in these countries was different, or perhaps the quarantine established by the neighboring governments had done its job, but the fact remains that the plague had gone no further. The foreign press avidly and noisily discussed the unprecedented calamity, while the government of the Soviet Republics, without undue noise, worked tirelessly to set things right. The Extraordinary Commission to Fight the Chicken Plague changed its name to Extraordinary Commission for the Revival and Reestablishment of Chicken Breeding in the Republic and was augmented by a new Extraordinary Committee of Three, consisting of sixteen members. A "Goodpoul" office was set up, with Persikov and Portugalov as honorary vice-chairmen. The newspapers carried their portraits, over articles with such titles as "Mass Purchase of Eggs Abroad" and "Mister Hughes Wants to Torpedo the Egg Campaign." All Moscow read the stinging article by the journalist Kolechkin, which closed with the admonition, "Don't whet your teeth, Mr. Hughes, at our eggs— you have your own!"

Professor Persikov had worked himself to the point of exhaustion. For three weeks the chicken events disrupted his entire routine and doubled his duties and burdens. Every evening he had to attend conferences of chicken commissions, and from time to time he was obliged to endure long interviews either with

Alfred Bronsky or with the mechanical fat man. He had to work with Professor Portugalov and Assistant Professors Ivanov and Bornhart, dissecting and miscroscoping chickens in search of the plague bacillus. He even hastily whipped out a pamphlet in three evenings, "On the Changes in Chicken Kidneys as a Result of the Plague."

But Persikov worked in the chicken field without real enthusiasm, and understandably so: his mind was elsewhere, grappling with the most important, the central, problem, from which he had been diverted by the chicken catastrophe—the problem of the red ray. Straining still further his already shaken health, stealing hours from sleep and meals, often falling asleep on the oilcloth sofa in his office at the Institute instead of going home to Prechistenka, Persikov spent whole nights puttering with his chamber and his microscope.

By the end of July, the frenzy subsided a little. The work of the renamed commission settled into a normal groove, and Persikov returned to his interrupted work. The microscopes were loaded with new preparations, and fish and frog roe hatched in the chamber under the ray with fantastic speed. Specially ordered glass was brought by airplane from Königsberg, and during the last days of July, mechanics working under Ivanov's supervision constructed two large new chambers, in which the ray attained the width of a cigarette pack at its source and, at the widest point, measured a full meter. Persikov merrily rubbed his hands and began to prepare for some mysterious and complicated experiments. To begin with, he spoke by telephone with the People's Commissar of Education, and the receiver croaked out the warmest assurances of every possible assistance and cooperation. After that, Persikov telephoned Comrade Fowlin-Hamsky, the director of the Livestock Breeding Department of the Supreme Commission. Fowlin-Hamsky gave Persikov his most amiable attention. The matter involved a large order abroad for Professor Persikov. Hamsky said into the telephone that he would immediately wire Berlin and New York. After this there was a call from the Kremlin, to inquire how Persikov's work was progressing, and an important and affable voice asked whether Persikov would like to have a car placed at his disposal.

"No, thank you. I prefer the trolley," said Persikov.

"But why?" the mysterious voice asked, and smiled condescendingly.

In general, everybody spoke to Persikov either with deference and awe or with an indulgent smile, as though he were a small, though overgrown, child.

"It is faster," Persikov replied, to which the resonant basso responded in the telephone, "Well, as you wish."

Another week went by, and Persikov, withdrawing still further from the subsiding chicken problem, devoted himself completely to the study of the ray. From the many sleepless nights and overwork, his head felt light, as though transparent and weightless. The red rings never left his eyes now, and Persikov was spending almost every night at the Institute. Once he left his zoological refuge to deliver a lecture at the Tsekubu Hall on Prechistenka about his ray and its effect on the egg cell. It was a colossal triumph for the eccentric zoologist. The clapping of hands sent the plaster crumbling and pouring from the ceilings; under the hissing arc lights, the black dinner jackets of the Tsekubu members and the white gowns of the ladies dazzled the eye.

On the stage, on a glass-topped table next to the lectern, a moist gray frog the size of a cat sat on a platter, breathing heavily. Many notes flew to the stage. They included seven declarations of love, which Persikov tore up. He was dragged by main force onto the stage by the Tsekubu chairman to bow to the audience. Persikov bowed irritably; his hands were damp and sweaty, and the knot of his black tie was not under his chin, but behind his left ear. Hundreds of yellow faces and white shirtfronts wavered in the mist before him, and suddenly the yellow holster of a revolver flashed and disappeared somewhere behind a white column. Persikov vaguely noticed it, but forgot it at once. But as he was departing after the lecture, walking down the raspberry-colored carpet of the staircase, he suddenly felt ill. For a moment, the bright chandelier in the vestibule turned black, and Persikov felt queasy and nauseous. He thought he smelled something burning; it seemed to him that blood was dripping, hot and sticky, down his neck. And the professor caught at the rail with a trembling hand.

"Are you unwell, Vladimir Ipatyich?" anxious voices flew at him from all sides.

"No, no," answered Persikov, recovering. "I am simply over-tired. . . . Yes. May I have a glass of water?"

It was a very sunny August day. It interfered with the professor, and therefore the shades were drawn. A reflector on a flexible stand cast a sharp beam of light on the glass table piled with instruments and slides. Leaning in exhaustion against the backrest of the revolving armchair, Persikov smoked. His eyes, dead tired but pleased, gazed through the ribbons of smoke at the slightly open door of the chamber, where the red sheaf of his ray lay quietly, exuding its faint warmth into the already close and tainted air of the room.

Someone knocked at the door.

"Yes?" asked Persikov.

The door creaked softly, admitting Pankrat. With arms held stiffly at his sides, and blanching with awe before the super-natural being, he said, "Mr. Professor, there's someone asking for you out there. His name is Destin."

The semblance of a smile flitted across the scientist's cheeks. He narrowed his eyes and said, "That's interesting. But I am busy."

"They say they have an official paper from the Kremlin."

"Destiny with a paper? A rare combination," said Persikov. "Oh, well, bring him in!"

"Yes, sir," said Pankrat, and he slipped out of the door like an eel.

A moment later the door creaked again and a man appeared on the threshold. Persikov's chair squeaked as he turned, and he peered at the visitor over his shoulder, above his glasses. Persikov was too remote from life—he was not interested in it—but even Persikov was struck by the predominant, the salient, characteristic of the stranger: he was peculiarly old-fashioned. In 1919 this man would have been entirely appropriate in the streets of the capital; he would have passed in 1924, in the early part of the year; but in 1928 he was definitely odd. At a time when even the most backward section of the proletariat—the bakers—wore ordinary jackets, and the military tunic had already become a rarity in Moscow—an outdated article of apparel irrevocably discarded by the end of 1924—the visitor wore a double-breasted leather coat, olive trousers, puttees, gaiters, and a huge Mauser pistol of antiquated construction at his hip, in a cracked yellow holster. The visitor's face produced the same impression on Persikov as it did on everyone else—an extremely unpleasant one. His little eyes looked out at the world with astonishment but, at the same time, with assurance; there was something brash and aggressive even in the short legs and the flat feet. His face was closely shaven, almost bluish.

Persikov frowned. He squeaked mercilessly with his chair, and looking at the guest no longer over his glasses but through them, he asked, "You have a paper? Where is it?"

The visitor was obviously overwhelmed by what he saw. Ordinarily, he had little capacity for embarrassment, but here he was taken aback. Judging from his little eyes, he was daunted most of all by the twelve-tier bookcase, reaching to the ceiling and crammed with books. And then, of course, there were the chambers, in which—as though in hell—there flickered the scarlet ray, diffused and magnified by the glass walls. And, indeed, Persikov himself in the penumbra beside the sheaf of light thrown out by the reflector was sufficiently strange and majestic in his revolving chair.

The visitor stared at the professor; sparks of deference leaped through the usual assurance of his eyes. He offered no paper, but said, "I am Alexander Semyonovich Destin!"

"Yes? And?"

"I was appointed manager of the model Soviet farm—the 'Scarlet Ray' Sovkhoz," explained the guest.

"And?"

"And so I've come to see you, comrade, with a secret memorandum."

"Interesting. But make it short, please."

The visitor unbuttoned his coat and pulled out an order, printed on excellent thick paper. He held it out to Persikov. Then, without waiting for an invitation, he seated himself on a revolving stool.

"Don't push the table," Persikov said with hatred.

The visitor turned a frightened glance at the table, at the far end of which, in a moist dark aperture, a pair of eyes gleamed lifelessly like emeralds. They exuded a deadly chill.

The moment Persikov read the paper, he rose from the chair and rushed to the telephone. A few seconds later he was speaking hurriedly and with extreme irritation. "Excuse me. . . . I cannot understand. . . . How can this be? I . . . without my consent or advice . . . But heaven knows what he can do with it!"

The stranger turned on his stool, extremely offended. "Pardon me," he began, "I am the manag—"

But Persikov waved him off with his hooked forefinger and continued. "Excuse me, I cannot understand it . . . And, finally, I categorically protest. I shall not sanction any experiments with eggs. Before I try them myself—"

Something squawked and clicked in the receiver, and even from a distance it was clear that the voice in the receiver, patient and condescending, was speaking to a small child. The conversation ended with Persikov, beet-red, violently slamming down the receiver and crying past it to the wall, "I wash my hands!"

He returned to the table, took the paper, read it once from top to bottom above his glasses, then upside down through his glasses; and suddenly he howled, "Pankrat!"

Pankrat appeared in the door as though rising up a trap ladder at the opera.

Persikov glanced at him and barked, "Get out, Pankrat!"

Without showing the slightest astonishment, Pankrat disappeared.

Persikov turned to his visitor. "Very well. I submit. It's none of my business. Besides, I am not interested."

The visitor was not so much offended as amazed. "But pardon me, comrade," he began, "but you are—"

"Comrade . . . comrade. . . . Is that all you can say?" Persikov broke in sullenly.

Well! Destin's face seemed to say.

"Pard—"

"Now, if you please," interrupted Persikov. "This is the arc bulb. With its aid you obtain, by manipulating the ocular"— Persikov snapped the lid of the chamber, which looked like a camera—"a cluster of rays which you can gather by moving object-lense No. 1, here, and mirror No. 2." Persikov turned off the ray, then turned it on again on the floor of the asbestos chamber. "And on the floor you may arrange whatever you please and proceed to experiment. Extremely simple, don't you think?"

Persikov meant to express irony and contempt, but his visitor never noticed it, peering into the chamber with intent, glittering little eyes.

"But I warn you," continued Persikov, "keep your hands out of the ray, because, according to my observations, it causes growth of the epithelium—and, unfortunately, I have not yet established whether it is malignant or not."

The visitor quickly hid his hands behind his back, dropping his leather cap, and looked at the professor's hands. They were stained with iodine, and his right wrist was bandaged.

"And how do you manage, Professor?"

"You can buy rubber gloves at Schwab's on Kuznetsky Bridge," the professor answered irritably. "I am not obliged to worry about that."

Persikov suddenly looked up at the visitor, as though examining him through a magnifying glass. "Where do you come from? And, generally, why *you*?"

Destin was finally offended in earnest. "Pard—"

"After all, one must know what it is all about! Why have you latched on to this ray?"

"Because it's a matter of utmost importance."

"Ah. The utmost? In that case—Pankrat!" But when Pankrat appeared, he said, "Wait, I must think."

And Pankrat vanished obediently.

"I cannot understand one thing," said Persikov. "Why this haste and secrecy?"

"You get me muddled, Professor," answered Destin. "You know that all the chickens have died out—to the last one?"

"And what about it?" shrieked Persikov. "Do you intend to revive them instantly? Is that it? And why with the aid of a ray that has not yet been studied sufficiently?"

"Comrade Professor," replied Destin, "I must say, you mix me up. I tell you, we must reestablish chicken breeding, because they're writing all kinds of rot about us abroad."

"Let them write."

"Well, you know!" Destin responded ambiguously, shaking his head.

"I'd like to know whose idea it was to breed chickens from eggs."

"Mine," answered Destin.

"Uhmm . . . I see. . . . And why, if I may know? Where did you learn about the properties of the ray?"

"I attended your lecture, Professor."

"I haven't done anything with eggs as yet! I am only preparing to!"

"It'll work, I swear it will," Destin cried suddenly with conviction and feeling. "Your ray is so famous, you can hatch elephants with it, let alone chickens."

"Tell me," said Persikov. "You are not a zoologist? No? Too bad. You'd make a very bold experimenter. . . . Yes. But you are risking to end up . . . with failure. And you are taking up my time."

"We shall return your chambers. What do you mean?"

"When?"

"As soon as I breed the first batch."

"You speak with such confidence! Very well. Pankrat!"

"I have men with me," said Destin. "And guards."

By evening, Persikov's office was stripped and desolate. The tables stood bare. Destin's men had carted away the three large chambers, leaving the professor only the first—his own little one, in which he had begun his first experiments.

In the August twilight, the Institute turned gray; the grayness flowed along the corridors. From the study came the sound of monotonous footsteps; without turning on the light, Persikov paced the large room, from door to window. It was a strange thing: on that evening, an inexplicably dismal mood descended both on the people who inhabited the Institute and on the animals. The toads had for some reason raised a particularly melancholy concert, twittering ominously, as though in warning. Pankrat went chasing along the corridors after a grass snake that had escaped from its case, and when he caught it, the snake looked desperate, as though it had resolved to flee wherever its eyes would take it, only to get away.

In the deep dusk the bell rang from Persikov's study. Pankrat appeared on the threshold. He beheld a strange picture. The scientist stood, lost and solitary, in the middle of the room and looked at the tables. Pankrat coughed once and stood still.

"There, Pankrat," said Persikov, and he pointed to the denuded table.

Pankrat was shocked. It seemed to him that the professor's eyes were tearstained in the dusk. It was extraordinary and terrible.

"Yes, sir," Pankrat answered lugubriously, thinking, I'd rather you gave me hell!

"There," repeated Persikov, and his lips quivered, like a child's whose favorite toy had suddenly been taken from it. "You know, my good Pankrat," continued Persikov, turning away to the window, "my wife . . . she left me fifteen years ago and joined an operetta . . . and now it turns out she is dead. Such a thing, my dear Pankrat. . . . They sent me a letter."

The toads screamed piteously, and the twilight shrouded the professor. There it was . . . night . . . Moscow . . . some white spheres lit up somewhere outside the window. Pankrat, confused and anguished, stood with his hands straight down his sides, rigid with fear.

"Go, Pankrat," the professor said heavily and waved his hand. "Go to sleep now, Pankrat, my good friend."

And night came. Pankrat ran out of the study, on tiptoe for some reason, hurried to his cubbyhole, dug up a half-filled bottle of strong Russian vodka from under some rags in the corner, and gulped down almost a tea glass full in one breath. He chased it down with some bread and salt, and his eyes cheered up a little.

Later that evening, already close to midnight, Pankrat sat barefoot on a bench in the dimly lit vestibule and spoke to the sleepless derby on duty, scratching his chest under the calico shirt. "I'd rather he'd hit me, I swear I would."

"Really crying?" the derby asked with curiosity.

"Sure as I sit here," Pankrat assured him.

"A great scientist," agreed the derby. "Naturally, no frog can take the place of a wife."

"Naturally," echoed Pankrat. He thought a while and added, "I'm thinking to bring my woman out here. . . . Why should she sit all by her own in the village? But she can't stand them snakes and vermin nohow."

"They're sure a nasty lot," agreed the derby.

No sound came from the scientist's study. And there was no light there, no bright strip under the door.

CHAPTER 8   Events at the Soviet Farm

Truly, there is no season more beautiful than August in the country—say, in the Smolensk Province. The summer of 1928, as we know, was of the finest, with spring rains just in time; a full, hot sun; and an excellent harvest. The apples were ripening in the former Sheremetyev estate, the woods stood green, the fields

spread out in yellow squares. A man becomes better in the lap of
nature. And even Alexander Semyonovich would not have seemed
as unpleasant here as he had in the city. He no longer wore the
obnoxious leather coat. His face was bronzed by the sun, his unbuttoned calico shirt revealed a chest overgrown with the densest
black hair, his legs were clad in canvas trousers. And his eyes were
calmer and kinder.

Alexander Semyonovich briskly ran down the stairs from the
columned porch, over which a sign was nailed, bearing a star and
the words THE "SCARLET RAY" SOVKHOZ, and went to
meet the light truck which had brought him three black chambers
under guard.

All day Alexander Semyonovich was busy with his assistants,
installing the chambers in the former winter garden—the Sheremetyev greenhouse. By evening everything was ready. A frosted
white bulb glowed under the glass ceiling, the chambers were
set up on bricks, and the mechanic, who had arrived with the
chambers, clicked and turned the shiny knobs and lit the mysterious red ray on the asbestos floor of the black boxes.

Alexander Semyonovich bustled about and even climbed the
ladder himself to check the wiring.

On the following day, the truck returned and disgorged three
crates, made of excellent smooth plywood and plastered all over
with labels and warnings in white letters on black backgrounds:
Vorsicht: Eier! ("Careful: Eggs!")

"But why did they send so few?" wondered Alexander Semyonovich. However, he immediately applied himself to unpacking the
eggs. The unpacking was done in the same greenhouse, with the
participation of everyone: Alexander Semyonovich himself; his
wife, Manya, a woman of inordinate bulk; the one-eyed former
gardener of the former Sheremetyevs, currently serving in the
Sovkhoz in the universal capacity of watchman; the guard, con-
demned to life in the Sovkhoz; and the general maid, Dunya.
This was not Moscow, and everything was simpler and friendlier
here. Alexander Semyonovich directed the work, glancing lovingly
at the crates, which looked like such a solid, compact gift under

the tender sunset light filtering through the greenhouse windows. The guard, whose rifle dozed peaceably by the door, broke open the clamps and metal bindings with a pair of pliers. The air was filled with the sounds of tearing and splintering wood. Dust flew. Pattering softly with his sandals, Alexander Semyonovich bustled around the crates.

"Easy, please," he begged the guard. "Careful. Don't you see—you've got eggs there!"

"It's all right," the provincial warrior grunted, drilling mightily, "one moment." *Tr-r-r* . . . and the dust flew.

The eggs were packed exceedingly well: under the wooden lid there was a layer of waxed paper, then blotting paper, then a firm layer of wood shavings, and finally sawdust, in which the tips of the eggs gleamed whitely.

"Foreign packing," Alexander Semyonovich said admiringly, digging into the sawdust. "Not the way we do things. Manya, take care, you'll break them."

"You've gone silly, Alexander Semyonovich," answered his wife. "Imagine, such precious gold. As if I never saw eggs. . . . Oh! How large!"

"That's Europe for you," said Alexander Semyonovich, laying out the eggs on the wooden table. "What did you expect—our measly little peasant eggs? They must be Brahmaputras, all of them, the devil take 'em! German."

"Sure thing," echoed the guard, admiring the eggs.

"I don't understand, though, why they're dirty," Alexander Semyonovich said reflectively. "Manya, look after things. Let them go on with the unpacking. I am going to telephone."

And Alexander Semyonovich went to the Sovkhoz office across the yard to telephone.

In the evening, the telephone twittered in the office of the Zoological Institute. Professor Persikov ruffled his hair with his hand and went to answer. "Yes?" he asked.

"The province calling, just a moment," a woman's voice answered through the hissing receiver.

"Yes, I am listening," Persikov said squeamishly into the black mouth of the telephone.

Something clicked and snapped, and then a distant masculine voice anxiously spoke into the professor's ear. "Should the eggs be washed, Professor?"

"What? What is it? What are you asking?" Persikov cried irritably. "Who is speaking?"

"From Nikolsky, Smolensk Province," the receiver answered.

"I don't know what you're talking about. I don't know any Nikolsky. Who is it?"

"Destin," the receiver said sternly.

"What Destin? Oh, yes, it's you. Well, what is it you're asking?"

"Whether they should be washed. They sent me a shipment of chicken eggs from abroad."

"Well?"

"They seem slimy somehow."

"What nonsense. How can they be 'slimy,' as you put it? Well, of course, there can be a little . . . perhaps some droppings stuck to them . . . or something else."

"So they shouldn't be washed?"

"Of course not. So you're all ready to load the chambers with the eggs?"

"I am. Yes," replied the receiver.

"Hmm," Persikov snorted.

"So long," the receiver clicked and was silent.

" 'So long'," Persikov mimicked with hatred, turning to Assistant Professor Ivanov. "How do you like this type, Pyotr Stepanovich?"

Ivanov laughed. "It's he? I can imagine what he is going to cook up with those eggs out there."

"The m-m-m-moron!" Persikov stuttered furiously. "Just imagine, Pyotr Stepanovich. Very well, it is possible that the ray will produce the same effect on the deutoplasm of the chicken egg as it did on the plasm of the amphibians. It is very possible that the hens will hatch. But neither you nor I can say what kind of hens they will be. Perhaps they won't be good for anything. Perhaps they will die in a day or two. Perhaps they will be inedible. Can I guarantee that they will be able to stand on their feet? Perhaps their bones will be brittle." Persikov became more and more excited and waved his hands, crooking his forefingers.

"Very true," agreed Ivanov.

"Can you vouch, Pyotr Stepanovich, that they will produce future generations? Perhaps this imbecile will breed sterile hens. He'll drive them up to the size of a dog, and then you can wait for progeny until the second coming."

"No one can vouch for it," agreed Ivanov.

"And what brashness!" Persikov whipped himself up still further. "What insolence! And I am ordered to instruct this scoundrel." Persikov pointed to the paper delivered by Destin (it lay on the instrument table). "How can I instruct this ignoramus, when I myself cannot say anything on this problem?"

"Was it impossible to refuse?" asked Ivanov.

Persikov turned livid, picked up the paper, and showed it to Ivanov.

The latter read it and smiled ironically. "Mmm, yes," he said significantly.

"And, then, mark this. I've waited for my order for two months —and not a sign of it. While that one receives the eggs instantly and generally gets every possible cooperation."

"He won't get anywhere with it, Vladimir Ipatievich. And it will simply end with their returning the chambers to you."

"If only they don't take too long about it. They are holding up my experiments."

"True, that's the worst of it. I have everything ready, too."

"The diving suits came?"

"Yes, today."

Persikov calmed down a little. "Uhumm, I think we'll do it this way. We can seal up the doors of the operating room and open the window."

"Of course," agreed Ivanov.

"Three helmets?"

"Three. Yes."

"Well . . . that means you, I, and someone else, perhaps one of the students. We'll give him the third helmet."

"We might take Greenmut."

"The one who is working for you with salamanders? Hmmm, he is not bad. Although, wait, last spring he could not describe to me the structure of the air bladder of the Gymnodontes," Persikov recalled with some rancor.

"No, he is all right. He is a good student," Ivanov defended him.

"We shall have to stay awake one night," Persikov went on. "And one more thing, Pyotr Stepanovich, did you check the gas? You never know with those 'Good Chemicals' fellows; they may send us some worthless trash."

"No, no," Ivanov waved his hands. "I tested it yesterday. We must give them their due, Vladimir Ipatyich. It is excellent gas."

"On whom did you try it?"

"On ordinary toads. Give them a whiff and they die instantly. Oh, yes, Vladimir Ipatyich, we must also do this—write to the GPU, ask them to send us an electric revolver."

"But I don't know how to use it."

"I'll take that upon myself," answered Ivanov. "We used to practice with one on the Klyazma, just for amusement. There was a GPU man living next door. A remarkable thing. Extraordinary. Noiseless, kills outright from a hundred paces away. We used to shoot crows. I think we may not even need the gas."

"Hmm, a clever idea. Very." Persikov went to the corner of the room, picked up the receiver, and croaked out, "Let me have that, oh, what d'you call it . . . Lubyanka."

The days were unbearably hot. You could see the dense, transparent heat wavering over the fields. And the nights were magical, deceptive, green. The moon shone brightly, casting such beauty upon the former Sheremetyev estate that words cannot describe it. The Sovkhoz palace gleamed as though made of sugar, the shadows trembled in the park, and the ponds were cleft in two—

a slanting shaft of moonlight, and the rest, bottomless darkness. In the patches of moonlight, you could easily read the *Izvestia*, with the exception of the chess column, which was printed in nonpareil. But, naturally, nobody read the *Izvestia* on such nights. The maid, Dunya, somehow found herself in the copse behind the Sovkhoz. And, by coincidence, the red-moustachioed chauffeur of the battered little Sovkhoz truck was also there. What they did there remains unknown. They took shelter in the fluid shadow of an elm, on the chauffeur's outspread leather coat. A lamp burned in the kitchen, where two gardeners were having their supper, and Madame Destin, in a white robe, sat on the columned veranda, dreaming as she gazed at the resplendent moon.

At ten o'clock in the evening, when all the sounds had died down in the village of Kontsovka, situated behind the Sovkhoz, the idyllic landscape reechoed with the lovely, delicate sounds of a flute. It is impossible to express how appropriate they were over the copses and former columns of the Sheremetyev palace. The fragile Liza from *Pique Dame* mingled her voice in a duet with the passionate Polina, and the melody wafted up into the moonlit heights like a ghost of the old regime—old, but so touchingly lovely, enchanting to the point of tears.

"Waning . . . waning," the flute sang, sighing and trilling.

The copses stood in breathless silence, and Dunya, fatal as a wood nymph, listened, her cheek pressed to the prickly, reddish, masculine cheek of the chauffeur.

"He plays good, the son of a bitch," said the chauffeur, embracing Dunya's waist with his manly arm.

The player was the Sovkhoz manager himself, Alexander Semyonovitch Destin, and, in all justice, he played extremely well. The fact of the matter is that the flute had once been Alexander Semyonovich's profession. Up until 1917 he had been a member of Maestro Petukhov's well-known concert ensemble, whose harmonies rang out every evening in the lobby of the cozy Magic Dreams Cinema in the city of Yekaterinoslav. The crucial year of 1917, which had changed many a career, had also turned Alex-

ander Semyonovich to new pursuits. He abandoned the Magic
Dreams and the dusty star-spangled satin of the lobby and plunged
into the open seas of war and revolution, exchanging his flute
for a deadly Mauser. For a long time he had been tossed upon
the waves, which had repeatedly cast him up, now in the Crimea,
now in Moscow, now in Turkestan, and even in Vladivostok. It
needed a revolution to bring Alexander Semyonovich fully into
his own. The man's true greatness was revealed, and, naturally,
the lobby of the Dreams was no place for him.

Without going into details, let us say that late 1927 and early
1928 found Alexander Semyonovich in Turkestan, where he had,
first, edited a large newspaper and, later, as the local member of
the Supreme Economic Commission, won wide fame by his remarkable work in irrigating the Turkestan territory. In 1928,
Destin came to Moscow and was awarded a well-deserved rest.
The highest Committee of the organization whose card the pro-
vincial-looking, old-fashioned man carried with honor in his pocket
showed its appreciation by appointing him to a quiet and honor-
able post. Alas! Alas! To the misfortune of the Republic, the seething brain of Alexander Semyonovich would not be quenched. In
Moscow, Destin collided with Persikov's discovery, and in his
room at the Red Paris Hotel on Tverskaya, Alexander Semyonovich conceived the idea of restoring the chicken population of
the Republic in a month's time with the aid of Persikov's ray.
The Commission on Livestock Breeding listened to Destin's proposal, agreed with him, and Destin came with a thick sheet of
paper to the eccentric zoologist.

The music floating over the glassy waters and copses and park
was already drawing to its finale, when something happened that
interrupted it before its proper end. Namely, the Kontsovka dogs,
who should have been asleep at that hour, suddenly broke out
into a deafening chorus of barking, which gradually turned into
a general anguished howling. Spreading and rising, the howling
rang over the fields, and now it was answered by a chattering,
million-voiced concert of frogs from all the ponds. All this was so

uncanny that for a moment it seemed that the mysterious, witching night had suddenly grown dim.

Alexander Semyonovich put down his flute and came out on the veranda. "Manya! Do you hear? Those damned dogs . . . What do you think is making them so wild?"

"How do I know?" answered Manya, staring at the moon.

"You know, Manechka, let's go and take a look at the eggs," suggested Alexander Semyonovich.

"Really, Alexander Semyonovich, you've gone completely daffy with your eggs and chickens. Rest a bit!"

"No, Manechka, let's go."

A vivid light burned in the greenhouse. Dunya also came in, with a flushed face and glittering eyes. Alexander Semyonovich gently raised the observation panes, and everyone peered inside the chambers. On the white asbestos floor the spotted bright-red eggs lay in even rows; the chambers were silent, and the 15,000-watt bulb overhead hissed quietly.

"Oh, what a brood of chicks I'll hatch out here!" Alexander Semyonovich cried with enthusiasm, looking now into the observation slits in the side walls of the chambers, now into the wide air vents above. "You'll see. Who says I won't?"

"You know, Alexander Semyonovich," said Dunya, smiling, "the peasants in Kontsovka were saying you're the Anti-Christ. Them are devilish eggs, they said, and it's a sin to hatch eggs by machines. They talked of killing you."

Alexander Semyonovich gave a start and turned to his wife. His face became yellow. "Well, how do you like that? Our people! What can you do with such people? Eh? Manechka, we'll have to hold a meeting. Tomorrow I'll call some Party workers from the district. I'll make a speech myself. We need to do some work here. A regular wilderness."

"Dark minds," said the guard, sitting on his coat at the door of the greenhouse.

The next day was marked by the strangest and most inexplicable events. In the morning, when the sun flashed over the horizon,

the woods, which usually hailed the luminary with the loud and
ceaseless twittering of birds, met it in total silence—this was noticed by everyone—as though a storm were just about to break.
But there was no sign of a storm. Conversations in the Sovkhoz
assumed a strange, ambiguous tone, very disturbing to Alexander
Semyonovich. Especially because the old Kontsovka peasant nicknamed Goat's Goiter, a notorious troublemaker and know-it-all,
had spread the rumor that all the birds had gathered into flocks
and cleared out of Sheremetyevka, flying northward, which was
simply stupid. Alexander Semyonovich, thoroughly distressed,
spent the whole day telephoning to the town of Grachevka, from
whence he finally obtained a promise that some speakers would
be sent to the Sovkhoz in a day or two, to address the peasants
on two topics: "The International Situation" and "The Question
of the Good Chicken Trust."

The evening brought its own surprises. Whereas the morning
had seen the woods turn silent, demonstrating with utmost clarity
how ominous and oppressive the absence of sound could be
among the trees, and at midday all the sparrows had taken off
somewhere from the Sovkhoz courtyards, by evening a hush had
also fallen on the pond in Sheremetyevka. This was truly astonishing, since everyone for forty verst around was familiar with the
famous croaking of the Sheremetyevka frogs. But now all the frogs
seemed to have died out. Not a single voice came from the pond,
and the sedge stood silent. It must be admitted that Alexander
Semyonovich completely lost his composure. All these events
caused talk, and talk of the most unpleasant kind—behind his
back.

"It is really strange," Alexander Semyonovich said to his wife
at lunch. "I can't understand why those birds had to fly away."

"How do I know?" answered Manya. "Perhaps it was because
of your ray?"

"You're just a plain fool, Manya," said Alexander Semyonovich,
throwing down his spoon. "No better than the peasants. What
has the ray to do with it?"

"How would I know? Leave me alone."

That evening brought the third surprise. The dogs set up their baying again in Kontsovka—and what a wild performance it was! The moonlit fields reverberated with the ceaseless wailing, with anguished, angry moans.

Alexander Semyonovich was recompensed to some degree by another surprise—this time a pleasant one—which occurred in the greenhouse. A succession of tapping sounds began to come from the red eggs in the chambers. *Toki . . . toki . . . toki . . . toki*, came now from one egg, now from another.

The tapping in the eggs was a triumphant sound to Alexander Semyonovich. He instantly forgot the strange phenomena in the woods and the pond. Everybody gathered in the greenhouse: Manya, Dunya, the watchman, and the guard, who left his rifle at the door.

"Well? What do you say?" Alexander Semyonovich cried jubilantly. They all bent their ears with curiosity to the doors of the first chamber. "It's the chicks—tapping, with their beaks," Alexander Semyonovich continued, beaming. "Who says I won't hatch any chicks? Oh, no, my friends." And overflowing with emotion, he patted the guard on the shoulder. "I'll hatch out such a brood, your eyes will pop. Look sharp now," he added sternly. "The moment they begin to hatch, let me know at once."

"Sure thing," the watchman, Dunya, and the guard answered in chorus.

Toki . . . toki . . . toki. The tapping started anew, now in one, now in another egg in the first chamber. And, indeed, the picture of new life being born before your eyes within the thin, translucent shells was so absorbing that the whole group sat on for a long time on the empty overturned crates, watching the raspberry colored eggs ripen in the mysterious glimmering light. It was not until very late that they dispersed to their beds. The Sovkhoz and the surrounding countryside were flooded with greenish light. The night was eerie, one might even say sinister, perhaps because its utter silence was broken by the intermittent outbursts of causeless howling in Kontsovka, plaintive and heart-rending. It was impossible to tell what made those damned dogs carry on like that.

In the morning a new vexation awaited Alexander Semyonovich. The guard was extremely embarrassed; he pressed his hands to his heart, swore, and called God to witness that he had not slept, yet he had noticed nothing. "It's a queer thing," the guard insisted. "I am not to blame, Comrade Destin."

"Thank you, my heartfelt thanks," Alexander Semyonovich stormed. "What do you think, comrade? Why were you posted here? To watch! Now tell me where they've disappeared! They've hatched, haven't they? That means they've escaped. That means you left the door open and went away. Well, you'll see to it that the chicks are here—or else!"

"There isn't any place for me to go. And don't I know my job?" The warrior was finally offended. "You're blaming me for nothing, Comrade Destin!"

"But where have they gone to?"

"How should I know?" the warrior exploded at last. "Who can keep track of them? What is my job? To see that nobody makes off with the chambers, and that's what I'm doing. Here are your chambers. Who knows what kind of chicks you'll hatch out here? Maybe you couldn't catch them on a bicycle, maybe!"

Alexander Semyonovitch, taken somewhat aback, grumbled a little more, then fell into a state of puzzlement. It was indeed a strange business. In the first chamber, which had been loaded before the others, the two eggs lying closest to the base of the ray were broken. One of the eggs had even rolled away a little, and fragments of the shells were scattered on the asbestos floor under the ray.

"What the devil," muttered Alexander Semyonovich. "The windows are shut—they couldn't have flown out through the roof!"

"What an idea, Alexander Semyonovich," Dunya cried with incredulity. "Who has ever seen flying chicks? They must be around somewhere. Tsyp . . . tsyp . . . tsyp," she began to call, poking into the corners piled with dusty flowerpots, boards, and other rubbish. But no chicks responded anywhere.

The entire personnel ran about the Sovkhoz yard for two hours searching for the nimble chicks, but nobody found anything. The day passed in extreme agitation. The guard over the chambers was doubled by the addition of the watchman, who had been given strict orders to look into the windows of the chambers every fifteen minutes and to call Alexander Semyonovich the moment he saw anything happening. The guard sat at the door, sulking, the rifle between his knees. Alexander Semyonovich wore himself out running here and there, and he did not have his lunch until almost two in the afternoon. After lunch he napped for an hour in the cool shade on the former ottoman of Prince Sheremetyev, drank some Sovkhoz-brewed cider, walked over to the greenhouse, and convinced himself that everything was now in excellent order. The old watchman sprawled on his belly on a piece of burlap and stared, blinking, into the observation window of the first chamber. The guard sat alertly at the door.

But there was also something new: the eggs in the third chamber, loaded last of all, began to emit strange sounds, gulping and clucking, as if someone were sobbing inside them.

"O-oh, they're ripening," said Alexander Semyonovich. "Getting ripe and ready, I can tell now. Did you see?" he addressed the watchman.

"It's sure a marvel," the latter answered in a completely ambiguous tone, shaking his head.

Alexander Semyonovich crouched for a while over the chambers, but nothing hatched in his presence. He rose, stretched himself, and declared that he would not absent himself that day from the estate; he would run down to the pond for a swim, and if anything began to happen, he was to be summoned at once. He hurried over to the palace bedroom; it was furnished with two narrow spring beds, covered with crumpled linen, and the floor was heaped with piles of green apples and mounds of millet, prepared for the coming broods.

Arming himself with a terry-cloth towel and, after a moment's thought, with his flute, which he intended to play at leisure over the smooth waters of the pond, Destin walked out briskly from the palace, crossed the Sovkhoz courtyard, and proceeded down the willow avenue to the pond. He strode energetically, swinging his towel and carrying the flute under his arm. Heat poured down from the sky through the willows, and his body ached and begged for water. A thicket of burdocks began on his right, and as he passed by, he spat into it. Immediately, there was a rustling in the tangle of broad, sprawling leaves, as though someone were dragging a heavy log.

With a fleeting twinge of anxiety, Alexander Semyonovich turned his head toward the thicket of weeds and stared with wonder. The pond had been soundless now for two days. The rustling stopped, the smooth surface of the pond and the gray roof of the bathing shed gleamed invitingly beyond the burdocks. Several dragonflies darted past Alexander Semyonovich. He was just about to turn to the wooden planks leading down to the water when the rustling in the weeds was repeated, accompanied by a short hiss, as of a locomotive discharging steam. Alexander Semyonovich started and peered into the thick wall of weeds.

"Alexander Semyonovich," his wife's voice called, and her white blouse flashed, disappeared, and flashed again in the raspberry patch. "Wait, I'll come along for a swim."

His wife hastened toward the pond, but Alexander Semyonovich did not answer; his entire attention was fixed on the burdocks. A gray-green log began to rise from the thicket, growing before his eyes. The log, it seemed to Alexander Semyonovich, was splotched with moist yellowish spots. It began to stretch, swaying and undulating, and rose so high that it overtopped the scrubby little willow. Then the top of the log seemed to break and lean over at an angle, and Alexander Semyonovich was in the presence of something that resembled in height and shape a Moscow electric pole. But this something was three times thicker than a pole and far more beautiful, thanks to the scaly tattoo. Still comprehending nothing, but feeling a chill creeping over him, Alexander Semyonovich stared at the top of the terrifying pole,

and his heart skipped several beats. It seemed to him that a sharp
frost had fallen suddenly over the August day, and it turned dark,
as though he were looking at the sun through a pair of summer
trousers.

At the upper end of the log there was a head. It was flat,
pointed, and adorned with a round yellow spot on an olive-green
background. A pair of lidless, open, icy, narrow eyes sat on the top
of the head, gleaming with utterly unheard-of malice. The head
make a quick forward movement, as though pecking the air,
then the pole gathered itself back into the burdocks; only the
eyes remained visible, staring unblinkingly at Alexander Semyonovich. The latter, covered with sticky sweat, uttered four words,
completely absurd and caused only by maddening fear. (And yet,
how beautiful those eyes were among the leaves!) "What sort of
joke—?"

Then he remembered that the fakirs . . . yes . . . yes . . .
India . . . a woven basket and a picture. They charm . . .

The head swept up again, and the body began to emerge once
more. Alexander Semyonovich brought the flute to his lips, gave
a hoarse squeak, and panting for breath every second, began to
play the waltz from *Eugene Onegin*. The eyes in the greenery instantly began to burn with implacable hatred of this opera.

"Have you lost your mind, playing in this heat?" Manya's merry
voice rang out, and Alexander Semyonovich caught the glimmer
of white out of the corner of his eye.

Then a sickening scream rent the air of the Sovkhoz, expanded,
and flew up into the sky, while the waltz jumped up and down
as with a broken leg. The head in the thicket shot forward, and
its eyes left Alexander Semyonovich, abandoning his sinful soul
to repentance. A snake, some fifteen yards long and the thickness
of a man, leaped out of the burdocks like a steel spring. A cloud
of dust sprayed Destin from the road, and the waltz was over.
The snake whipped past the Sovkhoz manager directly toward the
white blouse down the road. Destin saw Manya turn yellow-white,
and her long hair stood up on her head as though made of wire.
Before his eyes, the snake opened its maw for a moment; some-

thing like a fork flicked out of it, then it seized Manya, who was sinking into the sand, by the shoulder and jerked her up a yard above the road. Manya repeated her piercing death scream. The snake coiled itself into an enormous corkscrew, its tail churning up a sandstorm, and began to squeeze Manya. She did not utter another sound, and Destin heard her bones snapping. Manya's head flew up high over the earth, tenderly pressed to the snake's cheek. Blood splashed from her mouth, a broken arm slipped out, and little fountains of blood spurted from under the fingernails. Then, almost dislocating its jaws, the snake opened its maw, quickly slipped its head over Manya's, and began to pull itself over her like a glove over a finger. The snake's hot breath spread all around it, scalding Destin's face, and its tail almost swept him off the road in a cloud of acrid dust. It was then that Destin turned gray. First the left, then the right half of his pitch-black head became silver. In deadly nausea he finally broke from the road, and seeing and hearing nothing more, bellowing like a wild beast, he plunged into headlong flight.

CHAPTER 9   A Writing Mass

Shchukin, the agent of the State Political Administration at the Dugino Station, was a very brave man. Reflectively, he said to his assistant, the redheaded Politis, "Oh, well, I guess we'll go. Eh? Get out the motorcycle." After a silence, he added, turning to the man who sat on a bench, "Put down your flute."

But the gray-haired, shaking man on the bench in the office of the Dugino GPU did not put down his flute, but burst into a fit of crying and inarticulate moaning. Shchukin and Politis saw that the flute would have to be taken from him. The man's fingers seemed frozen to it. Shchukin, a man of enormous strength who could almost have been a circus strong man, began to unbend one finger after another. Then he put the flute on the table.

This was in the early, sunny morning of the day following Manya's death.

"You will come with us," said Shchukin to Alexander Semyono-vich. "You will show us the way around." But Destin raised his hands against him in horror and covered his face, as if to shut out a frightful vision.

"You'll have to show us," Politis added sternly.

"No, let him alone. The man is not himself."

"Send me to Moscow," Alexander Semyonovich begged, crying.

"You won't return to the Sovkhoz at all?"

Instead of an answer, Destin once more covered his face and horror poured from his eyes.

"All right," decided Shchukin. "I can see you really aren't up to it. The express will be coming soon. You can take it."

Then, while the station guard was trying to bring Alexander Semyonovich around with some water, and the latter's teeth chattered on the blue, cracked cup, Shchukin and Politis held a conference. Politis felt that, generally, nothing had happened and that Destin was simply a deranged man who had had a terrifying hallucination. Shchukin tended to think that a boa constrictor might have escaped from the circus that was then performing in the town of Grachevka. Hearing their skeptical whispers, Alexander Semyonovich rose from the bench. He recovered a little and, stretching his arms like a Biblical prophet, cried, "Listen to me. Listen. Why don't you believe me? It was there. Or where is my wife?"

Shchukin became silent and serious and immediately sent a tele-gram to Grachevka. He assigned a third agent to keep a constant eye on Alexander Semyonovich and accompany him to Moscow. Meanwhile, Shchukin and Politis began to prepare for the expedi-tion. They had only one electric revolver, but that should be pro-tection enough. The 1927 fifty-round model, the pride of French technology, devised for short-range fighting, fired only to a dis-tance of a hundred paces, but covered a field two meters wide and killed everything alive within this field. It was difficult to miss with it. Shchukin strapped on the shiny electric toy, and Politis armed himself with an ordinary twenty-five-round sub-machine gun and some cartridge belts. Then they mounted a motorcycle and rolled off toward the Sovkhoz through the dewy, chilly morning. The motorcycle rattled off the twenty verst between the station and the Sovkhoz in fifteen minutes. (Destin had walked all night, crouching now and then in the roadside shrubbery in paroxysms of mortal terror.)

The sun was beginning to bake in earnest when the sugar-white, columned palace flashed through the greenery on the hill overlooking the meandering Top River. Dead silence reigned over the scene. Near the entrance to the Sovkhoz, the agents caught up with a peasant in a cart. He ambled slowly, loaded with sacks, and they soon left him behind. The motorcycle dashed across the bridge, and Politis blew the horn to bring someone out. But no one responded, except for the frenzied Kontsovka dogs in the distance. Slowing down, the motorcycle drove up to the gates with the bronze lions, green with neglect and time. The dust-covered agents in yellow leggings jumped off, fastened the motorcycle to the iron railing with a chain and lock, and entered the courtyard. They were struck by the silence.

"Hey, anyone here?" Shchukin called loudly.

No one answered. The agents walked around the yard with growing astonishment. Politis frowned. Shchukin began to look more and more serious, knitting his fair eyebrows. They peered through the closed window into the kitchen and saw that it was empty. But the entire floor was littered with white bits of broken china.

"You know, something really must have happened here. I can see it now. Some catastrophe," said Politis.

"Hey, anyone there? Hey!" called Shchukin, but the only answer was the echo from under the kitchen eaves. "What the hell," grumbled Shchukin, "it couldn't have gobbled all of them at once. Unless they ran off. Let's go into the house."

The door of the palace with the columned terrace was wide open, and the interior was completely deserted. The agents even climbed to the mezzanine, knocking everywhere and opening all the doors. But they discovered absolutely nothing, and they returned to the courtyard across the vacant porch.

"Let's walk around to the back. We'll try the greenhouse,"

decided Shchukin. "We'll search the place, then we can tele-phone."

The agents walked down the brick-paved pathway past the flowerbeds to the backyard, crossed it, and saw the glittering windows of the greenhouse.

"Wait a moment," Shchukin whispered, unbuckling the re-volver.

Politis, watchful and tense, unslung his submachine gun.

A strange, resonant sound came from the greenhouse and from behind it. It was like the hissing of a locomotive. Z-*zau-zau* . . . *z-zau-zau* . . . *s-s-s-s-s*, the greenhouse hissed.

"Look out, careful," whispered Shchukin, and trying to step softly, the agents tiptoed to the windows and peered into the greenhouse.

Politis instantly jumped back, and his face turned pale. Shchu-kin opened his mouth and stood transfixed with the revolver in his hand.

The whole interior of the greenhouse was alive like a pile of worms. Coiling and uncoiling in tangled knots, hissing and stretching, slithering and swaying their heads, huge snakes were crawling over the greenhouse floor. Broken eggshells were strewn over the floor and crackled under their bodies. Overhead burned an electric bulb of dazzling brightness, bathing the whole interior of the greenhouse in a weird cinematic light. On the floor lay three black boxes that looked like huge cameras. Two of them, leaning askew, were dark; in the third, there glowed a small, densely scarlet light. Snakes of all sizes crawled along the cables and window frames and squirmed out through openings in the roof. From the electric bulb itself hung a jet-black spotted snake several yards long, its head swaying near the bulb like a pendulum. The hissing was punctuated by a curious rattling and clicking, and the greenhouse diffused an oddly rank smell, like a stagnant pool. The agents also caught sight dimly of piles of white eggs heaped in the dusty corners, an exotic giant bird lying motionless near the boxes, and the corpse of a man in gray near the door, next to a rifle.

"Get back," cried Shchukin, and he began to retreat, pushing

Politis back with his left hand and raising the revolver with his right. He managed to fire nine times, his gun hissing and flashing greenish lightnings at the greenhouse. The sounds within rose violently in answer to Shchukin's fire; the entire greenhouse became a mass of frenzied movement, and flat heads darted in every opening. A succession of thunderclaps reechoed over the entire Sovkhoz, and flashes played upon the walls. *Chakh-chakh-chakh-takh,* Politis fired his submachine gun, backing away. Suddenly there was the sound of strange, four-footed padding behind him, and with a horrible scream, Politis tumbled backward. A brownish-green creature with splayed-out paws, a huge pointed snout, and a ridged tail, resembling a lizard of terrifying size, had slithered around the corner of the barn and viciously bit through Politis' foot, throwing him over.

"Help!" cried Politis, and immediately his left hand was caught in the maw and snapped. Vainly trying to raise his right hand, he dragged his gun in the sand.

Shchukin turned around and began to rush from side to side. He fired once, but aimed wide of the mark, afraid to hit his comrade. His next shot was in the direction of the greenhouse, because a huge olive-colored snake head had appeared there among the smaller ones, and its body sprang toward him. The shot killed the giant snake, and again, jumping and circling around Politis, already half-dead in the crocodile's maw, Shchukin tried to aim so as to kill the hideous creature without hitting the agent. At last he succeeded. The electric revolver fired twice, throwing a greenish light on everything around, and the crocodile leaped, stiffened, stretched out, and released Politis.

But now blood gushed from the agent's sleeve and mouth, and leaning on his sound right arm, he tried to drag his broken left leg. His eyes were dimming. "Run . . . Shchukin," he sobbed out.

Shchukin fired several times in the direction of the greenhouse, shattering several windows. But then a huge spring, olive-colored and sinuous, leaped out from the cellar window behind him, swept across the yard, filling it with its enormous length, and in an instant coiled itself round Shchukin's legs. He was knocked down, and the shiny revolver flew out sideways. Shchukin gave a mighty cry, gasped for air, and then the rings concealed him altogether, except for his head. A coil slipped once over his head, ripping off the scalp, and the head cracked. There were no more shots in the Sovkhoz. There was only hissing. And in reply to it, the wind brought in the distant howling from Kontsovka. But now it was no longer possible to tell whether the howling came from dogs or men.

CHAPTER 10   Catastrophe

The night office of the newspaper *Izvestia* was lit by bright electric lights, and the fat editor at the stone table was making up the second page, containing dispatches "From the Union of Republics." One item caught his eye; he peered at it through his pince-nez and burst out laughing. Then he called the proofreaders and the makeup man and showed them the galley sheet. The narrow strip of damp paper carried the words: "Grachevka, Smolensk Province. A hen as large as a horse and kicking like a stallion has been seen in the district. Instead of a tail, it has a bunch of bourgeois lady's feathers."

The compositors roared with laughter.

"In my day," said the editor, guffawing broadly, "when I was working for Vanya Sytin's *Russkoye Slovo*, some of the men would drink themselves to the point of seeing elephants. They did. Nowadays, it seems, they're seeing ostriches."

The proofreaders roared.

"That's right, it is an ostrich," said the makeup man. "Shall we use it, Ivan Vonifatievich?"

"Have you lost your wits?" answered the editor. "I wonder how the secretary let it through—it's obviously just a drunken message."

"Must have been quite a binge," the compositors agreed, and the makeup man removed the report about the ostrich from the table.

Consequently, *Izvestia* appeared on the following day containing the usual mass of interesting material, but not a hint concerning the Grachevka ostrich.

Assistant Professor Ivanov, who read *Izvestia* regularly and thoroughly, folded the paper in his office, yawned, commented, "Nothing of interest," and began to put on his white smock. A little later, the burners flickered in his room and frogs began to croak.

But Professor Persikov's office was in an uproar. The frightened Pankrat stood at attention, his arms stiffly down at his sides. "I understand. Yes, sir," he said.

Persikov handed him an envelope sealed with wax and said, "You will go straight to the Department of Livestock Breeding, to that fool of a director Fowlin, and tell him right out that he is a swine. Tell him that I, Professor Persikov, said so. And give him the envelope."

A fine thing, thought the pale Pankrat to himself, clearing out with the envelope.

Persikov raged. "Damn them, they don't know what they're doing," he whimpered pacing the office and rubbing his gloved hands. "It's outrageous—a mockery of me and of zoology. Sending me piles of these damned chicken eggs for two months, but nothing I have ordered. As if it were so far to America! Eternal confusion, eternal nonsense!" He began to count on his fingers: "Let us say, ten days at most to hunt them up . . . very well, fifteen . . . even twenty. Then two days for air delivery, a day from London to Berlin. Six hours from Berlin to Moscow. Incredible bungling!"

He furiously attacked the telephone and began to ring someone.

His office was ready for some mysterious and highly dangerous experiments. On the table lay strips of paper prepared for sealing the doors, diving helmets with air tubes, and several cylinders, shiny as quicksilver, labeled "Good Chemicals Trust," "Do not touch," and pasted over with pictures of a skull and crossbones.

It took more than three hours before the professor calmed down and took up some minor tasks. He worked at the Institute until eleven o'clock in the evening, and therefore he knew nothing of what transpired outside the cream-colored walls. Neither the preposterous rumor which had spread through Moscow about some strange snakes, nor the dispatch in the evening papers, shouted by the newsboys, had reached him; Assistant Professor Ivanov was at the Art Theatre, watching *Tsar Fyodor Ioannovich*, and there was no one else to bring the news to the professor.

At about midnight, Persikov came home to Prechistenka and retired for the night. Before falling asleep, he read in bed an English article in the magazine *News of Zoology*, which he received from London. He slept. Moscow, alive and seething till late into the night, slept. Only the huge gray building on Tverskaya Street did not sleep. The building was shaken by the roaring and humming of the *Izvestia* printing presses. The night editor's office was in a state of pandemonium. The editor, furious, red-eyed, rushed about not knowing what to do and sending everybody to the devil's mother.

The makeup man followed him about, reeking of wine fumes and saying, "Oh, well, it's not so terrible, Ivan Vonifatievich, we can publish an extra supplement tomorrow. After all, we can't pull the whole issue out of the press!"

The compositors did not go home, but went about in flocks and gathered in knots to read the telegrams that were now coming every fifteen minutes throughout the night, each more fantastic and terrifying than the last. Alfred Bronsky's peaked hat dashed about in the dazzling pink light of the press room, and the mechanical fat man creaked and limped, appearing now here, now there. The entrance doors slammed continuously, and reporters came rushing in all night. All twelve telephones in the press room were busy; the central switchboard almost automatically answered every new call with "busy, busy," and the signal horns sang and sang before the sleepless young ladies at the switchboard.

The compositors clustered around the mechanical fat man; the former sea captain was saying to them, "They'll have to send down airplanes with gas."

"Sure thing," answered the compositors. "God knows what's going on there."

Unprintable, angry oaths shook the air, and somebody's thin voice screamed, "This Persikov ought to be shot!"

"What has Persikov to do with it?" somebody answered in the crowd. "It's that son of a bitch in the Sovkhoz; he's the one to blame!"

"They should have posted a guard!" shouted someone.

"But maybe it has nothing to do with the eggs at all!"

The building shook and hummed from the rolling presses, and it seemed that the unprepossessing edifice was blazing with an electric fire.

The dawning day did not extinguish this fire. If anything, the day intensified it, although the electricity went out. Motorcyles rolled into the asphalt yard one after another, alternating with cars. All Moscow had awakened, and the white sheets of the newspapers spread over it like birds. The sheets rustled from hand to hand, and by eleven in the morning the newsboys ran out of papers, despite the fact that *Izvestia* came out that month in editions of one and a half million.

Professor Persikov left Prechistenka by bus and arrived at the Institute. There he found a surprise. In the vestibule stood three wooden boxes, neatly bound with metal strips and covered with foreign labels in German. The labels were dominated by a single Russian line, written in chalk: "Careful—eggs."

The professor was overwhelmed with joy. "At last!" he cried. "Pankrat, open the creates at once, but take care, don't crush the eggs. Bring them into my office."

Pankrat immediately carried out the order.

Fifteen minutes later the professor's voice rose in fury in his office, which was littered with sawdust and scraps of paper. "What the hell, are they playing jokes on me?" the professor wailed, shaking his fists and turning the eggs in his hands. "He's a filthy beast, this Fowlin. I won't permit him to make a fool of me. What is this, Pankrat?"

"Eggs, sir," Pankrat answered dolefully.

"Chicken eggs, you understand, chicken eggs, the devil take

them! They're of no damned use to me. Why don't they send them to that scoundrel in his Sovkhoz?"

Persikov rushed to the telephone in the corner, but before he had time to call, Ivanov's voice shouted from the corridor, "Vladimir Ipatyich! Vladimir Ipatyich!"

Persikov tore himself away from the telephone, and Pankrat jumped aside, making way for the assistant professor. The latter ran into the room without, as his polite custom was, removing his gray hat, which sat far back on his head. He held a newspaper in his hands. "Do you know what happened, Vladimir Ipatyich?" he cried, waving in front of Persikov's face a sheet of paper headed *Extra Supplement* and graced with a brightly colored picture.

"No, but listen to what they did!" Persikov shouted in reply, without listening. "They've decided to surprise me with some more chicken eggs. This Fowlin is a total idiot, just look!"

Ivanov was utterly dumbfounded. He stared in horror at the opened crates, then at the newspaper, and his eyes almost jumped out of his face. "So that's it!" he muttered, gasping. "Now I see. . . . No, Vladimir Ipatievich, just take a look." He quickly unfolded the paper and pointed to the colored picture with a trembling finger. It showed an olive-colored, yellow-spotted snake, coiling like a terrifying fire hose against a smudged green background. The photograph was taken from above, from a light plane that had cautiously dived over the snake. "What would you say it is, Vladimir Ipatyich?"

Persikov pushed his glasses up on his forehead, then slipped them down again, peered at the picture, and said with extreme astonishment, "What the devil! It's . . . why, it's an anaconda, a river boa!"

Ivanov flung down his hat, sat down heavily on the table, and said, punctuating every word with a bang of the fist on the table, "Vladimir Ipatyich, this anaconda is from the Smolensk Province. It's monstrous! Do you understand, that scoundrel has hatched snakes instead of chickens, and they have multipled as phenomenally as the frogs!"

"What?" Persikov screamed, and his face became purple. "You're joking, Pyotr Stepanovich . . . Where from?"

Ivanov was speechless for a moment, then he regained his voice, and poking his finger at the open crate, where the tips of the white eggs gleamed in the yellow sawdust, he said, "That's where."

"Wha-at!" howled Persikov, beginning to understand.

Ivanov shook both his fists and cried, "You can be sure. They sent your order for snake and ostrich eggs to the Sovkhoz and the chicken eggs to you."

"Oh, God . . . oh, God," Persikov moaned and, turning green, began to sink onto the revolving stool.

Pankrat stood uttterly bewildered at the door, white and speechless.

Ivanov jumped up, snatched the paper, and underscoring a line with a sharp nail, he shouted into the professor's ear, "They'll have a jolly business on their hands now! I absolutely cannot imagine what will happen next. Vladimir Ipatyich, look." And he bellowed out, reading the first passage in the crumpled sheet that caught his eye, " 'The snakes are moving in hordes toward Mozhaisk, laying enormous quantities of eggs. Eggs were seen in the Dukhovsk district. Crocodiles and ostriches are overrunning the countryside. Special troop units and detachments of state police halted the panic in Vyazma after setting fire to the woods outside the town to bar the approach of the reptiles.' "

Persikov, turning all colors, became bluish white. With demented eyes he rose from the stool and began to scream, panting and suffocating, "Anaconda . . . anaconda . . . water boa! My God!"

Neither Ivanov nor Pankrat had ever seen him in such a state.

The professor pulled off his tie, ripped the buttons from his shirt, turned a livid purple like a man having a stroke, and staggering, with staring, glassy eyes, he rushed out. His shouts reverberated under the stone archways of the Institute. "Anaconda . . . anaconda," rolled the echo.

"Catch the professor!" Ivanov shrieked to Pankrat, who was dancing up and down on one spot with terror. "Get him some water! He's having a stroke!"

CHAPTER 11   Battle and Death

Moscow was ablaze with the frenzied, electric night. All lights were on. Every corner and every room were brightly lit by lamps with shades removed. No one slept in Moscow, which had a population of four million, except the youngest children, who knew nothing. In every apartment, distracted people ate and drank, without care, whatever was at hand; everywhere, people cried out; and every minute, distorted faces peered out of the windows from all floors, looking up at the sky, crisscrossed with searchlights. White lights flared up continually in the sky, casting pale, melting triangles over Moscow, then fading out. The sky hummed steadily with low-flying airplanes. Tverskaya-Yamskaya Street was the worst of all. Every ten minutes, trains arrived at the Alexander Station. They were made up helter-skelter of freight and passenger cars of every class and even of tank cars, all of them clustered with fear-crazed people, who then rushed down Tverskaya-Yamskaya in a dense stream. People rode in buses, on the roofs of trolleys; they crushed one another and fell under the wheels.

At the station, quick, uneasy bursts of gunfire rapped out every now and then over the heads of the crowd: the troop units were trying to stop the panic of the maniacs running along the railway tracks from the Smolensk Province to Moscow. Now and then, the station windows shattered into splinters with a crazy gulping sound, and all the locomotives howled incessantly. The streets were littered with discarded and trampled posters. The same posters, lit by fiery red reflectors, stared down from the walls. Their contents were already known to everyone, and nobody read them. They proclaimed a state of emergency in Moscow. They threatened penalties for panic and reported that Red Army units, armed with gas, were departing in a steady stream for the Smolensk Province. But the posters were powerless to stem the howling night.

In their homes, people dropped and broke dishes and flowerpots; they ran about, knocking against corners; they packed and unpacked bundles and valises in the vain hope of making their way to Kalancha Square, to the Yaroslavl or Nikolaev Stations. Alas, all stations leading north and east were cordoned off by the heaviest line of infantry. Huge trucks, with swaying, clanging chains, loaded to the top with crates surmounted by soldiers in peaked helmets, with bayonets bristling in all directions, were carting off the gold reserves from the cellars of the People's Commissariat of Finance and enormous boxes marked "Careful—Tretyakov Art Gallery." Automobiles barked and scurried all over Moscow.

Far on the horizon, the sky quivered with the glow of distant fires, and the dense August blackness was shaken by the steady booming of cannons.

Toward morning, a massive serpent of cavalry wound its way through sleepless Moscow, which had not extinguished a single light. Its thousands of hooves clattered on the paving stones as it moved up Tverskaya, sweeping everything out of its path, pressing everything else into gateways and store windows. The ends of its scarlet cowls dangled on the gray backs, and the tips of its lances pierced the sky. The rushing, screaming mobs seemed to recover at the sight of the serried ranks pushing relentlessly forward through the seething ocean of madness. The crowds on the sidewalks began to roar with hope renewed.

"Long live the cavalry!" cried frenzied female voices.

"Hurrah!" replied the men.

"They'll crush me! They're crushing! . . ." people cried somewhere.

"Help!" came from the sidewalks.

Packs of cigarettes, silver coins, and watches began to fly into the ranks from the sidewalks. Some women jumped down onto the pavement and, risking life and limb, ambled along the mounted columns, clutching at the stirrups and kissing the men's boots. Occasionally the voices of platoon commanders rose above the ceaseless chattering of hooves: "Draw in the reins!"

A gay and reckless song was struck up somewhere, and the faces under the dashing scarlet cowls swayed over the horses in the wavering light of electric signs. Now and then, alternating with the columns of horsemen with uncovered faces, came mounted figures in strange hooded helmets, with tubes flung over their shoulders and cylinders attached to straps over their backs. Behind them crawled huge cistern trucks with the longest sleeves and hoses, like fire engines, and heavy, pavement-crushing caterpillar tanks, hermetically sealed and gleaming with their narrow slits. Then came more mounted columns and, after them, more cars, solidly encased in gray armor, with similar tubes protruding outside and with white skulls painted on their sides, over the words "Gas" and "Good Chemicals."

"Save us, brothers!" the people wailed from the sidewalks. "Crush the snakes! . . . Save Moscow!"

Good-humored oaths reverberated through the ranks. Cigarette packs leaped from hand to hand in the brightly lit night air, and white teeth grinned at the crazed mobs from atop the horses. A song, subdued and tugging at the heart, began to spread along the ranks:

> ". . . no ace, no queen, no jack,
> We'll beat the reptiles' filthy pack . . .

Peals of "Hurrah!" rolled over the tangled human mass in answer to flying rumors that at the head of all the columns, in the same scarlet cowl as the rest of the horsemen, rode the graying commander of the horse army who had won legendary fame ten years before. The mob howled, and the rolling of "Hurrah! Hurrah!" rose up into the sky, bringing some solace to desperate hearts.

The Institute was dimly lit. Outside events reached it only in vague and fragmentary echoes. Once a volley of fire burst fanlike under the fiery clock near the Manège: soldiers were shooting down some looters who had tried to rob an apartment on Volkhonka. There was little automobile traffic here, most of it massing toward the railway stations.

In the professor's study, lit by a single small bulb, Persikov sat with his head on his hands, silent. Ribbons of smoke floated in layers around him. The ray in the box was out. The frogs in the terraria were silent because they were asleep. The professor did not work and did not read. Under his left elbow lay the evening edition of news dispatches on a narrow strip of paper, reporting that all of Smolensk was on fire and that the artillery was shelling the Mozhaisk forest systematically, sector by sector, to destroy the piles of crocodile eggs heaped in all the damp ravines.

Another report said that an air squadron had achieved considerable success near Vyazma, flooding almost the entire district with gas, but that the number of human victims in the area was impossible to estimate, because instead of orderly evacuation, the people rushed about in divided, panic-stricken groups in all directions at their own risk.

There was a report that a special Caucasus division near Mozhaisk had won a brilliant victory over herds of ostriches, hacking them all to pieces and destroying huge quantities of eggs. The division itself sustained negligible losses.

The government announced that, should it prove impossible to halt the reptiles within two hundred verst of the capital, the latter would be evacuated in orderly fashion. Workers and employees were enjoined to maintain perfect calm. The government would take the sternest measures to prevent a repetition of the Smolensk disaster. There, thrown into panic by the sudden attack of an army of several thousand rattlesnakes, the people had rushed into hopeless wholesale flight, leaving burning stoves that soon transformed the city into a mass of raging flames.

It was also reported that Moscow had enough provisions to last at least six months and that the Council of the Commander in Chief was taking speedy measures to fortify and arm all apartment buildings in order to fight the reptiles in the very streets of the capital in the event that the Red Armies and the air fleets failed to halt their advance.

The professor read none of this. He stared before him with glassy eyes and smoked. Only two other persons were at the Institute—Pankrat and the housekeeper, Marya Stepanovna, who was continually breaking into tears. The old woman had not slept for three nights, having spent them in the study of the professor, who adamantly refused to abandon his only remaining, now extinguished chamber. Marya Stepanovna huddled on the oilcloth sofa, in a shadowy corner, and kept a silent, sorrowful vigil, watching the kettle with some tea for the professor coming to a boil on the tripod over the gas burner. The Institute was silent, and everything happened very suddenly.

On the sidewalk outside there was an outburst of angry shouts, which made Marya Stepanovna jump and cry out. Flashlights and lanterns flickered in the street, and Pankrat's voice was heard in the vestibule. All this noise meant little to the professor. He raised his head for a moment and muttered, "They're going crazy. What can I do now?" Then he relapsed into stupor.

But his stupor was rudely broken. The iron doors of the Institute on Herzen Street rang with violent blows, and the walls shook. Then the solid mirrored wall in the next office split asunder. The window of the professor's study sang out and flew into splinters as a gray rock bounced into the room, smashing the glass table. The frogs began to scuttle in alarm in their terraria, raising a wild outcry.

Marya Stepanovna ran about wailing, rushed to the professor, and seized him by the hands, shouting, "Run, Vladimir Ipatyich, run!"

The professor rose from the revolving stool, straightened himself up, and curled his forefinger into a hook, his eyes recovering the sharp little glitter reminiscent of the old, inspired Persikov. "I am not going anywhere," he said. "This is stupid. They are rushing about like maniacs . . . If all Moscow has gone mad, where am I to go? Please stop screaming. What have I to do with it? Pankrat!" he called, pressing a button.

He probably wanted Pankrat to put a stop to the commotion, which he had always disliked. But Pankrat no longer could do anything. The banging ended when the Institute doors flew open; there was a distant popping of shots, and then the whole stone edifice shook with the thunder of running feet, with shouts and the sound of crashing windows. Marya Stepanovna clutched at Persikov's sleeve and began to drag him somewhere.

But he shook her off, drew himself up to his full height, and just as he was, in his white smock, he walked out into the corridor. "Well?" he asked.

The doors swung open, and the first thing to appear in them was the back of a military uniform with a red chevron and a star on the left sleeve. The officer was retreating from the door, through which a furious mob was pressing forward, and firing his revolver. Then he turned and dashed past Persikov, shouting to him, "Save yourself, Professor, run! I can do nothing more!"

His words were answered by the frenzied shriek of Marya Stepanovna. The officer jumped past Persikov, who stood still like a white statue, and disappeared in the darkness of the tortuous corridors at the other end.

People burst into the door, howling:

"Get him! Kill him!"

"Public enemy!"

"Loosed the snakes upon us!"

Twisted faces and ripped clothing milled in the corridors, and someone fired a shot. Sticks waved in the air.

Persikov made a step back, barring the door to the study, where Marya Stepanovna knelt in terror on the floor, and spread out his arms, as one crucified. He wanted to prevent the mob from entering, and he cried out with irritation, "This is complete madness. You are utterly wild beasts. What do you want?" And then he bawled, "Get out of here!" and completed his speech with the shrill, familiar cry, "Pankrat, throw them out!"

But Pankrat could no longer throw anyone out. Pankrat, trampled and torn, with a crushed skull, lay motionless in the vestibule, while more and more crowds stamped past him, paying no attention to the fire of the militia in the street.

A short man with apelike crooked legs, in a torn jacket and a tattered, twisted shirt, dashed out ahead of the others, leaped toward Persikov, and with a frightful blow of a stick opened his skull.

Persikov swayed and began to collapse sideways. His last words were, "Pankrat . . . Pankrat . . ."

The completely innocent Marya Stepanovna was killed and torn to pieces in the study. The chamber, in which the ray had long gone out, was smashed to bits, as were the terraria, and the crazed frogs were hunted down with sticks and trampled underfoot. The glass tables were smashed to pieces, the reflectors were shattered, and an hour later the Institute was a mass of flames. Corpses littered the sidewalk; the area was cordoned off by a line of troops armed with electric revolvers; and fire engines, pumping water from the hydrants, aimed jets at all the windows, from which great tongues of flame were breaking out with a dull roar.

CHAPTER 12   The God of Frost

On the night of August 19 to 20, an unprecedented frost descended on the country, unlike anything within the memory of the oldest citizens. It came and lasted two days and two nights, bringing the thermometer down to eighteen degrees below zero. Frenzied Moscow locked all its doors and windows. It was not until the third day that the residents of Moscow realized that the frost had saved the capital and the vast expanses which it governed and which had been the scene of the terrible catastrophe of 1928. The cavalry at Mozhaisk had lost three-quarters of its men and was near exhaustion, and the gas squadrons had not been able to halt the advance of the loathsome reptiles, which were closing in on Moscow in a semicircle, from the west, the southwest, and the south.

The reptiles were defeated by the cold. Two days and two nights at eighteen degrees below zero had proved too much for the abominable herds. When the frost lifted, leaving nothing but dampness and mud on the ground, leaving the air dank and all the greenery blasted by the sudden cold, there was no longer anything left to fight. The calamity was over. Woods, fields, and illimitable swamps were still piled high with varicolored eggs, often covered with the strange, exotic patterns that Destin, who had vanished without a trace, had once mistaken for caked mud. But now these eggs were harmless. They were dead, the embryos within them lifeless.

For a long time, the wide expanses of the land were still putrescent with innumerable corpses of crocodiles and snakes that had been called forth to life by the mysterious ray born under the eyes of genius on Herzen Street, but they were no longer dangerous. The fragile creatures of the rank and sweltering tropical swamps had perished in two days, leaving throughout the territory of three provinces a legacy of frightful stench, disintegration, and decay.

There were protracted epidemics. For a long time, diseases raged, spread by the festering corpses of men and beasts; and for a long time, the army combed the land, equipped now not with gases, but with sapper gear, kerosene tanks, and hoses, clearing the earth of the dead. It completed its work, and everything was finished by the spring of 1929.

And in the spring of 1929, Moscow once more was dancing, glittering, and flashing with lights. Again the rolling of mechanical carriages rustled on the pavements, and the crescent of the moon hung, as though suspended on a fine thread, over the helmet of the Cathedral of Christ. On the site of the two-story Institute that had burned down in August, 1928, there rose a new zoological palace. Its director was Assistant Professor Ivanov, but Persikov was no longer there. Never again did the persuasively hooked forefinger rise before anyone's eyes, and never again was the creaking, froglike voice heard by anyone. The ray and the catastrophe of 1928 were long discussed and written about throughout the world, but gradually the name of Professor Vladimir Ipatievich Persikov receded into mist, sank into darkness, as did the scarlet ray he had discovered on an April night. The ray itself was never recaptured, although the elegant gentleman and now full professor Pyotr Stepanovich Ivanov had made attempts in that direction. The first chamber had been smashed by the raging mob on the night of Persikov's murder. Three chambers were burned down in the Nikolsky Sovkhoz, the "Scarlet Ray," during the first battle of the air squadron with the reptiles, and no one succeeded in rebuilding them. Simple as had been the combination of lenses with the mirrored clusters of light, it was never captured again, despite Ivanov's efforts. Evidently this required something special in addition to knowledge, something possessed by only one man in the world—the late Professor Vladimir Ipatievich Persikov.

1925

Leonid Leonov
(1899 -   )

Born in Moscow, the son of a self-taught peasant poet, Leonov
attended the University of Moscow and served in the Red Army
during the Civil War. One of the most talented Soviet writers
and the author of numerous novels, including The Thief,
Skutarevsky, The Road to the Ocean, and others, as well as a
number of successful plays, Leonov is by no means a satirist.
"A Tale About the Furious Calaphat," which turned out to
be, perhaps unwittingly, such a devastating satire on Soviet
society, is a story told by a peasant guerrilla fighter to a group
of his comrades sitting at night around a fire in the woods during
a lull in one of the early peasant rebellions against the Soviet
government. It is from one of Leonov's finest novels, The
Badgers (1925).

A Tale About the Furious Calaphat

(From The Badgers*)*

by Leonid Leonov

My grandfather heard this story from his grandfather, who heard an Old Believer read it from a book.

It happened in the olden times. Life was more spacious then, and the air was purer. Fields and birds, woods and foxes, and cool springs leaping in the ravines. Kingdoms were so vast, a man's years wouldn't last him to walk from end to end. And the kings in those days were born glum and solitary, each one more savage than the next. A king would go up in his tower and look out over the forest at the fair view opening before him: clouds rushing in the sky, woods singing, rivers flowing. Sometimes the king's heart would sicken with boredom, and he would shout from his tower, "Everything is mine! The rivers and the woods, the swamps and the ravines, the peasants and the bears, the earth and everything alive under the sky!" The peasants heard him, but took no offense. Even the rooster crows from his perch about his barnyard, and then you feed him ants' eggs for it. It was no great matter. So the king sat there in place of a rooster. People lived in peace.

In the middle of those times, a little son was born to one of these roosters. And the boy began to grow and to increase in cleverness from day to day. In his ninth year, the son comes to his daddy and says, "You're living, Daddy," he says, "without sense or order. Your whole kingdom's out of kilter! Can you tell me how many blades of grass there are in your fields or how many trees in the forest? How many fish in the rivers or stars in the sky? Every blade of grass needs counting. You see, you don't know!"

His daddy scratched himself. "Well," he said, "we've lived this

137

way for twenty generations. We ate our fill and we slept soundly. We've done right well." "You're wrong," said the son. "There is a science called eometry, and you've got to live by it. We'll give a number to every fish. And every star and every growing shoot, both leafy and blooming. I'm going off to the mountains now, to study eometry."

No sooner said than done. He lifted his hut up on his shoulders and went into the mountains.

For eleven years he sat in his hut. Another would have plowed up heaps of earth in all those years, but this one thought of nothing but eometry. In a word, he learned it from A to Z. In his twentieth year, the son came to his father. "Hello," he says, "And how is your health?" The father saw him and got scared. "You've grown a lot," he says. And indeed he had: sometimes he would come out in a rainstorm, wave his hat in the sky, and sweep away the clouds. "Now," says the son, "I'm going to retire you. I'll take things into my own hands. And my name from this day on will be Calaphat!" (In their tongue it meant, "I'll get to the root of everything.") "I will astonish the whole world!" And so his daddy, he says, "If you're so smart, go sing your song, and we fools will listen."

Then he retired his father and began to toil in the sweat of his brow. He branded every fish, he issued passports to all the birds, and wrote down every blade of grass in a book. And everything around sickened. It was no joke: all nature got scrambled up. Even the bear got thin with worrying: was he a man or was he a beast, what with the passport in his hands?

And then Calaphat took it into his head to build a tower to the very skies. "I'll see," he says, "what kind of a view will open up from there. And, incidentally, we'll brand the stars as well!" From that moment on, it was the end of all things. He could think of nothing else but his tower.

One evening he met a little old man of the woods, in a hat made of tree bark, with a bark basket on his arm. "Quit all this strife," says the little old man. "Let your army go, don't do yourself harm, live in peace." "No," says Calaphat, "I'll build my tower." "But there are other ways to get up there!" says the old man. "I want to grow," answered Calaphat. "Aren't you big enough? I've heard tell that your sparrows have blown up to ten pounds apiece." "That's nothing," Calaphat bragged. "I've even got my lice up to five pounds each!" The old man laughed. "Why should you want to grow when a louse grows along with you? You'll be as big as a mountain, and the louse will be half a mountain. It'll eat you all the more!" Calaphat turned away from the little old man—the fool knew nothing of eometry.

And so everything began to swell. Men swelled with strength and rage, trees swelled with pride that they were of the earth, night swelled to twice the size of day. And Calaphat's tower grew and grew, up to the very skies. Twenty years had gone into building it! Twenty years for him—for us, twenty centuries. It needed a year to walk around it. Clouds broke against it and ran down the walls like rivers. One day the master mason came and said, "We can't go any higher. We're smack against the roof of the world. The men have no more strength left. The sun's too strong up here; it burns our heads!" And all the while the tower was being built, the land was overrun with crooks and swindlers—one for every brick.

Spring came, and Calaphat got ready to go up into the sky. He went into his tower and bolted every door, to keep the common people from following him.

He climbed for five years—up and up. At the end of the fifth year, the sky showed blue above him. Calaphat made one last push and jumped out at the top. He looked around, and his head dropped to his chest with grief. All his eometry had gone for naught.

While the king had been climbing his tower, the tower, unable to hold his weight, kept sinking into the ground. Calaphat had not risen a single inch: he'd take one step up and the tower would sink a step down, deeper into the earth. And all around, the woods were singing once again, the foxes running in them. The fields were fragrant with bloom, birds were caroling. Nature had thrown off Calaphat's passports. And that was the end of him and all his works.

1925

Vyacheslav Shishkov
(1873 - 1945)

An engineer by profession, Shishkov lived for many years in
Siberia, and a number of his works describe life in that region.
His best-known work is the historical novel Yemelyan Pugachev
(1944), which deals with the eighteenth-century Cossack and
peasant rebellion. Among Shishkov's earlier works are some volumes of what he called "jesting tales," from which "The Divorce"
is taken.

The Divorce

by Vyacheslav Shishkov

There lived on this earth of ours a man and his wife, Ivan and Marya Prirodov, both of them weavers. For ten years they lived together in peace and harmony. It's true there were some minor rows between them now and then, but that is normal, that's the way it's always been, according to every law. Everything in nature is a tooth for a tooth, a fang for a fang. Even ravening wolves in the forest fight. Why, then, should people live in total peace, if they're descended from a monkey?

But one day, just a short while ago, real trouble broke out, and, mind you, without a single drink. Unfortunately, it ended in divorce.

This trouble did not burst into their lives all of a sudden. It gathered on the sly, like a ball of twine: today a thread, tomorrow a piece of rope, the day after—a noose. And the noose tightened around their hearts.

The breakup was brought about by two faiths. One faith was in God, the other in ideology. And, then, there was Vera, with her red kerchief, also a weaver.

Being a weak female, Marya was religious. Ivan was a free-thinker. At the meeting, when it was decided to convert the church into a theater, Marya nearly started a fistfight.

In retaliation, and in conformity with ideology, Ivan took down all the icons from the wall at home, muttering, "Take a look at Vera. Why, critically speaking, you aren't fit to tie her shoe. How in hell did I ever live with you?"

"Phooey!" spat his wife.

The rest is clear of itself.

After the divorce, they came back to their room as strangers. The husband brought with him a pound of sausage. She brought some rolls and a herring. They munched their food silently, each in his corner. Ivan looked for a knife and could not find one, but his pride did not allow him to ask. He bit off a piece of the sausage, thinking, I'm a free bird now—I can go wherever I please; and he savagely tore off another piece with his teeth. Marya concentrated on her herring, washing it down with tea.

I could sure do with some tea now, thought Ivan. But I guess she wouldn't give me any. She's sore.

He went to the faucet, walking, for some reason, on tiptoe, and drank a glass of water. Then, as if to cover his faintheartedness, he sang with a careless air, "I wander out alone upon the ro-o-ad . . ."

Marya yawned, glanced at the clock on the wall—it was ten—and began to make the bed. "Turn around!" she cried to Ivan, as though he were a beggar nagging for a handout. "You're nothing to me now—just so much dirt. I've got to undress. Go and ogle your Verka."

Ivan turned away. Marya undressed, made the sign of the cross over the pillows, and lay down.

"Can I turn now?" asked Ivan, but there was no answer. Where was he to sleep? There was no sofa. Perhaps on the chairs? "Oh, what the devil! I'll lie down on the floor."

Marya slept soundly, Ivan restlessly. In the morning, Ivan had to turn away again.

At work, Ivan and Marya inquired among their fellow workers whether anyone knew of a room somewhere; any cubbyhole would do. But not on your life. Who has vacant rooms today?

"Back in the old times, you had all the rooms you wanted. But get divorced today and you're in for it."

The second night came.

"It's my turn on the bed," said Ivan. "It isn't your bed only; it belongs to both."

"Look away," said Marya, undressed, and lay down on the floor.

Ivan slept soundly, Marya restlessly: she turned and twisted; the floor was hard.

The third night came. Ivan was reading a newspaper. Marya took out a new nightgown trimmed with lace, spread it out, as if on purpose, right in front of Ivan's nose on the table, and began to draw pink ribbons through the lace. Ivan squinted at the nightgown, snorted, and could not get on to the next line. His mind suddenly refused to comprehend the words; his eyes saw only a woman's nightgown and a woman's body—his ex-wife's, Vera's, it made no difference.

"Turn away, I have to change," said Marya.

It seemed to Ivan that Marya's voice sounded differently. Ivan turned away to the mirror and rubbed his eyes. The small square of the mirror reflected a corner of the bed. Marya threw back the blanket, and the nightgown slipped off her shoulder. Ivan's heart jumped, stopped, then *knock-knock-knock*, it raced as though the bridle had broken loose. To keep from looking at the reflection of the firm female body, Ivan, true to ideology, tightly shut his eyes, but opened them again at once.

As he settled down on the floor, he thought to himself, I'll have to get a pallet. A hell of a thing, this divorce. Nothing was properly planned.

Marya thought a while and said angrily, "Get in! But mind you, back to back."

"Absolutely!" cried Ivan. "In conformity . . . and so forth."

What a pleasure! The air in the room was near freezing, but his back glowed with warmth. Still, one must remember ideology.

"Don't fidget, please," said Marya, falling asleep.

"I'm not fidgeting. . . . Just . . . well . . . it's nice."

On Sunday, the following conversation took place between them.

"When are you getting out of here? I'm fed up with you," said Marya.

"Where can I go, when there is such a shortage everywhere?"

"Go to your Verka, that's where!"

Ivan glanced up into Marya's eyes: fiery sparks, like crazy imps. "She has her own husband," he said sullenly. "What do you think? There's nothing between us; we're just friendly."

"Friendly?" screamed Marya. "So why'd you paw her at the dance? Out in the hallway?"

"Paw! So what? How can a man keep his hands off you women? When you're . . . well, you know . . . all sorts of combinations . . . A man can't help it."

"Can't help it?" her voice went up still higher. Then suddenly she was quiet. Controlling her sighs, she said, "Anyway . . . The fool that I am, what do I care? You're nothing to me now. Phooey! Just a stranger, no closer than that log of wood. Go have your fun with anybody you want."

"And you?"

Marya blinked rapidly and ran out of the room.

They went to bed—again back to back. Ivan fought the temptation to turn around.

As if guessing his feelings, Marya squeezed out through her teeth, "Don't you even think to touch me. I'm not your whore."

"Imagining things. . . . What do you take me for, a kid?"

"But you . . . Oh, go to hell!"

Ivan smiled ruefully in the dark. To curb himself, he tried to turn his thoughts in other directions: Twelfth category. . . . By what right? This Lukin hasn't been with us a year and gets promoted. Because he knows how to wag his tongue? And I just barely got the eleventh. Is that justice or isn't it? Sure isn't, thought Ivan, falling asleep. What's that? Would be a good idea to . . . punch him . . . what's his name, in the jaw. Ye-ah, Lukin, that's him . . . that's him. . . . Hold, hold . . . twelfth category. . . . So? Category? Catch him, land him one!

Ivan flung out his hand to catch the offender, but his hand encountered something soft, like firm dough.

And immediately after that, the offender gave him a hard pull by the beard, crying out, "None of your embraces, you! Get down on the floor if you can't keep your hands to yourself."

"Sorry . . . I got fuddled. It's the combination."

And again—back to back, and friendship sundered. Ivan lay quietly, blinking his eyes and unable to make out whether Marya was snuffling or giggling at him. They lay without speaking for a long time.

"Ivan," called Marya.

Ivan pretended to be asleep and snored lightly.

"All the trouble I have with you," sighed Marya, and turning her full, buxom body to her husband, she called quietly again, "Ivan."

Ivan snored. Then Marya touched his back lightly with her lips, smacked them, and said, "My darling . . . Vasil Vasilich."

"What! What's the matter?" Ivan turned to her quickly. "Who's this Vasil Vasilich of yours?"

"None of your business," said Marya and turned her back to him.

"Maybe it isn't," said Ivan. "Eh, Masha, Masha!"

"You can tangle with your Verkas—and God knows who else— and I'm to sit around and twiddle my thumbs? Swell chance."

"I've never tangled with anybody. My word, as an honest man. . . . Huh! Exchange you for some Verka? Don't make me laugh."

"No? You'll tell me that you loved me?"

"What else? Ah, Masha . . . " He shook his head deploringly and buried the tip of his nose in Marya's thick braid.

Marya quickly turned to him and cried, "Oh, you darned fool, you faker! Pretending, snoring like a horse . . . I've never known any man save you from the day I was born. And you lapped it up! I just thought I'd test you. Hah, Vasil Vasilich, may he croak, whoever he is."

"Masha! My little raisin!"

"Vanya!"

And in the morning Ivan said, "Queer things can happen in this world. Take us; we've lived together for ten years, and nothing out of the ordinary . . . everything just so. We'd even gotten a bit tired of one another. And now, the devil knows it. . . . I mean, as soon as we got divorced, I fell head over heels for you, like the most hopeless bourgeois. I mean, oh, what the hell. . . . And every minute, it got more and more proportional . . . I was fit to climb the wall or jump into the lake. That's what psychology can do. . . . We'll have to annul the divorce. . . . A stupid combination. It turned out rotten ideologically."

Marya sighed and said, "Would be nice to have a baby."

"Not a bad idea," said Ivan. "As for religious grounds, we'll regulate them somehow. And also, Masha, why don't we buy a spring mattress?"

1925

Boris Lavrenyov

(1891 - 1962)

Lavrenyov's early work alternated between the romantic and the
humorous. His stories and novels, skillfully told, dealt with contemporary experience. He was also the author of a number of
plays, including The Voice of America. "The Heavenly Cap" is
a witty grotesque developed against the background of the hungry
days of War Communism and the fantastic prosperity of the New
Economic Policy (NEP).

The Heavenly Cap

by Boris Lavrenyov

CHAPTER 1

The residents of the houses on the right side of Bolshaya Monetnaya Street kept track of the flow of revolutionary time by the professor of experimental physiology, Alexander Yevlampievich Blagosvetlov. But then, of course, in order to avert a possible accusation of partiality, the author must record that the residents of the left side did likewise.

It was during that unique, romantic time when the cities of the Republic, swept by gunpowder storms, were experiencing the initial period of general impoverishment, and all the clocks and watches, which had until then peacefully ticked away in the living rooms and on the spleens of their owners, had, in obedience to the laws of economics, been swallowed up by the villages.

In exchange for the watches, their owners received starchy and fatty substances. As for the timepieces, they were not infrequently hung around the necks of year-old citizens of peasant origin instead of rattles.

To the villages, the years described here were a period of primary accumulation.

But let us forget the villages. Although the exigencies of the day require assiduous courting of the mysterious elemental forces of the village, the author, steeped in the culture of cities, chooses an urban subject.

In those unforgettable days, city residents were engaged in the sole and universally obligatory occupation of government service.

Refusal to serve verged on treason to the homeland. Therefore everybody was in civil service—even the half-blind, even cripples, not only physical, but also moral—and the state, solicitous for the equal happiness of all its subjects, found work for each, according to his talents, for the six hours a day prescribed by the labor law.

Consequently, every socially conscious citizen was concerned with the question of time, since time, untouched by the general reevaluation of the universe, continued to be divided into hours, and among those hours was the one that marked the official beginning of work. And it was essential to determine this hour, at least with approximate correctness, if one was not to lose his minimum of calories or change his residence for another, as lacking in comforts as his own domicile, but substantially more restrictive of his freedom of movement.

Telling time, however, had become extremely difficult in the absence of the instruments evolved through centuries of scientific practice. It is true that there were individuals who somehow managed to do it. Whenever Aronchik Bleibas, the nephew of the watchmaker from Ertelev Lane, was asked, "What time is it?" he closed his eyes, sniffed with his narrow, always wet-tipped nose, and named a figure. Verification of such experiments by the clock on the City Hall tower proved that Aronchik was never wrong by more than ten minutes, and this assured him of lasting fame as a living clock. But such exceptional abilities could be attributed only to heredity; ordinary citizens found themselves faced with an insoluble dilemma.

CHAPTER 2

As we said at the beginning of this strange tale, Bolshaya Monetnaya Street was in a privileged position with regard to the computation of time.

Professor Blagosvetlov, who lived on this street (he too was mentioned in the opening lines of the preceding chapter), had managed, through all the revolutionary storms, both cosmic and legislative, to preserve intact his fine gold chronometer of English make. No one knew how it could have happened, and diverse interpretations were offered for this extraordinary phenomenon. The most widely current version, originating with the widow of a departmental director of the former Ministry of the Royal Court, a certain Malakicheva, was that the professor was busy in his laboratory canning human livers for the revolutionary army (human liver tasting exactly like calves' liver) and that, in reward for this, he was paid three times monthly, at the rate of two poods and eighteen pounds in American money.

There is no limit to the nonsense a stupid woman can invent! The author finds it necessary to refute with indignation this preposterous and patently reactionary slander. He knows better than anyone else that the professor, whose name was famous even beyond the frontiers of the Republic, was receiving two sets of rations from the state institution that had taken upon itself the burden of love for scientists and ballerinas: the academic ration and the so-called shock ration.

Concerning the origin of the latter term, there were numerous witty conjectures, but only the author knows the real truth. The lucky recipients of the shock ration were given dried fish of a very special quality. In order to make the fish edible, it was necessary to lay it on the edge of the stove and hammer at it with the butt end of an ax, without haste and at regular intervals, for approximately one and a half to two hours. This, and nothing else, was the true reason for the striking name of this ration.

At any rate, the two rations made it possible for the professor not only to preserve his chronometer, but also to maintain the existence of two organisms, one of which belonged to Blagosvetlov himself, the other to his lawful spouse, Anastasia Andreyevna.

Even during the most difficult years—1919 and 1920—the professor made daily visits, with the regularity of his own chronometer, to the physiological laboratory of the Institute of Exact Sciences, although the author must admit in all frankness that this served absolutely no purpose. Neither the professor himself nor the state derived any benefit from these visits.

For there was nothing in the laboratory but bare walls and

broken chemical utensils. On the dissecting table lay the skeleton of the last mongrel that had fallen victim to science in December of 1918, by this time gnawed to a fine polish by the laboratory rats. In summer, it was covered with a layer of dust; in winter, with hoarfrost. And, generally, wherever you turned, there was filth and desolation.

As for dogs, since 1919 they had become the object of culinary activities rather than physiological investigations, thus demonstrating the precariousness of basic scientific systems during the period of transition to socialism.

CHAPTER 3

It's a marvelous thing! Today, after the magnificent years of storm and stress, every writer has such an accumulation of material that it is pressing out, bursting out at every seam—there is no holding it back.

And the reason for this, my dear readers, is that, obedient to Heine's advice, we have spent several years on end beating drums and kissing canteen girls; and all this time we have hoarded our words deep within ourselves—as carefully and secretly as the miser knight hoarded his ducats. And when the drums were silenced and we brought our treasures home, the sacks that held them broke all at once. And now the gold is pouring out in an irrepressible stream, ringing, laughing, and weeping, and everything must out here and now, everything must be told, nothing must be forgotten or omitted.

It can be safely predicted that we shall not last long at this prodigal rate—two years or so and we shall find ourselves so dry that the only thing to do will be, perhaps, to start another revolution to find new topics.

The author must apologize for his entirely improper digression. It is a fatal trait inherited from a favorite late grandaunt. She was a great one for digressions, poor soul.

And so, the professor set out for work daily precisely at a quarter past nine. And he never permitted himself to deviate from this rule by even so much as two or three minutes. By this time, residents of his building who lived in rooms facing the street and served as lookouts were glued to their windowsills, sipping with delectation the excellent republican coffee made of richly browned corn.

As soon as the professor's stooping figure appeared on the sidewalk—in winter, dressed in a long overcoat with a raccoon collar; in summer, in tubular homespun trousers—his neighbors hastily drank down their coffee and emerged, in turn.

Their emergence was immediately noted by other eyes, faintly visible behind the foggy windows down the street. And so it went from house to house: human specimens poured out into the street with unbroken regularity, and the mechanism of civic duty, switched on by the professor, went into operation on Bolshaya Monetnaya with astonishing precision.

Tapping his cane on the pavement, the professor proceeded to the Zhdanovka Quay, climbed to the second story, and pulled the bell. He had to pull it only three times. After that, the door chain clinked and the professor was admitted within by the aged watchman, called Nestor, a historic name to which nature had taken care to append the most appropriate family name of Kotlyarevsky.

This second name gave rise to numerous misunderstandings in the laboratory. On one occasion, an itinerant commissar on a flying inspection tour glanced through the personnel list and was shocked to the point of tears. "No!" he exclaimed with emotion. "Academician Kotlyarevsky working as a watchman? What is the meaning of this? Couldn't they find a more fitting occupation for him? I shall call for an immediate investigation, and the culprits will suffer the full penalties. The Republic cannot allow such criminal failure to utilize our men of science!"

It was with great difficulty that the enraged commissar was finally persuaded that his ire was misplaced and that Nestor Kotlyarevsky, though resembling the academician in his documentary data, lacked the latter's high scientific qualifications.

Opening the door, Nestor Kotlyarevsky respectfully bowed to the professor with his usual greeting, "Good morning, Mr. Professor," to which the professor invariably answered, "Good morning, Comrade Kotlyarevsky."

In this connection, the author will permit himself to venture the observation, based on personal experience, that among men of equal age, those on the lower rungs of the social ladder are far more conservative in their habits than highly cultivated individuals.

The professor proceeded to his study and, with his coat pulled tightly around him, sat for a time in his chair, examining with unremitting attention the long cut in the dusty baize on his desk. An hour and a half later he rose and walked to the laboratory, where he seated himself by the dissecting table and with equal curiosity studied the mongrel's skeleton. For three more hours, devoted daily to this occupation, he sighed mournfully and rubbed his frozen hands.

At the expiration of these hours, Nestor would bring in three stunted logs of wood. One of them he would split with an ax on the tile floor, carefully placing it into the hollow of a broken tile in order to protect the rest of the floor. The splinters were then fed into the potbellied stove, where they smoked for a long time, causing the professor and Nestor to cough and suffocate; in the end, however, they heated up the iron walls of the stove, and for an hour the two priests of science warmed their fingers in the life-giving warmth. After another hour, the professor slipped one of the remaining logs under his coat, while Nestor took the other; and as soon as the professor's chronometer marked the expiration of the legal six-hour workday, the two went out together.

During the stormy years, this was known as highly qualified scientific work.

CHAPTER 4

With the end of the romantic era, both watches and dogs reappeared in the cities.

The people on Bolshaya Monetnaya now lolled peacefully between sheets laundered with real soap until the moment when the friendly hands of their clocks approached the requisite hour, and they no longer had to run to the windows. Indeed, many people had attained the happy state of being able to disregard clocks altogether, for in addition to government service, the erstwhile multitude of professions had come back into its own, and one of the most popular professions was that of being registered in the files of the labor exchange, which required no accounting of time, being everlasting.

Professor Blagosvetlov, forgotten by his ungrateful neighbors, nevertheless continued his daily visits to the laboratory, but his activities there were substantially different. The slit in the baize on his desk had been repaired, and a variety of test tubes and retorts was now in evidence. A fresh mutt kicked its legs daily on the dissecting table, and clear-voiced young republicans, under the professor's guidance, enriched their native science with new researches. A new tile had been set into the floor, another into the edge of the stove in the professor's kitchen, to replace the one mutilated by two years of hammering at the shock-ration fish. In wintertime, bundles of dry wood crackled in a regular round oven.

The only thing that had changed was the watchman, since Nestor Kotlyarevsky had departed from the revived Republic, somewhat in advance of his famous namesake, from which event persons of mystical bent might have drawn all sorts of conclusions. However, the name of the new watchman, Pimen, had its own historic connotations, and thus the order of things had not really been broken.

The life processes of the organisms of the professor and Anastasia Andreyevna were now sustained by a personal salary and individual credit at the PEPO, clearly demonstrating the superiority of state capitalism over wartime communism.

Everything would have been splendid, in accord with the latest conditions of existence, and the author would have been compelled, willy-nilly, to end his tale at this point if the professor had not discovered one spring day that his hat, which had selflessly served him from the very first days of the war and had witnessed the greatest ideological cataclysm in the world, had acquired an excessive number of holes, which rendered it inconsonant with the prosperous and flourishing state of the Republic.

When he left the laboratory that day, Blagosvetlov altered his customary itinerary and boarded the trolley going to the Avenue of October 25. Clanking along on its rails and splashing through the muddy spring puddles with its resonant wheels, for all the world like a brazen young hooligan, the trolley brought the professor to the Apraxin Market and set him down in the thick of the milling crowd under the vaulted arcades, which bore such a striking resemblance to the mouth of a Russian oven.

Struggling through the crowd and, by force of still uneradicated habit, apologizing civilly whenever he jostled anyone with his elbow, Alexander Yevlampievich finally, after giving the matter deep and concentrated thought, made his choice. He stopped before a window where an array of ordinary human hats and caps surrounded a cap of enormous size, capable of holding eight professorial heads and exhibited with the express purpose of drawing the prospective customer's attention.

As befits an experimental physiologist, Professor Blagosvetlov was a complete innocent in matters of applied economics, and the gigantic cap attracted him irresistibly. He looked at it with a shy smile, thinking, What a remarkable phenomenon, advertising! One might ask, why should anyone trouble to make such a cap? What for? Who can wear it? Unless, perhaps, an elephant in a circus. It might be thought, on the face of it, that such an absurdity would drive away any sensible buyer. Yet you cannot pass it by without stopping. An interesting example of reflex action.

On completing this clear and well-rounded thought, the professor, for some reason, drew himself up, smoothed down the new spring coat he had purchased at the PEPO, and resolutely stepped into the store.

At the noise of the opening door, the owner, who had been arranging his wares on the shelves, turned with alacrity to the customer.

The professor noticed that he had a long, yellow face, resembling a slice of pumpkin, and hairless, like an old woman's. This extraordinary facial apparatus reinforced the professor's conviction that he had made the right choice.

"What can I do for you, citizen?" the storekeeper asked, resting his bony fingers on the counter and leaning forward. His opened mouth made a narrow slit across his face, as though the pumpkin slice had cracked in half.

"I? . . . I . . . oh," the professor mumbled in confusion, suddenly unable to find the needed words. "I must replace this . . . this hat."

The storekeeper took the professor's hat, looked at it in the light, and tenderly smacked his lips. "An excellent hat! A splendid hat!" he even closed his eyes. "An admirable hat! Such hats were worn before the war only by the most elegant gentlemen. But now, if you pardon me, citizen, it has somewhat lost its shape."

"I . . . well . . . I mean . . . it is really quite funny." The professor became altogether confused. "You see, through all those years when we had no wood . . . well, I slept in it. I am bald, you see, and I was afraid of catching a head cold."

"That's reasonable," the storekeeper answered mildly. "I myself had two otter hats in a similar situation. I used to turn them out, with the fur inside, then I would put them on my feet and tie them on with a string. And I can tell you, my feet were never cold. And, then, I had a customer, an old gentleman, a former court chamberlain, an eminent personage—" Here the store owner broke off the thread of recollections and, with an amiable grin, inquired, "And what type of a headdress would you wish, citizen?"

"I . . . something like this one . . . felt . . . gray," the professor muttered, tenderly stroking the remains of his hat with his fingertips, like a man apologizing to a beloved woman for infidelity.

The storekeeper threw a critical glance at the professor and, stretching his hand across the counter, touched a button on the professor's coat. "I'll tell you, citizen, if you don't mind, I'd like to give you a bit of advice. Today, a hat is out of style. In fact, it's even unsafe—I mean, in the sense of social categories. If you excuse me, who wears a felt hat nowadays? A Nepman!* And what's a Nepman, if I may ask? A Nepman is like a splinter of an abolished way of life, something contemptible, not quite a man—an ape, only burdened with obligations. And, let us say, if the finance inspector should visit you, then, having a felt hat, you may altogether undeservedly be clamped into the wrong category."

"What would you suggest, then?" asked the discouraged Alexander Yevlampievich.

"Now, pardon me if I ask your occupation, citizen."

"I am a professor . . . a physiologist," Blagosvetlov mumbled uncertainly.

"There, a representative of scientific knowledge, you might say. If you were a civil servant, up to the fifteenth grade, I would offer you an ordinary cap. But for a thinking man, such a cap is not substantial enough. You need something to inspire understanding at a glance. I have it! A kepi! Yes, just the right thing! A most magnificent head covering. I have just one—and exactly your size!"

He turned and brought down a cap from the shelf. "There! The finest cloth. Prewar manufacture. Made by the Stieglitz factory."

"But, allow me," the professor said, recoiling, "what an incredible style!"

"Style? Don't you worry. *Dernier cry.* Look at it in the light."

He brought the cap to the door. The cap was made of yellowish, coffee-colored cloth, and its top, of extraordinary size, rose over the rim like a huge balloon with half the air let out. Besides this, it had another peculiar feature: its visor, long and flat, was covered with vivid turquoise cloth, and the tip of the crown was adorned, at its very center, with a pompon made of thin strips of the same turquoise material.

"But the visor? The visor? Why is it blue? Why the pompon?" the professor cried indignantly.

"If you forgive me! Seeing as the Republic is now in close

* A Nepman was the *nouveau riche*, the aggressive, get-rich-quick type of businessman who sprang up during the period of the New Economic Policy (NEP) in the early 1920's.

friendship with awakened China, the style is pure Nanking and the color of the heavenly empire. Truly a heavenly cap, expressing the awakening of the sleepy East."

"But it's indecently bright. It's good for some youngster, not for me," the overwhelmed professor argued.

"My dear citizen! How can you say this? Are you an old man? Why, you could still be an eligible bachelor, what with current female excesses. And, then, if you allow me, your complexion is even extraordinary for the present era. Nowadays everybody is gray or yellow, but your physiognomy is quite full-blooded. And everybody knows, even those who don't understand anything, that pink and turquoise go very well together."

"But I have a gray beard. People will laugh at me!" Alexander Yevlampievich offered a visibly weakening objection.

"Don't you worry about that. Who cares what evil-minded people make fun of? Take, for example, Comrade Lenin. The ignorant bourgeoisie also made fun of him on account of the Soviets, and what came out of it? But try it on," and the storekeeper nimbly slipped the cap on the professor's bald head.

Alexander Yevlampievich glanced into the mirror. The azure glow of the visor had indeed set off the delicately pink complexion of which the professor was secretly proud. Still, the general picture was absurd and rather startling. "No . . . I somehow don't like it. Perhaps something else?" he asked limply.

"Ah, don't argue, sir! It's a wonderful cap; you won't find another one like it. And, the main thing, look at the cloth. Nowadays, you pay six rubles for an article, wear it three months, and it falls apart. But this is a Stieglitz product—it will last you for decades, and it's only two and a half."

"Why so cheap?" the professor wondered.

"Cost price. Old stock. That's what I paid for it, that's what I'll sell it for. You'll be satisfied, take my word for it!"

The professor removed the cap and turned it in his hands. The price was indeed remarkably low, and he began to vacillate, for he had never been distinguished for strength of character or firmness of will. Suddenly his eyes caught sight of a little circle of gold braid over the visor and, within it, embroidered in red silk, a tiny snake. "And what is this?"

"This? It's something like a medical emblem. To tell you the truth, I had the cap made to order for a medical professor, but he died before it was ready. And so it remained."

The reference to the medical professor dealt the final blow to Alexander Yevlampievich's persisting distrust of the dazzling cap, but he made one last timid attempt at resistance. "Perhaps it should be ripped off?"

"It can be done. As you wish! But it will leave a mark. And why rip it off, if I may ask? After all, you are also engaged in medical science. Shall I wrap your hat?"

"Wrap it," the professor sighed brokenly. Then he put on the cap and got out his wallet.

Back in the street, he started out toward his trolley. Then he remembered that he still had to get a haircut, and, slowly dragging his galoshes, he ambled off to the barbershop.

He did not notice that his appearance on the sidewalk caused a commotion verging on panic. A young and fashionably dressed female citizen bumped into him. Her gray, penciled eyes flashed with gay astonishment, then they narrowed; her lips spread out, and snorting into his face, she rushed past. Being sufficiently myopic, the professor did not see any of this.

The purchase of the cap had evidently inspired him with a desire for a more youthful look. At the barbershop, he ordered his venerable square beard trimmed down to a small goatee. After this operation, he felt fifteen years younger and so turned homeward.

At home he encountered the first blow. He entered Anastasia Andreyevna's bedroom directly from the hallway, without removing his cap, anxious to boast of his purchase. To his astonishment, Anastasia Andreyevna, who was darning her husband's knitted underpants, dropped them and jumped up terrified from her chair. "What do you wish? Who let you in?" she squealed, and then, before the professor could open his lips to answer, she gasped, "Sasha! Good heavens! What has happened to you?"

"I . . . bought this . . . to replace the old hat," the professor answered, somewhat puzzled.

"You bought . . . this! Have you gone mad? This clown's cap, at the age of fifty-four? You look like an idiot! And what did you do with your beard? What has possessed you? Take this rubbish off at once, I won't stand the sight of it!"

The professor was by nature timid but hot-tempered. In his old companion's indignation and anger, he discerned a threat to his independence, and he flared up. "What? Do I ever interfere when you choose to bedeck yourself back and front with all sorts of stupid trinkets? Just imagine—fifty-four! Do you expect me to wear a coffin on my head? Do I have a right to do what I want? I will not take a woman's despotism!"

"He's gone completely insane!" Anastasia Andreyevna clapped her hands together in horror. "But you must understand, you look like a cretin in that cap!"

Although the professor secretly felt a strange embarrassment and was almost ready to accuse himself of excessive haste in his purchase, his wife's angry voice only irritated him, and he also began to shout. "And you look like a cretin without any cap! I know what I'm doing. I shall ask you again to keep your unsolicited advice to yourself." And, stamping out through the door, he threw back at her, "Old cow!"

Anastasia Andreyevna looked at the slammed door, tapped her forehead with her knuckle, and asked the walls and the chairs with a helpless air, "Well, tell me in all honesty, did you ever see such a fool?"

CHAPTER 5

The next five days brought the professor a good deal of vexation. Acquaintances shied away from him as Polynesians do from taboo objects; they stared at his extraordinary cap with the most indelicate air. The young citizens of the Republic in his laboratory guffawed behind his back without restraint and nicknamed him Spotted Medusa.

Anastasia Andreyevna sulked; at dinner the cutlets were burned and gritted on the teeth like pebbles.

It was quite obvious that all the foundations of his life were rocking because of the accursed cap. If he would only throw it out into the garbage heap and buy a new hat, everything would return to normal equilibrium.

But an inexplicable, angry obstinacy took possession of the professor—an obstinacy that often springs up in natively shy people when they encounter resistance to their whims.

He became thin and sallow, but he stubbornly persisted in wearing his dazzling head attire and even jauntily pushed its florid mass back on his head, which unexpectedly lent his modest face something of the devil-may-care look of a cavalry officer.

At any rate, one morning, as he was wending his way to the laboratory, he met two Red Army soldiers. At the sight of the professor, one of them, smooth-faced and ruddy like a young girl, said to his comrade with admiration, "There's a dashing old-timer for you! Just put him on a horse, and send him to Budenny's cavalry!"

Of course, it was quite absurd, but these words made the professor feel suddenly young and hearty. Continuing on his way to the temple of science, he pushed out his chest and tried to step out briskly, as though keeping time with a certain lively inner rhythm.

At that moment, he illustrated the ancient adage about those whom Jupiter chose to deprive of reason.

Little by little, the people who knew Alexander Yevlampievich began to grow accustomed to the azure aureole over his brow and the coffee-colored balloon waving over his bald head and no longer noticed the unseemly frivolity of the devilish cap. As for people he did not know, the professor himself never noticed them, thanks to the nearsightedness we mentioned earlier.

Even Anastasia Andreyevna calmed down, her cutlets resumed the requisite tenderness, and a full reconciliation took place between husband and wife, in celebration of which the professor decided to buy his wife a gift—an embroidered scarf for the piano.

In the morning, he set out again in trolley No. 2 for the Avenue of October 25, and the gray, ordinary day was unexpectedly marked by . . .

But there is no need to anticipate and show all the cards to the reader in advance. This may be done only in novels—and only by venerable novelists—but the author is a modest man, and he must first win his readers.

The professor duly bought the desired scarf, cream-colored and embroidered with enchanting, truly exquisite, inimitable roses in lacy, cutwork style. The embroidery was so delicate, so fine, so transparent that Alexander Yevlampievich paid eighteen rubles for it without protest and turned back to his penates.

True, he loitered a while in the crowded Gostiny Dvor, stood for at least six minutes before the window of the Leather Goods Trust, and stepped in to see a watchmaker of his acquaintance, to have his chronometer checked, but these innocent occupations did not take more than fifteen minutes altogether.

Arriving home, he kissed Anastasia Andreyevna on both cheeks, after which she handed him a letter from his son.

The son of Alexander Yevlampievich, who had graduated from a military-medical academy, developed an interest in the study of malaria and had been sent to Kushka, where, as we know, nature produces for the benefit of the inhabitants of the fortress only two commodities of wide consumption: two-inch scorpions and tropical malaria.

The professor sat down at the dinner table, tied his napkin around his neck, and spooning up his cabbage soup, read with lively interest the latest data concerning the origin of malaria nidi. It was only after he had finished the letter that he remembered the present and said to his wife, "I've brought you something, Tasenka. Take a look in the hallway. It's in my coat pocket, a little package."

Anastasia Andreyevna, flushed pink with pleasure, went out, but did not return for a long time. The professor looked at the door with some wonder and was on the verge of getting up, when Anastasia Andreyevna appeared on the threshold holding the opened gift in her hands.

Her face was happy, but somewhat troubled. Approaching her husband, she tenderly touched her lips to his bald head. "Thanks, Sashenka! It's a lovely scarf. But, my dear, how absentminded you've become! Why did you leave your chronometer in your coat pocket? It's lucky it wasn't stolen!"

The professor looked down at his wife's hand and saw a gold watch in the hollow of her palm. Its chain hung down, swaying and gleaming warmly. "Strange," he said, putting his hand out to the watch. "How did it happen?"

But before he touched the watch, his hand recoiled, and he jumped up. "It isn't my watch!" he cried. "I have no chain, I have a cord!"

Anastasia Andreyevna stood numbly, her eyes alternating between her husband and the watch.

The professor unbuttoned his jacket, felt his spleen, and pulled out of his vest pocket the chronometer, which swayed on its round, silken cord. "Here is my chronometer," he continued, completely bewildered. "And this—this is not mine!"

"But how could it get into your pocket, dear?" his wife gasped.

"Let me see it," the professor said firmly and picked it up with a strange, jerky movement, as though the gold were red-hot and burned his hand. He turned the watch this way and that, opened the lid, and brought it up to his eyes, to examine the face. "No . . . it isn't mine," he said in a flat voice. "Mine is English, and this is a Longine. An excellent make, but that doesn't explain anything. I am completely at a loss to understand it!"

He went on examining the watch, held up the heavy chain with his fingers, and suddenly turned pale. The chain was broken, or, rather, it had been cut with some sharp instrument, evidently several links below the ring that had held it in the vest buttonhole. The professor quickly put the watch back on the table; in fact, he almost threw it back. "It was snipped off . . . snipped off!" he breathed in a tragic whisper.

"But how did it come to you?"

"Ah! . . . How can I tell? I know as much as you do. Incredible!" The professor was so agitated that his hands and eyebrows were trembling.

"Calm down, Sasha." His wife put her hand on his shoulder. "Just try to remember carefully where you were."

"Wait . . . wait. First I took the trolley, then I bought a newspaper at the corner of Sadovaya, then I went to the store for the scarf. After that, I took a stroll along Gostiny . . . looked at some store windows. Then I stood for a long while near a shoe store. On the way home, I stepped in to have Ivan Parmenych check my chrono—" The professor broke off and happily clapped his hands. "But, of course! What an old fool! The watch must have lain on his counter, and I automatically . . . But what will Ivan Parmenych think? What a business! I'll take it back." He snatched up the watch and hurried toward the door.

"Sasha! Where are you going? Finish your dinner, then you'll go."

"Oh, no! Oh, no!" the professor cried indignantly. "The man must be out of his mind looking for it; he must have called the police. There may be a detective on the way here already."

He quickly kissed his wife's hand and ran off with extraordinary energy.

Anastasia Andreyevna waited a long time for his return, but it was almost eight o'clock when the entrance door slammed and Alexander Yevlampievich staggered into the room in his cap, coat, and galoshes. To his wife's silent question, he raised his hand with the gesture of the blind Oedipus. Heavy silence hung over the room like a lead ball.

"What is it? Why don't you say something? For God's sake!" cried Anastasia Andreyevna.

"The watch . . . does not belong to Ivan Parmenych," the professor said, forcing the words out hoarsely, and dropped into the armchair so heavily that the carved walnut legs creaked and whimpered.

CHAPTER 6

In the morning, at a family council, it was decided that the professor would advertise the watch in the lost-and-found column of the newspaper. Alexander Yevlampivich had hardly slept that night; his face was drawn, and two violet plums had sprung up under his eyes.

Saying good-bye to him in the foyer, Anastasia Andreyevna sighed deeply. "Sasha, dear, don't worry about it so much; think of your health. You've aged ten years in a single night. Nothing dreadful has happened, some silly misunderstanding. After all, it isn't your fault!"

"That's all I need, that it should be my fault!" the professor snapped angrily and pulled his cap violently down over his nose, instead of at the former jaunty angle.

The advertisement was printed, but nobody came to claim the watch, and it went on ticking peaceably on the desk, wound up regularly by the professor, whose heart was torn with doubts and suspicions throughout this procedure.

Exactly three weeks later, the professor went once again to the Avenue of October 25, prompted by the need to purchase half a dozen pairs of socks.

He had almost recovered his composure by now and was even showing the watch to visiting friends and telling them its fantastic history.

When he returned home with his purchase, he wanted to hang up his coat, but found that the hanger was torn. The professor was a methodical and tidy man, and he immediately proceeded to his wife, his purchase in one hand, the coat in the other, to ask her to restore the hanger to working order.

Anastasia Andreyevna took the coat, spread it on her knees, took a needle from the velvet mushroom, and began to repair the damage, while the professor paced the bedroom diagonally and talked with animation about the ice breaking on the Neva.

Suddenly he stopped midway, hearing something metallic drop

on the floor at Anastasia Andreyevna's feet. He bent down with youthful agility and remained squatting, with extended fingers and an open mouth.

Anastasia Andreyevna threw aside the coat and, bending her head, saw, lying on the floor at the tip of her left shoe, a flat gold cigarette case, gleaming with a diamond monogram. She started and looked at the panting professor. "What is this, Sasha?" she asked, trembling with terror and staring at the cigarette case with the eyes of a bird facing a cobra.

"I d-don't know. . . . A c-cig-arette case," the professor said, stuttering shrilly.

"But where did you get it?"

The professor stood up and clutched at his heart. His face turned gray and long, and beads of perspiration stood on his nose. "I feel ill . . . my heart," he said in a strained voice, and he sat down on the floor.

Anastasia Andreyevna screamed and rushed with express speed through the bedroom, hallway, and foyer and flew down the stairs to the lower landing, where their old family doctor, Serafim Serafimovich Archangelov, lived.

When she returned to her apartment, dragging the doctor by the hand, the professor was lying on the floor in a dead faint. After he was lifted to the sofa and given an injection of camphor, he moaned weakly and slowly regained consciousness.

"Sashenka, my dear! Do you feel ill?" Anastasia Andreyevna asked, crying.

The professor's teeth unclenched. He tried several times to say something, but he hiccuped and swallowed the words.

It was only when Dr. Archangelov bent closely over his face that he finally understood.

"C-cig-cigal-lette-case."

"What cigarette case? What cigarette case is he talking about?" the doctor asked, turning in perplexity to Anastasia Andreyevna, but she only shook her head.

The professor wearily closed his eyes and began to breathe more regularly.

"I think it is best to give him complete rest. Let him lie there for a half hour or so. I shall write out a prescription for bromide and chloral hydrate. His heart is all right; there is no need to worry. It's only a light spasm caused by excitement. The pulse is rapid, but that will pass. Let me have a pen and paper, please, Anastasia Andreyevna."

As he was signing the prescription in the study, Archangelov chewed at a corner of his tar-black robber's beard, which left exposed only his bulbous nose and small, sharp, yellow eyes, and listened with curiosity to Anastasia Andreyevna's jumbled story of the recent shocking events in the professor's life.

"Amazing! Adventures straight out of the *Arabian Nights*. I can't understand it at all. You say he brings home valuable objects in his coat pocket? So! Interesting! And may I see the coat?"

Although Anastasia Andreyevna had no idea why he wanted the coat, she willingly brought it.

Serafim Serafimovich carefully examined the coat with the air of a man who expected an actual devil to jump out of it with crashing thunder. Then he felt the lining and put his huge paw into the pocket.

His beard stood out like a fan, his lips twitched, and he announced triumphantly, "Ah-ha! Something else here!" And he drew out his hand, bringing to light something glittering that, on closer inspection, turned out to be a pair of earrings. The diamonds and sapphires in his palm sparkled in the cinnabar rays of the setting sun with pink and blue stars.

"Hell! Excellent earrings! The diamonds are at least a carat and a half each!" he said delightedly, without noticing that Anastasia Andreyevna had stopped in the middle of the room, as immobile as Lot's wife staring at the charred ruins of Sodom. "Hmm, yes! A first-rate acquisition. Easily worth fifteen hundred!" he continued imperturbably, rolling the earrings in his palm the better to admire their glitter.

Anastasia Andreyevna recovered at last. "Serafim Serafimovich! What can we do? How would you explain it?"

The doctor chewed the tip of his thumb with a melancholy

air, which he always did in moments of perplexity, and answered slowly, "I cannot understand it. I suppose, in the Middle Ages, Alexander Yevlampievich would have been burnt at the stake for dealings with the devil."

"Good God, that's all we need!" sobbed the professor's wife. "But what's to be done now?"

"I hardly know what to suggest," Archangelov answered without removing his thumb from his mouth. "It seems to me that it might be best to take these things to the police and tell them everything. Let Alexander Yevlampievich rest overnight, and in the morning he can go directly to the criminal investigation office. That's the best thing to do."

"Do you think—" Anastasia Andreyevna flushed and broke off. "Could Sasha suddenly have gotten . . . this . . . what d'you call it . . . kleptomania?"

The doctor reflected a few moments and said decisively, "No! Kleptomaniacs usually remember their thefts and perform them consciously. It's in the nature of kleptomania that a man cannot refrain from stealing, but he knows what he is doing. No, this is not kleptomania!"

On concluding this scientific explanation, the doctor bowed out with dignity.

After his departure, Anastasia Andreyevna returned to the bedroom.

The professor had completely regained consciousness and was sitting on the sofa, clasping his head with transparent, old fingers. He glanced at his wife as though he were looking through her and muttered, "I feel so weak. What's to be done?"

"Go to bed, Sasha! You must rest. Tomorrow morning you'll go to the police with the things and tell them the story."

And Anastasia Andreyevna told him about her conversation with the doctor.

The professor obediently allowed himself to be put to bed, drank a glass of hot milk, swallowed a dose of chloral hydrate, and fifteen minutes later he was whistling delicately through his nose.

Anastasia Andreyevna huddled in a chair by his bedside,

wrapped herself in a warm Orenburg shawl, and sat there until dawn, helplessly wrinkling her forehead.

CHAPTER 7

In the huge and untidy gray room of the criminal investigation office, a detective with close-cropped blond hair sat behind the reception table. His enormous nose, which hung over his upper lip, had evidently been deeply slashed in childhood and was now clearly divided by a white scar into two parts, like a twin pod. He raised his head reluctantly and listened with unconcealed skepticism to the professor's jumbled and halting monologue.

"Let me see the things," he said in a tight, gummy voice.

The professor took out a small bundle, carefully unwrapped it, put the cord back into his pocket, and laid out the cigarette case, the watch, and the earrings on the desk.

A momentary look of curiosity flashed like summer lightning over the stony face of the man with the pendent nose, and he whistled quietly.

The professor caught a polite but crafty grin in his indifferent eyes.

"But these are stolen articles, citizen! In fact, I have a report concerning this cigarette case, filled out with all the necessary formalities. What can you say to that? Eh?"

The professor shrugged his shoulders with dignity. "I find your question very strange. I came to you precisely because I wished you to explain whose things they are and how they came to me. I cannot tell you anything at all."

The detective blew his nose and grinned. "First time here? Never been apprehended before?" he rapped out after a pause, fixing his eyes on the bridge of the professor's nose.

The professor was taken aback, but a moment later he understood and turned purple. "Comrade, I ask you—" he began, raising his voice, but the detective civilly interrupted him.

"Don't be hasty, citizen! We shall clear it up in a minute. . . .

Antoshchuk! Bring me the file on Group No. 2. May I have your documents, citizen."

The professor's lips began to tremble with indignation at the insult, and he surprised himself by spluttering saliva as he shouted, "What right have you? Are you insane? I am Professor Blagosvetlov. I have— Here are my documents! Here, cards from KUBU, the Academy of Sciences, the university, a letter of thanks from the Soviet of People's Commissars!" He flung his shrill angry words at the detective, while his documents plunked one after the other on the desk.

The big-nosed detective collected them and examined each with exaggerated attention, even holding them up to the light. "Funny thing. Unquestionably not a fake," he said, addressing no one.

The professor felt his heart beginning to flutter again. His heartbeats seemed to fail, then suddenly hammered at his chest like the surf on a coral reef. "I should like to sit down," he said angrily. "I feel unwell."

"Comrade Lychkov! Give the citizen a chair. Sit down, citizen, and don't upset yourself. We are just doing our duty."

Antoshchuk brought two huge folders from the back room, and the detective began to turn the pages on the table.

A succession of glum physiognomies, *en face* and in profile, began to flicker before the professor. He closed his eyes.

Occasionally, the detective stopped at some photograph, looked up at the professor, and the empty silence of the room was broken by his glutinous mumbling: "Sintsov, Grigory, alias Lukichev, alias Markin. Nickname, French Nostril. Repeated arrests . . . buyer of stolen goods . . . age, forty-seven. . . . No, that's not it."

He ran through all the pages of the folders with astonishing speed, then firmly brought his hand down on the cover. "Calm yourself, citizen! This is our job. To tell the truth, I didn't suspect you. I see, a little old codger, talks intellectual, an educated beard. But I had to check, because we get such makeup artists here, they'll play you any part. We pulled in one of them fellows three days ago. The men bring in—if you pardon me—an archbishop. Honest! Everything proper—a robe, a cowl, a pastor's staff. They got him at Sennoy. He was walking around blessing the peddlers in the market. And then they nabbed him, blessing a stallkeeper with the right hand and slashing away at his pocket with the left. I must admit, I thought at first there was some mistake. Although the priests are certainly having no picnic in the workers' and peasants' state. Still and all, for an archbishop to come down to such things! . . . And, mind you, the documents were all there—and all straight. Agathon, Archbishop of Kiev, on a mission for the Living Church. But soon as the chief came in, he grabbed him by the beard first thing, and it came right off in his hand. The fellow's face was smooth as a turnip. We recognized him in a moment, without any photograph. Mitka Podtyazhka, pickpocket. Seven arrests! But don't you worry, Citizen Professor, as you have everything in perfectly natural order. Just leave the things here with your statement and go on home."

"But I would like to know how these things got to me?" the infuriated professor insisted.

"As for that, citizen, I couldn't say, I don't know myself. Couldn't be none other but a misunderstanding of nature."

"Well, then, can you protect me against a repetition of such misunderstandings? That's what I need, instead of your stupid tales."

"This, citizen, is not within my powers. If it's a question of preventing a burglary, that can be done sometimes, if you have a good detective force. But an inanimate object—how can you keep track of it? For the life of me, I can't understand your case. Good-bye, citizen. Here's the receipt for the things, if you please."

The professor went out, spat on the sidewalk, and flung the receipt into the mud.

At home, telling Anastasia Andreyevna how he had been taken for a thief, he became agitated again and even burst into tears. Then he retired to his study, intending to work on the proofs of his *Course in Experimental Physiology*, but his head ached, the lines of print coiled into circles. He finally lay down on the sofa and fell asleep without undressing.

CHAPTER 8

The next two weeks were almost uneventful in the professor's household, if we discount the fact that on Friday, after a trip to the center of town, the professor found in his pocket a gold and enamel brooch. However, on careful examination, it transpired that the brooch was only gold plated.

The discovery of the brooch left the professor quite unmoved. He treated its appearance with stoical indifference and was even secretly a little irked that it was only brass. This seemed like something of an insult, a mockery.

In the evening, he went to a meeting of the Learned Council, which lasted until half-past eleven. His colleagues at the meeting noted that his mind was extraordinarily fresh that day and that he formulated his ideas with classical lucidity.

He left the meeting in the company of a professor of pathological surgery, Yershov, and rode with him until the corner of Bolshaya Monetnaya. There he stepped down from the trolley and plunged into the oozing-wet April night.

The author would like to ask the reader whether he has any idea of what night was like in the Petrograd district after midnight in 1924, in the seventh year after the birth of the Republic. The author is certain that the reader does not have even an approximate notion of it, since the reader hangs out most of the time at various Avenues of October 25, around the dazzling temples of the great mute—all sorts of "Piccadillys," "Grand Palaces," and "Parisians." In such places, night has no resemblance to night. It is garish, noisy, and brazen, like the paint on a caracul-coated lady's lips, whose violent scarlet makes our cabbies swear sympathetically. Everything clatters, jingles, gleams, and scintillates, and there is no rest till morning for the earth in her tight corsets of asphalt and paving stones.

But in the Petrograd district all is silence. The sky is so far overhead, you'd need a ladder to climb it—and at that, a ladder

so long that even the State Fire Department hasn't built one
like it yet.

At eleven o'clock the lights go out in all the windows, and the
houses stand like solid grayish-purple cubes, except perhaps for a
dreamy little light somewhere under a roof, where a crazy poet is
scribbling verses. It's a strange thing: you might say that we have
almost reached communism, we've turned our whole life upside
down, and still we haven't managed to root out the poets.

Even the night-lights in the gateways are out, and no one
pays any attention, for what decent policeman in the Petrograd
district will venture further than the gateway nearest to his post
on the Kamenno-Ostrovsky or Bolshoy?

In the murky gloom, everything seems unreal, artificial, like
stage scenery, and this lends the landscape a certain dry, dead
quality. There is no sense of life, no aroma; even the puddles
made by tomcats and passing humans in the alleys have no smell.

Night is a strange time indeed in the Petrograd district!

Bolshaya Monetnaya gaped like a black, lifeless canyon, its
only sound the clicking of heavy drops from drainpipes. The professor unhurriedly sloshed along on the wet, gutted asphalt, wending his way home.

When he reached the gates of the burned-down building, its
naked skeleton barely visible against the velvet, starry sky, a man
separated himself from the wall across the street and walked with
a swinging gait toward the professor. In his light, rapid stride
there was something stealthy and predatory, and Alexander Yevlampievich suddenly felt an unpleasant emptiness at the pit of
his stomach. He slowed his steps, as though this might avert an
encounter with the stranger. But the man only broke the
straight diagonal and suddenly loomed up directly before the professor.

He wore a short quilted coat and a flat little hat, and the ends
of the scarf around his neck flew up behind him like wings.
Stopping before the professor, he raised his right hand with a
quick, light movement.

Alexander Yevlampievich started and put up both hands to shield his face, but at this moment somebody seized him by the throat from behind. His mouth opened to scream, but something rough and soft was stuffed into it. After that, a smart blow behind the knees sent him sprawling without a sound on the pavement.

The man who had first approached him bent down and peered into the professor's face. "The old geezer," he said, almost regretfully.

"Never mind!" said another voice, rougher and drier. "Smack him a couple on the jaw. He'll know better next time."

"I'm afraid he'll croak if I touch him."

"The louse! . . . Let me!"

The professor, numb with terror, felt two violent blows on his cheeks, delivered from behind, and green sparks danced before his eyes.

When he ventured to open them again, there was no one in the street. He was lying alone, supine, and his back shivered with the chill of the wet asphalt.

The professor drew his breath, sat up, and felt his sides. In the side pocket of his coat, he found his wallet; and in the vest pocket, his fingers felt the circle of his chronometer.

Everything was intact and in place. He froze with astonishment. The adventure had been so quick and strange that it seemed like a dream, a moment of delirium; only the wet asphalt under his seat recalled him to reality, but even that seemed almost to drift past his consciousness.

The professor listened. From far off, strong heels tapped on the sidewalk, and a light tenor voice approached, singing, "O night of magic dreams . . ." The passerby was walking on the opposite side of the street.

"Comrade," whimpered the professor piteously, "help me, I beg you!"

The tapping broke off, and a young voice, as crisp as an autumn apple, with a trace of an alien accent, asked, "Help you? Who are you?"

"A professor," answered Blagosvetlov, unaware of the full absurdity of his reply under the circumstances.

"A professor?" the voice crackled with wonder. "But what are you doing there?"

"I was robbed. I am sitting on the sidewalk."

The heels clattered on the pavement as the passerby ran across the street.

Alexander Yevlampievich saw a young face with a slender, beaked nose. "But why do you sit there if you were robbed? What a strange man!"

"It is hard for me to get up. I . . . I was very frightened," the physiologist mumbled in confusion.

The passerby helped the professor to rise and stood before him, smiling vividly.

The new moon, breaking through the murk, shone into his face and obliterated his eyes behind the round lenses of his glasses, which gleamed with a mysterious moon-green light.

"I thank you, young comrade!" The professor seized the hand of his deliverer and shook it with all his strength. "You have saved me from death! Who are you?"

The passerby was silent for a moment, then answered slowly, splitting off syllable after syllable like icicles: "My name is Hector von Zelies. I am a scientist. I came to Russia a short time ago. But that is beside the point, Professor. Don't speak of death aloud at night. She walks about nearby and waits for a careless call."

The professor glanced around nervously. The tone of his nocturnal companion was frightening. And the professor said, "You are right! We should not speak of death. I am infinitely grateful to you, and would be even more grateful if you extended your kindness and helped me to get home. It is there, on the next block."

"With pleasure! Even across the whole city! Across the world!"

The professor took out his handkerchief and wiped his hands. They were just starting when he felt the chill air on his bald head. He touched his head and found that his cap was gone.

Thinking that he must have dropped it when he fell, he bent down.

"What are you looking for?" asked his companion.

"I dropped my cap. I cannot see it. You have sharper eyes, my young friend, won't you take a look?"

The young man walked several steps back and forth in a strange, dancing walk and said, "No, I don't see it, either. Not even with my astral vision."

"Those scoundrels must have filched it. Oh, well, thank God for that."

His savior was curious. "Did they take much from you?"

"That's the odd thing about it—nothing. They only gave me two violent slaps on the face and ran off. I must say that the cap was my only loss."

"Peculiar robbers," Zelies said reflectively. "You don't suspect anyone?"

"No. No one."

"Perhaps it was a revenge of some sort? Or a romantic affair?"

The professor raised his hands in protest. "My young friend, how can you! A romantic affair at my age!"

The young man was embarrassed.

"The point is," the professor began, walking arm in arm with his companion, "that I have lately had a series of most fantastic adventures, altogether out of keeping with either my age or my social position."

"Namely?"

The professor cleared his throat and began his tale. They reached the gateway of the professor's house, and Alexander Yevlampievich, leaning his elbow on a projection of the wall, described in detail all the astonishing events that had intruded into his life.

The young man stood before him, flashing his moon-green eyes, hopping from foot to foot, and looking like a magical bird about to take flight. "Have you sought the help of the authorities?" he asked when the professor had finished his story.

"Oh, well, you know, I tried the criminal investigation office, but nothing came of it."

"Oh, no, Professor! What happened to you points to the fateful intervention of unknown powers into your destiny. I can see it is an utterly mysterious and dread affair. I would advise you to appeal immediately to the chief prosecutor."

"I hesitate to trouble him about such trifles. He may think I have gone mad."

"On second thought, the chief prosecutor may not help you, either. I sense the hand of secret forces. There is something political in it." The moon-glinting eyes of the young man flamed still more brightly; he was obviously engrossed in his conjectures.

"You think so?" asked the professor, shaken by this hypothesis.

"I am certain! One day a watch is dropped into your pocket; the next, they may slip in some infernal machine. Today they stole your cap, tomorrow they may slice off what propped the cap." Von Zelies glanced around and lowered his voice to a whisper: "Tell me, Professor, are you a materialist or an idealist?"

"I? As a representative of exact science, I . . . of course, I subscribe to a materialist world view."

His nocturnal companion jumped up and seized the professor by the shoulder. "There! I thought so. Perhaps they are avenging themselves upon you for that. You know, there is a sect of avengers for the disparagement of the supreme powers of nature, for disrespect to the master of the universe."

The professor shivered and nervously pulled the janitor's bell. "Thank you again, my dear friend," he said in parting. "I have never suspected that it might be so serious. I shall certainly do as you suggest. Good-bye. Drop in, if you don't think it boring to visit an old man!"

"Thank you, Professor. I am delighted to know you. I wish you a good night and good health," answered his companion and merrily clicked away with his heels, continuing his journey.

As the professor was entering the gateway, he turned for a last look at his deliverer and almost fainted with terror. He distinctly heard the clicking heels quite near him, but nowhere in the street was there the slightest sign of a human figure.

CHAPTER 9

Beginning with this chapter, the author proposes to put his cards on the table. In it, he will finally rid himself of the infernal cap or, to be more exact, provide a man who will bring the affair to its conclusion.

At any rate, the author intends honestly to fulfill the obligations assumed by him, for he is a man of conscience, and he understands that it is improper to draw a royalty for simply twiddling his thumbs.

The professor slept that night, neither well nor badly. He did not mention his nocturnal adventure to his wife, not wishing to worry his faithful comrade. After breakfasting on tea with milk and a buttered roll, he proceeded to the office of the chief prosecutor.

The prosecutor was still a fairly young man, with a neatly trimmed little British moustache over his upper lip. He wore a gray, excellently tailored suit and had equally gray, sharp eyes. He made the professor sit down in a low, comfortable armchair and moved over the cigarette case on the table. Then he asked with utmost cordiality how he could be of use to so eminent a scholar.

Modestly lowering his eyes, Alexander Yevlampievich described with his characteristic logic and exactness the startling events of the past month, including the disappearance of the notorious cap. "I do not know whom to suspect, but this clearly seems to suggest a plot against my health and life, perhaps even with some political overtones."

The prosecutor listened to the story, puffing at aromatic cigarettes. At particularly striking moments, he sharply threw up his pointed, blond little goatee and tapped his fingers on a marble paperweight. As the professor was concluding his story, he smiled faintly and glanced out of the window at the swollen, turbid Fontanka.

Then he pulled on his cigarette deeply and slowly and with obvious pleasure, and his answer came in a cloud of smoke: "The story you were kind enough to narrate, my dear professor, is so astonishing, so unheard of and fantastic in our sober time, that I am at a loss to comment on it, even tentatively. From the point of view of the existing laws, there is one circumstance which permits itself to be regarded as a basis for initiating judicial procedure." (The prosecutor had not been a prosecutor very long, and he relished forensic terminology much as a five-year-old citizen relishes her Kraft caramel.) "I am referring to the fact of the armed assault. This is what we jurists call corpus delicti. . . . But why did the robbers steal the cap? What can be so attractive in a cap to a street bandit?"

"Well, you see," the professor mumbled, "the cap was really somewhat out of the ordinary."

"And what was so extraordinary about it?"

"It was . . . of a rather unusual style, like . . . a beret, and then it had . . . a . . . turquoise visor and a similar . . . pompon on the crown." The professor squeezed out the words with difficulty, feeling that the polished floor of the prosecutor's office was opening up under his feet.

The prosecutor jerked up his goatee, puffed out a huge cloud of smoke, and it seemed to the professor that a shower of sparks flew out of the prosecutor's mouth together with the smoke. He even recoiled for a moment, until he realized that those were simply particles of dust whirling in the sunshine.

"If I understood you correctly, Professor," said the prosecutor, "it was indeed a most extraordinary cap. But, if you pardon my indiscretion, what could have prompted you, at your venerable age and with your social position, to acquire such a . . . well, such unusual headgear?"

The professor turned as red as a ripe tomato. He was ready

to drop through the floor and felt like a schoolboy caught by the teacher in the act of cheating. He answered in a scarcely audible voice: "I . . . it was . . . I mean . . . I was persuaded to . . . The owner of the store . . . he insisted that the style was very . . . becoming."

If the professor were not staring at the floor, but at the prosecutor's face, he would have noticed, even despite his extreme myopia, that the man's impassive mask shook for a moment with a spasm of sardonic laughter.

But the prosecutor managed to preserve the full dignity of his judicial rank and wiped the treacherous smile from his lips. "Well, I see nothing extraordinary about that. Each of us occasionally indulges in inexplicable tastes. I knew a man who was able to eat sausage only when—will you believe me?—when it was beginning to smell," he said civilly, hoping to reassure the professor. Then he added, "At any rate, I cannot congratulate the robber with a particularly great or profitable prize. Nevertheless, this obscure affair needs looking into, and with your permission, I shall immediately summon the chief of the criminal investigation squad."

The professor gloomily raised his hands. "I was there. It didn't do any good. They thought I was a thief and even checked their rogues' gallery albums to see if I had a record of arrests."

The prosecutor finally allowed himself to laugh. "Don't worry, Professor. I promise you there won't be any such mistake in my presence. Besides, you spoke to an ordinary detective on duty, but I am calling in a man of European caliber, a remarkable expert."

The prosecutor lifted the receiver. "Criminal investigation? Get me Pavel Mikhailovich. . . . Ah, Pavel Mikhailovich, how do you do! Can you come here at once? Yes, yes, to my office. A most curious case. Yes. I think you'll be very interested; it's right up your alley. Good! I'll expect you." He turned to the professor. "Will you pardon me if I ask you to wait a little, over there?" He pointed to a little sofa in the back of the room, behind a round table. "In the meantime, I shall see my other visitors. And to make sure you won't be bored, permit me to offer you a most fascinating thing, an album of unusual cases of photographic evidence. I can assure you there is nothing like it anywhere in the world."

The professor thanked him and settled down in the corner with the album.

The prosecutor saw his visitors, while Alexander Yevlampievich examined the album, occasionally glancing sideways at his host. The latter sat with his back to the window. The dazzling spring sun poured through the window, filling the office with a golden mist. At moments, this made the prosecutor quite transparent, and the professor clearly saw through his body the trees of the Summer Garden and the polished red porphyry of the Etruscan vase on its high pedestal.

The prosecutor's voice recalled Blagosvetlov to reality: "And now, Professor, permit me to introduce to you, Pavel Mikhailovich Presnyakov, our best detective."

The newcomer was an extremely tall man with a lean, rubber-flexible figure. He pressed the professor's hand with his long, tenacious fingers and, in one sweeping movement, folded himself and threw his light, gaunt body into the depths of a leather armchair.

"If you allow me," said the prosecutor, "I shall relay to Pavel Mikhailovich all the facts of the case, to save you the trouble of repeating the story. And you can make any corrections or additions you think necessary."

Presnyakov sat sunk in the armchair, with his hands crossed on his knee. A short, smoke-darkened pipe swung rhythmically from his teeth. His black-cherry eyes seemed apathetic and absent, but in the depth of the pupils there was a spark of close attention. From time to time, he raised his hand and knocked the ash from his pipe. "Do you have anything to add to the prosecutor's story?" he asked, thrusting his rubbery body forward.

"No . . . everything seems exact and complete."

There was no longer any apathy in Presnyakov's eyes. They glimmered with sharp purple sparks. "One question! Where did you buy the cap?"

"I am sorry, I don't remember the name of the owner of the store. But it was at the Apraxin Market, opposite the yellow house with columns. There was a huge cap with a raspberry-colored band in the window."

"Thank you. That's quite enough. Well, I'm off!" Presnyakov rose and filled his pipe with a new portion of the strongest tobacco.

"What do you suggest, Pavel Mikhailovich?" asked the prosecutor.

"Hm . . . nothing as yet."

"But when?"

"Tomorrow. . . . By the way, Professor, where can I reach you if I should need you to close the case?"

The professor gave him his telephone numbers at the laboratory and at home.

"Excellent. I believe I shall be able to inform you of a successful solution." Presnyakov said his good-byes and left.

The professor looked after him with involuntary awe. "Does he really know?"

"Oh-ho! I can tell you, he is an extraordinary man. If he has promised, you can be sure the case is well in hand or, rather, in the cap," the prosecutor allowed himself to pun.

"I am very grateful to you. Perhaps this idiotic affair will finally come to an end. Permit me to express my deepest gratitude."

"Not at all, Professor! It is my duty to protect the rights and lives of our citizens. I am delighted to see you, even if the reason for your visit was not the happiest one."

CHAPTER 10

The rusty mongrel tied to the metal frame on the dissecting table shivered, and its round, translucent, brown eye squinted in terror at the glittering lancet in the professor's hand.

The students of physiology craned their necks.

The professor brought down his hand and touched the lancet

to the bare canine belly, which shrank spasmodically from the steel. The dog whimpered.

But its hour had not yet struck on the clock of fate, and it was granted a brief but important reprieve.

Behind the backs of the students the beery voice of Pimen boomed out suddenly: "Alekhsan Lampovich, you're wanted on the teliphone."

The professor put down the lancet and went to answer.

The students looked at him with as much curiosity as they had looked at the dog a moment earlier, for the always deliberate and self-possessed professor had almost galloped to the telephone; he tripped on the way, flushed red as he picked up the receiver, and listened with a confused, helpless air.

In the silence, they heard Alexander Yevlampievich promise someone that he would come at once, gulping his words excitedly. Then he threw down the receiver, announced that the class was dismissed for the day, and slipping off his smock as he ran, rushed out of the room.

"What's wrong with him?" asked one of the students.

"He's in bad shape. The old man must be up to his ears. Did you see how nervous he was? Right away, he says, I'll be over at once. The dame must have given him hell."

But while the young neophytes of physiology were making such frivolous conjectures, the professor, his old hat pulled over his ears, was running down the staircase. At the entrance, for the first time since the beginning of the new era, he hired a cab.

At the criminal investigation department, in the office of the chief, adorned with photographs of corpses and similar innocent tokens of the profession of criminal investigation, Alexander Yevlampievich was awaited by Presnyakov.

Today he was even more rubbery than at their first meeting. As he pressed the professor's hand, he folded and unfolded himself with astonishing flexibility and speed. "Welcome to our precincts. Hm . . . you were quick. You see, Professor, don't take offense . . . hm . . . but I should like to show you . . . hm . . . some very curious things, which you . . . hm . . . probably never dreamed of. And yet, you've had so many extraordinary experiences this past month that you may not, after all, be too astonished at what's to come."

"But what is it you wish to show me?"

"Some exhibits in the Grand Guignol manner. Jack the Rippers and the like—a tragicomedy with quick changes of costume. A magical spectacle. But first I must ask you to step here for a moment."

He drew aside the hanging over the door to the next room. "I shall call you back in two minutes."

The door slammed shut behind the professor. He found himself in a small room. On the walls hung flat glass cases with photographs. Between them, in fanlike arrangements and in bundles, hung crowbars, skeleton keys, chisels, wrenches, screwdrivers, blowtorches, files, and knives. They formed themselves into patterns, glorifying human ingenuity.

In the case opposite the door was a photograph of a severed head. The professor glanced at it quickly, and suddenly the head winked at him with a colorless eye.

He backed away to the door, but fortunately Presnyakov appeared in the doorway and exclaimed, "Come in, please, Professor!"

The professor sidled into the office. He took two steps and was stricken numb—so numb that his knees felt cold, something pulled at the pit of his stomach, and the skin on his back puckered with gooseflesh.

In the corners before him—and he saw it with utmost clarity, for a pair of pince-nez straddled his nose, sitting askew, like a peasant woman on a horse—stood two silent figures. Their stark immobility made them look like wax manikins, and this immobility was unutterably terrifying. But most terrifying of all was that their heads were covered by exact, absolute duplicates of the professor's own luckless cap.

The professor jumped back in panic and, looking for protection, glanced around at Presnyakov. But how great was his astonishment when his eyes alighted on the accursed caps on the heads of two other manikins. Between them, he caught sight of Presnyakov's face, contorted in a fit of wild laughter, and this was the poor physiologist's last clear visual impression, for in his great excitement the pince-nez had dropped from their appointed place.

"You don't understand anything, Professor?"

He heard Presnyakov's question as through a curtain of delirium. Alexander Yevlampievich mumbled something altogether senseless, his weakened legs gave way, and he collapsed like a heavy sack on the chair that Presnyakov had quickly pushed over to him.

He regained consciousness feeling a trickle of water pouring into his mouth, with a strong smell of valerian.

Presnyakov's voice beat against his ears: "Forgive me, Professor! What an ass I am! I never thought this little comedy would upset you so. I must confess, I have a bit of a mania for theatrical effects. Before I took up criminal investigation, I worked for a long time in a pantomime show. Drink it down, drink it down— and calm yourself. Hey you, actors, march!"

The motionless manikins came out of their corners and moved toward the door in single file. The professor tightly shut his eyes in order not to see them.

Presnyakov shouted to someone: "Mazanov! Take them back to the cell. Bring in the hatter!"

The professor, who sat with his back to the door, could not see the man who entered, but his ears caught the conversation.

"Stand here. So you know nothing about the cap you sold to Professor Blagosvetlov?"

A breaking voice barked hoarsely, "I don't know, Comrade Citizen Chief! I am not guilty, whatever you say!"

"You don't know? And do you know this citizen?"

Presnyakov seized someone by the hand and pulled him over to the professor's chair. The professor saddled his nose again with his glasses and saw an effeminate face, like a slice of pumpkin, twisted with astonishment and fear. He recognized the owner of the hat store.

The hatter blinked in confusion and flung himself down on his knees. "Don't ruin me, Comrade Chief," he bleated like a sheep. "Don't ruin me—I swear by the mother of God, I'll confess everything. The first time in my life I've taken such shame upon myself. I will confess. . . . I stole a piece of cloth, I cut an extra cap. May I not leave this place if I ever do such a disgraceful thing again. The devil take it, that filthy rag! Ruined my business for a yard of cloth!"

"That's better," said Presnyakov, rubbing his hands. "So you're through playing the fool? Off with you! I'll be talking to you later."

The policeman pulled away the howling, protesting hatter.

The professor sat as though pinned to his chair.

Presnyakov filled his pipe, lit it, folded himself in half, and threw himself into an armchair with his customary rubbery movement. "You don't understand anything, Professor? Really? But it is so simple."

"Ah, stop tormenting me. . . . I cannot stand it any longer!" moaned Alexander Yevlampievich.

"Instantly!" Presnyakov bounced up and fixed the professor with eyes that flashed like pistol shots. "In a moment . . . You see, you were mistaken for a fence . . . a receiver of stolen goods. Hm . . . exactly. For a fence. Those four in the caps, whom you have just seen, they are also . . . hm . . . fences. . . . By accident, you purchased a cap which is the identifying mark of the receivers for a large gang of thieves. And so . . . hm . . . they began to slip you stolen articles. Then one fine day you were seen by a leading member of the gang who knew all the fences. Naturally . . . hm . . . he was surprised . . . and followed you home. This led to the nocturnal attack, for the purpose of recovering the uniform which you had no legitimate right to wear. It was fortunate that he realized the misunderstanding, or you might have paid with your head. That is all. The rest is our own professional secret."

"I . . . I can't take any more. . . . Permit me to go home," the professor gasped, hiccuping.

"Of course. By all means! Hm . . . but allow me to present

you with a memento—the cause of all your misadventures." And
Presnyakov held out the cap, which smiled at the professor tenderly with its turquoise pompon.

But the professor waved it off and recoiled as from an ampule
filled with plague bacilli. "No! No! To the devil with it! I won't
touch this rag."

"As you wish. . . . Mazanov! . . . See the citizen professor to
the door."

On the Avenue of October 25, the professor stepped into the
Leningrad Clothes store and, with an air of great dignity, purchased an expensive felt hat.

He left the store with his head high. The April sun, breaking through a round cloud, poured its silver brightness on the
professor, the sidewalk, the avenue, and the whole city, and everything became clear, definite, and natural.

The professor felt a strong pang of hunger. He consulted his
chronometer, which confirmed the advent of the lunch hour, and
turned his steps homeward.

1925

Yevgeny Zamyatin
(1884 - 1937)

Born in Tambov Province, a naval engineer by training, Zamyatin
was one of the most remarkable Russian writers of the twentieth
century. He was the guiding spirit of the Serapion Brotherhood,
a group formed by several of the most talented, original, and
independent younger writers in the early 1920's. The group, which
included such writers as Zoshchenko, Vsevolod Ivanov, and
Konstantin Fedin, was opposed to the increasing regimentation
of literature and felt, with Zamyatin, that "real literature can
exist only when it is produced by madmen, hermits, heretics,
dreamers, rebels, and skeptics."

Zamyatin's style is brilliant and varied. Some of his stories
(especially those dealing with an almost mythical Old Russia)
read like ballads. The landscape is stark, the people larger than
life, the events tragic or comic on a grand scale. Other stories
deal with contemporary life, seen in a grotesque, surrealistic light.
Still others are tongue-in-cheek jokes, ribald inventions he calls
"impious tales." A writer of subtle wit, great verbal skill, and
most meticulous craftsmanship, he was also the author of a
number of interesting plays and the prophetic novel We (never
published in the Soviet Union), which anticipated Orwell's 1984
and Huxley's Brave New World.

Zamyatin was never in favor with the Communist authorities.
He was viciously and relentlessly criticized for "inconsonance
with the Revolution." Trotsky branded him "an internal émigré."
In 1931 he was, surprisingly, permitted to leave Russia; he settled
in France, where he lived until his death in 1937.

Comrade Churygin Has the Floor

by Yevgeny Zamyatin

My most esteemed citizens—and also lady citizens, who are giggling there, way in the back, in disrespect to the moment that is an evening of recollections about the revolution—I ask you, citizens: do you desire to join my recollections to yourselves as well? In that case, I will beg you to sit without any giggles and refrain from interfering with the preceding orator.

First of all, maybe I ought to apologize that my recollections, as against all the rest, are an honest-to-goodness bitter fact. Because everything that was said here was as smooth as writing, but my story isn't writing, but just as it naturally happened in our village of Kuyman, in the Izbishchensk district, which is my beloved homeland.

Our whole nature out there is situated in a solid forest; there is nothing like a more-or-less provincial town in the distance, and the life that goes on in those parts is dark and ignorant—like, you might say, among the zebras or some such tribe. Myself, of course, included—without social consciousness up to the age of sixteen, and even believing in religion. But now, of course, all that is quit and finished, and amen. My brother Stepka—may his soul rest in paradise!—was about twenty-five, and long-grown in height besides, though somewhat literate. Aside from Stepka, we had another hero—the cooper's son Yegor, who'd also shed his life's blood at the front.

But as all of this existed at the moment of capitalism, there was also the enemy class three verst away, in the person of the former spider—I mean, the landowner Tarantayev—who naturally sucked our blood and brought back from foreign lands all sorts of things, like, for example, naked statues. And these statues were set out in his garden, just like that, especially one with a spear, some sort of a god—not our own Christian Orthodox one, but a god all the same. And there were parties in the garden, with songs and lanterns, and our peasant women used to stand and gape behind the fence, and Stepka, too.

Stepka, he wasn't nuts or anything, but queer somehow, and he had something damaged inside, so they never even took him in the army, and he remained like an unemployed member of our household life. Everybody envied him, front and back, and he sat sighing and reading books. And what kind of books, I ask you, did we have at that Tsarist moment? Not books, but, if one may say so, dregs of society or, to make it short, fertilizer. And the whole public library, if you allow me, was in the form of the lay nun Agafya, forty-three years old, who read the Psalter over the dead.

Well, naturally, Stepka filled himself up on those books and started playing the fool. At night, sometimes, I'd wake and look down from the bunk, and there he was, all white, before the icon, hissing through his teeth, "Do-o-st hear-r me? Do-s-s-st hear?" Once, just for fun, I say to him, "I hear, I hear." And he gives a start and jumps this high! But then I couldn't hold it any more, with laughter bursting out of my nose. He gave me such a shaking, my lungs and my liver didn't know which was which—took me a good long while to catch my breath.

Then in the morning, Stepka bowed low to our father's feet. "Let me go into a monastery," he begged. "I can't live daily like the rest of you, for there's an unknown dream stuck in my breast." And daddy said to him, "Stepka," he said, "you're a practical fool and nothing else. Tomorrow you're going to the city, to work with Uncle Artamon." Stepka began to argue, saying all sorts of words out of the Holy Writ. But our daddy, he wasn't no man's fool, and with a streak of cunning besides. So he said to Stepka, "And what does it say in your Writ? That every son of a bitch must listen to his mother and his father. Them are the true holy words." And so he wiped Stepka's organ of the nose with the Holy Writ himself, and Stepka gave in and went off at dawn to Uncle Artamon, who was working as a retired watchman in a factory.

And here, as they say, is a bird's-eye picture of life for you: here, for example, is a factory turning full steam, and somewhere on the African border there are impossible cliffs of mountains and a frightful battle going on, but we in our woods see nothing; the women bawl like calves without their men, and on top of it all there's a bitter frost.

In the course of time, the cooper's daughter-in-law received a letter from her husband Yegor at the front that he was made a hero, first class, with the Cross of St. George, and she was to expect him home any day now. Naturally, the woman rejoiced and put on clean stockings. One afternoon, it was St. Nicholas' Eve, my daddy and I came out to look, and there was Yegorka, the cooper's son, in a sleigh, waving his hand and saying words we couldn't catch, steam pouring out in clouds from his mouth in consequence of the cold frost.

I was, naturally, all excited to see the hero, but my daddy says to me, "We'll wait awhile, give him a chance to make a junction with his woman first." And just as he said it, Yegor's woman bursts into our house herself. Her eyes white, terrible, her hands shaking, and she cries in a black voice, "Help me, in God's name, help me to manage with Yegor!" Well, we think, he must have trounced her—we must stick up for a female creature. So we washed our hands and went with her.

We come in and take a look: the samovar is boiling, the bed is made up on the bunk, everything right and proper, and Yegor himself is standing quietly by the trunk. Except he isn't standing: he's propped against the trunk like he was a sack of oats, and his head is level with the trunk. As for his legs, there's not a stump left—cut off clean under the belly.

We were stunned and just stood there without any consequences. After a while, Yegor began to laugh in a queer, ugly way—it set my teeth on edge to hear him—and he says to us, "Well? A fine hero, first class? Got your eyeful? Now lift me up on top of the woman, with your help." And so his woman lay down on the bed, and we lifted up Yegor from the floor and laid him down in the proper way. After which we went out, and

I banged the door and caught this here finger in it, but didn't even feel no pain to speak of: I walk and keep on seeing in my eyes the imagination of Yegor against the trunk.

In the evening, of course, the village gathered in Yegor's house, every man and woman of us. Yegor was on the bench under the icons, either standing against the wall or sitting, whichever way you'd put it. And everybody who came in shook his head at the fright of it and kept silent, and he kept silent and smoked. And I stood there by the stove and could hear the roaches crawl out and rustle on the wall.

Luckily now, the cooper came, the father, and took out a bottle of vodka from his pocket. Yegor, naturally, drank down a glass and just began to pour another when somebody's kid bounced in from the street, yelling happily, "The *barin*! The *barin*!" We look, and it's a fact: the *barin* Tarantayev comes in the door. All shaven, with a fine, luxurious smell around him—you could tell he was accustomed to light food. He just nodded to us and turned straight to Yegor. "Well," he says, "congratulations to you, Yegor, congratulations." And Yegor grinned with his face on one side, unpleasant-like, and said, "And may I take the liberty, just what do you congratulate me for?" The *barin* says to him in reply, "In view as you're our pride and a hero who has suffered for the homeland." And he lifts up the sacking around Yegor's lower parts and bends down with his nose to look.

At that moment, Yegor's face got all twisted, he scrunched his teeth, and whacked him on the neck, once and again. The *barin* got so flustered with excitement, he poked Yegor, who keeled over on his side like a sack and couldn't get up, but just yelled, "Get him! Get him!" I jumped up to the *barin* with the rest, my heart shaking like a rabbit's tail, and there was nothing in the world I needed except to grab him by the throat. In short—the class war. *Barin* Tarantayev, red-faced, opened his mouth to speak, but tripped against our hateful eyes as if he'd stepped into a bed of nettles—and dashed double-quick for the door.

Under the impact of this victory, the peasants quieted down and told Yegor he was sure a hero, first class. Yegor naturally tossed off another glass and gradually made a speech that how was he a hero when he'd squatted down at the front into a hole to do his rude necessity, when it came down from above, smack on his feet? "But we shall soon," he says, "make an end to all this deception of the people's vision in the form of war. Because," he says, "we know without contradiction that now we've got one of our own, a muzhik, at the Tsar's court, Grigory Yefimych by name.* He's over all the ministers, and he'll show them where the hell they get off." When our peasants heard this, well, they were all moved with feeling and yelled with rejoicing that now, of course, both the war and the gentry were done for, finished, and we all relied our hopes on Grigory Yefimych, being he was in power and our own muzhik. And I'll tell you, fellow citizens, that now, of course, I understand everything quite expediently about this Grigory Yefimych, but at that time the news just sent my blood into a pulse.

And now, the rest of it. Namely, after Yegor insulted the *barin* on the neck, there was a strained rupture between us and that spider. He'd even posted a purebred Circassian at his gate, with a dagger for the prevention of entry. Before that, we used to go to the estate for newspapers and such, but now we lived in total woods, like zebras, and knew nothing at all about the course of events on the distant globe of the earth, like, for example, in Petersburg.

By and by, the former Christmas came around, then Shrovetide, frost, and thaw. And on Shrovetide my daddy receives a sudden letter from Stepka in the city. As we had no liquidation of literacy to speak of at that time, and the only reading man, as you might say, was Yegor, a peck of folks piled up at his house to hear Stepka's letter. And Stepka wrote that it was now inconvertibly known at his factory that all the business about God was nothing but a superstitious fact; as against it, there was a book called Marx. Also, he said, a certain important killing had taken place in the capital city of Petersburg, and, therefore, he said,

---

* The reference is to Rasputin.

wait and see what big things happen next in the near future. As for the wages at the factory, they were as miserable as could be, only nine and a half a month, and he was soon arriving in his own person.

Yegor stood on the bench, propped up against the windowsill, and he added with his hands, "You see," he yelled, "what did I tell you about Grigory Yefimych? It's all his work, don't have no doubt about that!"

Although the letter was unclear about the killing and kind of incomplete about God in the matter of prejudice, we had a feeling in our bones that all these things weren't to no purpose, and so we actually waited. We had no idea what we were waiting for, but, if you know what I mean, it was like a brute dog—pardon the expression—worrying before a fire. That's how we were. And besides, there was a terrible frost, everything quiet, and a woodpecker tap-tapping in the woods. And all of us, just like the woodpecker, harping on one thing—Grigory Yefimych.

In due time, a day or two went by; then it was dusk, and we see a mounted messenger on a black horse galloping straight for the Tarantayev estate and, over behind the estate, the setting sun, all swollen from the cold, and red. Yegor is, naturally, our general in chief, and he says, "It's starting. Keep an eye on the estate without cease and bring me back reports."

Just to be sure, we posted up two sentries: myself and another fellow, the hunchbacked Mitka. So we sit in the bushes, blowing on our fingers to keep them warm, and we can hear every nervous noise in the manor yard, and the dogs barking, and we're shaking. After a while, we look: without an evil word, the gates fling open and a crazy sled pops out, with the lady Tarantayev and her girl, both of them bawling, and after them the mounted fellow on his black horse, yelling at the lady like she was a dog, "Alé!" And then the sled goes one way, and the horseman the other—straight at us. The hunchbacked Mitka tried to pull me into the bushes, but my blood boiled up all of a sudden, as if I'd filled myself with alcoholic fumes and didn't know what I was doing. I waved my arms and ran straight at the horseman. Naturally, he stopped and says, "What's happened?" and his horse snorts in my face. And I say right out, "Nothing here, but what is happening out there, with you people?" "That," he says, "ain't nothing to do with you. *Alé!*" But I stare him in the eye and say with expression, "And how," I say, "about Grigory Yefimych? Does that have anything to do with you?" And he answers with a certain little laugh, "Your Grigory Yefimych is done for. Thank God, he was bumped off a long time ago!" And he gallops off in the direction.

So I rushed full speed to Yegor. His house is chockfull of peasants, everybody in tense expectation. As I started to report, my innocent heart of a sixteen-year-old got into my throat, and I cry bitterly for the lost happy dream in the form of Grigory Yefimych, and I see that everybody else sits with a sigh, stunned-like. And in conclusion of this sad intermission, Yegor announces his orders: everybody is to disperse home till morning for various natural necessities, like food and soporific rest.

Then gradually comes this significant morning when you in Petersburg see the triumph and the jubilee of the revolution, with flags and all, but in our parts there wasn't nothing like it at all. Still, as a man might say, the things that happened were, of course, the distant thunder in full connection, and on top of everything there was this frightful frost. So we gathered in front of Yegor's house in felt boots, and we lifted up Yegor into a basket filled with hay, like, in a manner of speaking, on a platform, and put him into a sled. After which Yegor announced from the basket that the hours were struck and we couldn't take it any longer, so we'd storm the Tarantayev manor in force. Let the *barin* give us a full accounting of how they'd killed our defender Grigory Yefimych, and, maybe, God willing, he was still alive. Naturally, we all unanimously marched along the snow, and the snow was so blue in the sun, it made your eyes water, and inside of us everything boiled wild as in a dog that sat ten years tied to a chain and suddenly broke loose and went off on a rampage.

The moment Tarantayev's purebred Circassian saw us in full numbers, he shut the gate and raised a row and all sorts of excitements inside, including the voice of the *barin* Tarantayev telling us that unusual events were going on in the capital and so we'd best go home without grievous consequences and wait for speedy developments. And Yegor shouted to him from his basket that we'd waited enough, we'd eaten two barrelfuls of waiting, and now we were obliged to find out the facts, and let him open up the gates at once, because we'd break them down anyway.

Then we heard a silence and a whispering, after which the gates creaked, and we saw the pleasant view with the pines along the road and, in the sight of all, the statue with a spear, which still had a useful role before it in coming events. Naturally, we marched inside in solid ranks. Namely, Yegor in front in his basket, and the rest of us behind, bunched up any which way. And the *barin* leading with his hind back to us, sprinting at top speed to the goal of his house. Suddenly, there's a revolver from out of nowhere in Yegor's hand, and he yells, aiming at the *barin*, "Halt!" As soon as this offal of society saw the revolver, he stopped without another word next to the god with the spear, himself stiff like an alleged statue. Then he says to us, "You're simply making a mistake. I am myself a man out of the people's freedom." And Yegor says to him sternly, "So you're at one with Grigory Yefi-mych? Speak up!" To which the *barin* answers in trembling words, "Why, no," he says, "how can you say that? We're all very happy that this scoundrel Grishka was killed off." At this, Yegor saw red and yelled to every side, "You hear him, fellows? The 'scoundrel,' he says! 'Very happy,' he says! You so and so!" and so on, with all sorts of swearing remarks. "And now," he says, "we'll pop you off your own self with this revolver."

Naturally, being he was a specialist, Yegor was a trained hand at every military killing and didn't give a spitting damn. But we still had a certain shade of feeling inside—it was kind of against the grain to do in a fully living man. And while we were, so to speak, exchanging opinions, the *barin* Tarantayev, he stands there without a sign, like a total corpse. Only once, I remember, he wiped the dripping of his nose.

And here a new fact appeared on the road outside the gate, in the form of a man running toward us full speed and waving his hands. Gradually, as we look, it turns out to be Stepka from the city, in accordance with his foregoing letter. His face shines, a tear is creeping down from his eye, and he waves his arms like they were wings, like he would any moment fly up on the will of the air, like a certain bird. And he keeps yelling, "Brothers, brothers, we've had an overthrow and a revolution, and my heart is just about to crack from impossible freedom, and hurrah!"

We couldn't tell what it was all about, only we felt that Stepka was exploding, as they say, from an overflow of soul, and even his yelling sent goose pimples up and down our backs, so there was general hurrah and an elemental excitement, like at the superstition of Easter. And Stepka gradually clambered up a bench next to the statue, wiping his tears with his mitten and saying, in addition, that the Tsar in the form of Nicholas was retired and that all the rotten palaces should be wiped off to the foundation from the face of the earth, and let there be no more rich men, but let us all live like a poor proletariat according to the former Holy Writ, but nowadays, however, all this was coming to pass according to the science of our dear Marx.

Then every man of us confirms this in the form of "Hurrah!" and Yegor yells from his basket, at the top of his voice, "We thank you, our hero Stepka, from our Orthodox Christian hearts! With God's blessing—smash their whole luxurious budget!"

And Stepka grabbed an ax from one of our peasants, jumped up to the statue, the one with the spear, and swung at it from the fullness of his soul to smash it. But at this moment, the *barin* Tarantayev seemed to wake up from out of his corpse and cried, "This is a precious statue, innocent of any guilt, and maybe that I brought it overland all the way from Rome itself, as it's a countless, costly image, by the name of Mars."

And we see Stepka's hand drop without consequences, and he says with expression, "Brothers! Just as I pronounced to you this dear name, suddenly we find his true image right before us in the form of a statue. I take this as an omen from on high and propose that we all bare our hats."

I ask you, fellow citizens, to take into account that we were then an altogether dark and ignorant people—as you might say, plain Hindus. In consequence of which, we all unanimously pulled off our hats, and so, without our hats, we grabbed this dear image under the backside and hoisted it into the sled next to the basket in which Yegor existed. And Stepka adopted a resolution: to let the *barin* Tarantayev go harmless for the good service that he revealed to us this image; but as a lesson against riches, let him watch how we exterminate his budget. Every man of us confirms this again in the form of "Hurrah!"—with pleasure that a program is shaping up without the spilling of a live man. But all the same, sad fate came out contrary to our expectations.

Namely, we advance on the house, with our vanguard in the form of the sled with the statue and Yegor in the basket, and walking alongside of it, our Stepka and the *barin*, with his arms tied up. And the windows glitter at us like suspicious eyes, and I particularly remember one, the attic window under the very roof, with a pleasant-looking pigeon sitting up there. And Stepka turns back his beautiful smile of happiness and yells from out of his soul, "Brothers, it's more than I can stand! What an extraordinary first and last day of the new life we're having this day!"

And just as he says it, we see the pigeon flutter up, and from the attic window comes an insignificant puff of smoke. And then, maybe in just another tenth moment of a second, there is a terrible crash in the form of a shot, and our Stepka with the foregoing smile drops nose down into a snowdrift.

We stand there like stunned posts and have no time to get our wits back, when another shot knocks off the statue's fingers, and then Yegor, with a frightful shout of profanity, sends two bullets from his revolver into the attic window and one back into the *barin* Tarantayev, who lies down next to Stepka in his dead form. And Yegor, in a hateful state of feeling, fires three more shots at him, with the addition of words: "And this is for Stepka! And this for Grigory Yefimych! And this for everything!"

And then, of course, there was general hollering and the final merciless degree of events—or, to make it short, total extermination. And you could see all over that innocent snow pieces of

broken glass and other utensils, like a sofa that gave up the ghost
with its feet up in the air, and the broken corpse of Tarantayev's
purebred Circassian, as it was naturally he that fired from the
attic, and he was pierced by a bullet from Yegor's military hand.
And also I remember, up on a twig, a gilded cage, and an unknown
aristocratic bird jumping up and down in it and squealing with
its last voice.

In the course of time and according to nature comes the night
and the well-known system of stars, looking as though nothing
had happened, and only a premature red dawn rises from the
darkness—or, in short, the last flames of the former manor house.
And with all that, there is total silence in the village, and all the
dogs howling; and in the community house, Stepka lies under
the icons in the form of a victim with a smile, and next to him the
statue, and the nun Agafya, forty-three years old, reading the
Psalter, and the village folks with various tears.

And that's the end of our diversified dark events as in a dream,
and after it comes the dawn of an entirely class-conscious day.
Namely, a visit from an actual orator. And then we learned in the
right and proper manner about the whole current moment, and
that Grigory Yefimych, or, in short, Grishka, was no hero, but
even on the contrary, and that this statue of ours occurred by
reason of a mistake of sound.

And in conclusion, I see that the lady citizens which first sat
with a look of laughter, they now have the opposite look, and I
support it entirely, seeing as all this is the bitter fact of our dark
culture, which, thank the Lord, today exists on the background
of the past. And here I will put a dot in the form of a sign and
retire, my dear fellow citizens, into your unknown ranks.

1927

Mikhail Zoshchenko
(1895 - 1958)

Zoshchenko was the most popular Soviet satirist and humorist. Born in the Ukraine, in a landowning family, he grew up in St. Petersburg, where he attended, but did not graduate from, the Law School of the University of St. Petersburg. He served as an officer in the Russian Army during World War I, was wounded and gassed, but volunteered again in 1918 for service with the Red Army. The author of innumerable satirical short stories and longer tales, he was a master stylist, capturing the inimitable and virtually untranslatable jargon that sprang up after the Revolution, when the lower and almost illiterate classes appropriated the language of the upper classes and put it to their own fantastic uses. His stories reflect the million absurdities of a society in a state of violent and abrupt collapse and transition.

By the 1930's, as satire became less and less tolerable to the country's rulers, Zoshchenko's position in Soviet literature became increasingly difficult. Subjected to persistent hostility and pressure, attacked for "inconsonance" with the times and "adulation of the West," and chronically ill as a result of his war injuries, he finally began to lose his earlier sparkle and pungency. During World War II, he wrote a number of "serious" and extremely feeble stories about Russian heroism and suffering at the hands of the Germans. His autobiography, Before Sunrise (1943), was violently attacked as antisocial and even amoral in its pessimism. In 1946, after a campaign of merciless persecution, Zoshchenko was expelled from the Soviet Writers' Union and hence, under Soviet conditions, from literature. A partial "rehabilitation" in the 1950's permitted him to publish some short pieces, but he never recovered from his long ordeal. His last works were pallid efforts by a broken man.

The Housing Crisis

by Mikhail Zoshchenko

The other day, my dear fellow citizens, a cartload of bricks went down the street. So help me, it did!

Will you believe me, my heart went hammering with joy. It means we're building. They wouldn't be carting bricks for nothing. A house is going up somewhere. And so it has begun—touch wood!

I'll bet, in twenty years, or even less, every citizen will have a whole room to himself. Or even two, if the population doesn't grow too fast, or, say, if they let everybody have abortions. Maybe even three per head. With a bath, too.

What a life it's going to be! One room for sleeping, another for receiving guests, a third for something else—who knows, who can figure it out now? There will be plenty of things to do in such a free and happy life.

In the meantime, though, it's a bit tight in the matter of square footage. The crisis makes things kind of hard.

I can tell you all about it, my friends; I've lived in Moscow myself. In fact, I've just come back from there. I've felt this crisis on my own hide.

I come to Moscow, you see, and there's no place to go. I walk around the streets with all my things. Nothing doing anywhere. Not only no place to stop, no place even to leave my few bags and bundles.

For two weeks, I'll have you know, I walked the streets with my things. I grew a beard and lost most of my belongings. And still I kept tramping from street to street, a light passenger, empty-handed, looking for a place to live.

Then I see a man coming down the staircase in some house. "For thirty rubles," he says, "I can fix you up in the bathroom.

The apartment is first-class, a princely apartment. . . . Three toilets . . . a bathtub. . . . You can make yourself at home in the bathroom. Running water right at hand. Fill up the bathtub and dive to your heart's content the livelong day."

So I tell him, "I'm not a fish, comrade," I say. "I have no call to dive all day. I want to live on land. Won't you reduce the rent a bit on account of the wetness?"

And he says, "I can't, comrade. I'd be glad to oblige, but I can't. It's not entirely up to me. It's a communal apartment, you see. And the rent for the bathroom is fixed."

"Well," I say, "what am I to do? All right. Take my thirty and let me in, but quick. For three weeks I've been tramping the pavements. I'm afraid I may get tired," I say.

All right. They let me move in, and I settled down.

And the bathroom, I must tell you, was really in grand style. Wherever you turned—hot-water tanks, faucets, a marble bathtub. And, incidentally, nowhere to sit down. The only place was the edge of the tub, and then you'd slip inside, right into all that marble.

So I spent another thirty for a wooden lid and lived along in comfort.

A month later, incidentally, I got married. She was a young, good-natured little thing. Without a room.

I'd thought at first that she would turn me down when she saw the bathroom and that I wouldn't live to see my future happiness and domestic bliss, but she didn't object. She only frowned a little and said, "Well," she said, "there are good people living in bathrooms, too. If worse comes to worse, we might put up a partition. Make a boudoir here, say, and a dining room there . . ."

"A partition would be fine, citizen," I said to her. "But the other tenants won't allow it, the devils. They keep saying—no alterations!"

All right. So we lived in the room as it was.

Before a year was out, a baby was born. We named him Volodka, and we went on living as before. Bathing him right there in the bathtub. Living.

And, do you know, it worked out fine. The baby got a daily bath and never caught a cold.

There was only one inconvenience. In the evening, the communal tenants would barge into the bathroom to wash up.

And while they were taking their baths, my family, the lot of us, had to move out into the corridor.

I begged and I pleaded. "Citizens," I'd say, "can't you take your baths on Saturdays? Where is it heard of, bathing every day? Give us a chance, have a heart, consider our situation."

And there were thirty-two of them, the bastards. Each one of them swearing. And even offering to punch me on the jaw, just in case.

What could a man do? We managed somehow.

Then one fine day, my wife's mother arrives from the provinces and settles in our bathroom, behind the hot-water tank. "I've been waiting a long time," she says, "to rock my grandchild's cradle. You can't deny me this diversion," she says.

So I tell her, "I'll be the last one to deny you. Go to it, my dear old lady, rock to your heart's content. The devil take you. You can fill up the bathtub," I say, "and dive all you want with your grandson."

Then I say to my wife, "If you expect any more relatives to drop in on you, fellow citizen, please tell me now. Don't keep me in suspense."

And she says, "I don't know. . . . Unless my kid brother comes up for his Christmas vacation . . ."

I did not wait for the kid brother and departed from Moscow. I am sending money for my family's support by mail.

1925

Poverty

by Mikhail Zoshchenko

What would you say, my friends, is the most fashionable word nowadays?

The most fashionable word today is, of course, "electrification."

I wouldn't argue—it's a great thing, lighting up Soviet Russia. But in the meantime, it has its bad sides, too. Not that it costs a lot. It doesn't. It costs no more than money. That isn't what I'm talking about.

Here's what I mean.

I was living, my good people, in a huge house, and the whole house was lighted by kerosene. Some of the tenants had smoky wick lanterns, some had table lamps, others had nothing but tallow candles. It was a sorry state of affairs.

And then they began to install electric light.

The first to install it was the deputy. All right, so he did. He was a quiet man, he made no fuss about it. All the same, he got a queer look about him and kept blowing his nose with a thoughtful expression.

Still, he kept quiet, he didn't let on.

Then my dear landlady, Elizaveta Ignatievna Prokhorova, comes in one day and says, would I like to have light in my room. "Everybody's doing it," she says. "The manager himself has electricity now."

Well, I didn't say no. . . .

We installed the light, turned it on—good heavens! What a mess! What filth and corruption all around!

In the old days, I used to go to work in the morning, come back in the evening, drink down my tea, and go to bed. And the kerosene lamp never showed up any of it. But now that we had electric light—somebody's old shoe in the corner, torn wallpaper sticking out in shreds and tatters, a bedbug scuttling off at a trot, beating it from the light, some rags here, spit there, a cigarette butt, a flea doing a merry dance! . . .

Heaven have mercy! A man could howl at such a sight.

There was a sofa in my room. I'd always thought it wasn't a bad sofa—a pretty decent one, in fact. I'd often sat on it to relax a bit in the evening. But now? I switched on the electricity— heaven and earth! My, oh, my, what a sofa! Everything poking out, everything hanging, all the entrails coming out. How could I sit down on such a sofa? My soul rose up in protest.

No, I think to myself, I'm not living in luxury. You take one look and you want to run. It's enough to sicken you. Everything drops from your hands.

Then I look at my landlady, Elizaveta Ignatievna, going around with her nose down, rustling with something in her kitchen, tidying up.

"What are you puttering with, my dear lady?" I ask her.

But she only shakes her head. "I had no idea," she says, "that I was living so shabby-like."

I looked at her few sticks of furniture. Yes, indeed, I think, it's not so fancy. Filth and corruption, rags and rubbish of every kind. And all of it bathed in bright light, staring you in the eye.

I began to come home, as one might say, with a heavy heart.

I'd come in, switch on the light, admire the bulb, and bury my nose in the pillow.

For a while, I turned things over in my mind. When I got my pay, I bought some whiting, mixed it with water, and went to work. I stripped off all the wallpaper, slaughtered the bedbugs, swept out the cobwebs, repaired the sofa, painted the room, made everything shipshape. A pleasure! The soul sings and rejoices.

Well, it was fine, but it didn't last. I threw away all that money for nothing. The landlady cut the wire.

"It seems a bit on the shabby side, somehow, with the light," she says. "What's the good of lighting up such misery—so the bedbugs can have a good laugh?"

I begged and I argued—it got me nowhere.

"You can move," she says. "I don't wish to live with electric light. I've got no money for fancying up apartments."

But that's easy to say, comrades. How could I move after throwing away all that money for decorating? I had to give in.

Yes, my friends, light is a good thing, but sometimes it's not so good, either.

1925

The Wedding

by Mikhail Zoshchenko

Of course, Volodka Zavitushkin was a bit hasty. What's true is true.

Volodka, it might be said, had never really taken a good look at his bride. Honestly speaking, he'd never even seen her without a hat and coat. Seeing as all the principal events unfolded in the street.

As for the time Volodka Zavitushkin came with his fiancée to introduce himself to her mama just before the wedding, he introduced himself without taking off his own coat. In the hallway. On the run, so to speak.

Volodya Zavitushkin first met his bride in the streetcar. About five days before the marriage. He sits in the streetcar and suddenly he sees a young lady before him. Such a cute little young lady, nice and neat. In a winter coat.

And so this same young lady in the winter coat stands before Volodka, holding on to the strap, so as the fellow passengers won't tip her over. And with the other hand she clutches a package to her chest. And, naturally, there's a crush in the streetcar. People are pushing. It's simply hard to stand.

So Volodka took pity on her. "Sit down," he says, "on one of my knees. It'll be easier riding that way."

"Oh, no," she says, *"merci."*

"All right," he says, "in that case let me have your package. Just put it down on my lap, don't be shy. It'll still be a bit easier to stand."

No, he sees, she won't part with the package, either. Or maybe she's afraid he'll swipe it. Or something.

Volodka took another look at her and simply lost his wits. Lord, he thinks, what sweet young ladies ride in streetcars.

And so they ride along this way. Two stops. Three. Four. Finally, Zavitushkin sees that the young lady is pushing her way to the door. Volodka also gets up. And it was there, at the door, that they got acquainted.

They got acquainted and went on together. And then things happened in such a rush, and with no expense, that two days later Volodka Zavitushkin proposed to her.

Whether she agreed at once or no, on the third day after that they went to the civil records department and registered their marriage. They registered, and it was after this that the principal events unfolded themselves.

After registering, the bride and groom went to her mama's place. And the house, of course, was in total commotion. The table being set. The rooms full of guests. In short, a family celebration—and everybody waiting for the newlyweds.

All sorts of young ladies and gents running around, setting dishes, opening corks.

As for his young bride, Volodka Zavitushkin lost her in the hallway.

To make things worse, all sorts of mamas and relations crowd in on him with congratulations and pull him inside, into the room. They bring him in, and they talk to him and shake his hand and ask questions. They want to know what trade union he belongs to.

Volodka sees—there's no way he can recognize his bride. The room is full of young ladies. All of them dashing around, running

here and there. For the life of him, he cannot tell her from the
rest. Good Lord, Volodka thinks, I've never been in such a pickle
in all my life. Which one of them, after all, is my legal spouse?

So he wanders off around the room among those young ladies.
Edging up now to one, now to another. But they seem kind of
unwilling and show no special pleasure.

Volodka began to sweat a little. I'm in a fix, he thinks. I cannot
find my own wife.

The relatives began to look at him in a queer way: what kind
of a young man is this, running around like a maniac, throwing
himself at all the girls?

So Volodka took up a position by the door and stands there in
total decline. At least, he thinks, if they would sit down to the
table right away. Maybe that would straighten out the situation.
The one that's going to sit down next to me, she'll be the one.
Wouldn't be bad, he thinks, if it's that little blond. Or who
knows, they may stick me with some ape, then go and live with
her.

In the meantime, the guests start sitting down at the table.

The young bride's mama pleads with them to wait a little
longer. But there's no holding them—they simply make a rush
for the grub and the drinks.

Volodka was dragged off to the place of honor. And next to
him they seat a young lady.

Volodka took one look at her and breathed easy. Well, he
thinks, so that's her. Not bad at all. She's even prettier without
a hat. The nose ain't pushing out so much.

Out of the fullness of his feelings, Volodka Zavitushkin poured
out some wine for her and for himself and started off congratu-
lating and kissing her.

And it was then that the principal events ensued.

All sorts of shouts and yells went up.

"He's an abnormal maniac," they yelled, "the son of a bitch!
Throwing himself on all the girls. His young spouse ain't come out
yet to the table, she's dressing up, and he starts practicing with
somebody else."

What happened then was absolute rot and nonsense.

Volodka should, of course, have turned it all into a joke. Instead, he took offense. In the excitement, some relative or other popped him on the head with a bottle.

Volodka yells, "To hell with you! Filled up a houseful of skirts, and I'm supposed to tell between them!"

At this point the bride makes her appearance, in a long white robe. "So that is how it is," she says. "Well, don't you think you'll get away with it. You'll suffer."

And again, of course, there are screams and moans and hysterics.

The relatives naturally began to chase Volodka from the house.

And Volodka says, "Let me have some grub at least. I haven't had a bite to eat since morning with all this bother."

But the relatives ganged up and kicked him out on the staircase.

The next day Volodka Zavitushkin stepped in at the civil registry department after work and got himself a divorce.

They did not show the least surprise. "That's nothing," they said. "It happens."

And so they gave him his divorce.

1929

Earthquake

by Mikhail Zoshchenko

At the time of the famous Crimean earthquake, there was a fellow by the name of Snopkov living in Yalta.

He was a cobbler. An individual artisan. He had a little workshop of his own in Yalta. Not even a workshop—a small stone hut, a booth.

And he worked with a pal of his, just the two of them, partners.

They were both from out of town. And they repaired shoes for the local population and also for the citizens who came for water cures.

They weren't doing so bad, either. In wintertime they definitely starved, but in summer they had more than plenty of work. Some days there wasn't even time to take a drink. Well, of course, for a drink there's always time. As for anything else . . .

And so it was on that day, too. I mean, just before the earthquake, namely, I think, on Friday, September 11, the cobbler Ivan Yakovlevich Snopkov got tired of waiting for Saturday and helped himself to a pint and a half of good old Russian vodka.

Particularly as he was done with his work. And particularly as he had two bottles stacked away. So why should he wait? He went ahead and helped himself. Particularly as he didn't know yet there was going to be an earthquake.

And so with the pint and a half under his belt, the man naturally fooled around a bit in the street, sang something or other, and started back home. He came back home, stretched out in the yard, and fell asleep without waiting for the earthquake.

Whenever he had an extra drink, he always stretched out in the yard. He didn't care for sleeping under a roof in a drunken state. He didn't feel so good under a ceiling. He couldn't breathe. It made him dizzy. And he always demanded clear, open skies.

And so this time, too. On September 11, just before the earthquake, Ivan Yakovlevich lapped himself full of vodka, got good and plastered, and fell asleep under the cypress in the yard.

There he was, sleeping, dreaming all sorts of interesting dreams, and right alongside the famous Crimean earthquake was going on. Houses rocking, the earth booming and shaking, and Snopkov lies there, sleeping to his heart's content, and doesn't give a hoot for anything.

As for his pal, he made a getaway from the start and found himself a quiet spot in the park, so's he wouldn't get hit by some falling stone.

It wasn't till early morning, maybe around six o'clock, that our Snopkov got around to opening his eyes. He opens up his eyes under the cypress and can't make head or tail of his own yard. Particularly as the stone booth was down in a heap. Well, maybe not altogether in a heap, but one of the walls had cracked and crumbled down, and the fence had keeled over on top of it. The only thing that didn't change was the cypress; everything else was kind of difficult to recognize.

So he opens his eyes, Snopkov, and thinks, Holy mother, where'd I get to? Could I have wandered off somewhere the other day in my drunken state? Such queerly broken households all around! But whose could they be? No, he thinks, it isn't good to get so plastered. Alcohol, he thinks, is an unhealthy drink; not a damned thing sticks in your memory.

And he began to feel awful uncomfortable in his mind. Eh, he thinks, look where I've wandered off to. It was lucky, he thinks, I lay down in a yard, but what if it was in the street? Some car could have squashed me, or a dog could have chewed something off. No, he thinks, I'll have to go easier on drink—or maybe quit it altogether.

He started feeling miserable from all these thoughts. He felt so blue, he took the remaining half-pint from his pocket and drank it down right on the spot, from all that aggravation.

He drank the liquor down and got fuddled all over again. Particularly as he hadn't eaten in such a long time and his head was weakened from the previous binge.

And so he got tipsy again, got up on his feet, and went out into the street.

He's walking down the street and doesn't recognize a thing with all that liquor in him. Particularly as everybody's going around in droves after the earthquake. Everybody's out in the street, nobody stays inside. And everybody's half-dressed, carrying feather beds and mattresses and such.

And so Snopkov goes down the street and his heart grows cold. Heavens, he thinks, where am I? What kind of a hell's hole did I fall into? Could I have gotten to Batum by steamship? Or maybe I've gone all the way to Turkey. Look at all them people going around undressed; you'd think you're in the tropics.

He walked along in this pickled state, and he was almost sobbing.

Then he came out on the highway and kept going, without recognizing anything.

He went on and on, and finally he dropped by the wayside from exhaustion and excess of alcohol and fell into a dead sleep.

He wakes up—it is dark. Evening. Stars are shining up above. And he feels chilly. He feels chilly because he is lying there by the roadside without his clothes and without his shoes. In nothing but his underpants.

He lies there by the roadside, picked clean from head to foot, and he thinks, Good God, he thinks, what is this? Where am I lying back here now?

And then he really got scared. He jumped up on his bare feet and started down the road.

He must have walked about eight miles in the heat of his excitement, then he sat down on a stone.

He sat down on this stone and bowed his head. He felt awful. He didn't know the neighborhood and couldn't get his mind straight on anything. He was getting more and more numb inside and out. And he was dying for some food.

It wasn't until morning that Ivan Yakovlevich Snopkov found out what was what. He asked a man who was passing by.

This man who was passing by said to him, "Why, if I may ask you, for example, are you hanging around here in your underpants?"

And Snopkov said, "I really can't make head or tail of it myself. Tell me, if you'll be so kind, where am I?"

And so they got to talking. The passerby says, "It's close to twenty miles from Yalta. You've sure gone a hell of a long way!" And then the man told him all about the earthquake, what was destroyed where, and what was still being destroyed where.

Snopkov got very upset about the earthquake and hurried back to Yalta.

And so he walked across the whole of Yalta in his underpants. Although nobody was surprised, seeing as it was an earthquake.

Although, come to think of it, nobody would have been surprised anyway.

Afterward, Snopkov added up his losses. They'd taken plenty from him. Sixty rubles in cash; his jacket, worth about eight rubles; his pants, worth about a ruble and a half; and his sandals, almost new. So it came to almost a hundred rubles, not counting the damaged booth.

Now I. Y. Snopkov has decided to go to Kharkov for an anti-alcohol cure. Because it costs too much this way.

What does the author mean to say by this work of art?

The author is raising his voice energetically against drunkenness. The sting of this literary satire is aimed precisely against drinking and against alcohol.

The author wants to say that a drinking man can even sleep through an earthquake, let alone other, more delicate things.

Or as one of our placards says: "Do not drink! Under the influence of liquor, you may embrace your class enemy!"

You sure may—as simple as that!

1931

Ilya Ilf

(Ilya Fainzilberg, 1897 - 1937)

and

Yevgeny Petrov

(Yevgeny Katayev, brother of
Valentin Katayev, 1903 - 1942)

*Ilf and Petrov, leading Soviet satirists, were both born in Odessa,
which produced some of the best and wittiest writers of the early
revolutionary years, including Isaac Babel and Yury Olesha. In
1927, Ilf and Petrov formed a literary partnership. Together, they
wrote innumerable sketches, stories, and feuilletons. Their most
popular works were the hilarious novels* The Twelve Chairs *and*
The Little Golden Calf, *which were fantastic elaborations on
the grotesqueries and absurdities of the NEP period.*

How the Soviet *Robinson* Was Written

by Ilf and Petrov

The editors of the illustrated fortnightly *The Cause of Adventure* complained of a shortage of good stories capable of capturing and holding the attention of young readers.

There was no lack of manuscripts, but none of them was quite up to the mark. There was too much slobbering seriousness in them. To tell the truth, they were more likely to cast gloom upon the spirit of the young reader than to capture it. And that was what the editors wanted—to capture and to hold.

Finally, they decided to commission a serial novel.

A messenger was dispatched posthaste with a note to the writer Moldavantsev; and on the very next day, Moldavantsev was sitting on the plump sofa in the editor's office.

"You understand," the editor explained, "the story must be entertaining, fresh, full of interesting adventures. In short, it must be a Soviet *Robinson Crusoe*. A story the reader won't be able to put down until he finishes it."

"Robinson Crusoe, hmm? It can be done," the writer pronounced laconically.

"Not simply a *Robinson*, but a Soviet *Robinson*."

"What else? Not a Rumanian one, surely!" The writer was not a man to waste words. It could be seen at once that he was a man of action.

And, indeed, the novel was ready on the dot. Moldavantsev did not depart too far from the illustrious original. A *Robinson* is a *Robinson*.

And so, a Soviet youth is shipwrecked. A wave casts him up on a desert island. He is alone, defenseless in the face of mighty nature. He is beset by dangers: wild animals, lianas, the coming rainy season. But the Soviet Robinson, full of zest and energy, overcomes all the seemingly insuperable obstacles. Three years later a Soviet expedition finds him, in blooming health. He has conquered nature, built a cottage, surrounded it with a ring of green gardens, bred rabbits, sewed for himself a Tolstoy blouse of monkey tails, and taught a parrot to wake him every morning with the words, "Attention! Throw off your blanket! Throw off your blanket! We shall now begin our morning calisthenics!"

"Very good," said the editor. "And that touch about the rabbits is excellent. Most topical. But, you know, I am not too clear about the underlying idea of the work."

"Man's struggle with nature," Moldavantsev declared with his customary brevity.

"Yes, but there's nothing specifically Soviet here."

"And what about the parrot? He takes the place of our radio. An expert announcer."

"The parrot is good. And the ring of gardens is good. But somehow one doesn't sense the Soviet public spirit. Where, for example, is the local committee? And what about the leading role of the trade unions?"

Moldavantsev suddenly came to life. The moment he saw that his novel might be rejected, his reserve vanished. He became eloquent. "But how can you have a local committee? The island is uninhabited!"

"Very true, it is uninhabited. But there must be a local committee. I am not a literary artist, but if I were you, I would bring it in. As a Soviet element, you know."

"But the whole plot is built around the fact that the island is unin—"

At this point, Moldavantsev glanced up into the editor's eyes and broke off. The eyes were of such springlike, vacuous innocence, there was nothing in them but the emptiness and blue of an early March sky. Moldavantsev decided to accept a compromise. "Come to think of it, you're right," he said, raising his shoulders. "Of course! Why didn't I think of it at once? I'll have two men rescued from the shipwreck: our Robinson and the chairman of the local committee."

"And also two committee members," the editor added coldly.

"Oi!" squealed Moldavantsev.

"Never mind 'oi'! Two members—and one girl activist, to collect membership dues."

"But what do we need the dues collector for? From whom will she collect?"

"From Robinson, of course."

"The chairman can collect from Robinson. It won't do him any harm."

"Now you're mistaken, Comrade Moldavantsev. This is absolutely inadmissible. The chairman of the local committee must not waste his time on trifles and run around collecting dues. We are fighting against such things. He must concentrate on the serious work of leadership."

"All right, we'll have the collector, too," Moldavantsev yielded. "In fact, it will be better so. She will marry the chairman—or even Robinson. It will make the book livelier."

"No. You must avoid cheap vulgarity and unwholesome eroticism. Just let her collect her membership dues and keep them in a fireproof safe."

Moldavantsev began to fidget on the sofa. "But, if you don't mind, how can there be a fireproof safe on a desert island?"

The editor pondered the problem. "Wait, wait!" he exclaimed. "You have a marvelous passage in the first chapter. Together with Robinson and the members of the local committee, the wave casts up a number of things . . . "

"An ax, a rifle, a compass, a keg of rum, and a bottle of antiscorbutic medicine," the writer enumerated triumphantly.

"Cut out the rum," said the editor quickly. "And then, what's that bottle of antiscorbutic for? Who needs it? Better make it a bottle of ink! And a fireproof safe. That's a must!"

"You and your safe! The dues can be kept in a hollow in a baobab tree. Who will steal them?"

"What do you mean 'who'? What about Robinson? And the local committee chairman? And the members? And the store commission?"

"The commission was also rescued?" Moldavantsev asked anxiously.

"It was."

A silence followed.

"Perhaps the wave cast up a table, too? So they could hold their meetings around it?" the author asked sarcastically.

"Ab-so-lute-ly! People must be provided with proper working conditions. Let's say, a pitcher of water, a bell, a tablecloth. The tablecloth can be of any kind—red, green. I'm not one to interfere with the work of the creative artist. But this, my friend, is our first and foremost task: we must show the reader a picture of the masses, the broad strata of the laboring people."

"A wave cannot cast up any masses." Moldavantsev was suddenly obstinate. "This is entirely at odds with the plot. Imagine! A wave suddenly casting up thousands of people on the shore! Who ever heard of such a thing?"

"And, then, we must also have some healthy, optimistic, life-affirming laughter," interposed the editor. "That can never do any harm."

"No! A wave cannot do it."

"A wave? Why a wave?" the editor asked with astonishment.

"How else could the masses get to the island? After all, it's uninhabited!"

"Who told you it's uninhabited? You confuse me. No, no, everything is clear. There is this island. Or, still better, a peninsula —it's more secure somehow. And a number of entertaining, fresh, interesting adventures take place on it. Trade-union work is carried on. Sometimes inefficiently. The girl activist exposes some shortcomings, let's say, in the collection of membership dues. She is supported by the wide masses. And the repentant chairman. At the end, you can have a general meeting. This will be very effective—in a literary sense. And that's it!"

"And Robinson?" mumbled Moldavantsev.

"Oh, yes, I am glad you reminded me. Throw him out altogether. A preposterous, totally indefensible figure of a whining pessimist."

"I see. Now everything is clear," said Moldavantsev in a sepulchral voice. "You'll have the story tomorrow."

"That's all, then. Go home and create. And, incidentally, you began with a shipwreck. Let's leave out the shipwreck. The story will be much more engrossing without it. Right? Fine. Good-bye."

When he was alone, the editor laughed gleefully. "At last," he cried, "at last I will have a real adventure story—and a most creditable work of art at that!"

1933

Mikhail Koltsov
(1898 - 1941 ?)

Born in Kiev, Koltsov was a militant and active Communist agitator. His feuilletons served one purpose only—the furtherance of the Party's policies. He went to Spain as a correspondent for *Pravda* during the Spanish Civil War in 1936, and is said to have been the model for Karkov in Hemingway's *For Whom the Bell Tolls*. In the grim concluding lines of "Stupidity"—an unequivocal call for police action—he carries the official conception of the role of literature and, particularly, of satire to what is perhaps its logical conclusion. In any event, these lines clearly reflect the spirit of the day, for the story appeared in the period of the "great purges." Koltsov himself was arrested in 1938 and disappeared. He is said to have died in a concentration camp several years later. His work was not republished until his "rehabilitation" in the late 1950's.

Stupidity

by Mikhail Koltsov

The small rooms occupied by the management of the Yelan Co-operative Society were seething with activity. The front door slammed continuously, admitting and letting out visitors with canvas briefcases. In the foyer, the teakettle was being heated for the fourth time for the leading personnel.

The director, Comrade Sparrows, stuck his head out of his room into the office. "What about the latest instructions? How many days is it that we've been planning to wire them to the field? Bring me the text for signature!"

They brought him the sheet of paper with the text. The instructions concluded with the energetic words: " . . . build up your stocks."

"And where is the number? We cannot wire instructions without numbers."

The sheet fluttered off to the records department and returned bearing a weighty, impressive number: ". . . build up your stocks 13,530"

Sparrows dipped his pen, looked with stern disapproval at the fat drop of ink, shook it off contemptuously, and wrote his signature after the number.

The instructions were wired. They slid along the telegraph lines and then were taken from the station by messengers to the various villages.

The messengers froze and buried their blue noses in acrid-smelling sheepskin collars. The instructions were warm; they rested deep in the bosoms of the messengers' coats.

The representative of the district cooperative society in Ionovo-Yezhovka unfolded the telegraph blank, smoothed it out, picked up the receiver, and in a loud voice read the orders from the central cooperative office from beginning to end to the representative of the district executive committee: " '. . . build up your stocks 13,530 sparrows.' Did you get it?"

"I have it. All except the end—I didn't hear right. What stocks are we to build up?"

"It says 'sparrows.' "

"I see, I see. . . . Clear enough. And how many sparrows must we stock?"

"It says '13,530.' Do you have it?"

"I see. I see. It's quite clear. And who signed it?"

"No signature. There's no need for a signature. It's simple enough: you'll have to stock up and deliver thirteen and a half thousand sparrows. This little order should be expedited first thing, without delay. Telephone the chairman."

When he heard about the new instructions, the Ionovo-Yezhovka chairman did not allow himself to be discountenanced. He stated frankly and openly that the stocking of sparrows was a new sort of job for the residents of Ionovo-Yezhovka. They'd done all sorts of jobs, but what they'd never done, they'd never done. They'd never stocked sparrows. However, it could be done. Ionovo-Yezhovka wouldn't let the center down. It could be done; but first, morale had to be raised, the masses had to be inspired with the will to work.

The chairman of the Soviet, together with the two district representatives—the representative of the district executive committee and the representative of the district cooperative branch—arranged a meeting with the active Party members and reported to them on the latest instructions concerning the stocking of sparrows.

This was followed by a meeting of the general citizenry of Ionovo-Yezhovka. Some of the citizens had at first been seriously alarmed. When they learned that all the center wanted was sparrows, their spirits rose.

One of them even got up and made a short speech, to the accompaniment of ripples of light laughter in the hall: "I don't know about other things, but don't you worry about sparrows. We'll get you plenty. We won't stint on sparrows."

The laughter seemed suspicious to the presiding officials. The chairman of the meeting said sententiously and sternly, "There! Look sharp, now!"

The campaign was launched without a hitch. The population of the village plunged into the job of stocking sparrows with an energy appropriate for the most urgent and vital tasks. By orders of the local authorities, not only adults but also schoolchildren were mobilized for the work.

In order to fulfill the assignment with the greatest speed and efficiency, the hunt went on not only in the daytime, but also at night. With lanterns.

At the very height of the sparrow campaign, several visitors came to Ionovo-Yezhovka, in connection with other matters: the district prosecutor, Karlov; the people's judge, Semerkin; the representative of the district militia, Dzyubin; and a committee from the district executive committee, to inspect the local work. They found the rural cooperative in a whirl of activity.

"You've come at the wrong time. We're in the midst of sparrowstocking."

"Of what?"

"Of stocking sparrows. We must say, you've set us quite a figure in the center. Thirteen and a half thousand! We don't know how we'll do it. It's lucky the population is working actively."

The district officials had heard nothing of sparrows. But none of them wanted to show himself out of touch with current economic tasks. Everyone kept silent. Some even commented sympathetically, "Just go on with the work. And while we're here, we'll also do our bit to help."

The presence of guests from the district center raised the general morale still higher. Then one day someone arrived from the neighboring village, Alexandrovka. At Alexandrovka, they had also received instructions from Yelan and had also begun to stock up; but they had written to the center requesting that the figure be lowered.

The local workers gloated. "We've beaten Alexandrovka! We've beaten them hollow! They're way behind, the devils. And we—we shall yet overfulfill the assignment!"

And then misfortune struck. Some cats got into the barn, where two thousand sparrows were kept, and gobbled up two hundred birds.

A special protest meeting was called in this connection. At the meeting, the representative of the district executive committee said, with his eyeglasses glinting ominously, "We regard the fact that cats devoured two hundred sparrows as wrecking, as sabotage of the crash assignment. We intend to bring the guilty parties to justice. But we must reply to the action of the cats by redoubled effort to raise our stock of sparrows."

A number of other acute problems arose in the process of the campaign. To clear them up, the instructor of the cooperative society, Comrade Yenakieva, made a special trip to Yelan.

On arriving at the district center, Yenakieva came to the main office and declared, "I have assumed personal direction in the matter of stocking sparrows. The work is proceeding satisfactorily on the whole. But there are a number of unsolved problems, and I have made this special trip for the purpose of clearing them up. First of all, our peasants want to know the rates at which they will be paid for supplying the sparrows, and we the cooperators have no knowledge of these rates. Secondly, there is a bottleneck in packaging materials. Incidentally, we also need an answer to the following question: in what form are we expected to supply the sparrows—live or dead? It would also be desirable to have an exchange of experiences with other organizations. For example, we are now stocking live supplies. For this purpose, we put out millet as bait. We also spread handfuls of twigs on the threshing floors to attract the sparrows. . . . When we get the rates of compensation and the packing materials, the work will unquestionably be speeded up. It is further important to find out . . ."

Comrade Yenakieva's report and the ensuing scandal complete the story of the sparrow campaign. This provincial story of an idiotically misinterpreted and witlessly fulfilled instruction should not, perhaps, be taken too seriously. After all, it shows little more than innocent stupidity. But it is time, at long last, to take up arms against that delightful quality as well! And can we, generally, speak of stupidity as an innocuous, natural, "objective" quality?

The Party appreciates and sets a high value on a disciplined approach to the fulfillment of its assignments. And this is precisely why it is essential to smash to a pulp all those who, speculating on this discipline and abusing it, transform the fulfillment of directives into a travesty, and unquestioning performance into buffoonery.

The sparrow campaign in the village was observed by leading officials from the district center: the prosecutor, the judge, and the chief of militia. Who would believe that these esteemed personages—no, not personages, apes!—thought of the sparrow hunt as a normal, sensible enterprise? . . . No! Each of them inwardly wondered at the comedy. But each remained silent.

We are today going over the Soviet and the cooperative systems from top to bottom. We are getting rid of everything rotten, alien, harmful. We should not make an exception for people who play the role of fools. Such "naïve elements" as those who stocked up sparrows can be educated in one place only. In prison.

1936

E. Bermont, Arkady Vasiliev, L. Lagin, N. Vorobyov, Boris Laskin, and E. Vesenin

These writers are among the better practitioners of latter-day Soviet satire. Working within an extremely rigid system of prescriptions and limitations, which has inevitably prevented true individualization of style or originality of approach, they nevertheless manage to write with considerable, if only occasional, wit and skill.

A Timid Soul

by E. Bermont

Even when Mikhail Mikhailovich Ranev finally goes to bed, his thoughts, like black flies, give him no rest all night.

And, indeed, how can you keep track of everything? Just recently, for example, they stepped on the toes of an important comrade whom it would have been best to leave alone. And yesterday, on the contrary, they did not hit hard enough at another important comrade, whom, at the moment, it would have been most advantageous to hit.

Life is difficult for the timid soul of a rabbit when it has chosen an altogether unsuitable body—that of an editor of a certain organ of the press. Poor, poor rabbit, he must walk the path of tigers!

And so a messenger rushed down the long corridor of the editorial offices, with round portholes like a ship. "Gvozdikov is wanted by Mikhail Mikhailovich!"

The theater critic ambled sluggishly to the editor's office. He was in a sour mood: he knew that the limit of the editor's critical daring was a blast at the Planetarium show or at the jazz in the foyer of the Enchantment Motion Picture Theatre.

With his head bent low, Mikhail Mikhailovich was reading slowly: " 'Unfortunately, Shakespeare's remarkable play did not receive adequate treatment in production. The director, Kontsupsky, proved unequal to his task.' " The editor stopped. "But wait a moment, wait, Gvozdikov! Wasn't this Kontsupsky awarded a decoration?"

"Yes, he has a decoration. And he is an Honored Artist."

Mikhail Mikhailovich hiccuped with displeasure. "How many times have I asked you not to omit mentioning ranks and titles

239

in your reviews. . . . After all . . . I must . . . oh . . . have some guideposts."

Carefully inserting all the titles, Ranev read again: " 'Unfortunately, Shakespeare's remarkable play did not receive adequate treatment in production. An Honored Artist and holder of a medal, the director, Kontsupsky, proved unequal to his task.' Hm, hm. . . . How does this look, Gvozdikov?"

The reviewer was gloomily silent.

"Hm . . ." the editor went on, "Now you are saying that a decorated director proved unequal to the play of an undecorated dramatist. . . . How can that be?"

"But this is Shakespeare!"

"So what if it's Shakespeare? I could understand it if a director who has a Badge of Merit failed to do justice to a play by a dramatist with a Banner of Labor. That would be natural. But this . . ." And he spread his hands, adding, "We'll have to take it out."

The reviewer's spirits rose. "Take out Kontsupsky's name?"

"No! We'll cross out that he failed with Shakespeare. . . . I am in favor of ruthless criticism myself, but not like this, Gvozdikov. . . . Don't forget, we are now celebrating Shakespeare's anniversary . . . three hundred and seventy five years!"

But the terrors of the rabbit soul did not end with theater reviews. If Ranev's eye caught an item in which the reporter stated that "the quality of the syrups in the stores and soda plants is extremely low," his mood would instantly darken. "This is a g-g-generalization," he would stutter. "D-do you mean to say that they sell poor syrups in the Red capital of the most advanced country in the world?"

"What has the Red capital to do with it, Mikhail Mikhailovich? Try and taste it yourself. The cranberry syrup, for example—"

But the editor would not allow the reporter to finish. "Well, then, say so. Say that certain cranberry syrups in some of the soda-water manufacturing plants, through the fault of a few of the workers . . . Now, that would be sensible and useful criticism."

One day Ranev entered the office of the editorial secretary with a face dark as a cloud. In his hands was a crumpled galley sheet. He angrily drew his nail across a dispatch. "Read it!"

"A tornado and heavy rains swept over Novorossiisk. Many windows were broken."

The secretary, an imperturbable football, boxing, and bullfight fan, looked up at him in surprise. "Well, what's wrong with it?"

"And here is another item—a tornado with rain over Tuapse. Also with broken windows."

"Well?"

The editor lost his temper. "What do you mean 'well'? You must have some political sense. What we get here is a generalization. Tornadoes with rain all over the country. . . . No, no, leave the item about Novorossiisk, but drop the one about Tuapse."

And Mikhail Mikhailovich turned to the door. But in a moment he returned. "Or, better, write that Tuapse enjoyed a bright, sunny day, the beach was crowded with bathers, and the city theater presented Korneychuk's *Bohdan Khmelnitsky* with great success."

"And what's the *Bohdan Khmelnitsky* for?"

"As a counterbalance to the tornado. A tornado means disorder, problems, and *Bohdan Khmelnitsky* is an achievement . . ."

The fear of "generalizations" had taken such a grip on the employees of Ranev's paper that even the chief of the want-ad department called the editorial secretary every five minutes. "I have here four ads in a row saying that a single engineer is looking for a room with conveniences. . . . Shall I print them?"

"But why not?"

"After all, you know, it's a kind of generalization . . . What will Mikhail Mikhailovich say?"

Incidentally, I must confess that I dictated this story to a typist employed under the above-mentioned rabbit soul.

At about the tenth line, she started anxiously and asked, "Isn't this a generalization?"

But I reassured her. "Don't worry, Tamara, go on typing. This is a perfectly specific instance."

1939

The Crystal Vase

by Arkady Vasiliev

I heard the story of the crystal vase from Dr. Druzhkin. He assured me that all of this was the absolute truth, without an iota of fiction, and that he had merely altered the names of the characters, out of respect for the ethics of the medical profession. Here is the story he told me.

I lived at the time in the provincial city of V. One night—it was considerably past midnight—I heard someone knocking desperately at my window. When I opened the door, a woman's figure rushed toward me. I immediately recognized Marya Yefimovna Zabaluyev, the wife of an acquaintance, an official in the economic apparatus.

Before I could say a word, Marya Yefimovna clutched at my sleeve, repeating the same words over and over through a flood of tears: "Come, Doctor, come! It's dreadful!"

A minute later I was ready to travel to the end of the world. But the journey was much shorter, since the Zabaluyevs lived on the same street with me. On the way, I tried to find out from my weeping companion what had happened to her husband, the esteemed Pavel Nikolayevich.

In reply to my questions, Marya Nikolayevna only cried still more hysterically, repeating the same phrase: "It's so dreadful! It's so dreadful!"

As we approached the Zabaluyev home, I heard something resembling the roaring of a bear and the crashing of broken china. While Marya Yefimovna was opening the door, a crystal powder box flew out through the window and shattered at my feet.

Marya Yefimovna stood aside, allowing me to enter first, and whispered with a sob, "Good God, he's reached my dressing table!"

I entered the apartment and saw a strange spectacle: the entire floor was littered with broken dishes. On a chair in the middle of the room stood the master of the house himself. He had a poker in his hand, and he used it with dexterity to knock off the crystal pendants from the magnificent chandelier.

At the sight of her husband disposing of the chandelier, the wife, forgetting all caution, rushed toward him, but was stopped in her tracks by his calm greeting.

"A-ah, it's you, Masha! Who is that with you? Doctor, hello, my friend! Just a moment, I'll be right down."

Pavel Nikolayevich knocked off the last pendant, unhurriedly climbed down from the chair, and trying not to step on the broken glass, came toward me, holding out his hand. "How do you do, Doctor! I am delighted to see you. I've been doing gymnastics, as you see. Mashenka, why do you stand there? Ask the guest to come in, prepare some tea."

Completely recovering her courage, Marya Yefimovna returned to her role as mistress of the house. "Tea? And did you think of what we'll drink it from? You have smashed every bit of crockery and glass."

But Pavel Nikolayevich did not listen to her. He stretched out on the divan, and a moment later his mighty snores proclaimed that my violent host had fallen into a sound and prolonged sleep. I examined him: his heartbeat was calm and regular. His pulse was strong.

Several days later I learned the prehistory of this incident.

In the same town there lived a certain Georgy Nikolayevich Ruchkin, who occupied a prominent post. There had long been rumors among the local officials that Ruchkin was about to be promoted to a high and responsible position in the capital. These rumors either simmered down or flared up with new force. Later, Ruchkin's subordinates began to say quite openly that their chief was slated to become a deputy minister.

Of course, Comrade Ruchkin himself did nothing to assist the spread of these rumors. Whenever any of his zealous admirers began to build conjectures in his presence, Ruchkin would only smile mysteriously and concentrate on the details of some current matter.

Pavel Nikolayevich Zabaluyev was not employed directly under Ruchkin; he merely had occasion to visit him now and then in the course of his duties. When he learned that Ruchkin might soon become a deputy minister and therefore his chief, Zabaluyev lost all his peace of mind. He began to drop in on Ruchkin at least three times a week, inventing more and more pretexts for these visits. He would either come for Ruchkin's valuable advice on how best to organize some enterprise or beg "dear Georgy Nikolayevich" to give his "opinion concerning the existing system of accounting in regard to material assets."

As soon as they completed the discussion of the topic at hand, Zabaluyev invariably turned the conversation to life in Moscow. Pavel Nikolayevich would dreamily roll his eyes up to his forehead and lisp ecstatically, "The Bolshoy Theatre! The Tretyakov Gallery! The Forel Cafe! Good God, all that culture!"

Ruchkin pretended that he did not understand the hints; only an enigmatic smile played on his full lips.

Returning home after these visits, Zabaluyev ranted and raved. "It's a sphinx, not a man! Try and get a crumb of information from him!"

Zabaluyev was at his wit's end, but before long everything became quite clear. During one of his trips to the district center, he learned that a conference of the local leadership was to take place two days later. One of the points on the agenda was the announcement concerning the change in Comrade Ruchkin's status.

Pavel Nikolayevich decided that it would be unforgivable, at the very least, to appear empty-handed at the meeting devoted to farewells to an honored leader. He immediately telephoned the crystal-manufacturing plant under his jurisdiction and placed an urgent order for a vase with Comrade Ruchkin's portrait and an inscription: "To the Esteemed Georgy Nikolayevich from his Disinterested Friend P. N. Z."

After two days at the district center, which were spent in constant agitation, Pavel Nikolayevich dropped all his work in mid-course and returned to his hometown. He hurried to the conference directly from the station.

At the door he was met by the director of the crystal-manufacturing plant, who handed him the carefully wrapped vase. Zabaluyev pushed his way through the crowded foyer and went onstage from behind the wings. He deposited his present on the speakers' table and, pleased with his idea, looked around and slipped back into the hall.

At last, the conference opened. After elections of the presidium and a short vote on the agenda, the chairman gave the floor to the speaker from the capital. Zabaluyev did not know the gray-haired man in a modest black suit who mounted the podium.

"Before proceeding to discuss our current tasks," said the visiting speaker, "I must report to the meeting on the decision we have adopted concerning Comrade Ruchkin."

The hall became silent. Zabaluyev fidgeted on his chair and, craning his neck, smiled at Ruchkin.

The gray-haired man unhurriedly drank some water and went on: "Comrade Ruchkin has been warned repeatedly that his methods of work require thorough revision. The toadying and the bureaucratic atmosphere he has been fostering could not but affect his entire work. The directing organizations have decided that Comrade Ruchkin can no longer be trusted and therefore cannot continue in his high post. And so . . ."

If a thousand-ton bomb had suddenly exploded or if the ground had been shaken by an earthquake, Zabaluyev would probably have gotten less of a fright. His first thought was, The vase!

But the vase was already unwrapped. Its blue facets flashing in the light, it was being passed from hand to hand on the stage. Zabaluyev distinctly heard someone's deep basso exclaim admiringly, "It's Ruchkin all right! An excellent likeness!"

Zabaluyev did not remember how he sat it out till the intermission. And the most terrible thing happened during intermission: he was invited backstage, into a room where the entire presidium was assembled.

The gray-haired man asked, "You ordered this vase? Please tell me what prompted you to do it?"

Zabaluyev's first impulse was to deny everything, to say that it was not he who had ordered the vase, that there was some mistake. But his glance fell on the vase, and he saw his gift at close range for the first time. The workers at the factory had outdone themselves in an excess of zeal: under Ruchkin's portrait there was an undulating inscription, written in full, without initials: "To the Esteemed Georgy Nikolayevich from his Disinterested Friend, Pavel Nikolayevich Zabaluyev."

Pavel Nikolayevich uttered a single word: "Guilty."

The gray-haired man said, "Ruchkin refuses to accept your gift. Take back the vase and be kind enough to remit its full price to the factory tomorrow. The bill is inside."

Someone pushed the vase into Zabaluyev's hands. Losing all sense of firm ground under his feet, he muttered dully, "At least give me a newspaper to wrap it."

The gray-haired man answered dryly, "This isn't a store. You may go."

The door opened, and Zabaluyev stepped into the crowded foyer. He was noticed. People stretched out their hands, voices asked to see the "unique little artifact." He picked his way carefully, pressing the crystal vase to his chest. And it was only when he was out in the street that he fully realized everything that had happened to him.

Two boys and the corner militiaman witnessed the spectacle of a tall, burly man jumping up and down on a beautiful blue vase until it was reduced to dust.

What happened after that was really quite simple. Pavel Nikolayevich stepped in to see a crony, poured out his soul, and poured in so much vodka that, on coming home, he turned to smashing everything that even remotely resembled crystal. And it was at this occupation that the doctor found him.

Intrigued by this story, I asked the doctor to tell me the end.

The doctor asked with astonishment, "What other end do you want? That was all. I heard that Zabaluyev was demoted."

"And how is his health?"

"Excellent. But he cannot endure the sight of anything made of glass or crystal and uses mostly plastic and aluminum dishes."

"And what would you call his fit?"

"What fit?"

"Oh, when he was smashing dishes at home."

The doctor laughed and said, "The Latin name for it is *Failurus Sycophantus*."

1947

Grandmother's Cake

(A Cautionary Fairy Tale)

by L. Lagin

Grandmother baked a cake, neither big nor small, neither high nor low. A cake of ordinary, normal size. But tasty, with mushrooms.

This grandmother worked as a cleaning woman in an office. Her grandson worked there, too, and it was the grandson's birthday.

And so the grandmother brought the cake to the office. "Help yourselves, darlings. Have some cake, with tea if you want. Or just plain, without tea."

When they saw the cake at the office, they simply gasped with admiration:

"Heavens, what a cake, what a fine cake!"

The clerk Ivanov said, "Let's eat it!"

And the clerk Petrov said, "Right, let's eat it."

And he took out a knife to cut the cake. He was a great one for eating—one, two, and it's done.

But the chief clerk—Sidorov was his name—said, "No, you'll either drive me crazy or make me wither away before my time. I won't allow you to eat cakes without the permission of the assistant office manager!"

So he ran off to report to the assistant manager. "Permit me," he said, "to report: Grandmother baked a cake, neither big nor small, neither high nor low—regulation size, so to speak. And as the aforesaid grandmother brought the aforesaid cake to the office under your authority with the concrete proposal that the office employees partake of it, I should like to have your instructions as to the disposition of this matter."

"A cake?" asked the assistant office manager.

"Yes, sir, a cake."

"With mushrooms?"

"Precisely. With mushrooms."

"Uhum! And a fresh one, at that! At least if the damn thing weren't fresh. But no, it's a fresh one! No, I refuse to take such a responsibility upon myself. Let the office manager assume the responsibility."

And so he went to report to the office manager. "Permit me," he said, "to report: Grandmother baked a cake, neither big nor small, neither high nor low—regulation size, so to speak. And as said grandmother brought said cake to the office under your authority with the concrete proposal that the office employees partake of it, what are your instructions as to the disposition of this matter?"

"A cake?" asked the office manager.

"Yes, sir, a cake."

"With mushrooms?"

"Exactly. With mushrooms."

The office manager thought and thought. Then he said, "You know what? Write a memorandum. I'll take the memorandum to my chief. And just as the chief says, so it will be."

No sooner said than done. The clerk Ivanov and the clerk Petrov and the clerk Sidorov sat down, and for four days they wrote the memorandum, under the general supervision of the office manager.

"Permit us," it said, "to report: Grandmother baked a cake, neither big nor small, neither high nor low," and so on, and so forth. Then they took the finest India ink and drew the plan of the cake and its views in cross section, from above, from the side, from below. Then they checked, verified, correlated, and bound the document and took it to the chief of the office chief.

The chief read it. "What's this?" he asked. "Are you pulling my leg, or what? Grandmother is treating you to cake? Eat it in good health!"

But they still would not leave. They stood there, shifting their weight from foot to foot, looking miserable.

"Do you have any other questions?"

"Yes, sir, Comrade Chief."

"What is it?"

"Could we possibly have your resolution in writing, just in case?"

At this point the chief lost patience. "Out!" he says. "Get out of my sight! Go and do as you're ordered."

Well, there was nothing to be done; they went to carry out the chief's orders. But the cake had in the meantime dried and hardened till it was like stone. No knife could cut it.

So they got an ax—and *cr-rash!* it came down on the cake.

The cake is whole, but the ax is smashed to pieces.

"Bother! All this trouble on my head!" said the office manager, and he ordered his subordinates to write a memorandum saying that "Grandmother baked a cake, neither big nor small, neither

high nor low," and so on, and so forth. "And consequently we
request your permission to write off one (1) ax," and so on, and so
forth.

Phooey!

And that's the whole tale.

1954

A Glass of Water

by L. Lagin

It happened recently that a rather large institution in a fairly big
city held some sort of conference. It may have been to confirm a
plan, to confess mistakes, or something else along such lines. At
any rate, that is of no importance to our story.

The important thing is that at all the conferences, meetings, and
similar assemblies of this particular institution, the speakers were
served tea. And not simply tea, but tea with sugar and lemon. The
speakers, naturally, enjoyed it, and the cost was small. Mind you,
we are by no means opposed to the serving of tea and lemon. We
are talking of something else altogether.

You see, there was in that institution a certain up-and-coming
man, who was liked and respected both by his colleagues and by
his superiors. Let us call him, for the sake of convenience, Sidorov.
This Sidorov was coming up in the world not by the day, but by
the hour, and everybody was saying that he would get an important
and, mark you, a well-deserved promotion in the very near future.
He was also a pretty good speaker.

And so it was Sidorov's turn to address the conference. He got
his share of applause in the hall. He got his share of applause

from the presiding table. And Sidorov began his interesting and constructive speech.

At this point, a young woman came out upon the stage (the conference was held in the clubhouse) and brought over to Sidorov the glass that was due him as a speaker.

But the glass was different from those served to the previous speakers. Instead of tea with lemon, it contained the most ordinary boiled water.

Many of the rank-and-file participants in the conference began to whisper among themselves: "Did you see? Sidorov! and suddenly they give him plain water! . . . Ve-ry interesting!"

At the presiding table there were also whispers: "Something's up, comrades! There's something in the wind! There is no smoke without fire!"

And even Sidorov himself, for all that he was a fearless man (he had medals all across his chest), blanched when he saw what the waitress had brought him. He blanched, his legs became like water, he mumbled something indistinct, garbled his well-prepared speech, broke off in the middle, gave up, and walked off the stage without a single handclap. And, in all fairness, there was nothing to applaud in such a speech.

Since then, Comrade Sidorov has gone downhill. No one applauds him any more. Indeed, he seldom gets up to speak at all. And his speeches are much less sensible and interesting than they were in the old tea-drinking days. Perhaps it is because he has lost confidence in himself or something.

For the last three months, he has been showing everybody and anybody who would look and listen a letter from the chef at the club certifying that he had been served plain water not for some special reason, but simply because the kitchen had run out of tea. But no one believes it. And, between us, he does not believe it too much himself.

And, indeed, everybody else gets sweet, strong tea with lemon, and Sidorov—why just Sidorov?—gets a glass of ordinary boiled water! There is something in it!

Sidorov s whole career has gone to the dogs. Well, perhaps not altogether to the dogs, but until such time as everything is thoroughly cleared up.

But how can it be cleared up when there is nothing in the whole business that you can properly take hold of? And as for documents, there are none except the letter from the chef. We know these little letters!

1955–1960 (?)

For the Birds

by N. Vorobyov

It was a hot day in July. The rooster Asmodeus squatted under an elderberry bush, languishing with heat and greedily gulping the air. He never dreamed that at this quiet midday hour he would become the victim of a preposterous incident that would make him the laughingstock of the poultry yard.

At the exact moment when Asmodeus, overcome by drowsiness, nodded off to sleep, state farm zoologist Makar Khizhnyak stole up to him from behind and grabbed him with both hands. The rooster fought back, pecked at his kidnapper's hands—to no avail. Makar slipped into the house, sat down, squeezed the rooster tightly between his knees, and picking up some instrument from the shelf, began to do something with it—*click-click, click-click*.

You're cooked, my friend, Asmodeus thought gloomily, closing his eyes.

But what a queer thing! The instrument kept chattering, but there was no pain, only feathers flying in all directions. Could he be clipping me? The rooster cautiously opened his left eye and looked around.

Sure enough: Makar was shearing him as though he were a common, ordinary sheep. He had denuded his neck and back and was now starting on the proud, curved chest.

The rooster could endure it no longer. "Cr-r-rimin-owl!" he screeched at the top of his voice, and he slapped the offender so violently with his wings that Makar dropped the scissors and recoiled. The half-naked rooster leaped up to the windowsill, down on the table, up on the cupboard. Dishes rang and clattered, and a storm of multicolored feathers whirled through the room.

The door creaked open, and Makar's wife appeared on the threshold. For a moment she stood wordlessly, unable to understand what was happening in her house. Then a terrible thought made her start and turn pale. "Makar, darling," she said to her husband tenderly, "lie down on the sofa. I'll go and call the doctor."

"What are you hinting at!" Makar shouted angrily. "I am engaged in scientific work and will beg you to refrain from disturbing me. The discovery of hen shearing will belong to nobody but me, Makar Antipych Khizhnyak, zoologist at our experimental poultry-breeding station. Do you understand?"

His wife did not know it, but Makar was really trying to work out a scientific problem. On the previous day, he had had an earnest conversation with Afanasy Petrovich Bidnenko, senior zoologist at the same poultry-breeding station. They had sat on the porch, enjoying the fragrant breeze from the gardens and talking.

"I have a most tempting idea," Makar Antipych had said, blowing out a ringlet of smoke.

"And what is this idea?" Afanasy Petrovich was curious, and he too blew a ring.

"I am thinking of organizing chicken shearing."

"What for?"

"What do you mean 'what for'? To harvest raw materials. If one hen yields twenty grams of down and feathers, a hundred will produce a pillow, a thousand a whole feather bed!"

"You may be right," Bidnenko said doubtfully. "But I'm afraid people may laugh at us. They may say, 'you loafers, you can't turn out enough eggs and meat, so you're trying to cover up with feather beds?'"

"That's not the point," Khizhnyak reassured him. "We can't catch up with the leading collective and state farms anyway. But a new invention—I am talking about the shearing—will bring our station fame and glory. And before you know it, we'll have our dissertations made to order, too!"

"If that's the case, Makar, go to it!" Bidnenko was suddenly enthusiastic. "What the devil, let the feathers fly!"

And Makar "went to it."

He sheared one hen and drew his first scientific conclusion: "The shearings may be classified into two grades: down, collected from the region of the belly; and feathers, from the rest of the body."

He sheared another hen and composed a new chapter for his scientific treatise: "The shearing should begin at the head. The large feathers on the wings and tail should not be touched. . . . The procedure can also be applied with equal success to turkeys, geese, and ducks."

By the time he denuded the rooster Asmodeus, Makar had already envisaged himself as the father of scientific poultry shearing. His style of writing became ornate, pompous, and thoroughly self-satisfied. In his further notes, Makar Khizhnyak produced stern scientific admonitions such as the following: "I properly regard the sale of unshorn fowl at any time subsequent to my proposal as indirect economic sabotage."

Thirst for the fame of a pioneer has taken complete possession of Makar Antipych. Today he is tirelessly dispatching his scientific arguments in every possible direction. "I consider my proposal and my experiments to be the first in the history of poultry breeding," he reports to the Regional Administration of Incubator Stations, to the Central Department of Poultry-Breeding State Farms, to the Ministry of Agriculture . . .

"But perhaps it is really a valuable discovery?" we asked some poultry experts.

"No," they answered shortly. "It is nothing but the product of an idle mind."

You'd think that the specialists from the above organizations would answer Makar Khizhnyak with the same laconic clarity. But no! Some of them have sent him streamlined, oily letters: we'll talk it over; we'll think about it. Others (and these are in the majority) have "relayed" Makar's missives "along the appropriate channels." And all these missives have descended like an avalanche upon . . . the Kuvaldin District Executive Committee.

The district is in the midst of feverish activity. The collective farmers are harvesting corn and sugar beets, preparing feed for the winter. The workers of the district executive committee should by rights be out in the field. But they do not have a moment to spare. They are pondering their answer to Khizhnyak and trying to decide: should roosters be sheared, or should they not be sheared?

Meanwhile, Makar Antipych continues to besiege the various government institutions of the Republic and of Moscow itself. Agonizing over the fate of the hens who are still running around in the full glory of their down and feathers, he warns, "We must not lose a moment's time—we must shear! Here are the complete instructions for scientific shearing:

"The operator should take the hen or any other fowl and tie its feet with soft tape; a piece of cloth, some fifteen to twenty centimeters wide and a hundred centimeters long, should then be drawn between its feet. After that, the operator should seat himself on a low bench, some twenty-five to thirty centimeters high, and hold the fowl between his knees, with its head toward him. With his free left hand, he should take the bird by the head and begin to shear, starting with the neck, some four to five centimeters below the head."

And in every letter, Makar Antipych invariably reminds the addressee: "I was the first to devise this."

Let us venture to disillusion our hero. The palm of primacy really belongs not to him but to the employees of the Solomensk Scientific Research Station. Here, too, there were some idle dreamers with time on their hands. The senior scientist Perekatilov and the Bachelor of Agricultural Sciences Vertyachkina grappled with this vitally important subject considerably earlier.

Of course, Makar Antipych has certain grounds for defending his laurels: he shears the hen with scissors, while Perekatilov and Vertyachkina simply pluck it "with forefinger and thumb." And that's a bird of quite a different feather!

But how many, we may ask, how many of these chicken barbers are still laboring in our science?

1954

Festival in the Town of N.

by Boris Laskin

Under the shade of giant Lombardy poplars in the park of the southern town of N. stood a monumental plywood structure with a heavy glass sign over the door: "City Philharmonic Society."

Through the open windows of the Philharmonic Society came the sounds of laughter, voices, fragments of melodies. The musical organism lived its own complex, restless life.

In the director's office there was silence. Comrade Mamaysky himself was not yet there. A light breeze ruffled the posters announcing visiting artists. In the most prominent spot, in the center of the office, stood a clay bust of the great chemist Mendeleyev. Comrade Mamaysky had little interest in chemistry. The bust had found its way into the office by accident. The purchasing agent, Kuvaldin, bought it in a secondhand store, mistaking the creator of the periodic system of elements for the composer Glinka. Subsequently, Kuvaldin immortalized his bold assumption in the inventory book by the entry: "Glinka—one."

And so there was silence in Comrade Mamaysky's office. Sud-

denly the door swung open, and the director entered. The stamp
of inspiration was on his brow. Mamaysky sat down at his desk,
pressed the bell, and called out, "Polya," since the bell was not
working.

The secretary, Polya Kulikova, a plump young woman with
straw-colored hair, entered the office.

"Go to the bookkeeping department and bring me the payroll
ledger."

Polya disappeared and returned a moment later with the ledger.
It was a weighty volume, about as thick as the telephone directory
of a big city.

"Catastrophic inflation of personnel!" This rather dry phrase
of somewhat legalistic tinge was a most apt description of the
state of affairs in the wilderness of the City Philharmonic Society.

Nevertheless, Mamaysky's far from average talents as a manipu-
lator had helped him to create a masterpiece of organization, in
which a variety of administrative and service personnel bore novel
titles, fascinating in their diversity.

Citizen Barnacle, F. F., whose services were not provided for
under the regular table of organization was given the impressive
title of Musical Eccentric.

The director's personal chauffeurs, the brothers Kirill and Me-
phody Zuyev, were listed briefly and somewhat intriguingly as
Marble Men.

The planning economist, S. P. Panibratsky, appeared in the
payroll as the Inspector of the Orchestra. It must be said, incidentally, that the demanding creative tasks before Panibratsky
were considerably facilitated by the fact that there was no orchestra.

"Everything shipshape, as in the best of houses!" Mamaysky
said cheerfully to Mendeleyev.

But Mendeleyev, still offended at Kuvaldin, remained stubbornly silent.

" 'Skoromnik, M. U.,' " read Mamaysky, " 'Chief of the Section of Original Genres.' "

The section of original genres included salaried magicians,

prestidigitators, and tamers of snakes (semivenomous). The latter addendum was made at the demand of the Department of Labor Safety. Under the same heading came soloists on the saw, on cans, copper plates, and other articles that irresistibly suggested metal scrap.

Next on the list was the ticket agent, Cossack, Y. S., whose job also was not to be found in the personnel plan. This aging man with the melancholy eyes of an antelope was described laconically and all-embracingly as an "artist."

Mamaysky shook his head with irony. "Artist! Just imagine, another Rossi!" he said, meaning Moissi.

This "artist," Cossack, Y. S., was quite remote from any creative endeavors. A modest messenger, whose task was to obtain railway tickets whenever the need arose, he combined his duties with ownership of a vegetable garden, which he was diligently cultivating when Polya Kulikova burst breathlessly into his yard.

"Comrade Cossack," cried Polya, "be calm! A commission has come from Moscow to investigate our personnel. The commission has gone over the personnel lists. Everything is in order with the administrative staff. We have only six names. As for the artists, the chairman of the commission said that he was very interested in the artists."

"And so?" asked Cossack.

"They want to see and hear our artists. And you know very well that our artists—"

"In short," said Cossack with mounting anxiety.

"Tomorrow the commission will audition you as an artist."

Cossack sank on a bed of radishes.

"Take yourself in hand," said Polya. "Mamaysky hopes that you won't let him down. Prepare your repertoire at once."

With these words Polya Kulikova disappeared.

The "artist" rose from the radish bed. He realized that he must act. And act at once.

Most of the rooms in the city hotel were occupied by artists. Thirty minutes later the pale Cossack was in the corridor of the hotel. He stopped at room number 7, occupied by the Zaitsevs, the husband and wife team who had created a most effective act called "The Human Arithmometer." Mrs. Zaitsev wrote on a blackboard set up on the stage the eight-digit figures named by members of the audience; at the count of three, Zaitsev, dressed in a frock coat and turban, would turn around, glance at the terrifying combination of figures, and a few moments later announce to the audience the results of multiplication, division, or any other arithmetical operation suggested.

Cossack stood hesitantly at the door of the Zaitsevs' room, from which he heard the voices of the husband and wife.

"Add it up, Kolya," said the wife. "Radishes—four and a half, butter—nineteen, meat—twenty-nine."

"Fifty rubles," said Zaitsev, erring only by two and a half. In domestic computations, Zaitsev liked to deal in round figures. This was how he rested from performances.

Cossack entered the room. Five minutes later the couple was informed of the situation.

"There can be serious complications," said the Human Arithmometer, "both for you and for Mamaysky. This is as clear as two times two is four," he added, somewhat coyly.

"Listen, Nikolay Ivanovich," pleaded Cossack, "explain your technique to me. I shall put on your tailcoat. The comrades on the commission will call out their staggering figures. I shall multiply them somehow and give any answer. Who will check it?"

"You are a child," said Zaitsev. "That's exactly what they are here for—to check. We must think of something else."

"But what?"

"Wait! You are a Cossack. Dazzle them with your skill in horsemanship."

"You are joking," Cossack said mournfully. "What has horsemanship to do with it? I am not a Cossack by profession, only by name."

"I simply don't know how to advise you. Go to room number 10. It's the home of Matilda Prokhorova and her company of trained mice."

"That's no solution."

"Why?"

"Because, first, I am afraid of mice, and, second, our buffet waitress, Zina, is already there. She is also listed as a performing artist."

"In that case you're in trouble. But perhaps you ought to go and see 'Two-Sharashkin-Two'? They are tightrope walkers. There is still a lot of time until tomorrow."

"I have difficulty enough walking on solid ground and you talk to me of tightropes. If you are in such a gay mood, I'd better go."

And Cossack went. When he came home, he thought and thought and finally came to a decision.

The festival of the talent on the Philharmonic payroll started at noon. A piano stood on the summer stage. In the front row sat the members of the commission and Mamaysky, whose face expressed approximately the following: What can I do, comrades? I knew we would be in for it someday.

The chairman of the commission glanced at Mamaysky and said loudly, "Well, shall we start?"

"We shall," answered Mamaysky.

However, the scene looked oddly like a silent movie: Mamaysky's mouth opened and closed, but no one heard a sound.

The first to come out on the stage was the master of ceremonies, a bald man with the soft movements of a horse thief. After telling the audience a joke that he had found the night before in a dog-eared copy of *The Alarm Clock* magazine, the master of ceremonies made his exit, followed by a menacing look from Mamaysky, and a pair of ballet dancers ran out upon the stage.

Ignoring the sheet music before him, the accompanist, whose eyes were glued on the commission members, began to play Delibes' "Pizzicato," and the ballet soloists—the senior economist, Zaykin, and the typist, Clava Raspopova—performed their dance with the haste of passengers hurrying to catch their train.

But, then, of course, the performance itself could scarcely be described as a dance. It was a series of extremely fanciful com-

binations, resembling simultaneously a wrestling match, a session
of hygienic massage, and morning calisthenics.

After the energetic economist had dropped the prima ballerina
on the floor, not without a good deal of grace, the chairman of
the commission said, "That is enough. Who is next?"

The next performer, the cashier, Kluyev, was introduced as a
"master of the literary spoken word." Lisping cheerfully, he ran
through the poem "Wait for Me."

Cossack did not watch the performances of his colleagues. He
nervously paced the corridor backstage, warming up his voice.
Cossack had decided to crash the line as a vocalist, and he was
now rehearsing—and frightening chance passersby with sounds
that resembled the barking of a male coyote.

"Your turn," Cossack was told.

He raised his head high and began to ascend the steps with the
face of a man on his way to the scaffold.

When Cossack appeared on the stage in a boy's size frock coat
and yellow slippers, known playfully as "Verochka's style," Mamaysky knew that it was time to give up.

Cossack looked at the members of the commission with glassy
eyes, cleared his throat, and his face suddenly assumed a pensive
expression. The last time Cossack had sung was in 1913, at a
graduation party at the university, and it may not be amiss to
state that the graduation was his brother's, not his own.

"Rapid as Waves Are the Days of Our Lives," declared Cossack,
then nodded to the accompanist.

Cossack began to sing.

Such incredible roulades flew over the hall that the commission
members, who had heard a thing or two in their lives, unanimously lowered their eyes, and the chairman closed his altogether.

Mamaysky fixed Cossack with the stare of a fakir trying to
charm a cobra. But it was too late. With the desperation of a
man who was ready for anything, Cossack, who had just barely
finished his first vocal offering, suddenly clapped his hands with

wild abandon and burst into song again: "Eh, Dunya-Dun-ya, Dunya, little berry, little love!"

Embellishing the refrain with a fiery tap dance, Cossack ranted and stormed on the stage.

He did not hear the chairman of the commission say to Mamaysky, who was in a state of deep trance, "The picture is clear. It will do for today. We'll see the rest tomorrow."

In the meantime, Cossack left the stage and departed from the theater.

He walked across the city in his concert garb, and people cautiously stepped aside to let him pass.

Night came. The participants in the second round were preparing for the next day's ordeal.

The waitress, Zina, trembling with revulsion, was rehearsing with the mice in Matilda Prokhorova's room.

The music librarian, Polubakov, described in the payroll ledger as a juggler, was energetically smashing dishes.

The city did not sleep.

1954

Childhood Friend

by Boris Laskin

When he returned from his after-dinner walk, Nikolay Illarionovich Khvostukhin, a thickset, robust, balding man of about forty-five, noticed a man's coat on the hanger as he was undressing in the foyer. Wondering who the guest might be, Khvostukhin caught sight of his wife, Raisa Pavlovna.

She was coming out to meet him, holding her finger to her lips. "Wait a moment."

"What has happened?"

"Sh-sh. Some comrade of yours is here to see you."

"Who? What comrade?"

"A childhood comrade."

"What childhood?"

"Oh, my God, yours. A childhood friend."

"Did he give his name?"

"He did when he came in, but I forget. He said you grew up together and went to the same school."

"So why did you forget his name?" Khvostukhin grumbled with annoyance, nodding at the coat.

"You will recall it when you see him. Great thing . . ."

"Where is he?"

"In the dining room."

"Did he say what he came for?"

"I've no idea. Kolya, I beg you, make it short. Here are the tickets; I'm putting them in your outside pocket. You see? In case of something, just show him the tickets and explain that we are in a hurry to get to the theater. That's all. I'll dress in the meantime."

Khvostukhin glanced through the slightly opened door of the dining room. Some stranger sat on the sofa turning the pages of a magazine. Who can it be? Khvostukhin thought, straining to remember. He seems to be about my age, but I can't for the life of me remember who he is!

He shrugged his shoulders and resolutely walked into the dining room, like a swimmer plunging into cold water. "Sorry," he said with exaggerated gaiety, "whom do I see?"

The guest put aside the magazine and rose from the sofa. "Nikolay! Hello! Hello, old man!"

Throwing his arms around Khvostukhin, the guest did not notice the puzzled expression on the face of his host. I haven't the faintest idea who it is embracing me, his eyes said plainly.

The host smiled with embarrassment. "Good heavens! Whom do I see! Of all people!" exclaimed Khvostukhin, shaking his guest's hand.

"You don't recognize me?" the guest asked gaily.

"Wait, wait, wait . . ."

"I can see you don't recognize me. Come on, try to remember. I'll wait."

Straining his memory, Khvostukhin muttered, "Wait, wait . . ."

"Remember Grishka Sokolov?" asked the guest.

Sighing with relief, Khvostukhin sank on a chair. "Good Lord! . . . Why, Grishka, how are you? I barely recognized you."

"You couldn't."

"I certainly did!"

"You couldn't have recognized me."

"But why?"

"Because I am not Grishka."

"What do you mean you're not Grishka?"

"Just as I say; I'm not Grishka."

"Come on. Stop pulling my leg."

The guest shrugged. "Why should I pull your leg? I asked about Grishka just because you could not possibly mistake anyone else for him. There's no one like him."

Khvostukhin was embarrassed. "But of course. . . . He was fair."

"Grishka? . . . Dark as a raven."

"That's what I'm saying—fair . . . as a raven," Khvostukhin mumbled, flushing.

"Never mind." The guest patted his host on the shoulder. "I'll have to confess. Remember Genka Vinogradov?"

Expecting another trick, Khvostukhin winked at his guest. "I remember Genka all right, but you're not Genka."

"How do you like that! Then who am I?"

If I knew who you were, thought Khvostukhin, and repeated uncertainly, "No, you're not Genka."

"And I tell you I am Genka, Genka Vinogradov."

"No. If you are really Genka, show me your passport."

The guest frowned. "Do you ask all your old friends for their passports? Anyway, I am Genka. Genka Vinogradov. I give you my word."

"Now I do recognize you," Khvostukhin declared boldly.

"As a matter of fact, you do not recognize me," said the guest. "You simply took my word for it."

There was an uncomfortable pause.

"My, my, how many years it's been," began Khvostukhin. "Just to think of it, how many years . . ."

"Yes. 'Time is an extraordinarily long thing,' as Mayakovsky wrote."

As he scanned the face of his childhood friend, Khvostukhin caught sight of Raisa Pavlovna behind his back. She stood in the next room and, raising her hand, was pointing at the clock. Her gesture meant: Time to wind up. We'll be late to the theater.

"Look here," said Khvostukhin. "Perhaps you'll . . . well . . . I mean . . . have some dinner? Although, to be truthful, I've had mine already."

"Thanks. I've also had my dinner."

"Really?"

"Really. I have such a habit—to have dinner every day."

"But where did you dine?" asked Khvostukhin, relieved that the conversation had finally taken a more tractable turn.

"In a restaurant."

"And where are you staying?"

"At the Moscow Hotel, for the time being. I'll move in a few days."

Khvostukhin nodded. "Mm, yes . . . so that's how things are. Well, and generally, how is life treating you?"

"I'm living. And you?"

"No complaints," Khvostukhin answered, offering the guest a cigarette. "Working."

"I think you are in the main administration?"

"Yes. I am chief of the main administration. Just returned from a business trip the other day."

The guest inclined his head to the window. "There's a blue Zim outside. Yours?"

"Mine. The job requires it. You can't manage without a car."

"Naturally. Have you seen any of the old crowd?"

It would have been better if I had asked the question instead of him, thought Khvostukhin.

"I'm asking, have you seen any of the fellows?" the guest repeated.

"Oh . . . some of them."

"Whom?"

"That fellow . . . what's his name? . . . Ivanov!"

"Pasha?"

"Sasha—I mean, yes, Pasha."

"Well, and how is he?"

"He? . . . He, well . . . he's working."

"I think he was in Gorky, on a Party assignment, then he went to Kuibyshev. A talented man, a good worker. He was the same in childhood, wasn't he?"

"I'll say," confirmed Khvostukhin, vainly trying to remember which Ivanov they were talking about.

"I had a letter from Victor Sharokhin, from Altay," the guest continued with animation. "He's become such a famous mechanic—a big man!"

"Good fellow," Khvostukhin said with feeling.

"And Lyuba Nekrasova, remember her?"

"Lyuba? Nekrasova? . . . There was such a girl . . ."

"A Candidate of Science."

"Mm, yes. . . . People don't stay put. They grow," Khvostukhin commented. "And how is your personal life?" Having taken over the initiative, Khvostukhin began to feel more self-assured. "I hear that you, well . . . I guess you got married?"

"I did."

"Right. Any children?"

"A son."

"Not bad." Khvostukhin folded his arms on his chest and rocked them. "Rocking, eh? . . . Wah-wah."

"Well, how shall I put it? The 'wah-wah' days are kind of over by now. The fellow is going to college."

I guess I put my foot into it that time, thought Khvostukhin.

He said hurriedly, "Ah-h. Of course. So he walks already! Not bad."

Glancing at his watch, he took out a notebook from his pocket, dropping the theater tickets on the floor. Leafing through the notebook with a worried air, Khvostukhin did not notice that his guest bent down to pick up the tickets and put them on the table with a smile.

"You are probably in a hurry," said the guest.

"You see . . . I'd forgotten altogether. This evening I have—"

"A conference?"

"Yes. There's a matter I must attend to."

"Well, in that case I'll go."

Catching a note of resentment in his guest's voice, the host protested. "No, no, stay a while. Where are you staying?"

"I told you. At the Moscow Hotel, for the time being."

"Oh, yes. What's the room number?"

"Room 607."

"This time you stopped at the hotel. All right. But in the future, whenever you come to the city, come right over from the station with your things, right here to my place. . . . Call me up. If there is any problem with getting a hotel room, I'll give orders—that'll help."

"Thanks," the guest bowed, and he sighed for some reason. He narrowed his eyes a little and looked attentively at Khvostukhin, who took out a briefcase from somewhere and became absorbed in some papers, forgetting his guest's presence.

After a while the host asked absently, "And how are the old folks?"

"They both died," the guest answered in a low voice.

Khvostukhin underlined something with a pencil. "So you will . . . I mean . . . Give them my regards when you see them. All right?"

Slowly shaking his head, the guest said, "All right."

"Don't forget now. And how is your health?"

The guest paused for a moment, then he said, "I'm in bad shape. I have cancer, measles, typhoid, and meningitis."

"Really? Good fellow! I'm delighted for you." Khvostukhin raised his eyes to his guest. "Well, uhm-m . . . And how are you fixed with an apartment?" And without waiting for an answer, he buried his nose again in his papers.

"My apartment burned down to the ground, with all the furniture, during the flood. And, generally, the whole house burned down."

Putting aside the papers and glancing into the next room, where his wife had long been waiting nervously, Khvostukhin turned his eyes to his guest and said, gaily rubbing his hands, "Well, then, so everything is fine. May God grant, as they say, that it won't be worse in the future. Am I right?"

The guest did not reply. He was looking out of the window.

"Pu-pu-pu," Khvostukhin played out with his lips, rising. "I shall call you in a day or two. We must get together."

"We've sort of gotten together already," the guest said dryly, putting out his cigarette in the ashtray. "Guess I'll be going."

"But where are you rushing?" asked Khvostukhin, seeing his guest to the door.

"Business."

"What kind of special business do you have there?" Khvostukhin remarked patronizingly. "I haven't even asked you—what system are you working in?"

"We're in the same system now. I was appointed to the ministry six days ago."

"Oh, I see!" Khvostukhin removed his tie. He still had to change. "Well, call me in case of anything."

"Try to get you on the telephone! No, better come and see me. Fourth floor, second office in the hall. Good-bye."

"At last!" said Raisa Pavlovna when the door had closed after the guest. "What did he come for? Some business?"

"No." Khvostukhin waved his hand. "I think he dropped in to get on the good side of me, just bootlicking. You see, we're in the same system now. 'Come and see me,' he says. 'Fourth floor, second office—'" Khvostukhin suddenly broke off. "Wait a moment, where did he say? Fourth floor, second office! . . . Wait! On the fourth floor are the deputy m-m-min— One minute!"

"What is it?"

"One minute." With a blanched face, Khvostukhin lifted the receiver and dialed with feverish speed. "The clerk on duty? . . . This is Khvostukhin speaking. . . . What? . . . Yes, I'm back. . . . We have a what? . . . A new deputy minister? . . . First deputy?" Khvostukhin mopped his forehead. "What's his name? . . . Vinogradov? . . . Gennady Vasilievich? . . . Yes? . . . Delighted to hear it."

Khvostukhin put the receiver into his pocket. Then, realizing what he had done, he lifted it out and carefully deposited it in its cradle, as though it were made of fragile glass. "There," he said helplessly. "There. So."

"Kolya! What has happened?" Raisa Pavlovna cried in alarm.

"What? Eh?"

"Come to the theater. You'll tell me everything on the way."

Khvostukhin stared at his wife. One might have thought he was seeing her for the first time. "I'm not going anywhere!"

"What happened? You were sitting and talking . . ."

"Sitting and talking," repeated Khvostukhin.

"Did you recognize your childhood friend?"

Khvostukhin looked at the telephone, then at his wife, then again at the telephone, and said quietly, "No. I did not recognize him. He recognized me."

1955

On the Left Foot

by E. Vesenin

In his dreams, the aspiring scholar Ivan Semyonovich Pushkov already saw himself as a Candidate of Science. Naturally! To begin with, he had chosen for his dissertation a most vital and pertinent topic: "Concerning the Regular Alternation of the Left and the Right Foot as a Decisive Factor in the Training of Will-power in Man." Secondly, his academic sponsor was Pavel Petro-vich Golenishchev himself. In the College of Transportation and Psychology, Golenishchev enjoyed indisputable authority, and a great deal, or, to be more exact, a great many, depended on him.

Golenishchev confidently guided Pushkov to the defense of his dissertation. With the carping meticulousness characteristic of jewelers and philologists, he polished the dissertation and weighed every word of the candidate's paper, which was to be read at the coming defense.

"It is most essential, my friend, to confine your paper precisely to twenty minutes," he admonished Pushkov. "Not a minute longer! Otherwise . . . Remember what happened at Romash-kin's defense? Yes. The whole Learned Council will fall asleep—and you won't wake them with a brass bell. . . . Twenty minutes! But not a second less, either, or you may be judged insufficiently scholarly."

The official opponents were urged by Golenishchev not to be overzealous in their praise: "Season your comments with a touch of criticism, so that no one will accuse you of partiality."

And he promptly went on to dictate to Pushkov the answers to the future comments of his opponents. "We want to make certain that you are not caught unawares. And don't forget the main thing—thank your opponents most warmly for their criticism."

Golenishchev could be depended on completely. He made pro-vision for everything, to the last detail: the color of the folder for the dissertation; the names of those to whom copies of the paper were to be sent—with gift inscriptions; the names of those to be invited to the defense, as well as those to be invited after the defense to the banquet at the Mount Elbrus Restaurant.

All the more mundane preparations were entrusted to the as-sistant dean, Kvasov, who had a wealth of experience in organiz-ing the details of other people's scholastic achievements, especially in their banquet stage. He was always ready to arrange the traditional presentations of a magnificent basket, crystal vase, or desk set to the guest of honor, "in the name of friends and admirers" (the choice of the gift depending on the preference of the recipient and the sum he had provided for the purpose).

Just before the defense, Golenishchev had a personal chat with every member of the Learned Council. Of course, none of them had read the dissertation, but each had willingly promised to attend the defense and, of course, to support Pushkov. "With you as his adviser, how could the dissertation be anything but brilliant?"

Naturally, Golenishchev did not remain in debt to his colleagues. He cordially promised one to support his doctoral dissertation; another, to appear as an opponent at the defense of one of the latter's students; a third, to drop a word at the ministry in behalf of his niece.

Old Tuberosov was somewhat more difficult. Firmly convinced that science had stopped with him, he voted "against" all aspirants for academic degrees as a matter of principle.

But Golenishchev found a key even to Tuberosov's heart. "Pushkov," he said to him, "is a product of the glorious Tuberosist school. He refers to you virtually on every page of his dissertation and quotes you extensively."

Tuberosov melted and said he would think about it. This represented a major victory.

The energetic activity of Golenishchev and Kvasov inspired confidence in success. And yet a little worm of doubt still gnawed at Pushkov's heart. "After all, the vote will be secret. And who can see into another man's soul?"

Golenishchev ridiculed his fears. "My vote is assured. And the rest will go along. The members of the Council may think as they please about the dissertation, but nobody will want to quarrel with me. In my lifetime, I have seen degrees awarded for worse dissertations. You can take Golenishchev's word for it!"

The fateful day came.

Pushkov moved as under hypnosis: automatically he mounted

the platform, opened the folder, buttoned and unbuttoned his coat, adjusted his tie, and began to read his paper in an oddly sepulchral voice.

Profusely citing "names," Ivan Semyonovich produced an array of irrefutable arguments proving the enormous role of feet in man's life, and he brought the full force of his logic and erudition against those who maintained false positions, giving preference to hands: "Throughout human history we can trace the primacy of feet over hands, and not only over hands. Note how this postulate is supported in proverbs and folk sayings: 'The hand is the foot's servant—it shoes the foot,' 'The feet don't feed the belly; the belly feeds the feet.' Furthermore, we have a proverb recording the melancholy fact that 'when the foot slips, the head weeps.'

"Where do we find the finest examples of ideal cooperation?" Pushkov asked, and answered: "In the coordinated action of the feet! At the same time, what do we see in the realm of the hands, where the right hand does not know what the left is doing? The folk in its wisdom is a thousand times right when it says, 'One hand kills the other, but one foot lifts the other.'"

No one interrupted Pushkov, and his speech flowed on with increasing freedom, smoothness, and confidence: "Scientific analysis shows that, at all the crucial moments of man's life, from birth to the grave, the prime role belongs to the feet. Looking at a baby, we say with tender emotion, 'The child has gotten up on his feet,' 'The baby took his first step.' We speak lovingly of 'the patter of little feet.' And vice versa, when age approaches, we admit sadly, 'his feet can barely carry him,' 'he has one foot in the grave.' A man dies, and here, too, the feet come into play. People say, 'He kicked the bucket,' or, 'He was carried out feet first.' And when a man achieves success? Then he 'stands firmly on his feet.' Or take a man who lives on a grand scale. How can he do it? He must be 'on a good footing' with his superiors, he 'stands on his hind legs' before them, he 'trips over his feet' to please them, and he does not disdain to 'step on the feet' of his neighbor and rival. Such is the great role played by the feet in man's existence.

"Even in questions of love," Pushkov continued, "the feet are at the fore. Take the enamored Chatsky in Griboyedov's *Woe From Wit:* 'With the first light of dawn, I am on my feet and at your feet.' And Tatyana Larina! What were her first words to Yevgeny Onegin after many years of separation? 'What brings you to my feet?'"

The closing portions of the paper rang out loudly and solemnly under the lofty ceiling: "If we wish to raise a generation capable of keeping step with the epoch, we must bring up our children with a full and conscious mastery of the intelligent alternation of the feet. It is high time we put an end to the superstition which says that a man is in a bad humor because he got up on the left foot. The assertion that the left foot is the source of ill temper and tyranny is entirely fallacious. It may have been true of the heroes of our great nineteenth-century writers Shchedrin and Ostrovsky, heroes who blamed their actions on 'the whim of my left foot.' But in our own day and age we must return to the left foot its proper position of leadership and exclaim with the poet, 'Who is that stepping out with the right? Left! Left!'"

The final words, declaimed with especially effective, well-rehearsed emotion, were greeted with applause. The speaker thanked his responsive audience and, quite exhausted, descended from the platform, mopping his bald, perspiring brow.

Official opponent Mizintsev was given the floor. "For the sake of objectivity," he declared, mindful of Golenishchev's instructions, "we are compelled to point out a rather substantial shortcoming. The speaker has neglected the enormously rich archives of the Assyrio-Babylonian era, when, as we know, the cult of the foot attained unprecedented proportions. Nevertheless, the scholarly value, both theoretical and practical, of the work of Ivan Semyonovich Pushkov, who has manifested great erudition and an admirable breadth of scope, unquestionably merits the awarding of the degree."

The speech of the second opponent and all the subsequent comments were favorable and resembled one another like cigarettes of the same brand.

Suddenly the venerable, silver-haired ancient in a silken skull-cap who sat at the Council table—it was, indeed, Tuberosov himself—seemed to wake up and, halting in the middle of the latest profile he was drawing on the pad before him, lisped out maliciously, "And has the esteemed aspirant attempted to establish the effect of the problem he has investigated on the development of the ballet?"

The experienced Golenishchev had foreseen the possibility of some such nasty trick on Tuberosov's part and hastened to the aid of Pushkov, who was completely dumbfounded, since Tuberosov's question had not been provided for in the scenario. "The effect of the regular alternation of the feet on the development of the ballet and bicycle sports," Golenishchev replied with utmost dignity, "will be examined by the aspirant in a separate monograph."

The members of the Learned Council began to fill out the secret ballots. Golenishchev nodded encouragement to Pushkov. Kvasov stood behind the door waiting for the cue for his gala entrance with the basket of flowers.

If a man with two left feet had suddenly appeared in the conference room, he would not have produced as much astonishment as the chairman's announcement of the results of the secret vote: eleven "against," and only two "for."

The first to disappear was Kvasov. He handed the doorman the unused basket of flowers, with instructions to deliver it to Pushkov's home. Then he hurried to the restaurant and, for the first time in his long banquet practice, canceled the ascent on Mount Elbrus.

Bidding good-bye to Golenishchev, all twelve members of the Council pressed his hand with warm sympathy, indicating that they had done everything in their power.

The catastrophe crushed Ivan Semyonovich Pushkov completely. With blank eyes he looked around him, muttering, "I don't understand a thing. Nobody criticized the paper. They even praised it. What is this? Whom can you believe?"

"That is exactly what I ask—whom can you believe?" stormed Golenishchev. "No one! You can't trust anyone! To let me down like this? They won't forget it!"

Three of the professors—Grechikhin, Kuzkin, and Tuberosov—were descending the wide staircase of the college in profound silence. They were also amazed at the results of the vote. By the time they had reached the street, Professor Grechikhin could no longer restrain himself. Offering his colleagues a ride, he asked Kuzkin, "So you also voted 'against'?"

"As you see. But what is it precisely that troubles you?"

"Well, really! This Golenishchev has lost all sense of proportion—he sticks us with his half-baked idiots, and we are expected to assume the responsibility."

"Exactly! Why on earth?"

"Well, that's what I felt—why on earth? But I thought that I would be the only one against."

"Hm . . . I had the same idea. We shall certainly hear from Golenishchev now!"

"Not at all. We can still be of use to him. The important thing is this. How many votes were there 'for'? Two! Obviously, one was Golenishchev's. I shall tell him that the second one was mine."

"Hm . . . that is exactly what I was planning to do."

"Oh, well," old Tuberosov, who had been silent all the way, broke in at this point, "I suppose I should confess: the second vote in favor was mine. I cannot understand it myself. Some devil must have prompted me. I happened to glance at the blank that Dean Duletov was filling out. He voted against, and since, as you well know, we are at knives' points, I voted 'for' as a matter of principle, just to spite him."

"But, Dormidont Heraklitovich, we know very well that you are always at knives' points with Golenishchev as well. No, no, we had better get together on this. Let each of us say that the second vote was his. Golenishchev cannot verify it, anyway."

"Very well, let's have it your way," agreed Tuberosov. And with their spirits restored, the three members of the Learned Council drove off to Mount Elbrus to celebrate, this time at their own expense.

Golenishchev, meantime, continued to rage. "Against whom did they lift their hand? I will remind them of it! Klepikov, Tuberosov's student, is just about to defend his dissertation. I'll rouse everybody. We'll give them such a rap on the knuckles, they will rock on their feet. Mark Golenishchev's word!"

Pushkov's wife guided her stunned husband into a cab and nagged him all the way home. "I knew you wouldn't get the degree today—I felt it in my bones. I knew you wouldn't make the grade. On what foot did you get up this morning? . . . On the left? No wonder. You've no one but yourself to blame."

1955

Yury Kazakov
(1927 -   )

Born in Moscow, Kazakov graduated from the Gorky Literary Institute in 1957. One of the most original and talented of the younger Soviet writers, he is the author of numerous short stories written in an emotional key very different from that of "Socialist realism." He is concerned with the individual and his experience in confronting the world of men and of nature and, often, in confronting his own inner world. He writes in a style of considerable purity and beauty. While he is by no means a satirist, his "Goblins" is a gentle spoof—aimed at the persistence of "religious superstitions"? or, perhaps, at the claims of the purveyors of "atheist propaganda"? Kazakov, like the other members of the relatively more independent younger generation of writers, has been criticized for a variety of "sins," including aestheticism, decadence, and pessimism.

Goblins

by Yury Kazakov

Zhukov, the director of the village club, had overstayed in the neighboring kolkhoz. It was a hot day in August. Zhukov had come early, he had managed to go everywhere and see everyone, but the visit had been unsuccessful. Everybody was in a hurry. It was the height of the harvest season.

Zhukov was very young; he had been working at the club less than a year. A native of Zubatov, a large village, he was now living in Dubki, in a little room next to the club.

He had intended to leave as soon as he had finished his errands. There had even been a car going his way, past Dubki. But he had changed his mind, deciding to pay a visit to the teacher first; he wanted to have a talk with him about something intelligent, cultural. The teacher, as it happened, was away hunting; he should have returned long ago, but something had delayed him. And Zhukov drearily began to wait, already realizing that he had made a mistake and should have gone with the car.

He waited about two hours, smoking, looking out of the window, and conversing dully with the landlady. He had even dozed off, but was awakened by voices from the street: the herd was being driven home, and the women were calling to the cows.

At last he tired of waiting, and irritated by the frustrating day, he drank a glass of sour apple cider for the road—which immediately set his teeth on edge—and set out for his own kolkhoz, about ten miles away.

On the bridge, Zhukov caught up with old Matvey, the night watchman. The old man, in a shabby winter hat and a well-worn sheepskin coat, stood with his feet spread wide apart, holding up his gun with his elbow and rolling a cigarette. He looked sullenly at the approaching Zhukov.

"Ah, Matvey!" Zhukov recognized him, although he had seen him only twice. "Out hunting, too?"

Without answering, Matvey slowly began to walk, squinting at his cigarette. He took some matches from an inside pocket, lit up, inhaled several times, and began to cough. Then he put the matches back, his nails scraping on the flap of his coat, and said, "Hunting! I watch the orchard at night. In a tent."

Zhukov's mouth was still prickling from the cider. He spat and also lit a cigarette. "I bet you sleep all night," he said absently, thinking that he had been a fool to refuse the ride; now he would have to walk.

"Sure—try and sleep!" Matvey said significantly after a silence. "I'd be glad to sleep, but they won't let you."

"They're thieving?" Zhukov inquired ironically.

"Huh, thieving!" Matvey grinned dourly, then suddenly stepped out more freely. He seemed to relax and lean back slightly, like a man who had finally emerged into the open after long constraint. While they had been walking, he had not given Zhukov a single glance, but peered in all directions across the twilit fields. "No, they're not thieving, but they come . . ."

"Who comes? The girls?" asked Zhukov and laughed, remembering Lyubka and thinking that he would see her soon.

"Oh, them . . ." Matvey mumbled inaudibly.

"Come on, grandpa! Don't drag it out!" Zhukov spat. "Who comes?"

"The goblins, that's who," Matvey said mysteriously, giving Zhukov a sidelong glance.

"Blathering!" Zhukov mocked him. "Tell it to your old woman. What kind of goblins?"

"Just wait," Matvey replied morosely. "You'll fall into their hands, then you'll know what kind."

"You mean devils?" Zhukov asked, assuming a serious expression.

Matvey gave him another sidelong glance. "Hm," he mumbled vaguely. "Black. Some with a greenish cast . . ."

He took two cartridges from his pocket and blew off the coarse tobacco dust adhering to them. "Here, take a look," he said, showing Zhukov the paper wads inside them.

Zhukov looked down and saw the crosses scratched on the paper with indelible pencil.

"Charmed!" Matvey said with satisfaction, putting the cartridges back. "I know the right words!"

"They bother you, eh?" Zhukov asked mockingly, but immediately made a serious face again to show the old man that he believed him.

"Not too much," Matvey answered gravely. "They don't come up close to the tent. Just . . . they'll come out of the dark, you know, one by one, and gather under an apple tree . . . rustling . . . standing there in a row, little ones, side by side." Matvey lowered his eyes to the road and made a long sweeping movement with his hand before him. "They stand there and play songs."

"Songs?" Zhukov could no longer control himself, and he burst out laughing. "They're as good around here as my club members— amateur musicians! What kind of songs?"

"Um, different ones. Sometimes they're real sad. And then they call, 'Matvey, hey, Matvey! Come here! Come here!' "

"And you?"

"And I say, 'Oh, you such and such to your mother! Scat from here!' " Matvey smiled lovingly. "And when they start to creep up to the tent, I load the charmed bullet and *cra-ack* at them!"

"Do you hit them?"

"Huh, try and hit them!" Matvey said contemptuously. "Who can kill the unholy ones? I just chase them off a bit till morning, until the first cockcrow."

"It's bad," Zhukov said after a silence and sighed. "It's really bad."

"Eh? What's bad?" asked Matvey.

"I'm talking about my work. My atheist propaganda isn't doing so well, that's what!" said Zhukov, frowning and looking at Matvey. "I suppose you babble in the village, too, scaring the girls?" he asked sternly, suddenly remembering that he was the director of the club. "Goblins, indeed! You're a goblin yourself!"

"Eh?" asked Matvey again, and his face became stony and hostile. "You will be going through the woods now?"

"Well? What if I do?"

"You will? Look out, then—don't be too sure of getting home." Matvey turned away. Without another word, without bidding Zhukov good-bye, he walked rapidly across the field to the orchard looming darkly in the distance. Even his back expressed his anger.

Alone on the road, Zhukov lit a cigarette and looked around. The twilight was becoming deeper, the sky was fading in the west, the kolkhoz behind him was almost invisible; only some roofs showed darkly here and there among the poplars, and the electric windmill rose above them.

On the left, he could see a birch wood stretching jaggedly to the horizon. It looked as though someone had scratched a row of vertical lines with a white pencil on a dark background, spacing them widely at first, then, farther off, more closely, and then drew out a faint white line across the dim horizon.

Also on the left there was a lake, set motionless, like a bright stone, in its banks—the only shining spot in all that darkness. A fire was burning near the lake, and its smoke blew over across the road. The dew was falling, and the smoke was damp.

And on the right, in the gloomy shadows and clearings, between the dark promontories of the forest, electric cable towers marched from hill to hill. They resembled a row of huge, silent creatures cast down to earth from other worlds and moving soundlessly, with upraised hands, in a westerly direction, toward the kindling greenish star—their home.

Zhukov glanced back again, still hoping he might catch a car. Then he set out along the road. As he walked, he constantly looked across at the fire and at the lake. There was no one near the fire, and not a soul was visible on the lake. The lonely fire, lit by an unknown hand for some unknown purpose, gave him an eerie feeling.

Zhukov walked hesitantly at first, puffing at his cigarette, glancing around, and waiting for a car or a companion. But no one could be seen either behind him or before him, all the way to the horizon, and Zhukov finally made up his mind and began to stride in earnest.

When he had gone about three miles, it turned completely dark. Only the road glowed dimly, broken here and there by mist. The night was warm. But when he stepped into a pool of mist, the chill enveloped him. Then he emerged into the warmth again, and these transitions from chill to warmth were pleasant.

How ignorant our people are! thought Zhukov. He walked with his hands in his pockets, knitting his eyebrows and recalling Matvey's face, recalling how malevolent and scornful it had become when he had laughed at him. Yes, he thought, we must, we must improve our atheist propaganda. We must wipe out superstition, root and stem! And he felt an even stronger desire to speak to someone about things cultural and elevated.

He began to think that it was time he moved on to the city, to continue his education. And, as always, he immediately visualized himself conducting a chorus—not in the kolkhoz club, where he did not even have a proper stage with wings and where the fellows smoked and giggled in the hall, but in Moscow. And his chorus was a hundred strong, a regular academic choir!

As always, these thoughts filled him with a sense of elation, and he no longer noticed anything around him. He saw neither the stars nor the road, and he walked unevenly, clenching and unclenching his fists, working his eyebrows, humming snatches of music, and smiling without fear that someone might see him. He was glad now that he was alone, without companions. He came to an empty barn by the roadside and sat down on a log to rest and smoke.

Once there had been a farm here, but after the neighboring kolkhozes had been merged, the farm was razed, and only the barn remained. It stood empty and open, and it seemed to have no doors. Its warped dark frame leaned at an angle, and in the gaping hole, inside the barn, the blackness was especially dense.

Zhukov sat, resting his elbows on his raised knees, facing the road, with his back to the barn, and smoked, gradually cooling off, his mind no longer on the city and the conservatory, but on Lyubka, on how best to snatch a proper kiss, when suddenly he felt that someone was looking at him from behind.

All at once he realized that he was sitting in the dark, alone in the midst of empty fields, among mysterious, somber shadows that might be bushes—and might not be bushes.

He remembered Matvey, his coldly vengeful, ominous face, and the mute, deserted lake, with a fire burning for no known purpose.

Holding his breath, he slowly turned and glanced at the barn. The roof of the barn hung suspended in the air, and stars were glimmering in the gap. But just as he looked at it, it settled back upon the walls and something ran thumping into the field behind the barn with a muffled, monotonous wail—"O-oo. . . . O-oo. . . ."—sounding farther and farther away.

Zhukov's hair stood on end, he leaped up and vaulted out upon the road. Well! he thought in terror, I'm done for! and he bounded down the road. The air rushed past his ears, and in the bushes on either side something was crashing, snorting, breathing coldly on his back. I must cross myself! thought Zhukov, feeling something snatching at him from behind with clammy fingers. "Lord, into Thy hands . . ." He crossed himself, stopped, out of breath, unable to run any farther, and turned around.

There was no one on the road or in the fields, and the barn was no longer visible. Zhukov wiped his face with his sleeve, his eyes fixed on the road, said hoarsely, "Ha!"—and started, frightening himself. Then he cleared his throat, listened, and said again, trying to keep his voice steady, "Ho! Ho! Hey!"

Recovering his breath, Zhukov set out once more with rapid strides, calculating feverishly how much farther he had to go. He peered with a sinking heart into the night and the darkness around him, remembering that the wood of which Matvey had spoken so ominously still lay ahead.

The road descended to the river, and Zhukov, dazed as in a dream, bounded with long leaps across the bridge over the murky water bordered by tangled willow thickets. Something hooted under the bridge, but Zhukov did not stop to think whether the

sound had been real or imagined. Wait—I will get to you! Zhukov
thought with angry fear about Matvey, climbing up the hill where,
as he knew, the wood began.

The wood announced its presence with dew and dampness.
Something was breathing powerfully from its depths, sending into
the warm air of the field the dank, close odors of mold, mushrooms, water, and decayed pine needles. At the right of the road,
in the wood, there was impenetrable darkness. At the left, in the
fields, the air was somewhat brighter. Stars shone overhead. There
were more and more of them as the evening deepened into night.
The sky, though black, suffused a pallid, misty light, and trees
were outlined against it in firm silhouette.

An owl broke heavily from a branch in the wood, swept by with
a faint rustling sound, and settled somewhere else, farther ahead.
Zhukov heard it, but could not distinguish it from the surrounding gloom. He only saw the branch sway up and down, blotting
out the stars.

As he came nearer, he frightened it off again, and it began to
fly in circles, out over the field and back into the deeper darkness
of the wood. Now Zhukov could see it. The horizon beyond the
fields still glowed with a last faint remnant of the sunset. Not
even a remnant—simply, the sky there was more rarefied, more
insubstantial, and the owl was a dark, silent spot as it flitted
across.

Following its flight over the field out of the corner of his eye,
Zhukov stumbled on roots and thought with heavy fear about it.
He did not dare to glance toward the wood or look behind. But
when he finally looked forward, down the road, his back ran cold:
before him, a little to the left, the goblins, who had crept out of
the wood and crossed the road, were standing, waiting for him.
They were little, just as Matvey had said.

One of them tittered.

Another moaned in a thin, high voice, like the voice behind the
barn: "O-oo. . . . O-oo. . . ."

And a third cried out like a rooster, triumphantly: "Kolya!
Kolya! Come here! Come here!"

Zhukov's teeth clicked, and he froze with terror. He could not even cross himself—his hand refused to rise. "A-a-a!" His howl spread through the woods.

Suddenly he realized that those were little fir trees. Trembling like a hunting dog before it points, he took a step in their direction, then another.

Behind the little firs, something rustled and scudded away into the field with a startled cry.

A bird! Zhukov guessed, joyously catching his breath and moving his shoulders under his soaked shirt. Sprinting past the firs, he got out a cigarette and matches, but thought at once that if he lit a match, they'd see him throughout the woods. He did not know and did not dare to think of who would see him, but he knew that they would.

Zhukov crouched down, glanced at the earth around him, pulled his jacket over his head, and lit the cigarette under the jacket. I'll cut through the field, he decided. He could no longer bring himself to walk along the road, which led off through the wood. The fields were bad enough, but somehow less terrifying.

He crashed through the dense nut grove bordering the wood, came out into the open, and strode off through the field, making wide detours around everything dark in his path and constantly glancing over his shoulder to the right. The owl was still flying. All around him there were little squeals and whisperings, and from afar, from hollows and ravines deep in the wood, came cries or moans that quivered for a long time on the air, rolling like echoes from tree to tree.

At last the wood ended, and the dim, dusty road wound its way once more among the fields. Zhukov returned to it and, whimpering with fear, broke into a fast trot—without glancing back—pressing his elbows to his sides like a runner. He ran, the air boomed in his ears, and the wood receded farther and farther, until it became no more than a faint dark line. Zhukov had already made up his mind not to look at anything and was beginning to feel better. He even began to hum something monotonous and unnaturally gay, timing it to the rhythm of his running—"Tee-ta-ta! Tee-ta-ta!"—when suddenly he stopped short in mid-motion, and his eyes bulged.

The thing he saw this time was neither a tree nor a bird, to which he had already become accustomed, but something living, moving in his direction across the field. It did not resemble a man or a cow or a horse, but was altogether indefinite. Zhukov clearly heard the snapping of the weeds, a strange, soft bouncing, and a faint knocking.

"Who is it?" a loud voice called.

Zhukov was silent.

"Anyone from hereabouts?" the voice asked anxiously, already from the road.

Zhukov finally understood that he was being spoken to, that a man was approaching him, wheeling a bicycle, but he was still unable to answer. He merely panted.

"Zhukov?" the man said uncertainly, approaching and peering at him. "Why, hello! But why didn't you answer? And I was wondering who it might be. Do you have any matches? Give me a light."

Zhukov recognized Popov, a member of the district committee of the Komsomol. Zhukov's hands shook so violently that the matches in the box rattled as he handed them to Popov.

"Where were you coming from?" asked Popov, lighting his cigarette. "I lost my way. I was heading for your village and missed the turn. I was already at Gorki, so I cut across the field back to this road. . . . But what's the matter?"

"Wait . . ." Zhukov said hoarsely, feeling faint and dizzy, "wait. . . ." He stood still, smiling guiltily, unable to master his weakness. Sweat poured down his body, and his breath came in short gasps. There was a strong smell of dusty plantain in the air.

"You aren't sick?" Popov asked with concern.

Zhukov nodded silently.

"Come on, sit down!" Popov said firmly and turned his bicycle. "Hold on to the bars. Come on!"

Popov started the bicycle at a run, then jumped into the saddle, making it swerve sharply, blew at the strands of hair that had fallen on his forehead, and pedaled off toward Dubki.

Zhukov sat perched on the frame, feeling uncomfortable and ashamed. He felt how heavily the bicycle was rolling on the dusty road. Popov was breathing hotly on his back and bumping him with his knees. Both were silent most of the way.

At last they saw the lights of the kolkhoz, and Zhukov stirred. "Wait, now," he said.

"Sit, sit!" Popov gasped, out of breath. "It's not much further; we'll just get to the health station."

"No, no, stop now," Zhukov said, wrinkling his face and stretching out his foot to catch the earth.

Popov stopped with relief. They jumped down from the bicycle and stood for a while silently, not knowing what to say. In the nearby stable, the horses heard human voices and clattered restlessly with their hooves on the wooden floor. A strong, pleasant smell of manure and tar came from the stable.

"Give me a match," Popov asked. He lit a cigarette and spent a long time mopping the sweat from his face and neck with obvious enjoyment. Then he unbuttoned his shirt collar altogether. "Well, how are you? Any better?" he asked hopefully.

"It's better now," Zhukov said hastily. "I had some cider. That's what it must have been."

They slowly walked along the street, listening to the subsiding sounds of a large village settling down for the night.

"How are things at the club?" asked Popov.

"Fair. It's harvest time, you know, people are busy," Zhukov answered absently. Then he suddenly asked, as if remembering something, "Do you know the word 'goblins'?"

"What? What did you say? 'Goblins'?" Popov thought for a moment. "No, I haven't heard it. What do you need it for, a play?"

"No. It just came to my mind," said Zhukov.

They reached the club building and shook hands.

"Take the matches," said Zhukov. "I have more at home."

"All right." Popov took the matches. "Drink some milk—it's good for an upset stomach." He mounted his bicycle and rode off to the kolkhoz chairman's house.

Zhukov walked through the dark hallway and unlocked his room. He drank some cold tea, smoked, listened to the radio in the dark, opened the window, and lay down.

He was almost asleep, when everything seemed to turn in him suddenly. He saw, as from above, the fields at night, the solitary lake, the dark procession of cable towers with upraised arms, the lonely fire; he heard the life that filled those vast expanses in the deep, dark hours of night.

He began to relive his entire walk, but now it was with a quick sense of happiness, with an embracing warmth for the night, the stars, the smells, the rustling sounds, and the cries of birds.

He felt again the need to talk with someone about things cultural—about noble, elevating subjects, like eternity. He thought of Lyubka, jumped down from his cot, pattered barefoot across the room, dressed, and went out.

1960

Anonymous

"Letters to Auntie" appeared in the magazine Oktyabr in 1963.
They were presented as anonymous letters from a provincial, only
slightly edited for publication by V. Livshits. But whether they
are a literary hoax or genuine letters does not change their value
as witty satirical pieces.

Letters to Auntie

The "Letters to Auntie," with which we have decided to acquaint our readers, are purely personal documents. However, you must not think us guilty of indiscretion in making public a private correspondence; the letters are being published with the knowledge and consent of both the correspondent and the addressee.

It must be said that both of them—the correspondent, a member of the planning department of a certain provincial enterprise, and the addressee, his venerable aunt, retired on pension—were quite astonished to learn that these ingenuous letters had evoked the interest of the editors.

But it is precisely their spontaneity and even naïveté that may, in the editors' view, appeal to the readers of our journal.

A few necessary deletions were made in preparing the letters for publication.

First Letter

Dear Auntie,

I hasten to inform you that I have arrived safely. The other passengers in my compartment turned out to be the nicest people. One, like myself, was going to Moscow on an assignment from his enterprise; two others were returning from assignments. This gave us all a sense of community, and we spent the whole night playing preference on a suitcase. I won forty-seven kopecks.

The conductor was also a very decent fellow. At three in the morning he knocked at the door of our compartment, thinking there was a fire, but it was only our smoke. Everybody had a good laugh.

Incidentally, a waiter comes through the cars at frequent in-

tervals, selling sandwiches, beer, and even cognac. So you need
not have worried.

What else can I tell you about my journey? The car was comfortable. True, when we wanted to take a nap (there were still
four hours to Moscow), the conductor removed our bed linen,
and we had to doze on pillows without pillowcases. I say doze
rather than sleep because at dawn the radio on the train wished
us good morning and began to play records. One of them, in fact,
was repeated several times—the one that says, "You and I are
not married." I know the words by heart now.

For the convenience of passengers who may not feel inclined
to listen to music at dawn, there is a regulator under the table in
each compartment. You can lower the sound or even switch it off
altogether. I switched it off. After that, I learned twice again that
"you and I are not married"—from the speaker in the corridor.
It blared out the information at full volume, but here you could
do nothing; no one could switch it off.

I am telling you this, Auntie, so you will understand why I was
a trifle shaky when I left the train. But this passed very quickly,
and soon I was quite myself again, running from one taxi to
another with my suitcase and basket.

Don't imagine that there were no taxis at the station; there
were long lines of vacant taxis with their green lights on. But every
time, it somehow happened that they would not take me. I noticed
that the drivers were collecting groups of three or four people
into their cabs and driving off. But I always remained outside any
group. Finally, I managed to get into a taxi by myself. The driver
turned on the meter and asked me where to go. When I said
Cheremushki, he turned off the meter and said that his shift was
up. Another driver had no more gasoline when he heard the
address. A third made me get out, saying that his tires were worn.

An experienced visitor to Moscow later explained to me that it
isn't every taxi driver who will take you where you have to go.
Some prefer to go where they have to go. They are a cranky lot and
have their favorite routes, from which they will seldom deviate.

Nevertheless, in the end, I too succeeded in finding a taxi.

What can I tell you, Auntie, about Moscow? I have not seen it for several years. Moscow is beautiful! The widest thoroughfares, streams of automobiles, wonderful new houses. As was to be expected, I was especially impressed by the new district—Cheremushki. There is much greenery here, much fresh air, many children, and, unfortunately, many similar street names: Cheremushkinskaya Street, Cheremushkinsky Crossing, Cheremushkinsky Lane, the New Cheremushkinskaya Street, New Cheremushkinsky Crossing, and some other Cheremushkinskoye and New Cheremushkinskoye, so that, by the time I found Semyon Semyonych, my driver and I had become fast friends.

I delivered your parcel. Semyon Semyonych was most grateful, especially for the raspberry jam and the book of Voznesensky's poems. In Moscow, he said, you cannot get it; in the outlying provinces you can.

Semyon Semyonych cordially invited me to stay at his home, but I did not want to impose on anyone and decided to take a room in some hotel nearer the center of town. Especially since, in the course of my wanderings through Cheremushki in the taxicab, I had seen many posters with a pretty girl in a white apron and cap saying: "MAKE USE OF THE SERVICES OF OUR HOTELS."

I must tell you, Auntie, that this appeal is purely abstract in character. Moscow has a great many hotels, but evidently the number of people wishing to use their services is greater. At any rate, such posters are still premature.

In short, by evening I telephoned Semyon Semyonych again and asked for shelter.

As for the taxi driver with whom I had made the rounds of the Moscow hotels, he ended up with a sincere affection for me, having fulfilled his daily mileage norm with me. At the end of the trip, we were calling each other by our first names.

The hospitable Nadezhda Fyodorovna made my bed in the dining room, on a sofa which turns into a bed when you pull out the seat. Now I shall lie down and try to sleep, although I am not sure I can. Too many impressions. The faces of hotel clerks flicker before my eyes, and in my ears there is a constant humming of "but you and I are not married." Good night, Auntie!

I will now continue the story of my visit to the capital, as I promised. I shall not go into the details of my work here; that would bore you. It will be enough to say that everything is going smoothly.

In the morning, when I awakened on the sofa bed, Semyon Semyonych and Nadezhda Fyodorovna were already gone. Only their son Styopa, a fourth-grade student, was home. He attends the afternoon session at school. Like a good host, Styopa served me breakfast and entertained me with conversation. We thoroughly weighed the chances of the various football teams in the coming games, and then Styopa astonished me with his virtuoso skill in twirling a large thin hoop around his waist. This is done by means of rhythmic vibrations of the whole body and, according to Styopa, promotes your general physical development. I recalled that this device is called a hula hoop and that *Krokodil* * usually shows Western dandies and idlers of both sexes at this occupation. But Styopa explained that in *Krokodil* it is a hula hoop, but in school, at gym classes, it is a gymnastic hoop and that a hula hoop is bad, but a gymnastic hoop is good. Frankly, I never quite grasped the difference. But I like the exercise. I think I shall buy a hula–gymnastic hoop, or a gymnastic–hula hoop, for you and me, Auntie. It will help me fight against obesity, and it will help your rheumatic back.

And now I shall tell you how I traveled to my main office in a bus without a conductor. In such a bus the passenger drops his coin into the box, tears off his own ticket, and rides to his destination. It is an excellent idea, in conformity with the present level of social consciousness among the population. And it is true that when you drop your coin yourself, without the urgings of a con-

---

* *Krokodil* ("Crocodile") is the leading Soviet magazine of humor and satire.

ductor, you become imbued with a feeling of profound self-respect. And you begin to regard your fellow travelers in the bus with special friendliness. But this is something I understood only later. At the moment when I was about to drop the coin into the metal box, someone shouted anxiously, "Don't drop it!" I quickly pulled away my hand, thinking that the box was out of order and I might get an electric shock. But the box was in order, and I was stopped because a certain citizen, who had dropped a coin earlier, had to receive forty-five kopecks' change from his fifty-kopeck piece and was collecting this sum from other passengers, that is, from those who paid their fares after him.

I gave him my fifteen-kopeck piece, and now I had to collect my ten kopecks' change from others. A little old woman in a plush hat gave me six kopecks and demanded one kopeck change. I did not have a kopeck, but the man who paid fifty kopecks had two kopecks, so that now the old lady owed him one kopeck, and he owed me four. At this point a citizen who looked like a professor intervened and said that I was confusing everything: I, he said, had to collect four kopecks not from the man who paid fifty kopecks—he was still thirty-three kopecks short—but from him. But he did not have four kopecks; he had a twenty-kopeck piece, which he was now—what was he doing?—giving to the man who had paid fifty kopecks. Thus, the fifty-kopeck man had to collect only thirteen more, but the old lady would have to give her kopeck to him, the professorial citizen, and he would have to collect fourteen kopecks more from others.

I asked a woman sitting across from me to hold my briefcase for a moment, then I took out a notebook and pencil and proved without difficulty that the citizen of professorial appearance was mistaken. But he had a slide rule with him, and according to the slide rule I was mistaken. At this point the whole bus joined in on our calculations, and I did not notice when I passed my stop.

This little incident by no means invalidates the idea of self-service in my eyes. Simply, something still needs to be thought through. Or perhaps it doesn't. Who knows, these mutual computations may even be beneficial—a kind of mental gymnastics, a mathematical hula hoop?

After supper I took a stroll through the Moscow streets, admiring advertisements and store windows, which I think are very beautifully decorated.

However, even here some things made me wonder. Take, for instance, the advertisement that says, "Tea is a tasty and wholesome drink." Is it really necessary to convince anyone of that? And if it is, why not advertise, "Bread is a tasty and wholesome food"? It is inconsistent.

My very best wishes to you, Auntie. Don't forget to water my geranium.

                                                              Your Vasya

Second Letter

Dear Auntie,

When I recall what I wrote you in my first letter, I see that my attention is drawn to secondary things, rather than the important ones. Indeed—a man has not been in the capital so many years, then finally he comes, and instead of describing the university building, the Luzhniki Stadium, or the Metro,* he stares at signs, reads advertisements, and investigates the system of computations in a self-service bus.

However, all these things—the university, Luzhniki, the Metro—have been described many times before me, and so much better than I could dream of doing. There is really nothing that I could add. Only, perhaps, that the new stations of the Metro differ from some of the older ones, built in the "Triumph" style, by their good taste and simplicity. And so I hope, dear Auntie, that you will not mind if I continue telling you about all sorts of things,

* The Moscow subway system.

both important and trivial, that I come across in Moscow, just as they strike my attention.

For example, today, after visiting the main office, I strolled through the Moscow streets, looking at the Muscovites and thinking, How well people have begun to dress, such modern and attractive clothing! During the early postwar years the predominant colors were khaki and dull gray. But today the streets are bright with all the colors of the rainbow. Especially, of course, on the women. And I like this very much; it puts you in a better mood, it pleases and delights the eye. And yet our textile plant at home continues to pour out dreary fabrics that make you think of dismal, rainy days. And, again, take the matter of styles. In Moscow, Auntie, you meet any number of young girls wearing slacks and high hairdos, and young men in narrow trousers and brightly colored shirts, worn loosely over the trousers. Our city executive committee chairman would be appalled at the sight! But here nobody bothers. It is permitted. No administrative penalties. No fines. No threats of deportation from the city. And it made me think: perhaps we are too puritanical in the provinces? After all, there was a time when we gave up caftans and crinolines and, later, overcoats with shoulder capes and ladies' cloaks. Why shouldn't we, in our day, give up wearing wide trousers, long gabardine coats, and jackets nipped in at the waist?

I lunched at a small restaurant, furnished with light, handsome tables and chairs. The service was prompt and polite, and the food tasty. I said to my neighbor at the table that this restaurant was evidently firmly rooted in good traditions. But my neighbor mumbled, spooning down his fish soup, that it was too early to speak of traditions: this restaurant had only been opened two days before. We'll be able to talk of traditions, he said, after five or six months. Then we'll see what sort of traditions they are. Something in his tone suggested that this was a man saddened by wide experience in life. If I am in Moscow again after a year or two, I must try to come back to this restaurant. Just for curiosity's sake.

After lunch I took care of a few more business matters. Then, on a crowded street, I saw a large assemblage of people, and, naturally, I hurried to the spot. The people were gathered around a glassed-in billboard, over which there was a sign: "DO NOT PASS BY!" I did not pass by and began to study the cartoons posted on the board. This was much like our own "KROKODIL IN THE STREET." It pilloried violators of the public order. One would be foolish to assume that there are none among the millions of Moscovites. There are! And here they are exposed to the general view. You showed yourself in a disgraceful state? You caused a row? Up on the board with you, my good man, let everybody know what you are. Ivan Ivanovich Nikiforov, engineer of the SMU Plant No. 39, or Sergey Petrovich Kulebyako, of the regional dramatic theater. . . . This method of public persuasion, it seems to me, should be a strong deterrent both to those who have already found themselves on the board and to future candidates. On the whole, I would say that it is a good method. But when I looked more closely at the caricatures and the verses under them, I cannot say I liked them. In Moscow, with its wealth of artistic talent, all this might have been executed on a higher level. You can easily see that the drawings are not by Kukryniksy.* And the verses are on the order of the following:

> "Tipsy Sokolov, Boris,
> Smashed a window with ease.
> Why on earth did he do that?
> You can ask the dirty rat."

Such verses in the home city of a master like Sergey Ostrovoy!

In this verse the offender was called a rat. In others they are called "mugs," "snouts," "swine," and so on. Is this a good thing? Don't think, Auntie, that I am trying to defend rowdies and hooligans. Certainly not. But I think it is wrong to descend to their plane and answer abuse with abuse. In my opinion, this is a wrong educational method. Before you know it, the educator may get so carried away by his educational zeal that he will end up on the board himself—for using foul language.

* Popular Soviet cartoonists.

I stepped into a food store to buy something for supper. It was a self-service store. In the doorway, I had the following conversation with a store employee (I almost said a saleswoman, but she does not sell anything, she only lets the customers in):

SHE: Citizen, take a basket and check your briefcase.

I (taking a wire basket): Thank you. The briefcase isn't in my way.

SHE: Naturally, it isn't. Maybe it even helps. . . . Come on, come on, check it, that's the rule. Bags, briefcases, and valises must be checked at the door. You pick them up when you leave.

I: But why?

SHE: So you don't slip something in. All we need is to look away a moment and you'll shove a can of sardines or something else into your bag. And then we have to pay. All sorts of things happen.

I: Such things don't happen with me.

SHE: I wasn't talking about you, but generally.

I: And why don't you sew up the customers' pockets as they come in? You never can tell, some fellow may slip a jar of apricot jam into his pocket—and good-bye!

SHE (oblivious of the irony): We have no instructions concerning pockets.

I (changing my mind about shopping at this store): Inefficiency! At this rate, you'll go bankrupt before you know it! As for me, I'd rather shop at an ordinary store, without self-service. They don't stress their confidence in the customers by allowing them to go to the shelves and counters, but neither do they insult us by demanding that we check our bags and briefcases.

And I proudly walked away.

Don't imagine, Auntie, that this is done in all the self-service stores. I suppose that the director of this particular store had ordered the confiscation of bags and briefcases on his own initiative, which is scarcely to be welcomed.

In the evening, we went to a movie theater, the Russia. It is quite a distance from Cheremushki, but Semyon Semyonych and his wife wanted to show me the new theater and, incidentally, to see it themselves; they had never been there. I have generally noticed that many Muscovites, permanent residents of the capital, let years go by before they find the time to go to the Tretyakov Gallery or the Moscow Art Theatre or any of the places that visitors rush to see as soon as they arrive. The aborigines use the excuse that all these places are always within reach, just around the corner, and they can go whenever they wish. It's a wrong psychological attitude.

Dear Auntie, the Russia is a magnificent movie palace! Modern, spacious, bright. It is so beautiful that it would simply be embarrassing to show poor films there. But we were lucky, we saw a good film. Afterwards, at supper, we got to talking about movies generally, and I learned with astonishment that some of the movies that you and I have, unfortunately, seen at home were not exhibited in Moscow. It turns out that if a movie is not simply inferior but absolutely wretched, it is not released for the Moscow screens. It is, however, sent to us, in the provinces.

And I must say, I consider this unfair! If trash is to be shown at all, let everybody see it. And if it isn't, then no one should see it. And the second alternative, it seems to me, is the preferable one.

And now, dear Auntie, I shall conclude for the day.

Do not water the geranium with cold water—make sure the water is at room temperature.

With fond regards,

Vasya

Third Letter

Hello, dear Auntie,

Your nephew Vasya sends you respectful greetings.

My assignment here is finished. As I had planned, I shall spend two or three days longer in Moscow for my own enjoyment, and then—back home. The other day I was in Luzhniki. I was tremendously impressed by the sports palace. True, what I found there was not a basketball match, but an evening of readings by young poets; however, these readings obviously contained an element of sports as well: who'll beat whom? The second part of the program was devoted to singers and acrobats, and this combination of sport and poetry was reminiscent of ancient Greece: there, as we know, they also held simultaneous competitions of discus throwers, poets, and musicians.

I had no difficulty in obtaining a ticket for the Moscow Art Theatre, but some difficulty in getting one for the Contemporary Theatre. I did not get to see a young people's café. I stood in line for two hours on Gorky Street with a number of young men and their girl companions, and suddenly it occurred to me: here am I, a man considerably past his youth; do I have the right to take up space in this café, where space is at such a premium, when even the young are unable to get in? And so I quietly left the line and went to the Ice Cream Café where I could easily find a table, get my order, and reflect at leisure on why, after all, these young people's cafés are not made more widely available to young people, if they—the young people—have such a strong desire to sit in their own cafés? And what, generally, is the meaning of these "cafés by age"?

In the mornings I still converse with Styopa, a fourth-grade pupil, a sober and reasonable young man, but possessed of one noble passion. Styopa is a collector, and he collects matchbox labels and candy wrappers.

Indeed, he owns some unique specimens. What would you think, Auntie, of such a slogan as "Livestock Breeders! Cow-ize Our Pastures"? Or: "Novelists! Novelize Our Magazines"? I believe you would shudder. I also shuddered when I found in Styopa's collection a matchbox label showing a man releasing fry into a lake and urging, "Fishermen! Fish-ize Our Waterways!"

Among the candy wrappers, I found some similarly interesting examples. One wrapper has a picture of a small girl holding a piece of candy high over her head. Near her, a lovable little pup is jumping eagerly—he also wants to taste the candy. But the girl is nobody's fool; she won't share it with him. This brand of candy is called "Try and Take It from Me!" I suppose this series of educational wrappers might be continued indefinitely. My imagination suggests such names for candy as "I Won't Give You Any!" and "Mine!" and even an entire assortment of chocolates called "Get Along, Get Along, God Will Give You!"

I have carried out all your errands, Auntie. I bought the buttons, too, but not at the GUM, for it is not so easy for a stranger to find the needed department in that palace of trade, with all its galleries, rows, and passages. It is true there is a telephone that you are invited to use for inquiries. But the telephone was silent, while a pleasant female voice over the store radio urged you to purchase things, now a camera, now a fishing rod, and now an accordion, and explained how to find your way to the places where they are sold. It said nothing, however, about buttons. One might, of course, wait around until the voice remembered buttons, but I had little time, and so I bought the buttons in a small notions store.

I want to tell you about my visit to still another store, namely, a flower shop. The point is that it was Nadezhda Fyodorovna's birthday, and I decided to bring her some flowers. And as soon as I reached this decision, my mind's eye conjured up an image of a blue-eyed, fragile flower girl, as though freshly off the pages of Balzac (I trust, dear Auntie, that you will appreciate my erudition and style!). With an enchanting smile, condescending and yet encouraging, she helps me to find my way among all those gladiolas and cinerarias, and with the taste that only women possess, she selects for me a modest and beautiful bouquet. My mind's eye also envisaged the modest price of the bouquet—say, two rubles or so, but no more, since I had already exceeded my budget.

Well, then, I go into a flower shop. Along the walls, in pickle barrels, there is a row of dim, dusty, wilted shrubs. On the walls hang dreary wreaths made of roofing iron, which is generally in such short supply. And on the counters stand baskets of flowers, some of them real. There is no salesgirl.

As I examine the baskets, I hear a heavy snorting behind me. I look back and see a hulking, unshaven man in a quilted cotton coat.

"We ain't got none," he says in a hoarse voice.

"None of what?"

"No khyacints."

"And must you have just hyacinths?" I ask.

"Me? What the devil I need them for? They're all asking for khyacints, so I have none."

"And who are you?"

"I'm the salesman."

There is Balzac for you, Auntie!

"We have wreaths," the salesman says. "Twenty-five rubles and up. Or maybe you don't need one yet?"

"I don't need one yet," I say. "But I want a small basket of flowers. Live. Not artificial. For two rubles or so."

"For how much?"

"Two."

And here, Auntie, he burst into a most insulting fit of laughter. It turns out that there are no such prices here. I ended up by buying one of the baskets for six rubles and thirty-five kopecks, and though it was very heavy, I walked out of the store with a great sense of relief.

Oh, yes! I saw the blue-eyed girl after all! Right there, near the flower shop. She wore a janitor's apron and was sweeping the sidewalk with a huge broom. And I wondered at the inappropriateness of professions that is occasionally observed among us.

Well, Auntie, I guess that is all. Time to wind up.

Good-bye, I'll see you soon. I shall not write any more. If possible, move my geranium further away from the stove.

Your Vasya

1963